Copyright ©

In this work of fiction, the characters, places and events are either the product of the author's imagination or they are used entirely fictitiously. Any resemblance to actual events or persons, living or dead, is entirely coincidental.

This book is copyright material and must not be copied, reproduced, transferred, distributed, leased, licensed or publicly performed or used in any way except as specifically permitted in writing by the author, as allowed under terms and conditions under which it was purchased or as strictly permitted by applicable copyright law. Any unauthorized distribution or use of this text may be a direct infringement of the author and publisher's rights and those responsible may be liable in law accordingly.

Twitter: @rlockeyauthor

Book cover illustrated by Danielle Fenner

PROLOGUE

"This is the Beam of Zrelyar?"

"Yes, my Queen."

"What is its purpose?" she asked, studying the peculiar green beam of light reaching over her.

"We think—"

"You don't know?!"

"—that it's simply an attraction. I am extremely sorry that we do not know more."

Queen Lasapra studied the light. *Could it be some sort of high-energy laser, or a way to control the weather, perhaps?* she thought.

"Has a physicist studied the beam?"

"No, my Queen."

She scowled, glancing at the two soldiers standing nearby. *They guard it without knowing what it is!*

"What did my…" she said. *No, you're in control now, Lasapra. They're gone.*

The supervisor trembled as the Queen met her gaze and issued a command. "Find out what it is. Hire anyone you need."

"Yes, my Queen. Of course."

Lasapra nodded, turning around and glancing at the flat city ahead; the cheaper buildings were concealed underground.

I am the Queen of Zrelyar. I should know everything about this city!

She was led back to her palace, repressing her anger as people clapped upon sight of their new ruler.

I can't trust any of them.

CHAPTER 1

Vekkilar awoke to the sound of thunder and saw that her brother had disappeared from the adjoining room. She slipped out of bed and dressed into a pair of pale blue robes laying nearby, her sight focused on the hall to her right.

"Kol?!" she called out, stepping into the red quartz corridor ahead.

She admired the artwork hanging from the walls as she walked, her gaze focusing on her favourite painting—it depicted a pink brain, held by two slender hands, being dipped in a barrel of melted gold. The strange image reminded her of wealth and knowledge, both being essential for life in Zrelyar. The painting was called *Vanité*; she did not know the meaning and assumed it was from an ancient dialect.

"You decided to get up, then," she heard. Turning to the end of the corridor, she saw her brother Kolansar standing beside a door, wearing a pair of red robes that closely resembled hers. She glared at him and followed him into the room he had stood in front of, her eyes immediately fixating on the artwork sitting on a metal easel mounted to the wall.

"Shame you got up early to paint that," she responded with a smirk. Kol ignored her and approached a small pillow sitting on a shelf, occupied by a small, ovoid creature known as a Ukrifar.

"Here, Kretai," he said, taking a handful of meat chunks and tipping them onto the pillow; they were swiftly consumed. "Unlike Vekk, you have manners."

"Is she coming with us now?" Vekk asked, watching Kretai clean the fallen crumbs from the shelf.

"We'll get her later," Kol responded, following his sister as she ascended the black-tiled stairs that led to the living room and crossed into a spacious kitchen. Living underground had its advantages; they were protected from the acid rain and thunderstorms that struck regularly and had additional space for gardens that brought colour to the dark city.

Vekk and Kol passed a small seating area and viewed the multiple canvases of nature hung above, equal distances between; each were like soldiers standing in line. Bright white lights hid inside the ceiling, illuminating the room with a professional and modern atmosphere.

Nearby, a black slab hung from the ceiling,

held up by a glass pole that protruded through its centre. Vekk sat at the head of the dining slab in a metallic chair while Kol walked to the fridge in the kitchen to prepare breakfast, noting the colour of their home contrasted with the darkness of the pollution outside, visible from the skylight above him.

Their refrigerator was compact under the polished granite counter, simply accessible through voice commands. Kol called for their meals, a plate full of plants and mint green-coloured water, which were delivered on a large pedestal that raised through the counter's surface.

Vekk, unnerved by the silence, looked at Kol as he garnished their meals and asked, "Does Leritri need our help or are we free today?"

"I don't know," he muttered, disgruntled from his early awakening and lack of sleep. They fell back into silence until Kol brought the food. Taking their condiments from the wired shelving nearby, they ate to prepare themselves for a day they had not planned.

"No one on our street has been raided in over a month now," Vekk said, noticing Kol's low mood. "I'm sure we'll be left alone now."

"I wish we were born rich," Kol said, shovelling his food into his mouth. "We'd have more privacy."

"By Queen Lasapra's grace, we're living better than most," Vekk said, glancing down at the light reflecting off her golden skin; she was highly aware that it differed from the standard deep red or green skin that was common for Quarailians—their species.

Quarailians were easily recognisable with their slender bodies, which were adapted to agility activities and allowed them to outrun prey. Their ears stood away from the sides of their head, which increased the sound they could hear when spoken to directly. Two rectangular indents lay in their foreheads at a slant, left over from an ancient age where they served an unknown purpose.

Since they remained within Zrelyar for most of their lives, many Quarailians had long, flowing hair. Short hair was typically black, turning white as it grew longer; a few random strands matched the colour of their skin. Unaccustomed to danger, Vekk had allowed her hair to grow long while Kol cut his hair short as a style preference.

Vekk realised she had been silent for a few minutes. "We should see if Leritri needs our help."

"I heard you before," Kol told her. "Sorry, yes we should."

"It's just—"

Something scratched at the door.

"I'll let him in," Kol said, standing up and giving her a knowing smile. He walked upstairs to open their front door, locked with at least five different mechanisms. He opened the door to see a wolf-like creature standing obediently in the rain, whose back was covered in a fur resembling green moss while its skin was like wood. Its forehead sprouted two small horns that curved around the back of its ears—it was an Alpha Garisal, making it larger than the rest of the species.

"Sorry Arkriat," said Kol. Arkriat ran inside, away from the royal guards that patrolled the street behind him and over to the dining slab. Kol rushed downstairs and pulled Arkriat away from his meal, sitting back down as the Garisal walked away.

"I'll feed him," Vekk said and stood up, attempting to distract Arkriat from the food remnants that remained on the table. However, he finished quickly and ran downstairs to their bedroom. Kol left the rest of his food in the kitchen and followed, accompanied by Vekk.

"We need to get Kretai before we leave," Kol mentioned. They walked downstairs and entered her room, watching her fly onto the back of Arkriat and use the dense plate-like surface to conserve energy as the Alpha Garisal carried her.

"It'll be good to see her again," Kol said as he listened to the heavy footsteps passing outside.

"Did you know she has records dating back to the city's founding?"

"I expect she has records of Quelliare's

creation," he muttered. Quelliare, their home planet, was billions of years old but had only been inhabited for several million.

They continued out of the shed that marked their home, the only part above ground. They glimpsed the rich sector that stood above the ground; the buildings were composed of rectangular blocks stacked atop each other. They surrounded the carbon-black palace of the Queen, which stood tall in defiance of the turbulent weather.

The siblings walked quickly across the street to Leritri's residence to avoid the menacing glare of the patrolling soldiers. The street was cold, partly due to the rain falling in a coordinated strike on the people below; the unpredictable and heavy weather was a regular occurrence.

Lightning lashed the spires of the tallest buildings, doing little damage to the reinforced exteriors whose design kept the workers safe. The sun, almost invisible to Zrelyar as it hung behind the purple clouds, pushed through with rays of light, although doing little more than to imply that it was morning as the sky remained in darkness.

As they approached Leritri's house, they saw how the distant buildings towered above ground compared to the hut that was used to access her home, with little more than a trembling roof constructed to protect a sliding glass panel. The siblings approached the entrance, with the glass panel sliding away, and walked down into her kitchen.

"Leritri?" Kol called out. They looked around for her and heard a quivering response.

"By the fire, come over!"

They walked fast to find Leritri in her cushioned chair positioned by a holographic fire. She was one hundred and ninety-five years old, an old woman considering the average life expectancy of a Quarailian was around two hundred years of age.

"Hello," she said weakly, her hands clutching her seat to keep herself upright. Her tired mind longed for the communication that her neighbours brought; luckily, they were always interested in the stories that she had. Her knowledge extended many centuries and the wealth of artefacts and collections in her home reflected this.

"Hello. Do you need any help?" Kol asked.

Leritri watched as Vekk's eyes darted around the room. "Come. My house can wait," she told them.

Kol looked to his sister, who nodded. They lowered themselves into large red chairs while Arkriat and Kretai sat by the fireplace, absorbing the warmth from the electronics behind it and glaring at the swords that hung above.

The siblings chatted casually with her for approximately half an hour until Vekk asked her about the library of knowledge that lived in her home.

"Well," Leritri told her. "My books can describe Quelliare centuries before I was born. One story stands out in particular…"

She promptly began detailing a story that neither of the siblings asked for but were both intrigued by, noting the similarities to their own situation.

"Many centuries ago, Quelliare was united under one leader, a tyrant named Ooldar—the only leadership they had," she began. "The population was predominantly one species: Cristrials. They were manipulated into obedience."

"What's a Cristrial?" Vekk interrupted. "Are they extinct? I haven't heard of them before."

Leritri laughed. "No—Cristrials still live on Quelliare today. They regularly come to this city to trade goods, although they don't have as much power as they used to. Most of the power they had is now in the hands of the Quarailian Queen."

"What did Ooldar do that was so cruel?" Vekk asked with morbid intrigue.

"He stripped the area of valuable goods, leaving most of the surrounding land as mounds of dirt and stone; it ruined the landscape. Society was less structured at that time: fewer laws, less infrastructure and less common sense.

"Historical records state that one day, the people had had enough. His rebellious subjects plotted against him for months, disguising plans however possible," Leritri explained.

"How?"

"I'm not sure," she responded. "Some of my books refer to chests and lockets, in which plans were folded up and hidden inside of."

"How did it end?"

"Eventually, they stormed his palace, quite a weak building at the time, and surrounded him in his throne room," she told them. "His own guards turned upon him and he was swiftly removed from the throne, which was destroyed later to prevent it from happening again. A government took his place and restored Quelliare to its former beauty."

Vekk, intrigued by the story, interjected. "Was Ooldar killed?"

Leritri smiled and said, "Yes, he was decapitated. Ooldar couldn't be trusted and I just hope that we haven't made the same mistake with our Queen Lasapra. She hasn't cared for her people just as King Ooldar hadn't."

Leritri smiled once again after seeing the siblings in disbelief and said. "I'll discuss it with you later. Would you be able to help clean my kitchen first? The refrigerator smells particularly awful."

The siblings were suddenly less enthusiastic about the nature of their visit and wandered over to the kitchen, catching a glimpse of a soldier removing a man from his home; Leritri's kitchen skylight gave them a decent view of the street above. They were incredibly intrigued by the tale of Ooldar and were surprised that Leritri had such a fascination for brutal endings.

As they cleaned, Vekk considered the new perspective Leritri had given them on the state of the planet. Unbeknown to her, Kol had a similar shift in mindset and was furiously scrubbing as if the counter was Zrelyar itself.

Perhaps it's worse than I realised, he thought.

"Good Garisal," Vekk heard in the other room. She quickly realised this was likely Leritri petting Arkriat, the only creature she could see from the confines of her chair.

"Should we get her a Garisal?" Kol suggested jokingly.

"No," Vekk replied, mostly fixated on her cleaning.

"Do you think Leritri is right?" Kol asked.

"I don't really know. I doubt the Queen would appreciate that sort of thinking, though."

"We couldn't do much anyway."

"That's true. We'd need an army—and courage."

After they finished cleaning her kitchen, they returned to Leritri.

"We're finished," Vekk said. "Come on Arkriat, Kretai!" However, Arkriat was more than comfortable where he was and refused to move. Vekk gestured more furiously until he finally stood up and moved towards her.

"Do you think you could be the rebellious subjects that stood up to their leader?" Leritri asked the siblings, standing up surprisingly fast to pay them.

Vekk stared at her. "Leritri! We could never do that."

Leritri sighed. "You need to protect our future—your future. You are our saviours; don't throw that away! You will open your eyes when it actually impacts you. You won't waste any more time."

Taken aback, both siblings simply nodded, then walked to the entrance in silence.

Upon opening the door, Kol said. "Do you think it's the old age?"

"Probably," Vekk replied, looking fearfully at the violent lightning strikes. "We should get inside—it's too risky to stay out."

As Kol began to agree, the sound of horns echoed throughout the city and people ran from their homes into the streets. The thunderstorm subsided temporarily but the rain remained constant, as if ordered to stay by the Queen herself.

"It's a parade," Vekk said calmly as the siblings wandered towards the rushing crowds of people, who eagerly ran to the large road that extended down the centre of the city to the main gate. They pushed the people aside and stood behind the guards that protected the parade.

A royal tank labelled 'Queen Lasapra's Command' hovered down the street, with Lasapra herself perched atop a golden throne with a red canopy. It was followed by another tank, which showcased the 'New Developments by the General of the Royal Guard', as was written in silver on the front. It was occupied by a tall man staring smugly at the crowds, his medium-length hair swaying in the wind and his skin blending into the vibrant red lights behind him.

These two vehicles preceded many tanks in a regimented form; many of the vehicles were recognisable by the people of Zrelyar due to the military's constant presence in the city.

"This reminds me of Queen Lasapra's coronation parade twenty years ago; that was incredible," Vekk heard someone say behind her. She expected celebratory comments—a royal parade was a citywide event.

"These vehicles look nice, but..." Kol began, but was unable to finish as he suddenly felt the eyes of royal supporters on him and Vekk. He stepped towards the row of guards but tripped over a discarded metal plate, pushing two guards into the centre of the parade.

Kol retreated into the crowd, followed by Vekk, as the guards managed to avoid the floating death traps and began to seek out the source of the push. A few minutes after, they could hear soldiers approach, interrogating citizens about the perpetrator of the incident.

"Who tried to kill our guards?"

"Withholding information is considered to be treason."

Vekk and Kol moved swiftly to avoid questioning as the ceremony continued, with no end in sight. Vekk felt uncomfortable in the crowds, knowing that she stood out from the other Quarailians.

"I think we should go," Kol said, pushing through the crowds, away from the parade. He was quickly stopped by a soldier who stood much taller than he did, who told him that attendance was mandatory and forced the siblings to wait until the royal event had ended.

Quarter of an hour later, the display of power had ceased and the crowds dispersed, returning to their daily lives. Vekk and Kol sat on a bench and eyed the guards walking past.

"We can't get on the wrong side of the law," Vekk told her brother, who glared at her and remained in silence. They stood up several minutes later after the fear had worn off.

"Let's go to the palace." Vekk said, assuming Kol's actions would be forgiven. "I want to see whether it's as intimidating as people say."

Kol looked at her incredulously, before they walked across the street and along the pavements nearby their home, preferring the sheltered areas to avoid the rain. Queen Lasapra's palace was clearly visible from most areas in Zrelyar and their section of the city was no exception, even under the canopies of museums and wealthier properties; the parade had mostly been forgotten as Vekk and Kol wandered into richer lands.

"The palace is visible from everywhere," Vekk said in awe.

"I wonder how old it is," replied Kol, intrigued about its design. "It must've been built way before Queen Lasapra."

"I'm sure her life is more active than ours," said Vekk, with a glare.

"Would you really want to be dealing with criminals and laws though?"

"Not really, no."

They walked into the open street, avoiding eye contact with the soldiers, who held loaded rifles in their arms as if cradling a child. Security measures appeared to loosen once they reached the wealthier areas of Zrelyar, although the streets were also less crowded.

"Wait," Vekk said. "I need to know if she's there."

She led them through the district, despite never having visited the area. Kol, Arkriat and Kretai followed blindly with the assumption that Vekk would become less cryptic as they reached her goal.

They passed into the wealthiest neighbourhood in the city and towards the palace entrance, which was full of rich and influential figures who waited to see their Queen. There were no plants in sight, with metal sculptures being favoured as a display of wealth and as a reflection of Lasapra's personal taste in art.

"Do you think Queen Lasapra has any pets?" Kol asked as they walked towards the balcony that lay in front of the palace doors and above the metal garden of statues, overlooking the Queen's domain.

"I doubt it," Vekk said. "I imagine that she's too busy running the city."

They stopped at a short distance away from the palace doors, looking over the grand entrance.

"I thought one of the governors was supposed to be giving a speech today on the needs of young people," Vekk said, feeling defeated.

Kol took out his holographic tablet and swiftly searched for information.

"She cancelled in protest," Kol told his sister. "She believes the pollution levels are too extreme and refuses to work until something's done about them."

"I've researched those levels before—I know they could be much worse than they are now," Vekk said as a spontaneous lightning bolt struck one of the spires atop the palace, with the only evidence being the flash of light through the grey air.

The siblings stood away in shock and watched the rain begin to fall heavily across the city. Arkriat became tense and urged the siblings to move swiftly with several gestures and movements.

As the storm persisted, another lightning strike smashed into the ground. Both Vekk and Kol felt the sheer amount of energy produced.

"Do you think we can make it home safely?" Kol asked with a fearful concern.

"I don't know," Vekk replied, surveying the area for their middle-class neighbourhood.

The storm continued to strike the nearby area. Miniature fires began but were quickly extinguished by the rain as people dashed for shelter in fear of the danger that awaited.

The city was prepared to deal with strong force, but the people were not. Lightning strikes dispersed tiny crowds and sent innocent families running in fear for their lives. Their world was burning, a regular occurrence, with no end in sight. The cold and the pain made Vekk and Kol shake, while Kretai squeaked as someone passed by.

The siblings looked over the railing ahead of them and saw a man on a Hovescape, a small board consistent of two blocks of metal that curved at the side, held together by a holographic platform between them. He was speeding in an attempt to make it home.

He failed.

As lightning struck nearby which caused his Hovescape to malfunction and explode, killing him in the process. Vehicle parts flew everywhere. Vekk fell to the ground, struggling to grasp the situation while Kol stood, wide-eyed and shaking.

"How...could..."

He could not finish the sentence. He was paralysed in terror while Vekk screamed at Arkriat and Kretai, who both rushed over to them from under a sculpture.

"We need to go home. Now," she told her brother, glaring into his traumatised eyes.

They stared at their home and began to run, hoping to distance themselves from the palace as much as possible. The power of the storm could no longer shake them as much as Lasapra's callousness had; they could not survive in a city where they would be forced to see death every time they stepped outside in a thunderstorm.

CHAPTER 2

"Speak to me Brookes," Arthur heard being spoken directly into his ear.

"You're at work."

"Brookes? Answer me!"

A man...and a woman.

"Arthur!"

"Sorry sir!"

Arthur ceased his thoughts of the figures that appeared in his mind and walked to greet awaiting customers. Serving customers at Cakecut Bakery was always emotionally draining, with a manager that protected his profit better than his employees. However, Arthur had worked there since he was sixteen and had become accustomed to the role of a cashier. He was now twenty-two which led to a desire to find his true passion, despite having no means to achieve it.

The bakery was currently themed around winter, which applied to every piece of visible decor including tables and chairs; Arthur had noted the juxtaposition of the hostile atmosphere and the environment that contained it. He was used to watching the frozen clock's hands glide like a boulder, although it provided a small source of enjoyment to the workers as it proved that time was actually passing.

As Arthur handed a frail elderly woman her croissant, a man, well-built and red-faced, stormed in, pointing his finger at the veteran employee. The man was far taller than Arthur, who was short in comparison to the average man—this made the customer's infuriated expression seem more daunting to him.

"You gave me the wrong order!" he yelled, quickly approaching the counter.

The customers rapidly moved away as Arthur was left alone to deal with the towering figure in front of him.

"I'm sorry sir, what was it that you ordered?" he asked fearfully.

"Two pastries! Did you not listen?!"

Arthur looked at the order that had been thrown onto the counter: an empty wrap. He could feel the eyes of both the customer and the manager on him, curious as to how he planned to correct the situation.

I wish I had those two aliens to save me right now, he thought.

Using his minimal training, Arthur simply gave him the two pastries he allegedly ordered and smiled weakly as he walked away. The disgruntled employee heard a sigh behind him.

King Cut was disappointed.

"King Cut" was the name that the employees had given to the manager due to his enjoyment in slicing into his workers with insults and demands, although none would dare use it in his presence.

Immediately after the incident, a staff meeting was called; this included the three employees who were working and the boss himself. The bakery was temporarily closed, leading Arthur to expect to be fired.

"Today one of our employees failed to follow our rules. I will not allow this," Cut announced, walking back and forth in front of them like a military officer.

"Yes, my lord," Arthur heard an employee whisper behind him.

The boss did not realise that all of his employees were stifling laughs as they did not respect his position; King Cut did not tend to take action and the employees expected the meeting to remain as pointless as the rest.

"We do not give away free food to customers. We 'Reply, Resolve and Register'. This employee may have 'Replied' and 'Resolved' but he certainly did not 'Register' that man's money. You will do better."

Is he actually going to do something this time? Arthur thought to himself. He hoped not—he had no other job opportunities.

And that figure. Who was he? Arthur was not a writer extraordinaire or an avid painter and could not hope to relay the figure he had envisioned to another human being.

"Brookes!"

Arthur snapped to attention as Cut summarised his lecture, fearing that he would take further action on his inaction.

"Remember my rules and do not show the weakness displayed by the one employee who was unable to follow them."

Is this a military operation?

"Now, open this bakery and make me the millionaire my father wants to see. Your salaries depend on it."

Arthur stood up and returned to the counter, relieved yet disappointed that he had managed to keep his job.

Is this what I want to do with my life? he thought, pushing his hair away from his face and looking around at the two other employees.

Arthur had dreamt of being an astronaut since he was around ten years old and had attempted to work towards this life goal. However, he was not naturally skilled in anything related to science or mathematics, which prevented him from even considering this aspiration. Being forced into a position away from his ambitions had left him resentful of both his past self and his parents for allowing him to leave without a good education.

He rested casually on the counter, waiting

for customers to realise that the bakery had reopened. Business was slow as usual and had further decreased due to dissatisfied customers.

Arthur heard a yell from the back room; King Cut was more frustrated than normal. Arthur could see the other employees tense as the boss stormed towards Arthur's co-worker and childhood friend: Rose. She stood back as her boss rushed over to her. Arthur had to stifle a laugh due to his exaggerated walk.

King Cut yelled to her face, "You're fired! Don't come back unless you're going to settle this out of court!"

Rose stammered, "W...why?!" Arthur peered into the back room, seeing the desk inside surrounded by shards of glass, with the boss's computer having few keys remaining. He walked back to see Cut standing close to Rose, who was clutching the door handle.

All of the torment he had felt that he had endured over the six years of working for Cut, combined with the mysterious figure he had envisioned had diminished his job satisfaction greatly, despite his enthusiasm being minimal since he began.

Arthur rushed over to the door and grabbed a circular table by its edges. He threw it to the ground and Cut turned around, infuriated.

"It wasn't her. It was you," he snarled.

It had actually been neither of them; Arthur

later learnt that Cut had received a message from his father that he would no longer fund his business—Cakecut Bakery had nothing else to keep it afloat. Sales were down and employees were disgruntled, which had caused him to attempt to remove anyone or anything else in his way to profit.

He had smashed his computer and chosen the first employee in view just to feel some form of satisfaction. However, Arthur had hated his apathetic behaviour since his first day and felt freedom in revolt.

Despite being energised by his rebellion, Arthur slowly backed away and placed his employee ID on a nearby table. The boss was preparing to do something; he did not know what. Arthur grabbed the ajar shop door and fled the bakery.

He knew that he was fired.

Now unemployed and alone, Arthur walked home, contemplating on the extreme change that his life had taken. A car may have given him less time to reflect on his actions but Arthur preferred to save the little money he had. He was accustomed to abrupt changes in his life; once again, he did not know what would happen to him.

I have time to find another job, he thought, struggling to hold his breath amongst the noxious car fumes from the traffic beside him. *Got nothing else to do, anyway.*

He turned right, holding his hand horizontally above his eyes to block the glare of the powerful sun. As the image of losing his job in the icy bakery faded from his mind, he hurried across the boiling concrete and saw his flat in the distance.

Reaching the unassuming brick building, he jogged up the stairs and unlocked the door to see a German Shepherd bounding its way towards him.

"Hi Shadow!" Arthur said. Shadow walked back inside to allow Arthur to enter. They both sat on the dusty brown sofa and greeted each other. Shadow was a three-year old German Shepherd dog covered in black fur with a dark brown-coloured stomach. His large ears and regularly happy face helped him to look friendly and welcoming, although he was willing to protect his home if needed.

"I've had a difficult day," Arthur said while fussing over Shadow. Shadow instantly improved Arthur's mood; he certainly needed it.

Shadow licked Arthur's face and jumped off the sofa to run to his food bowl. Arthur saw that he had eaten all of the food that he had left for him six hours ago; Shadow was a large dog and required a lot of energy, which was frequently exhausted.

He stood up and refilled the bowl, much to Shadow's delight. He then prepared his own quick meal: a bowl of soup. However, Shadow quickly finished the chunk of meat that had been prepared for him and rushed over to Arthur, who was eating peacefully.

Shadow sat next to him while he ate until he finished and threw his bowl onto the nearby kitchen counter. Sitting around for a couple of hours in despair, evening arrived and invited him on a walk with his dog.

We could both use one, he thought as he grabbed his coat from the hook. He readied Shadow's harness and clipped on his lead, leading him out of the flat door. He took him down the streets, contemplating his next plan and staring at the glowing stars.

He considered the potential possibilities of a new job, although it was unlikely he would be able to get something more than low-skilled work.

What if I worked with animals, dogs like Shadow, I could finally do something for others.

He tried to clear his head of the idea of employment for the moment; he wanted to enjoy the walk with his dog, surrounded by the narrow streets of his neighbourhood and the sound of the bell in the church, which was barely visible in the distance

On their walk, they met another dog of similar size to Shadow. It was a chocolate Labrador Retriever with large brown eyes and drooping, fluffy ears. Its owner was a forty-year-old man, who resembled Arthur's former boss. The dogs played while Arthur stood awkwardly, watching them.

They get on so well, Arthur thought. He wished for the mental freedom that Shadow had, carefree and excited at the prospect of meeting another person, knowing they will likely be friendly. However, the possibility of using his creative mind was intriguing to him, especially if he could work at home, away from others.

After the meeting, they turned back, exhausted. Two hours had passed and they walked back into the flat, with Arthur noting the strange beauty in the moonlight that shone through the dusty windows. He rested in bed and read a fictitious book on aeronautics, curious about the assumptions people had made about what lay beyond Earth; he soon fell asleep with Shadow resting beside him. For just a moment, he forgot about the inevitable struggles he was due to have. He finally slept, feeling his perspective change—his world change.

Two figures stood in the light; their features were unclear from the darkness in front of their faces. They watched Arthur, both of them motionless, and waited for him to move. He could not recognise anything; white clouds and fog engulfed his surroundings and left him wondering where he was.

Arthur strode towards the figures, his vision obscured by the blinding light. Around him, buildings randomly collapse while others stood strong.

Does anyone know where I am?

No direction, no context, no support, he felt alone. The atmosphere around him felt untrustworthy, as if waiting for him to make a mistake so something could strike.

The tense figures watched him as he involuntarily approached; the figure that appeared male turned to the female figure beside him; she did not reciprocate the glance. Oddly enough, one of the figures seemed familiar, despite both of their appearances being obscured.

His lack of sight, along with the crashing sounds close to his ears, led him to extend his arm, as if waiting for help.

Suddenly, a wave rose above the figure's heads and crashed to the ground. It threw itself towards Arthur and he ran.

Help me.

However, his escape attempt was futile as he felt wet hands grab his arms and thrust him backwards.

What?

"What?!" Arthur said loudly, as he awoke in panic. Shadow quickly lifted his head up in fear that there was an intruder, but quickly iden-

tified the source of the sound and laid back down. Arthur got up out of bed, trying to make sense of what he saw.

What's wrong with my mind? he thought, hoping for an explanation that no one could give him. He sighed, dismissing it as a dream and dressing for the day. Shadow followed him into the living room as Arthur made them both breakfast, his mind still a puzzle he was yet to solve.

While eating, he silently decided to go to the pool to relax and procrastinate his response to the dire financial situation that threatened him.

Leaving food for Shadow, he grabbed his bag and left for the pool. Arthur walked quickly and attempted to calm his hyperactive mind, to no avail.

Once he arrived, he was immediately greeted by a receptionist, who was quick to question him.

"Would you like to have lessons?" she quickly asked.

"What?" Arthur responded in confusion.

"Are you here for your class already?"

"No."

She asked several additional, albeit meaningless, questions about membership until Arthur asked, "How much for a one-time session?"

The receptionist replied, "It's £5.50 for

three hours." Arthur stood still and silent for a moment. He knew he would struggle to pay his rent and was apprehensive about using his money for luxuries. He sighed and decided to pay the amount anyway, desperately needing a break.

He passed through the changing rooms, changed and walked out to the pool. There was a family of four currently swimming together.

He waited by the side to avoid ruining their session and spoke to a nearby staff member who appeared to be a similar age to him, except she had a job.

He inquired, "Are there any job offers at the moment?"

The staff member, more focused on her work, bluntly replied, "I don't know."

"How long have you been working here?" Arthur asked, hoping it was recent.

"Five years."

Oh.

"Do you have any ideas where I could get a job?"

"There's a bakery—"

"Thanks for the help."

At last, the family left and Arthur got in. He felt relaxed, likely more than he should have been. Being free was the greatest feeling he had and helped him to think; thinking had not been entirely present throughout his life and opening himself up to deep thought for once was incredible.

He swam in the clear waters of his mind yet formed no plan for the future. He had left behind everything he knew in search of an actual opportunity but had been quick to assume that his ideal career would materialise in front of him.

He was unable to enjoy himself while the weight on his mind dragged him down. He swam a length of the pool and looked out from the deep end. Grasping for the nearest object, he wrapped his fingers around a metal bar and pulled on it with the intention of getting out.

The metal bar was attached to an object that dragged across the wet tiles, scratching the floor as it moved. Arthur looked up to see a metal lifeguard chair towering above him, balancing on its front legs.

He panicked and fell back into the pool, having partially climbed out beforehand. He retracted his hand and saw the lifeguard chair slam onto the wet tiled floor, its long legs stretching over the surface of the water.

Arthur slammed his hand on one of the legs in a futile attempt to push it away. Instead, it tilted and slid on top of him, landing directly above him as he darted beneath the water. He briefly wondered where the lifeguard was, before his mind became clear and the air left his body.

He sank, paralysed from shock as the large

metal chair drifted through the water directly above him.

He could not breathe. He gasped for air and tried to move but his body refused to work for him at this critical moment.

But it did not feel critical.

You're drowning. Why are you not panicking?

He felt oddly calm until his head smashed into the hard, tiled surface of the pool. He saw a flash of metal directly above him. Then, he saw darkness.

Confusion. Beeping. Awakening. Arthur awoke and saw a white ceiling filled with bright lights; it was a hospital. He tried to recollect his entry to the room but could not remember any such memory, even why he was there.

Have I ever left? Has my whole life actually been a dream? He thought. *No, it couldn't be...it was too vivid.*

He checked a nearby clock for the date.

14th May 2024. That's right, I think.

He struggled to remember anything from the previous day or the past week—except for the alien figures.

Was I abducted by a UFO?

A nurse saw that he was awake and walked over to him. "You're awake!" she said. "You've had an operation. Please don't move your head too much."

"Why?"

"You were found at the bottom of a pool, with a metal chair crushing you."

A few key memories flooded back. He had almost drowned. He remembered the painful impact of his head on the cold ground and the calm of his mind despite the knowledge of drowning in that moment, no great accomplishments; he planned to change that when he had the chance.

His surroundings were not inspiring; injured patients laid near him, their expressions displaying exhaustion and disappointment while nurses walked in and out of the ward to administer tests and checks.

Why did I need an operation for a concussion?

Arthur was confused but had no choice but to wait until he had been discharged and could go home.

Where is my home? What is it? What does it look like?

He lay for multiple days with his only visitors being nurses checking on his wellbeing. He allowed his mind to dwell in a fantastical reality as a form of entertainment while the people around him kept to themselves.

A highlight of his recovery was the visit of a dog. Arthur was wheeled out of the ward in case of other patients' allergies and saw a large, black German Shepherd running towards him.

Shadow!

He could remember. His dog, with whom he

created memories, had brought them back.

Who were those two figures in my mind?

Arthur snapped out of the depths of his mind as he realised the nearby hospital staff were staring directly at him.

"They came back," he whispered.

"What did?"

"Everything...I mean my memories. They were gone but—" Arthur stopped talking to avoid sounding delusional.

"That's great!" The nurse responded.

Don't overthink it.

Shadow jumped on the hospital bed, with nurses holding on to prevent Arthur from rolling into a wall. They were overjoyed to see each other, appreciating the familiar presence; Arthur did not think that dogs were even allowed in hospitals. After five minutes, Shadow was taken out of the corridor with a nurse, but it was not clear who was actually looking after the dog during Arthur's absence.

After roughly a week, Arthur was discharged from the hospital and taken to a car waiting outside. It had been recommended that he should not drive and was awaiting an unknown driver.

The driver's door opened to reveal Rose, the woman from Cakecut Bakery whom he had essentially risked his job for—she was repaying him.

"This wasn't how I planned to spend

my weekend," she said. Arthur laughed and climbed into the car with her support.

"I've been looking after Shadow while you were gone."

"How did you know?" Arthur asked.

"I was listed as an emergency contact for you."

"You're the only person I know here."

They spoke in the car, discussing the events that had occurred since Arthur had been fired. He was relieved to know that she had cared for his dog during his hospital stay. They arrived at his flat to see Shadow once again, happy as ever to see his owner.

Arthur told him, "Careful Shadow, I need to watch my head."

"You watched out for mine," Rose said laughing. "I've paid you back now, anyway." She had told Arthur that she still had her job at the bakery, which she was using to pay for university, despite the minimum wage pay.

"Of course," replied Arthur, kneeling down and petting Shadow.

"Well I think it's time for me to go then," said Rose.

Arthur stood up as she picked up her bag, ready to leave.

"Bye Shadow!" she said as she left, relieved to go home despite missing the dog she had cared for the past week. Arthur stood away from the door and by the window, looking out onto the streets below.

"I'm going to change my life," he said. "I'm going to become an astronaut."

He knew he would waste no more time. He knew that he would seek out the qualifications he needed and journey to find the source of his visions in the depth of space.

CHAPTER 3

Vekk, Kol, Arkriat and Kretai rushed away from the palace, towards the familiarity of their neighbourhood, as they hoped to avoid the same fate as the burning corpse. Kol glanced at a patrolling soldier and grabbed Vekk's shoulder, causing them both to slow down to avoid suspicion.

They walked quickly to their house and ran inside; Vekk and Kol lowered themselves onto two chairs and glared at the canvases of nature hanging from the wall. The death of an innocent person had struck down the doors to their mental cages, built from years of conditioning.

How?! Kol thought as his eyes moved to focus on a framed map on the other side of the room.

Both siblings felt that time had slowed, as if the universe hoped to taunt them for longer. Both Vekk and Kol were adjusting their knowledge on the severity of the pollution of Quelliare; they now knew it was far worse than they had previously thought. There was only inaction, even as a body lay in the middle of the street.

Arkriat and Kretai stood nearby, concerned for their owners as they did not understand what had just occurred. Vekk glanced at them and held back tears as she visualised Arkriat or Kretai laying lifeless on the ground. Kol began breathing rapidly due to the tense atmosphere; they took several minutes to calm down, reaching an empty, reserved state.

"I feel cold," Kol said in an emotionless tone and Vekk nodded in agreement.

What sort of horrible person would let this happen? she thought, before quickly realising the most likely reason.

Someone who doesn't care for her people.

"Is it as bad as we just thought it was? I don't think storms are unusual on other planets," Vekk said. *The sky's always been grey, brown or purple—always.*

Kol responded, "I don't know. Other planets don't seem to have weather as bad as Quelliare's."

He did not have a great interest in other planets but had a passion for art, although paintings of his dying planet tended to bring a dull atmosphere for their home. Vekk thought they were aesthetically pleasing, although she was not bothered about their furnishings and preferred to leave design work to her brother. Their home was adorned with pieces of art that had been both bought and painted by Kol, the latter being preferred due to pricing.

There were long pauses in conversation, mostly due to the siblings' difficulty in processing their situation.

"Does something need to be done?" Kol suggested, supressing his rage.

"Yes, yes it does," Vekk said. *If I have children, they deserve to live in a beautiful world—I'd like to see it too.*

She also knew that Leritri was not getting any younger; the siblings felt she deserved to smell the fresh flowers and to be able to see the children playing near her home. Vekk was not sure if Leritri had children of her own as she never spoke of them and preferred to talk about other people's lives.

"We need a plan," She said.

"What? We can't topple a whole government by ourselves!"

They both turned to face the skylight in the kitchen. It was hard to see out of, from their position, but the grey smog was unmistakeable.

"I'm sure there's another way to save Quelliare."

Kol sighed and said, "I hope so. We'll have to take Arkriat and Kretai with us."

"We need to find out what's going on first."

"Arkriat, Kretai stay here. I don't want you to be in danger."

Vekk and Kol left their house and

looked around. The storm had restrengthened slightly, causing thunder to attack the ears of Vekk and Kol.

"Avoid any lightning that comes down," Kol helpfully suggested.

"I know."

Searching for an obvious sign to begin, they soon realised that they lived in a world where weaknesses were hard to identify. The palace was visible from everywhere, a symbol of strength and surveillance, while the Beam of Zrelyar stood to its left—it was a beam of light that extended diagonally, its total length unknowable as its tip was obscured by the clouds that surrounded it. Its purpose was undisclosed to the general public but many theorised it was a powerful device or weapon.

"Those green clouds," Kol said, gesturing to the sky ahead of them, "is that from the Beam of Zrelyar?"

"I expect so," said Vekk. "We should inspect it."

They walked swiftly, hoping to avoid the lightning strikes and eager to find a simple solution to the great problem that lay ahead, having no knowledge of the government's methodology. They passed through the poorer streets where they saw people lying beside every building, watching the wealthy stride past them. Vekk and Kol were not affluent but had a respectable amount of money from inheritance, working for Leritri and selling Kol's paintings.

Vekk gave a dying man five Floras, the currency of Zrelyar. The name expectedly stemmed from the plants used to make the money itself. The flowers, known as Florunas, grew native to Quelliare and had powerful capabilities. They had not been seen for centuries, except for the occasional flower that was quickly harvested.

Vekk cared for one such flower that had been gifted to her by her mother who neither Vekk nor Kol had seen for eighteen years, along with their father.

They walked through the destitute Quarailians and entered the richer zone of the city, characterised by the houses standing above ground while the rest of the population were forced below.

Lasapra's Palace had been built directly within the richer districts and stood in the centre of the city. To the left of the building, the Beam of Zrelyar illuminated the area with a distinct green light—it came from a small metallic room that stood beside the road, surrounded by walls and guards. An odd, musty smell filled the air; Kol assumed that it came from the beam itself.

"I've never been this close," Vekk said. "The Beam of Zrelyar must be more than a landmark." The storm began to subside but the beam remained strong, clearly passing through the clouds and likely into the atmosphere. The siblings walked swiftly towards the building that housed the source of the beam, stopping at a distance as to not alarm the guards.

"They have weapons," Kol said. "I feel like we've gone too far."

"If we hadn't, there wouldn't be guards," Vekk said, imagining herself walking past Lasapra and usurping her throne. She swiftly ceased the thoughts, believing them to be absurd. "We need to find out what she's hiding in there. It could be the key to saving Zrelyar."

She rushed towards the guards, who switched to defensive stances, and stepped closer to the gate embedded in the thick concrete walls. She looked through a reinforced slit of glass in the door to the building and saw another door; it was labelled by a sign labelled 'SEWAGE DOOR'.

Kol recognised one of the guards from the parade; the General of the Royal Guard stood in front of the gate and unlocked it, glaring at her as he did so.

"This place is not for civilians. It would be in your best interests to leave."

Vekk slowly backed away, terrified. She looked at the door behind him and saw five slots in the door, likely connected to the lock.

"Wait!" Vekk yelled, desperately seeking a distraction. Luckily for her, Kol ran out and elected the quickest route of angering someone.

"You? The head of the guard? I was expecting someone much fiercer!"

The head of the guard looked furious but did not move, much to Kol's surprise and fear.

Taking out his gun and sliding the barrel through a gap in the gate, he spoke again, "How about you both run back home before I prevent that from happening?"

Neither of them were prepared to deal with weaponry but Vekk used this time to study the door; five unique indents lay in the centre of the reinforced block of metal that was seemingly impenetrable.

"Go!"

They ran from the wealthy district, fearing the storm that was the military might of the head of the guard. Vekk pushed her brother ahead of her to increase his chances of escaping, while recalling what she had seen.

"We need to get to the sewers."

"Are you joking? That man had a gun."

Kol was incredibly apprehensive about the situation but Vekk knew they could not turn back. Fortunately, Kol had looked around the city before, studying it for his artwork; he knew where to find sewer access. He led Vekk to a platform in the ground, which was much dirtier than the surroundings, and stood on it.

"Are you sur—" Vekk was unable to finish her sentence as they were pulled down by a lift, into the sewers. They stepped out, immediately smelling the variety of foul liquids covering virtually everything.

"This is disgusting!" Vekk exclaimed, attempting to avoid the various slimy substances on the floor.

"We'll get your transportation soon, Your Majesty," Kol said, moving away from the spilt chemicals.

They walked through the seemingly ancient sewers, unsure which direction to take until they saw a cleaner, modern section in the direction of the palace.

"Over there!" Kol said, pointing to the area. It was better maintained than the other parts of the sewer and appeared to have been recently renovated. It also served as a guide for the siblings as they waded towards it.

"Even Arkriat doesn't make this much of a mess!"

"It's a sewer, Vekk," Kol said. "Criminals don't get the best that Zrelyar has to offer."

"That's not always true," Vekk muttered, her mind picturing Lasapra in her seat of power.

They made their way into another section that was plated with metal, similar to the mysterious building they sought to enter. They walked up a flight of stone stairs to find another level with a door. The door had five individual, empty slots, identical to the one on the surface. There were two guards patrolling the area; Vekk and Kol remained hidden.

"We need a distraction," said Vekk.

"I can tell. Do you have something?"

Vekk managed to pull a loose metal plate from the wall and threw it away from her, towards one of the guards. It hit his foot and fell onto the clean floor, drawing his attention.

"Something just hit me!" he yelled.

"Bring it here, let's take a look."

The guard ran over to the other end of the corridor to show the other soldier what had been thrown and the siblings took their chance. They approached the door as the guards turned away and walked down the corridor to find the attacker.

Vekk and Kol quietly rushed to the door to hear a muffled conversation, mostly consisting of incoherent pieces of dialogue.

"Will he know?"

"He should not."

"What about…"

"…no."

Both Vekk and Kol were breathing heavily, perplexed as to what was going on. The meeting appeared to convene as the members headed to the door, which contained five slots similar to the one that they had seen upstairs.

"What shapes?" Kol asked quietly.

"What?"

"We need to memorise the shapes in—"

Kol took out a camera he had on him with the intent to show some of his photos to Leritri.

"Good idea," Vekk remarked as he took a photo of the door; the siblings ran back down to the lower level of the sewer as the guards returned, noticed them and pursued.

"Where's the exit?"

"I don't know!"

They ran through many sections of the sewer, unsure where they came in. They finally came across another lift, which they used to return to the surface.

"Well that worked out," Vekk said, surprised that they had not been pursued.

"Let's hope this whole thing works out," said Kol, overwhelmed by fear. They ran back home to Arkriat and Kretai and sat down to analyse the image of the door.

"There are five slots. Potentially for keys?" suggested Vekk, as they entered their home.

"But where are the keys?"

Neither of them could answer. Arkriat began to bark suddenly and ran towards the framed map on the wall, with Kol calling after him. He ran back towards the siblings with it in his mouth.

"Arkriat! How did you take that down?!" Vekk asked, surprised yet annoyed.

She took it out of his mouth and attempted to figure out what Arkriat wanted them to see.

"It's a map of the places where ancient civilisations fell. I thought it was just art?"

Vekk looked closer at the glowing map. "It must be more than that; it's a real map," she said, pointing to a red marker on the map. "This is roughly where Zrelyar is. There are five key locations..."

"Five keys?"

"Exactly, and most of them are close together." Vekk said, relieved that they had a starting point.

"We...we have this for a reason," Kol muttered, taking the map from Vekk, who stood up and walked over to her planted Floruna, taking it from its soil. She walked over to Kol and placed it into his hand. Kol looked slightly confused but trusted in his older sister's wisdom as she knelt down beside him and placed one hand on the Floruna.

"Where is my brother's pain?"

A Quarailian man stood before Vekk and Kol, beside a third, older sibling not seen in years; they were eighteen years younger than they were in the present day. The man stood in their home, holding the map.

"Keep this," he said." It is important for all of us, just not now." He proceeded to frame it and hang it on the wall. The three siblings were confused but simply nodded, hoping for an explanation.

"I have to go now but you will see me when

you are ready."

"Where are you going, father?" Vekk asked him.

"You'll see me in time. Remember to utilise your abilities, Vekk. When we meet again, I want you to show me this moment."

The three siblings did not entirely understand but continued to listen regardless.

"Thrakalir, protect your siblings and continue to improve your combat skills. I am sure they will be of use one day."

"I will father, they'll be beyond what I can do now," he responded.

"Kol, your artistic skills will be incredible someday and you should keep practising your artwork. I want to see some of your work when I see you again."

Kol nodded and began to cry as the man proceeded to walk away, leaving them alone.

Vekk and Kol, now seeing present day, sat still. Vekk did not realise that Kol remembered the memory in such detail; she stood up and sat beside him.

"He wanted us to do this," Vekk said. "I hoped that you'd have some idea of what the keys were for, though."

"If either of us was to know, it'd be you."

"Thrakalir probably knew…"

"We need to be those rebellious subjects that Leritri mentioned earlier."

Vekk placed the flower back into the soil where it continued to grow.

"Where—"

They heard multiple loud vehicles outside approaching their house.

Wh—

The glass skylight in the kitchen shattered with a powerful blow.

"Help!" Kol exclaimed, feeling a sudden attachment to his lost family.

"Run!" Vekk yelled.

They ran to the glass door, which had also shattered so they simply ran through the frame and stood at the entrance to their house.

The head of the guard, who they had previously been confronted by, announced from the roof of a tank, "I am Zavroon, General of the Royal Guard. Surrender, spies, or be killed."

The siblings ran behind their house and between two buildings, onto a main street, despite being exhausted from running earlier in the day. It was evening; they utilised the cover of darkness to escape.

They ran behind lamps and advertisements, hoping the military would attempt to reduce the amount of damage they caused. Unfortunately, the lack of buildings above ground gave little shelter.

Neither of them were even particularly athletic which made the escape much harder. Luckily, Arkriat and Kretai were faster than them, which made them unlikely targets and gave the siblings less to be concerned about.

They headed for the commercial part of the city, which had more above-ground buildings to hide behind. They slid through cracks between stores and pushed through groups of people to escape. However, the military was better equipped. They hovered above, hoping to scare the siblings into retreating into the hands of Zavroon.

The vehicle was a Hovercle-16-9. A flying vehicle lifted by an oval-shaped device underneath and a backup engine at the back of the vehicle in the case of an emergency. The vehicle itself was in the shape of a flipped trapezium with a curved window covering the front side and an opening through the back of the vehicle for access. Its black and grey paint gave a sense of intimidation, which made many people feel fearful of the vehicles, although some saw them as a source of protection.

Vekk was split up from Kol, and both Arkriat and Kretai were entirely out of sight so she decided to hide to catch her breath. She managed to lose the military's attention but continued moving soon after, knowing that they would be targeting her brother, Arkriat or Kretai instead.

Kol slid through a crowd of people, causing a stir that temporarily distracted some of the soldiers on foot. Arkriat ran over and began to growl, inciting further panic. Both of them ran together down a straight road, which did little to deter their pursuers, and both were beginning to tire.

Vekk stopped to see her brother from a distance and accidentally walked into Kretai, causing the Ukrifar to fall to the ground, although recovering quickly. Vekk held onto the Kretai and continued running.

Kol began to slow as he became fatigued, which allowed Vekk to catch up with him. The four of them kept running as a vehicle fired directly at them, narrowly passing between them and destroying the roof of a shop.

The shop began to collapse as Vekk spotted a mysterious bag inside that attracted her attention, despite the chaos around her, and took it, hoping for something useful. The four newly-branded criminals escaped the underground room, which collapsed onto the pursuing soldiers. The Vekk, Kol, Arkriat and Kretai sprinted to the gate of Zrelyar, which was locked.

They stood fearfully as the vehicles began to surround them. Escape would grant them freedom as the gate was too large for most of the vehicles to pass. Luckily for them, a well-timed lightning strike crippled the Hovercle-16-9s and sent them burning to the ground. Zavroon approached them, perched in his personal vehicle.

"Well, looks like I will have a gift for Queen Lasapra—a pair of aspiring, inexperienced criminals."

Vekk scanned the area, looking for any route of escape; they had only one route of escape.

She nudged Kol and jumped onto one of the Hoverength-3s, the name clearly being derived from its abilities in hovering and strength. The front was sloped, which Vekk took advantage of by climbing onto its roof and using its height to jump onto a load of scaffolding, allowing her to make her way over the wall. Both Kol and Arkriat followed while Kretai flew beside them and escaped to freedom, leaving Zavroon behind as he sat content despite the loss of the siblings.

Freedom. The air became a delicate breeze as they ran away from the city and everything became much clearer than anything they had ever seen in their entire lives.

The grass was a vibrant purple hue with small flowers sprouting to find the partially visible sun on the horizon. They encountered insects that they had never seen before which came in a variety of shapes and colours.

The city was still visible and appeared to have a grey cage of darkness above it, darker than the sky above them. Arkriat ran into the open field with Kretai flying behind, taking advantage of the freedom that they had never had, even with the remnants of the city's pollution hanging in the air.

Kol stood in awe at the incredible landscape that lay before them and visualised the scene as a painting. The new inspiration was appealing even to Vekk, who was surprised such a place could actually exist on Quelliare as she had never left the city. They knew that it was possible that many more beautiful places could exist, even with the pollution that had likely spread across the world.

"Let's...let's keep going," Vekk said softly. They slowly walked through the field, which was slightly less polluted than the city at the distance they were, although it was clear enough for them to admire the nature that could not dream of growing in the city.

"What if we ruled Zrelyar after saving it?" Kol suggested.

"What?" Vekk said, taken aback. "We never said we would even go near Queen Lasapra. I assumed we were just solving the danger that everyone is in and return to our normal lives."

"Do you really think we will be welcomed back? Even if we did destroy the beam, we would just be arrested and it would be replaced," Kol pointed out, as the atmosphere began to feel less idyllic due to the loss of their home and their status.

Good point, Vekk thought. However, they

were hardly prepared to leave Zrelyar and were certainly not experienced or confident enough to lead the Zrelyarian citizens.

They found a nearby hill, large enough to contain a cave entrance, boarded up with wood, which suggested that it had remained for some time.

"This is quite old," Kol noted. "No one alive today would use wood to block something. They'd probably use metal or just destroy the entire hill."

Both of them stared at the boards, trying to find a way to break it down.

"Check that bag you stole," Kol suggested.

"I didn't steal it!"

"So how did it come into your possession?"

"I...acquired it."

Vekk opened the bag to find some pieces of scrap and a couple of screws covering a larger object. She dug out a large block of metal, strong and durable.

"That's lucky," Kol said.

Vekk smashed the boards and after multiple attempts, managed to break a hole large enough for them to climb through. Kretai moved away, fearing something would burst out.

Discarding the bag and the block, Vekk and Kol clambered through the opening, with Kretai cautiously following behind. Arkriat stood outside, unable to jump through without being caught on the remaining boards. Vekk realised and called to Arkriat, who grabbed the block with his mouth and dragged it over to the entrance.

"We need to ensure that both Arkriat and Kretai are with us at all times," Vekk said, grabbing the block and smashing more of the boards. They quickly fell away and the siblings walked through the dark cave with Arkriat and Kretai, concealing any potential source of light.

"Do we have a torch or something?" Kol asked.

Vekk felt around the walls for some indication of hidden passages, as was depicted in many forms of media that they had seen. However, the films failed her and she found nothing.

"How about this?" Kol said, pulling a lever to reveal torches on the walls, now lit with fire.

"Ah," Vekk muttered, walking deeper into the cave; its brilliant orange walls were now visible.

"It's freezing in here," Kol said quietly. The stone walls did little to insulate them as night approached but they laid down regardless.

"I was hoping for something more comfortable but it's probably the best we'll do while out of the city."

"We don't even have food," Vekk said. "If there aren't any other settlements on this world, we'll starve."

Kol was visibly anxious from his sister's panic; he had looked up to her and she had taken care of him for the most recent years of his life and to see her without direction concerned him.

Arkriat and Kretai had fallen asleep but the siblings lay awake, trying to process the sudden turn their lives had taken due to their own actions. With little more to think on after hours of contemplation, they eventually fell asleep.

Morning came and awoke Arkriat, who proceeded to nudge his owners to notify them that he was hungry. They woke up, mostly surprised that they had not been disrupted.

"I slept quite well, surprisingly," Vekk noted. Both of them stood up and walked towards the exit, noting the extinguished torches.

"I guess we should get going if we want to find food," Vekk said.

"I guess so."

They marched up the hill outside, still desperate for food and shelter. They also had to care for Arkriat and Kretai, which was difficult without any nearby shopping centres or any form of a welcoming society.

"I'm constantly doubting myself. We're now criminals." Kol said.

"You really think that they'd let us back in? I doubt anyone else'll do this anyway," Vekk replied.

"I know."

They had become slightly accustomed to the improvement in surroundings yet felt uncomfortable with their sudden freedom, with minimal restrictions set only by themselves—the mental barriers held them back while they physically progressed forward.

Reaching the peak of the hill, they saw a large gate, guarded by a soldier similar to those that chased them out of the city. He wore a typical military uniform consisting of a jacket with trousers, alongside a helmet in the same shape of his head. He was stood to attention, despite the only people nearby being two criminals, who were barely old enough to work, and their pets. Slowly, they approached him.

"We need to pass."

"Who are you?" the guard asked, expecting identification or a permit or some sort.

"We...live beyond the gate. We were...picking flowers and got lost." Vekk told him uncertainly.

"If you're lost, how do you know you live beyond this gate?"

"My...friend works with the military and told me that I can reach my village through this gate." Kol said.

"Who is he?"

"Za...Zavroon." Vekk interjected.

"Oh, of course," he said, flustered, taking

out his key card.

The guard opened the gate and allowed them through. The siblings moved quickly to avoid his gaze as they were unsure how much longer they could maintain their deception. However, the guard did not pursue them and stayed at his post. They continued to walk further from Zrelyar and into a more beautiful landscape.

"General?" the guard whispered into his earpiece as he watched them walk away. "I've found them."

CHAPTER 4

Continuing their search for refuge, Vekk and Kol strode across the vivid, blooming purple fields, enjoying the sun's rise and rays that gradually became more visible.

Arkriat ran ahead, surveying the area for threats while Kretai took advantage of the warm winds. Ahead of them was a large blue-green jungle with towering trees—from a distance, it appeared to have large amounts of wildlife that could survive in an area where the pollution's grasp was weaker. While walking, Vekk quickly noticed the Florunas sprouting from the ground. She knew that finding one in the wild was an incredible sight; seeing multiple was like a miracle.

"Florunas!" Vekk yelled, running over to a small, glowing flower. She had a unique affinity for the beautiful pink flowers and they continued to aid her in exploring her supernatural abilities, which allowed her to identify another person's painful memories. Similarly, they were vital on the planet as they respired clean air and had acted as a barrier for the jungle ahead, preventing the pollution from poisoning the bright biome. They resembled mushrooms, with a round exterior surrounding the glowing centre of the flowers themselves.

Vekk took a flower and held it, before placing it in the bag. Kol did not understand why Florunas held such great importance to Vekk and usually left her to tend to the one that had been planted in their home, but seeing them in plentiful amounts in the field gave him an appreciation for their beauty. They were once exploited for their abundance but had become so scarce that most of the currency in Zrelyar was essentially ancient and replacements had to be made out of artificial materials.

They reached the jungle after about an hour and pushed their way through the deep blue bushes and green vines, passing many beautiful creatures. They found several pulsating crystals wrapped up in vines, which they passed through to find a completely different society.

They stepped into a village unlike anything that they had seen before. It appeared quite primitive yet modern due to the small sizing of the village with homes resembling huts fashioned from glass and frozen leaves, despite the obvious heat.

The houses stayed away from the centre of the village, which appeared to be a pathway to the grand temple that stood at the back of the area, with no clear way to access it. There was a large space in front of the door, which implied that there was a missing ramp or staircase to reach the entrance.

The people of the village were unlike anyone they had seen before. They appeared to have two different height ranges, from matching the height of the siblings to the height of the average Quarailian's lower leg.

However, the taller of the species grew beyond the Quarailians' average height and far above the smaller members of their species but both forms were clearly of the same race, as both their bodies resembled translucent crystals held together by vines.

Their thin crystalline bodies had vines wrapped around all of the joints, yet they could bend easily. They wore brown pieces of cloth around their arms, while the rest remained exposed.

"Cristrials," Kol whispered. Leritri had described them before; they were unmistakable.

They headed into the village where an older Cristrial man walked over to them, pulsating with orange energy.

"Hello. Are you here from Zrelyar? I promise we are not behind on any payments."

Everyone was watching their conversation, fearing them due to their species alone.

"We just left the city—we're independent from anyone in Zrelyar." Vekk said.

They watched the man visibly relax, slightly, and said, "Oh, in that case, welcome to our village! Is that a Garisal? I've never seen one of those in reality!"

"Yes...that's Arkriat," Vekk replied, still taken aback by her surroundings. "We've never seen a Cristrial before, only heard of them in myths and legends."

"Really?" the man replied, laughing. "Well, we have business in Zrelyar all of the time. I'm not sure why we would be portrayed as mythical."

Vekk and Kol smiled awkwardly as they were left to walk around the village. It was larger than it first appeared as they saw more homes behind the trees that were protecting the back of the temple.

As they walked towards the grand building, a young Quarailian woman wearing tattered green robes approached them. "Would you like some food? I expect the journey has been long."

The siblings concluded that she likely had not been far outside the village, considering the distance between it and Zrelyar was relatively short. However, they accepted, not having eaten since their escape.

Upon entering her home, they were greeted with the unusual smell of decaying wood and natural food, boiling in a pot placed on a pedestal. Upon further inspection, they could distinguish the foul stench from the smell of the jungle, a stench arising from a mixture that resembled a blue ocean contained in a round pot.

They sat down on a broken log as the woman scooped out the mysterious meal and placed it into two square-shaped bowls, giving the siblings a bowl each and allowing Arkriat and Kretai to eat whatever remained in the pot.

Out of desperation and curiosity, they tasted the exotic meal and were surprised by the results. An unfamiliar yet pleasing taste dissolved in their mouths, nourishing them better than anything they had eaten before.

"The temple brings many visitors," the woman said, beginning to mix another meal. "I was one of them."

"What significance does the temple hold?" Vekk asked.

"Power, knowledge and salvation."

"What do you mean?"

"For some, the temple is one of the first steps to freedom; the power to choose can irreversibly shape your future—remember to be careful in your conclusions."

"How do we know if we're making the right choice by entering?" Kol asked, holding strong eye contact amidst his worried expression.

"Allowing yourself to think freely is a decision in itself."

"Who are you?" Vekk asked, her posture becoming defensive as she turned slightly towards Kol.

"You chose to ask me my name—a question that tells you nothing about my nature."

"I didn't say I was asking for your name."

The woman smiled, seemingly in praise of herself for Vekk's response; the former's expression closely resembled a smirk.

"Good, you have begun to consider multiple perspectives. I am a protector for these people—you can ask any one of them and they will support my claim."

"I see. Thank you for the...delicacy," Vekk said, her eyes moving to look at the setting sun. As the siblings placed down their bowls and called Arkriat and Kretai, the four of them exited her home, into the foreign world outside.

Vekk closed her eyes and breathed the slightly fresh air, before suddenly reopening her eyes and scanning the village with a concerned expression. "As incredible as this place is, we need to keep moving."

"You were the one taking part in word games." Kol took another few glances at the homes behind him, before the four of them began to wander around the village in search of answers. They wanted to focus on finding food and shelter, but the lingering presence of the temple called to them.

Power, knowledge and salvation—one of the keys sits inside. Vekk and Kol thought the same idea as it dawned on them that they had no choice but to enter.

If only to sate my curiosity.

Vekk and Kol searched for a prominent religious figure, soon realising that they could not distinguish them from the other Cristrials. They decided to split up, personally interviewing the people of the village and unintentionally exacerbating the instinctual fear that the Cristrials had of them.

"Excuse me…"

"Can you help us?"

"So you can conquer us, as your people do?"

"Go away, spies."

Stereotyped and struck with surprise, the siblings had little choice but to give up. They wandered over to a wooden bench beside a small hut with every eye in the village focused on them. Vekk analysed the ancient temple from afar but saw no means of entering the building, except for the doorway, which was several metres above the ground.

The frail elder that had greeted them earlier calmly approached and did not immediately appear to hold any of the fear that the others had for the siblings.

"Hello again," he said, smiling. "I believe I can help."

"Do you know how to get into the temple? The door is too high for any of us," Vekk told him.

"There is a ramp that will extend out from the temple walls that will allow you straight into the door."

"Thank you! How do we extend the ramp?"

"Find it yourself," the man said with sudden apathy and walked off.

What? Vekk and Kol thought simultaneously.

"Maybe he got nervous," Kol suggested.

"I don't know," Vekk said. "We should be careful, regardless."

Approaching the temple, they placed their hands on the exterior. They felt the chipped surface, the cracks and the peeling paint acting as a cover for the stone-cold walls that held the temple together.

Kretai dug her claws into the descending temple walls, which were too steep for Vekk or Kol to climb. Arkriat could smell the scents of the decades of use the temple had experienced under the various owners, as well as the mark each had left behind.

"Over here!"

Kol directed his sister to an octagonal hole underneath the door. It was a small indent in the wall, about 5 centimetres deep. It was surrounded by a faint, circular mark around it.

"We need something," Kol helpfully suggested.

"A key." Vekk said. "Another key."

Kol took a photo of the keyhole, before they

backed away in fear of the Cristrials forcefully removing them from the village.

"We won't get the key from anyone here."

"Then where?"

Arkriat barked. The siblings looked towards the jungle, whose trees began to illuminate themselves, a golden stripe working its way up the bark. The two moons of Quelliare, known as Vennirein and Jarelin, casted a soft light from the sun onto the village, something it could not do to Zrelyar.

The draw of the bioluminescent trees proved to be overwhelming for Vekk, Kol and Kretai as they approached the exit to the village. Arkriat followed behind, continuing to bark as they entered the jungle.

They sought out clear, charted territory, hoping for some indication of the rare keys that locked away their people's freedom to live and breathe freely.

The jungle was silent, devoid of any fauna. Never having experienced a jungle, they slowed their speed at the sight of a biome they viewed as almost mythical.

"The trees are...beautiful," said Vekk, awed by life that had previously been held out of sight.

The deep blue jungle was accompanied by green flora that covered the earth beside their feet; it felt mossy, easily breaking apart as Vekk, Kol and Arkriat disrupted the precise ecosystem by walking directly through it while Kretai flew above.

Irregular spots of light shone through the broken roof of leaves, which rose far beyond any living being underneath; the siblings were surprised to see a world that civilisation had not conquered.

Vekk placed her hand on a glowing tree, feeling the heat radiating from its core. "What are these made of? I didn't think nature could glow like this."

I'm glad to have some decent surroundings for once," Kol responded, allowing Kretai to land on his arm while watching Arkriat scan the darkness for predators.

They continued their search for the key, stepping over small branches and colourful plants that sprouted from the ground.

"Do you think that the military is still looking for us?" Vekk asked, backing away from the tree and heading forwards, stepping over small branches and colourful plants that were half-submerged in the dirt.

"Probably," replied her brother. "That general was furious; he probably knows what we're after."

"Imagine if we succeed; we could reform the entire city."

"We would have to dethrone Lasapra and replace all of the law enforcement in Zrelyar," Kol said. "I doubt we could do all of that."

"Of course we c...did you hear that?" Vekk asked, positioning herself behind Arkriat.

Arkriat began to growl at the darkness as something began to approach from the thick bushes, quickly increasing in speed.

"Why did we expect an unexplored forest to be completely safe?" Kol asked rhetorically.

"We didn't know that it was unexplored!"

Arkriat's growling grew louder, as if repeated by hundreds of Garisals. Kretai let out a squeal in fear as the sound of hundreds of feet scraping the earth was heard.

Kol quickly backed away as a pack of Garisals, resembling Arkriat with a smaller stature and without horns, revealed themselves beneath the glow of the moons.

"Stay back!" Vekk yelled, making eye contact with one of the predators as Arkriat stood forward to protect his loyal owners. They were still outnumbered: six feral Garisals to one Alpha Garisal and three fearful beings.

"Run," Kol said calmly, as he followed his own command. Vekk sprinted ahead of him, leading him and their pets forth. The Garisals ran fast, but the Quarailians had evolved to thrive in a versatile environment.

They projected themselves off trees and threw loose branches towards their attackers. It did not harm the Garisals but gave the siblings the adrenaline to continue running.

Kretai lifted herself off Kol's shoulder and

flew ahead, preferring the speed of her wings to her unpredictable owner's shoulder. She squealed as a Garisal neared Vekk's foot, allowing the latter to spin and smash the side of her fist into its face.

"We could hide in those bushes," Kol suggested.

"They'll find us there. Keep running!" Vekk replied as she grabbed a broken branch for protection, soon deciding to throw it at the nearest Garisal—a pack leader.

Arkriat suddenly stopped, unbeknown to the siblings, and jumped at the Garisal in the head of the group, wounding it severely.

The other members of the pack slowed, allowing the siblings to gain a greater advantage over their pursuers and giving their Alpha Garisal time to catch up to his own loyal pack.

Under the cover of night, the siblings and their pets retreated into the deep jungle, having evaded their brutal pursuers. Crouching in a bush, they took the time to reclaim their breath.

"What now?" Kol asked his sister.

"The key," she said. "I don't know where it is. I don't even know where we are."

"Arkriat, find a door!" Kol ordered, unsure if the Garisal even understood the command. However, Arkriat did appear to have some understanding as he patrolled the perimeter in search of something unnatural. The siblings attempted to help but struggled to see any displaced objects in the darkness, especially with the threat of the feral Garisals occupying their minds.

"I found something!" Vekk said. Rushing over, Kol saw his sister digging her fingers into a faint, circular outline on a rocky hill nearby. Ancient markings were etched into the rock but meant nothing to either of them.

"Help me with this door," Vekk said.

"How do you know if it's a door?" Kol asked.

"I don't."

Pushing random rocks and trying to decrypt the markings, the siblings attempted to open the door but had little knowledge on anywhere outside of Zrelyar, making it difficult to understand the wall's purpose or the location of an actual door.

"What if the circle is part of the markings?" Kol suggested.

Vekk replied, "Depicting what? We don't understand the other markings anyway."

"What if it represents a planet," Kol said, "or a symbol?"

Kretai watched from the peak of the hill as the siblings struggled with the wall, arguing, discussing and hypothesising about the potential secrets within the symbols surrounding the area. Kretai fell back to avoid the flying stones from the siblings' interferences, falling farther than expected.

"Kretai!" Vekk yelled, climbing onto the top of the hill.

"The roof fell in," she remarked, shocked by the fragility of the grassy cover. Behind the stone markings lay a rectangular room with small openings in the wall that appeared to lead elsewhere. However, the room itself was small, barely above the Quarailians' knees. The openings were too small to fit through and left few options.

Kol climbed over the wall and analysed the room for himself while Vekk picked Kretai up to ensure that she was not injured.

"Only Kretai could fit in those doors," Kol audibly noted, "but I doubt she'll be able to locate the key since she doesn't know what it looks like."

"Can we break it open?" Vekk suggested.

"Seems a bit extreme," Kol said with an amused tone. "We have nothing to break it with anyway."

Arkriat suddenly leapt over the wall, relieved to find his owners as they scoured the area for indication of a weapon, with Vekk choosing to analyse the trees that had previously caught her attention. Placing her hand through a glowing tree's light, it began to sink as if in honey and she felt a strong, dodecahedral object within its centre. She felt the twelve individual sides and the sharp corners before pulling it out of the tree and staring in awe at the fascinating golden object.

"What is this?" Vekk asked aloud, despite being alone. She carried the object towards the doors, leaving the tree to lose its source of light.

She tried placing the object in front of the miniature doors, as well as throwing it—neither had an effect. However, she felt oddly sure of the object's abilities and tried simply rolling it towards the doors. It exploded and threw Vekk backwards, creating an entrance for the siblings.

"What was that?" Kol yelled in the distance. He ran towards her with Arkriat and Kretai to see the new entrance themselves. "How did you do that? Did you steal a grenade from Zrelyar?"

"No...those trees literally have bombs inside of them." Vekk responded.

Falling with the collapsing ground, the group fell into a pool of murky water, feeling the collapsed earth below their feet. The siblings managed to swim up to catch their breath, along with Arkriat. However, Kretai did not resurface.

"Where's Kretai?" Kol asked.

"I don't know," Vekk replied. "I'll check for her."

She swam down into the depths of the pool while Kol and Arkriat swam to a tunnel opening made of decaying green bricks; water dripped through the cracks; the water level had risen due to the amount of debris that had just fallen. They stood in the tunnel, waiting for the other half of their small group to arrive.

Vekk swam through the unclean water to find Kretai desperately attempting to swim upwards for air mid-way down the pool but failing due to a lack of strength. Vekk grabbed her pet and quickly swam towards the surface despite her lack of clear vision, fearing for Kretai. She threw the small creature above the surface of the water while struggled to regain air herself.

She swam towards the brick opening and grabbed onto Arkriat's leg; Kol pulled her out and watched as she coughed violently. "I'm not used to...nature."

"Swimming wasn't a necessity in Zrelyar."

"We weren't rich enough for that."

Vekk finished clearing her throat and led her brother down the tunnel, towards a solid wall. The newly-discovered corridor had partially filled with water, but had begun to drain through unknown means.

Where is the water going? Vekk wondered as the ground dried beneath her.

"Do you have any of those tree grenades?" Kol asked.

"No," Vekk said. "There must be a way to break down this wall. Nothing usually closes off this abruptly unless it was sealed."

"Not necessarily," Kol said, pushing on a brick that was unmoved by his actions. He then stepped away for a moment and looked around, before heading towards a pale brick to his left. He dug his fingers into its crumbling edges and pulled it out, seeing darkness behind it.

Vekk watched him struggle to remove the rest of the bricks, soon stepping in to help. "How did you—do you know what this place is?"

"No."

They removed the rest of the bricks and stepped into a small room, where a crystal hand was attached to the wall. Its palm was against the bricks, facing the indent that it perfectly filled.

"That's not from a Cristrial..." Vekk said, stepping towards the hand and looking at its short fingers. She waved her hand to dissuade Kretai from flying towards it while being unable to remove her eyes from it. "Cristrials don't have hands like us."

Kol carefully placed his fingers around it and removed it from the wall, noticing a small piece of metal inside. "Looks like a replica of the Survivor's Last Hand—that's literally its name."

"What does that have to do with anything?" Vekk asked.

"I don't know."

Arkriat began barking in the corridor. Vekk and Kol walked out to see that the wall had disappeared and had revealed the room behind it.

"Are you planning on keeping that?" Vekk

asked, looking down at the crystal hand that Kol was clutching.

Kol shrugged. "Maybe it'll help us."

Walking into a circular room, water continued to drip but the bricks began to shift into platforms. The group jumped onto one platform with no space to move. The room was illuminated by torches, which somehow continued to burn despite the room appearing to have long been abandoned.

The ground was flooded with opaque water as another door opened across from the previous entrance, with no apparent means of access as it stood above the ground.

Kol suddenly jumped to another platform while Kretai flew directly towards the exit.

"She has an advantage," Vekk muttered. The ground was moving quickly but did not provide access to the exit. The siblings and Arkriat jumped across platforms to get closer but they constantly moved and gave no respite.

Leaping up to the door, Kol dug his fingers into the cracks and pulled himself up, dropping the Survivor's Last Hand while leaping across.

"Vekk, Jump!" he called out to his sister, who was staying beside Arkriat to ensure his safety.

She jumped to another platform, expecting Arkriat to follow her. However, he instead stayed still as the platform rotated and moved backwards with no way to reach the door.

"Arkriat!" Vekk yelled, looking for another platform to jump onto.

"Vekk come on!" Kol yelled at her. She ignored him and jumped towards the previous entrance to reach her loyal Garisal. Kol stepped forwards to join Vekk but the exit began to seal itself off from the death trap, separating the siblings once again.

"Vekk!" Kol yelled in frustration. Kretai flew onto his shoulder and made a whining noise, ruminating about Vekk and Arkriat's fates.

"They'll be alright," Kol said quietly. *I hope so, anyway.*

He walked down a long, thin corridor and a staircase winding around a pillar that was consistent with the rest of the brick building until he reached yet another door.

"This place doesn't change," he pondered aloud.

Kol began to feel around the walls for a hidden button or lever until Kretai flew off his shoulder and onto the floor, activating a plate, which caused the dusty door to open. It caused cracking bricks to reach their breaking point yet remain in the unstable door.

Beyond lay a room built with clean grey bricks which had been maintained unlike the rest of the building, with the corners being graced by white, cylindrical pillars, pure gold wrapping around as far as anyone could see. The wall that held the door was built with wood for no clear reason and stood out against the rest of the well-built chamber.

Against the centre of the back wall stood a stone stele with a glowing red ruby in its centre. It was engulfed in markings and images that neither Kol nor Vekk would be able to decipher fully except for minor parts and details.

"Beautiful," Kol said, walking towards it.

"Arkriat, jump to me!" Vekk commanded while attempting to avoid the pool of potential death below. Arkriat stood incredibly still, too fearful to move in case of the platform collapsing or quickly rotating. The distances between the platforms felt greater despite little difference.

The water level looks lower. Vekk thought to herself.

"Arkriat, jump!" she repeated. The Garisal finally jumped to a nearby platform and Vekk managed to reach him.

A crash, a screech, a hum. The sounds were brief but reminded Vekk of the risk to both her and her pet's lives as the platforms began to rotate and sink into the ground.

Was this journey even worth it? she thought. *We haven't even found a single key!*

Vekk and Arkriat slowly sunk into the water and were forced to swim to find an exit. The water seemed to be flowing towards one wall, which had a section that sunk into the building.

"There!" Vekk called, unsure of where the water would bring them. The power of the water current was overwhelming and pushed them towards the wall regardless of their resistance. They moved quickly until they were thrown through a loosely boarded up hole. Water bursted through the hole, throwing them into a room that was unlike the rest of the building.

"Vekk? Arkriat?" Kol said, seeing his sister and their Garisal fall to the ground through the once fortified wall, discoloured water rapidly flowing through.

"The key!" Vekk said, gesturing to the ruby within the stele.

"It would be easier to get if you didn't flood the room," replied her brother.

"At least I'm alive," she said. "I would say that's important."

"Of course," responded Kol, attempting to pull the ruby from the stone before they drowned. Kretai climbed atop the stele to avoid the water while Vekk searched hurriedly for an exit.

Kol channelled all of his strength into pulling out the key and was successful.

Now we just need to escape, Kol thought.

Pushing a discoloured brick, Vekk opened a door to reveal a staircase to the surface.

"Perfect," she said. "I hope we can find our way out once we're up."

"As long as we make it up," replied Kol, making his way through the door and outside, followed by his sister and pets.

Upon reaching the surface, they found themselves in the middle of the jungle, the moons watching them through the spaces between the trees.

"I dropped the crystal hand," Kol muttered.

"It doesn't matter now," Vekk said. "I have no idea where we are."

"None of us do."

They walked along an overgrown path, hoping that it led to the village.

"Do you think the Cristrials will be happy to see us again?" Kol asked, carrying Kretai in his hands.

"I doubt it," she said. "Our first meeting wasn't exactly... hospitable, despite our best efforts. Leritri portrayed them as nicer people then they actually are."

"They probably haven't met a friendly Quarailian before," Kol said.

They walked for approximately an hour until they reached the walls to Cristrial civilisation again.

"We've never been left completely unsupervised for that long," Vekk said. "That was real freedom."

"We better thank Zavroon then," replied Kol.

Upon entering the village, the siblings immediately felt the eyes of the people glaring. Despite their heroic intentions, the people did not trust their visitors.

Running over to the temple, they walked briskly towards the key hole and placed the ruby inside. The scratch of stone was heard and the temple began to move. The siblings ran away as a large ramp extended from the temple walls, allowing them access inside.

The group turned to see the elders of the Cristrials staring at them with anger.

"We do not trust you in our holy place."

"I'm sorry," Vekk said. "But this will save everyone."

They ran inside, away from the gaze of the angered villagers into the ancient temple, half-buried in the jungle.

The siblings walked through the temple's damaged corridors, seemingly having once been the site of a great battle. The art painted on the walls was colourful yet peeling, leaving the empty grey brick behind.

The ceiling was low, trapping the heat within the cold temple. They walked quickly to complete their business and avoid the elders who appeared to disapprove heavily of their actions, despite the life-threatening cost to achieve them.

They entered a room with four separate corridors leading off, all dark except from the light in the connecting rooms. Finally able to see, the siblings took a moment to appreciate the architecture, not recognising its origins.

"Which way?" Kol asked, as if his sister knew the answer.

Vekk looked at the walls for a sign, finding little indication of a direction.

"What are we even looking for?" Vekk wondered aloud.

"A key, I assumed," Kol said. "I thought you might know."

Arkriat ran down the left corridor, away from the siblings and Kretai. They ran after him, hoping the Garisal knew where he was going.

"Arkriat hasn't been here before. How would he know what we want?" Kol asked.

"Perhaps he can sense something," Vekk replied.

"Sense? Is he telepathic?"

They ran through several corridors until they reached a room with a closed door, unlike anywhere else they had seen before in the temple.

"This temple is well-decorated," Kol said.

"It's hard to tell when most of it isn't lit," Vekk replied.

Beside the door were three square holes in the wall with writing above each. The wall read:

Red is Yellow

Green is Pink

Red and Blue

Red and Yellow

Red and Green

One colour combination was listed above each box, as if waiting for an answer.

"I don't understand," said Vekk. "It doesn't tell us anything."

"Cubes," Kol said, walking over to the opposite wall where small glass cubes of different colours stood in openings in the wall.

"We need to match them up somehow," Vekk said. "The first box involves red and blue. What colour is created from red and blue?"

"But red is yellow so it must be yellow and blue," said Kol, "that creates green, which is actually pink."

Vekk took the pink cube and placed it into the corresponding slot. The square had no indication of their method being correct, which left the siblings to assume they understood.

"The next two colours are red and yellow, or just yellow," said Vekk, placing the yellow cube into its appropriate slot.

"This looks correct," said Kol. "The last one is red and green."

"I know," replied Vekk. "We need to switch both colours to yellow and pink; what is that?"

"I think it's a sort of orange," Kol said with a lack of confidence. However, a light orange cube was the only option that fit his vague description so he picked the final cube and placed it into the wall.

Cracking was heard as the door began to open, revealing steps into the room that they hoped contained the knowledge or treasures that they had come for.

Walking down the steps, another door opened into a room, where part of the outside wall was exposed and the ruby key had fallen onto a pedestal, waiting for collection. Above, two metal chains secured a sheathed spear. The spear was long, with its pointed head appearing to have been dipped into a mint green mixture.

"The gem...and an ancient weapon?" Vekk said, walking up to the artefacts with great intrigue while Kol checked his camera.

"The gem is one of the keys," said Kol, putting away his camera. "I'm not sure about the spear though."

The spear suddenly came loose, along with its sheath, as the metal chains disintegrated and fell into Vekk's outstretched arms as she reached for the artefact.

Grabbing both items, Vekk moved it away from the key and took the ruby with her other arm. She handed the key to Kol who placed it beside his camera.

"What am I? A storage unit?" Kol jokingly asked his sister as she also passed him the weapon, which he secured to his back using the sheath.

The siblings, alongside Arkriat and Kretai, ran upstairs and navigated their way out of the temple. When they reached the exit, they could see the elders, who had not moved, watching them once again.

Vekk noticed the Quarailian woman they had met earlier. Despite labelling herself as their protector, she stood behind the crowd.

"I assume you have desecrated our beautiful temple," one called out.

"No…we just solved the puzzle."

The elder sighed. "Remove them from my sight."

A couple of Cristrials ran at Kol and Kretai, clutching sharp knives in their hands. Vekk and Arkriat pushed the villagers away, providing them with time to escape. After about one minute of distraction, they both ran to catch up with Kol and Kretai at the entrance to the jungle.

They escaped from their pursuers back into the wilderness with a weapon and a key, giving them much more encouragement than they had on arrival.

CHAPTER 5

The sun gave the spotlight to its counterparts of the night as the siblings passed through the deep jungle. The thickness of the leaves prevented a large amount of light from passing through onto the foliage underneath, shrouding the surrounding area in darkness.

"I don't know if those people were angry or just cautious," Kol said to his sister.

"I think they were scared," Vekk said in response. "They are probably used to Quarailians demanding taxes or bribes from their small village."

"I can't believe we made it through that temple," Kol said, changing the subject. "It was like a labyrinth."

"It was a new experience."

"Being chased from civilisation wasn't."

"We don't know how far this jungle stretches out," Vekk said as she glanced at the darkness ahead.

"As long as nothing forces us to find out."

As they walked, Kol suddenly snapped a stick with his foot, causing him to notice a large pile of sticks and leaves in front of him, at the foot of a giant jungle tree.

"Something has been here," he said.

Vekk examined the scene. "There aren't any remains. Whatever did this is either hiding or has been eaten."

Arkriat became suddenly agitated as a hissing sound raced through their ears.

"What was that?" Kol asked fearfully, in a hushed tone.

"Not Garisals," Vekk said.

Around ten snakes began to slither out from the roots of the tree, with black, wrinkled bodies and bright yellow stripes.

"What is that?! Run!" Vekk yelled.

Arkriat leaped at one of the evasive creatures, instead ramming his head into the tree. The tree, having been hollowed out to create a snake den, began to shake and lean towards the siblings.

"Kol!" Vekk shouted, running over to him.

"Vekk!"

The tree snapped from its base, plunging into the ground ahead. Vekk and Kol ran in opposing directions as it broke through the moss and opened up the ground, exposing a series of tunnels filled with snakes.

Kol heard Arkriat barking on the other side of the toppled tree, followed by footsteps. He then turned to Kretai, watching as a snake leaped in the air but failed to reach her. Kretai squealed and flew to him, settling on his shoulder as they fled into the forest.

Vekk ran, ignoring the urge to catch her breath. She assumed Arkriat was nearby as she refused to look back; the slithering creatures were likely behind and waiting for her to slow down.

After several minutes, her body ached and forced her to breathe. She relaxed once Arkriat came into sight, his legs covered in blood—the predators no longer chased them.

She recovered and continued forward, fighting her fears for her brother. She looked down at Arkriat as he walked beside her, his attention fixed on the darkness.

"We need to find Kol—no one would forgive me if I lost him," she said, before noticing a nearby cave; a break in the roof of leaves above allowed moonlight to shine around it. She looked at the narrow space and slid through the contorted opening, with Arkriat following behind.

They reached the other side and wandered into an opening to see a beautiful pond with grass growing around it due to the opening in the roof. Critters ran across the ground and Arkriat sat by the pond, watching the fish swim around inside.

"It's so…quiet," Vekk remarked. "I hope Kol found somewhere like this."

The calming sound of water, the drop of

a pebble and the run of various insects were sounds Vekk had never experienced in real life. She almost began to forget about her brother and Kretai, who were likely still lost as she wandered around and felt the blades of grass. Arkriat stared thoughtfully at the animals that walked around, maintaining his distance to avoid interfering with their daily life.

I'm glad that Kol has the spear. Vekk thought; she believed herself to be far safer than he was.

Until she heard a familiar growl.

Kol ran from the snakes, ducking and dodging various obstructions in his and Kretai's way. He pulled out the ancient spear and aimed it at the direction of the waiting predators, hoping to catch one off guard if it jumped at him.

He was completely isolated for the first time and had no support; he had to follow through on his basic instincts to run.

Just as Vekk used to say.

Upon the absence of their parents and older brother, Vekk had advised Kol on avoiding danger. At the time, she had never faced a dangerous situation herself and had elected to suggest the most obvious method, unbeknown to Kol.

Feeling the darkness trapping him, he silently hoped for Vekk's safety and carved a path through the forest, destroying foliage as he went. He reached a large clearing to find a small farm, characterised by a metal windmill with many rows of crops growing in the main source of light available in the middle of a jungle.

He ran to the door and slammed his hand on the door. He was greeted by a strange figure. It was a Kerrilas, a figure with black hair and a grey face, with his eyes of a similar shade, giving off a very daunting appearance. The species regularly traded in Zrelyar, which allowed Kol to recognise his features.

"Hello, I am Kolansar and I need help, desperately," Kol said. "Can I come in?"

The figure merely nodded and led him to the dining room where they sat together and discussed.

"Your purpose?" the Kerrilas asked him.

"My purpose? I...am looking for my sister," Kol told him, slightly confused.

"Her name?"

"Vekkilar"

"Her last location," the Kerrilas asked.

"In the jungle. There's a fallen tree where we were separated," Kol replied.

"Stay, I will check surveillance," he was told bluntly. "Have a drink."

The Kerrilas placed a strange drink in front of Kol. It was a deep blue colour and had a foul smell, served in a hollow glass sculpture.

"What is your name? It's difficult to address you without a name," Kol said to the Kerrilas before he left the room.

The Kerrilas paused for a moment.

"Yarsnael."

Kol stared at the concoction that stood before him on the table. It smelt too foul to consider drinking but he knew Yarsnael would not likely take kindly to his refusal.

Kretai sat by it on the table, staring at it but being similarly repulsed. Kol chose to sit and try to figure out how far Vekk could have gone and whether she and Arkriat could survive in the jungle without a weapon.

Yarsnael entered moments later, the same blank expression he had before.

"She was never here," he said. "She must be deeper in the jungle."

"We did leave separate ways. Maybe she's looking for me," Kol said.

"Your spear is interesting. Where did you acquire it?" Yarsnael asked.

"Oh, I found it," Kol said bluntly.

"The location. What is it?" he was asked with the same monotone voice but with a slight frustration.

"It's…it was given to me by a woman."

"Her name," he was asked, once again in a monotone voice.

"Zavroon," Kol replied quickly.

Yarsnael laughed, telling Kol, "That is the name of a military commander in Zrelyar. Your home."

"How do you—"

"No Quarailian has been found living anywhere else. Drink up."

Kol began to feel uneasy and thanked Yarsnael for his hospitality. He began to walk towards the door until he was stopped.

"Wait."

Kol turned around to see Yarsnael looking more serious than before.

"That spear belonged to my grandmother. I will tell you about her."

Kol was 'offered' to sit back down and listen, to which he reluctantly accepted.

Kretai sat beside him while Yarsnael told a hyperbolic story of his grandmother, a technique Kol would not have believed him to be capable of when they had first met.

Desperate to quench his thirst, Kol took a sip of the substance he had been given earlier. Suddenly, Yarsnael slowed down. Everything slowed down and Kretai stood up to attention, or at least it seemed as if he did. Kol began to choke, violently.

Kol saw the Kerrilas raise to his feet and walk over to him as he fell to the floor.

Yarsnael knelt down and whispered, "Our deal is done."

He attempted to throw up his drink, fighting against the toxins entering his body. However, his muscles failed him soon after as he fell unconscious with no indication of where he was.

Half an hour earlier, his sister looked around for danger, with no signals of where the growling came from.

"Stay with me," she commanded Arkriat, who sought out the source of the sound.

They were unexpectedly overwhelmed as a pack of Garisals jumped from the roof and surrounded them. Vekk grabbed one of the Garisals by his neck and threw it towards the other attackers. Arkriat attacked two of the Garisals at once, overpowering them with strength and his horns.

Vekk jumped over Arkriat to pull a root from a tree growing above and threw it into the mouth of a Garisal running at her. It slowed it down and gave time for Arkriat to jump at the creature.

Vekk climbed out of the roof opening and jumped back into the action, on top of two of the Garisals. They became disorientated and fearful as they retreated into the darkness nearby.

Another Alpha Garisal, who had a necklace hanging from its neck, attacked Arkriat from behind. Vekk grabbed it from the back and used it to pull the Alpha Garisal down, allowing Arkriat to recover and jump at it.

The necklace came off and the Garisals ran away, the pack leader standing down in shame. Vekk realised that the necklace was a symbol of power to the Garisals and she had removed this one, revoking its status as leader.

The Alpha Garisal sat sadly in front of them, waiting for a verdict on his life. Vekk stood looking at him, unwilling to hurt him any more.

"You don't need this," Vekk said, as if the Garisal could understand her. "Go! Lead your pack!"

Arkriat understood the message and communicated it to the Alpha Garisal who nudged the necklace and then Arkriat. Vekk placed it upon her Alpha Garisal who became excited at the sight of such a reward. The Alpha Garisal left, as did Vekk and Arkriat.

"We need to show Kol your new necklace," Vekk said as she searched for a possible route to find her brother. She ran straight in the direction that Kol had ran to, hoping to find him.

As they were walking quickly, Arkriat suddenly stopped and began to sprint in one direction, with Vekk following and struggling to keep up the pace. They ran past various creatures and glowing trees, too focused on a mysterious goal to appreciate the beauty.

They came across a clearing, with a farmhouse. As they walked up to the door, they heard a man choking and falling to the ground, as well as footsteps.

Vekk rushed into the farmhouse to see her own brother unconscious, on the floor, at the feet of a Kerrilas who was examining the ancient spear.

"What have you done?!" she gasped as she ran over to Kol.

"The second one arrives. Would you like some too?" he said in a low voice.

"Did you poison him?" Vekk asked in a panicked tone.

"He thought it was an exotic drink," he said laughing. "I'm surprised my employer was unable to take both of you down himself."

"Give me the antidote!" Vekk commanded, holding eye contact with his emotionless eyes.

Arkriat growled deeply at Yarsnael as he stood and laughed, lifting the spear up over Kol's dying body.

As he brought the spear down, Vekk grabbed the stick and sent the pole into Yarsnael's forehead, forcing him to let go. Arkriat kept him away as Vekk reclaimed the spear and searched for an antidote.

"Zavroon has it," Yarsnael told her.

"You work for him?!" Vekk said, quickly looking up.

"I was going to deliver the body to him but he has come to us."

The faint sound of vehicles—many vehicles—was heard as Vekk rushed outside to see Zavroon, mounted in a Hoverength, staring directly at her. Her eyes widened as he fired directly at her, Vekk narrowly avoiding death by leaping into the farmhouse.

The entrance collapsed and she was trapped inside with Kol and Yarsnael, along with Arkriat and Kretai She turned around to Yarsnael, who looked as calm as ever, and punched him in the face. He fell to the floor and Arkriat began to bark viciously at him. Kretai took cover under the dining table as another shot was fired from Zavroon's tank, destroying the front wall of the house.

"Incredible. Travelling all the way into my spy's own home. I see you planned your route accordingly," Zavroon mocked. Vekkilar spotted a small vial on his belt as he spoke, paying no attention to his words.

"Zavroon, come down here and fight me!" Vekk yelled.

Zavroon stifled a laugh and looked at her coldly.

"Why would I do that if I could take you down right now," he said sarcastically.

"You're worried about losing to an untrained civilian?" Vekk replied in a mocking tone.

"Fine, I will show you how veterans fight," Zavroon said, stepping down from his Hoverength.

They stood opposite each other in front of the military vehicles, allowing their anger to build. Vekk resisted the urge to escape while Zavroon appeared to be fully confident of his abilities.

Zavroon lunged at Vekk but she slid underneath and grabbed the vial from his belt.

Stunned for a second, he watched her run into the farmhouse and kneel down beside her brother.

"Is this it?!" Vekk asked Yarsnael furiously.

"Yes."

She removed the lid and hesitated before pouring it into her brother's mouth; she noticed a similarity to the ancient liquid stuck to the head of the Cristrial spear. Casting the vial aside to avoid the risk of deception, she grabbed the spear and gently nudged her brother with it, then thrusting it into the side of his neck. Kol immediately vomited onto the floor beside himself and sat up.

"Vekk?"

"Kol! I'm glad you're alive but we need to get moving," Vekk said, pulling him to his feet.

As they exited the building with Arkriat and Kretai, they saw that Zavroon had once again mounted his Hoverength and was preparing to fire.

"You should've stayed in the ashes that were your home; this won't be quick," Zavroon told them both as he began to tap the terminal in front of him.

Instead of running, both siblings charged at the Hoverength, contrary to Zavroon's expectations. The soldiers began to fire at them, struggling to avoid the other vehicles that surrounded their targets. Both siblings climbed onto Zavroon's Hoverength as Arkriat and Kretai darted at the soldiers, distracting most of them from firing at the siblings. Vekk reached the open compartment of the vehicle and clutched Zavroon's arm, placing all of her weight into her grip as Kol attempted to push him out from behind.

The general broke free and brought his forearm onto Vekk's face, knocking her onto the ground as Kol hit the control terminal with his foot while attempting to take control, accidentally causing the Hoverength to fire on another vehicle and setting off a small chain reaction. Both Kol and Zavroon were flung from the vehicle and the siblings, Arkriat and Kretai fled the confrontation. They ran behind the farmhouse and towards the deeper forest, slowing the enemy forces who struggled through the thick bushes in their heavy gear.

To circumvent this, the military task force deployed multiple aircraft. However, the dense jungle roof made it difficult to track them and allowed the siblings to escape.

They slowed and managed to relax slightly, knowing they were temporarily free of danger. Kol was still recovering from his poisoning and vomited on the ground, noticing that the ancient spear was on Vekk's back, intact.

"Why didn't you use the spear?" Kol asked

Vekk.

"I don't want to kill anyone," Vekk replied. "I'm not ready for that."

"I see," Kol replied, "and Arkriat's new necklace?"

"We...were given it by another Alpha Garisal."

Kol laughed. "I was clearly given the worse company," he said, feeling the poison in his body being neutralised.

"The amount of power they are using to stop us is far too excessive," Vekk noted. "There's only four of us with one old spear as our only weapon; they didn't even know about it until they saw us a few minutes ago."

"Perhaps we are the first to go this far in order to stop them," Kol said.

"I hope so," Vekk replied, eyeing a predator who slithered away upon feeling the glare of Arkriat.

They lay down beside a tree after agreeing to rest and slept until day arrived once again.

The jungle's artificial night began to dissolve as a bright light shone through the thick barricade of flora and fauna, awakening Vekk and Kol. Arkriat and Kretai had already awoke, with Arkriat patrolling the perimeter for threats and Kretai seeking the warmth of the siblings. Vekk gestured to the animals and they continued through the wavering patches of light. They quickly approached an opening, where the siblings gazed upon a new biome, vast in size and great in contrast to the previous land they had travelled across; it was a pale mesa desert with tall white spikes erect in the ground, distant from each other. They stood ahead of the towering rock formations, which created a maze-like pattern in the distance; the desert itself was miles below them, at the foot of a cliff of which they stood at the edge.

"There's no way down," Vekk said, staring over the ridge to see the vertical distance, which they would have to find a way to descend.

"We'll have to climb down," Kol said to her.

"Are you serious?" Vekk asked. "We have no climbing experience at all!"

"Well we can't jump," he said. Kol peered over the edge of the cliff to analyse the difficulty of the climb and knelt down to prepare himself to descend the great obstacle.

"Wait what are those? Vekk said, pointing to three, strategically placed mounds in the sand.

"I don't think sand is naturally square like that," her brother replied, stepping away from the cliff.

They stared at the ground, holding Arkriat back while Kretai flew over, unaware of the mounds below.

"Perhaps they're buildings," Kol said, just before the mounds began to move and reveal themselves as military vehicles.

"We need to descend, now!" Vekk commanded.

"What?—No!" Kol responded as Vekk knelt by the edge and mentally prepared herself to descend.

"Go, now," Vekk said in a hushed voice as she grabbed Arkriat and began to climb down, soon followed by her brother. Kretai flew quickly beside them, attempting to reach the ground as soon as possible.

Vekk almost fell due to the weight of the Garisal and was forced to leave him to make his way down without her support. He dug his claws into the wall of rock and slowly slid down due to his weight; Alpha Garisals were not built for climbing, as Arkriat had quickly discovered, but he clutched the rock as if it was prey.

A laser cut into the wall beside them, moving with precision to cut the weary siblings from the side of the cliff and forcing them to adapt, causing them drop faster down the wall and yelling at Arkriat to do the same.

As they climbed and dropped, the vehicles realised their targets' tactics and began to cut underneath the siblings. Kol was too slow to adapt as a laser cut next to his arm, singeing it and causing him to cry out as he fell from the cliff in agony.

"Kol!" Vekk yelled as she let go of part of the rock formation in an attempt to catch up to him. However, Kol managed to grab onto a rock to slow his descent. Falling quickly, he continued to grab any part of the cliff that he could, knowing that one particular vehicle was targeting him directly.

The vehicles were compact, with a small window in the front and a mechanism hidden in the vehicle, which fired a concentrated beam. It was painted black, which offered the soldiers inside little protection in the bright, hot desert and instead heated up the exterior.

Vekk was unable to keep up as she was forced to move constantly across the cliff to avoid the lasers that were attempting to predict her location. Kol managed to reach the ground, continuing to dodge incoming lasers with greater difficulty, as he was now unable to fall unpredictably.

Nearing the hot desert sands, Vekk dropped down the cliff slightly, only to send her foot at an awaiting laser. It singed her foot and caused her to fall completely to the ground. Arkriat continued to quickly slide down the cliff while Kretai stood on Kol's shoulder, hoping that he would divert some of the attention away from her.

Vekk struggled to stand, although the incoming lasers accelerated the process. She joined her brother in attempting to dodge and to distract the vehicles from their descending Garisal. Kretai flew towards a nearby ledge, unable to provide support due to her small size and weak body.

One of the vehicles began to ignore the siblings and aim at Arkriat, directing their lasers at his small feet; Arkriat panicked and retracted his claws from the wall. Vekk ran over to soften his fall but was thrown to the ground by his weight on impact. Kol used them both as a distraction and began to run at the rightmost tank as it directed its attention on Vekk and Arkriat, who were running in separate directions to avoid being hit.

Kol felt a deep anxiety as he ran, never having fought so directly before. He was still very young; he was not equipped for battling an enemy force, nor trained for such. Fortunately, the vehicle was too fixated on his sister, which allowed him to climb onto the roof where he was safe from the vehicle's weaponry.

He paced around the hot surface, before stepping back once the pilots climbed out of the vehicle and aimed two small guns at his chest. He glanced at the vehicle to his left, which had turned to face him but refused to fire as it waited for a resolution.

Vekk and Arkriat ran towards the leftmost vehicle, barely avoiding the lasers that were burning beside them. Quarailians had evolved to flourish in areas of varying heights and objects but the desert had none of these benefits; they had not adapted towards a flat, dry biome with virtually no wildlife.

Vekk threw herself into the sand to avoid the violent gunfire, before leaping onto the nearest vehicle, while Arkriat darted towards her and climbed onto the burning surface. She grabbed the corners of a hatch and pulled the door open, sliding inside with the Alpha Garisal.

It was surprisingly cool inside compared to the boiling exterior, although it was far more confined; two pilots used the control terminals inside and filled half of the space available. Arkriat jumped at the partially visible head of one of the pilots who fell to the ground in shock.

The other pilot was surprised by the intrusion but managed to quickly grab his weapon and aim it at Vekk, who froze in fear. Arkriat fought with the other pilot, who struggled to keep him away.

"Drop your weapon," Vekk was told by the pilot. She took the spear that was clipped to her clothing and knelt down to place it on the ground as the other pilot escaped out of one of the hatches, away from Arkriat.

The remaining pilot pointed his weapon at both of them as Arkriat moved to his owner's side, giving both him and Vekk a slim chance to escape or attack. He began to growl at the pilot, who began to aim his gun specifically at the Garisal, as if anticipating an attack. Vekk took the opportunity to deliver a blow to the guard's visor, shattering it. He fell to the floor as Vekk grabbed his falling weapon.

"Leave," she commanded, aiming the gun.

"I won't face the general's wrath. Kill me."

"'The General'?"

"General Zavroon. He is in charge of this operation."

Vekk was unsurprised yet she was determined to leave as quickly as possible.

"Help us then," Vekk offered.

The pilot appeared desperate to escape yet he had denied her offer to do so. "I'm not interested. You're criminals."

"Then get out," she said in an increasingly frustrated voice.

The pilot reluctantly escaped through the hatch to the vehicle in between the other two, both of which had been compromised. Vekk reclaimed her spear and stood by the window of the vehicle, searching for her brother.

Kol threw all of his weight onto one of the guards watching him, causing him to fall onto the hot metal surface; he immediately retreated onto the sand to escape the burning metal plating.

Kol quickly stood back up and climbed through the entry hatch, avoiding the other pursuer and locking the hatch to avoid further altercations.

Then he heard a click.

The pilots quickly fell from their chairs and electricity spread across the vehicle, locking down the other hatch and making every piece of technology unresponsive. Kol tried pushing the nearest hatch in an attempt to open it but to no avail; escape was impossible from his metallic prison.

The vehicle began to combust and explode, spreading electricity across the hot metal structure and tearing it apart. Kol was thrown by the explosion into the burning wreckage, smoke dancing out of the disaster and alerting all to the self-destruction of the vehicle. Plates and parts flew through the air and severely damaged the centre vehicle, one particularly dense part wedging itself into the window and cutting off the electricity supply, disabling the vehicle.

Vekk watched the event unfold from the fortified glass window of her stolen vehicle. She was shaken by the event and fell onto a seat, followed by anger as she placed her hands onto the vehicle controls. She clutched the orientation handles and rotated the vehicle to face the damaged tank that Kol had inadvertently disabled. Her hand then moved to the laser activation screen.

She drew the laser on the screen to fire directly through the helpless vehicle, watching a corpse fly through the air in front of her as it exploded. She bunkered down in the vehicle, holding Arkriat to prevent him from escaping as debris smashed into them, leaving dents and irreparable damage.

Kretai flew over to the wreckage where Kol had last been seen and searched for him, holding onto hope despite the chance of survival being minimal.

Vekk and Arkriat climbed out of the vehicle once the destroyed tanks lay in pieces on the ground. They ran to Kretai who was struggling to see due to the flames and thick smoke that remained.

"Kol!" Vekk screamed, throwing metal plates away as she attempted to forget the people that she had killed minutes ago in her emotionless daze. Arkriat began to drag an arm out of the wreckage, which Vekk noticed in her peripheral vision. She ran over to find Kol's charred body, in need of immediate medical assistance.

Arkriat pulled him away from the wreckage and left him on the ground for Vekk to analyse, who quickly knelt down and stared at her brother's lifeless appearance.

She held back tears as she took the spear from her back and looked at her brother, unconscious and burnt.

"I should've left him out of this," Vekk said to herself, the guilt mounting quickly.

She cleared some of the ash from his face

and placed the ancient spear on top of his chest.

She suddenly felt the beating of a pulse below the spearhead and quickly removed the spear; Kol did not move but he was alive. Staring at her brother, she hesitated about using the spear now that she was not pressured by enemies. Arkriat grumbled and took the spear in his mouth while Kretai stood on Kol's chest and felt for the deep cuts and bruises. She soon squeaked at Arkriat, who ran at Kol and thrusted the spear into his arms and chest.

Vekk stared, stunned by their actions, before hearing Kol breathing as the spear fell from his body. She watched in awe as he began to move and cough, choking on the residue of melted metal. He finally opened his eyes to see Vekk staring down at him, with the blinding sun behind her head.

"Am I dead?" he asked, feeling numb from the physical trauma.

"No, definitely not," Vekk said, repressing her ruminations, "but you might've been if Arkriat and Kretai hadn't stepped in."

"Maybe, but I doubt they took down that middle vehicle," he said, gesturing to the centremost wreckage as Vekk helped him to stand.

"I've done a terrible thing," she told him as she helped him to his feet. "I destroyed the middle tank; I've killed someone—maybe more than one."

"You killed someone?"

"I'm supposed to be protecting you! I'm not here to kill, I just want to find the next four keys and get back to Zrelyar, with the four of us still intact." Vekk said as they began to walk into the open desert.

"We don't need to do it again," said Kol, before attempting to change the topic. "What do you think will happen once we're done?"

CHAPTER 6

"I'll do it. I will become an astronaut," Arthur said excitedly. "I'll do it!" He stared at the crinkled paper which displayed his low grades that barely let him pass through school, which were weak but numerous. He was using one hand to research the next qualifications he needed on his old laptop and the other hand to hold the paper that he could not take his eyes away from. It held both his despair and hope in a few simple words, followed by a single number.

He managed to find a reliable course, which would allow him to gain Additional Development Levels, the new qualifications that would pave his way to university—for the small price of £10,000 per year.

I can't—

Arthur stood up and stood back from the laptop, imagining scenarios in which he would have to stay in his current lifestyle.

I'm not staying like this. I can't.

He had replayed the moment where he left the bakery every night and planned to end it as soon as possible.

"Come on Shadow!" Arthur called, grabbing the lead as his dog happily ran over. He clipped it to Shadow's collar and they left the flat, giving Arthur an opportunity to relax. He had taken a full-time job at a retail store, although it would not raise the £20,000 he would need and the even greater amounts needed for university.

People passing by complimented Shadow and some even took their dogs over so they could see each other; his menacing name did little to deter visitors.

"You hit the jackpot with him," one woman said to Arthur.

I wish I had financially, as well, he thought.

They continued with the walk, the sun setting ahead of them. They walked in near silence, with the exception of Shadow's feet pattering on the pavement rhythmically. Arthur took his phone out to call his best, and only, friend Rose for advice.

"Hello?" he heard.

"Hi Rose, it's Arthur," he said. "How's university?"

"Stressful. You're lucky you don't have to go through it," she said jokingly.

Arthur paused for a moment then said, "I was looking…to complete some AD-Levels."

He heard a stifled laugh from her.

"I'm sorry, Arthur, it's just that you don't have any qualifications that could get you in," she said.

"I do," he responded. "Just because they aren't high qualifications, doesn't mean that they aren't a pass."

"Right," she said. "You'll need a lot of money. You'll need multiple jobs to raise that much, even during your studies."

"I know,"

"I can recommend you to the same university I am at, but it's quite a distance from where you live."

"I'll take any help," he said. "Thanks for supporting me…towards the end, at least."

"No problem. Bye!" Rose said, abruptly hanging up the call.

"Right then," Arthur said, putting his phone away. He finished walking Shadow and entered their flat, sitting on the sofa and thinking over what his next move would be. Exhausted from another day of work and Shadow's walk, he relaxed with his dog until he fell asleep in the living room.

He woke up, finding himself dressed from the day before and almost late for work due to being away from the alarm beside his bed.

I'm not losing another job, he thought, running to change into his work uniform and throwing some meat into Shadow's bowl. He rushed off to work, forcing his problems out of his head.

Walking into work, he saw new staff at all of the counters. Surprised, he checked his e-mails but found no indication that he had been fired. He quickly walked to his boss' office, who was quickly sorting paperwork.

"What is it Arthur?" she asked.

"Have I been fired?" he asked anxiously.

"What? No!" she said. "We've replaced most of our staff members due to budget cuts; you're one of our best employees, despite the fact that you were nearly late today."

Arthur relaxed his shoulders and said, "I'm one of your best employees?"

"Your job isn't exactly demanding but I hope you can teach the new employees how to do their job properly. They're making me regret firing the others."

"Would I be able to have a promotion," Arthur said, seeing an opportunity to earn money for his education, "if I took on more responsibility?"

His boss was surprised by the bold question and stopped working for a moment. "I told you we have budget cuts," she said. "What do you want the money for?"

"Qualifications," he said. "I want to go further in life than this. No offence."

"None taken. I'll give you a small raise but you'll have to teach the new employees how to do their job efficiently," she told him. "And fire Greg."

"Thank you so much. I'll do that right away." Arthur said to her, slowly backing out as she continued to work.

Feeling thrilled with a greater purpose and income, he walked off to the storage department to carry out his new job, feeling dread overcome his cheery attitude as he sought out 'Greg'.

He walked over to the new recruits and saw many people; it was a disorganised ruin of boxes and displaced lids, which would take a long time to reorder.

"What is going on?!" Arthur said loudly.

He directed each worker to their appropriate workstation and attempted to explain their role. Greg was quickly identified as he misplaced products and distracted the other workers. Arthur stared at him for several moments before quickly approaching.

"You're fired," he blurted out as Greg turned to look at him with unearned confidence.

"You don't have the authority."

Arthur threw a box to the ground and gestured to the door.

"Ask the boss if you need to, I don't care."

Greg swore and pushed his way to the exit, throwing his ID card to the ground and smashing the door open.

"This job is going to get me to space," he muttered to himself, walking over to yet another new employee and waiting for the hours to pass.

As the day concluded Arthur quickly left, walking home as fast as he could, restricted by the serious concussion he had suffered days prior; the pain reminded him why he was following his ambitions now instead of later.

I could work even harder without the extra pain, he thought.

He made his way back to his flat, passing his neighbour carrying out a large piece of artwork. As Arthur shut his flat door, he stared at the wall as an idea came to him.

Art.

Shadow ran over to his owner as usual and was discontent with his lack of affection; the large animal jumped at Arthur, who immediately stopped daydreaming to greet his dog. They sat down as Arthur devised a plan to earn a greater income; he had a creative mind but had never had a use for it until now.

A day later, Arthur bought a canvas and painting supplies after work to see how much he could earn, despite not having painted since his childhood. He placed it on his desk and filled Shadow's food bowl to prevent the dog from eating art supplies. Arthur researched modern works of art online for inspiration, quickly becoming motivated to rediscover his craft. He painted for half an hour, attempting to make his first proper work of art a masterpiece.

Show people what you're thinking, he told himself. However, his inexperience was clear when he stepped away and saw nothing more than colours thrown on a canvas like a child who had never used a paintbrush.

Arthur stared at his work, his mind blank.

"Great start," he muttered.

Remembering the cost of the canvas, he sat back down to attempt to rectify his mistakes and to create a meaningful piece of art.

He painted a battlefield of two lone defenders of a village against an unstoppable force of tanks and thousands of soldiers who sought for nothing but war. The beige village burnt and would be left with red scars that would last for centuries, never to be repaired due to the warning that the remnants sent. Grey smoke filled the air, leaving only the most valiant soldiers to remain behind to fight despite the thick wall of grey that hung ahead of them. The thin black outline of the figures helped distinguish them from their surroundings that were little more than a mix of purples and greens. When Arthur placed down his brush, the work still did not represent his initial vision, although becoming closer to the image in his mind.

"I'm leaving this as it is. Anything else would probably make it even worse," he said aloud to himself.

He placed it at the back of his desk and researched the various methods of selling personal works of art, soon coming across a local art market.

A market that ran through his work hours.

It was solely for artistic work, which would help Arthur to study others and improve his skills, yet it would ensure strong competition. He booked a small stall, which was surrounded by larger ones, likely owned by artists with much greater experience.

He called his boss, booking the day off for the art market and began to hypothesise how his life would be if he could become an artist—a wealthy artist. He carried these thoughts to his bed where he slept ready for the next day where he would create yet another painting to build up stock—under the assumption that it would sell.

On the day of his artistic debut, Arthur awoke later than usual. He had the day to himself as he hoped to be able to make another change in his life; this time, he was focused on his career. *Going to space isn't cheap.*

He got out of bed and made breakfast. Shadow had become accustomed to his schedule and was surprised to see him preparing food later in the day.

Arthur quickly ate breakfast, throwing Shadow's food into his bowl. He placed his own bowl into the sink and ran to change into some semi-formal clothes; he was desperate to create a prominent first impression. He had an hour to reach the market and set up before the crowds came, which was harder than expected as he had become accustomed to minimal responsibilities and deadlines.

He decided to take Shadow with him instead of leaving him alone in a small flat, where he remained most of the time due to Arthur's long work hours, which caused the hopeful artist to feel guilty. At times, his neighbours would offer to walk him while Arthur was at work, but this a rare occasion.

They walked down to the town centre, now characterised by the many stalls, and found his small metal stand pre-prepared for him to organise his work. Arthur tied Shadow's lead to a post and unpacked his bag; he placed his most recent works at the front of the stall with the addition of his first piece, which he felt a certain connection to. The rest were placed behind him, which only consisted of two pieces of his art as he only had a week to make his stock. After he had set up his five products, he stood waiting for customers and looked around at his competitors.

One seller had painted portraits of many people, likely examples of what Arthur could produce for his own customers if he had far more training. The stall beside him was just brush strokes of various colours and tones with little obvious meaning. If anyone chose his work, they would likely have found a deeper, metaphorical meaning behind them.

However, Arthur's work was hardly comprehensible as he had just painted anything he could imagine in great detail. The most prominent scenes were of battles, particularly of animals or aliens, although they mostly deviated from the standard idea about the appearance of otherworldly creatures; they had come from figures and beings that Arthur had mentally detailed in his mind when he was bored.

The market began and crowds quickly entered. Arthur waited, voicing his thoughts to Shadow who just stared at him blankly. Nobody was approaching Arthur's stall, giving him an urge to adjust his art and doubt his own skills. But he waited.

Impulse decisions had not gotten him far before.

He stood waiting for half an hour when one person began to walk towards him, at last.

Nope. She's going towards the artist beside me.

He remembered why he was there, giving him the courage to wait for sales. A few moments later, someone did come to his stall, browsing the work for sale.

"Can I help you?" Arthur inquired eagerly.

"I'm…I'm good, thanks," the woman told him awkwardly.

He quickly noticed her look away from him to focus on the art and managed to withdraw some of his excessive enthusiasm, hoping that the potential customer would purchase a piece of art regardless of their awkward exchange.

She picked up a piece of art consisting of a night in a desert where a city lay in ruin and two figures fought outside the walls for control.

"How much is this one?" she asked.

"Twenty-five pounds?" Arthur replied, not knowing the value of his own work.

The woman paid the amount and left, allowing several more customers to visit the stall and, beyond his expectations, quickly bought the few pieces of art he had; he had to leave early due to insufficient stock.

"Wow," Arthur said, zipping up his bag and untying Shadow. "I need to buy a lot more canvases for next time."

How did they sell out so fast? There are far better pieces of art around me.

Before leaving, he asked for the date of the next event, which he soon learnt was a month away, providing him with enough time to build up a decent amount of stock to cope with demand. Just as he picked up his backpack to leave, a police officer approached his stall, looking around the empty stand.

"Are you Arthur, who works at Homephreys?"

"Y...yes, yes I am," Arthur responded nervously, lowering his backpack to the ground.

"Place your hand here," he ordered him, gesturing to the pole of the stand. Arthur soon obeyed and the officer quickly grabbed his wrist and handcuffed him to it.

"What?!"

The officer took hold of Arthur's free arm and cuffed him to the other pole using another pair of handcuffs, preventing him from leaving; the other sellers watched in shock as Arthur's bag was taken in the officer's escape. Everyone backed away from the area, unsure how to respond to the rogue who had robbed an artist's stall, seemingly without reason.

Arthur jumped through the stall and pulled at the cuffs, soon collapsing the weak stall as the poles flew away from the roof. He ran through the market like an escaped criminal and was directed by bystanders as he attempted to ascertain the officer's location. While passing through, he suddenly felt the two sets of dangling handcuffs being pulled, as he turned to see the man attaching both of them together. Arthur was powerless to prevent him and fell to the ground to the sound of loud barking.

He then heard the swinging of fists and a familiar voice as the animal barked aggressively. Shadow soon broke past the officer and snarled at him, who stood ahead of Greg, the man that

Arthur had fired.

"Don't disrespect my brother again!" The rogue officer yelled as Arthur struggled to free himself. The scene soon became chaotic as more police officers entered the scene, though this time they instead freed Arthur and arrested the man, began to shout and swear.

Arthur rushed to answer police questions and quickly walked home, now reunited with his backpack and dog. Arriving at the flat, he checked his backpack to ensure he was still in possession of his cash. Finding his wallet intact, he struggled to divert his attention from the events at the market.

Why can't anything go right for once?

He opened his laptop and checked his bank account online, expecting it to be fuller than before. He saw that he was £9,700 away from being able to afford AD-Level courses, although this did not include his art earnings, which was around £110. He quickly bought more canvases and planned his next work.

Months passed and Arthur continued to sell his artwork, which earned him most of his income; it was quickly rising, faster than it ever had before, which brought him closer to his aspiration. He bought large amounts of canvases and practised regularly between job shifts, where he had an opportunity to mention his artistic work in casual conversation to gain more customers. He continued to paint more simplistic pieces that resembled his first pieces of work to cater for a growing demand.

For the first time since leaving school, his life was improving; he spent a lot of time researching the job prerequisites to become an astronaut, with none of them providing him an opportunity to explore a universe beyond the solar system.

He had also began exercising at least twice a week; Arthur knew that it would help him to survive in new environments and pass the physical tests that awaited him. He was committed to completing his aspiration as quickly as possible while still taking time to relax and look after Shadow, although his chaotic schedule did not always allow for this. Eight months after his first art sale, he deposited his most recent earnings from the art market and realised he had reached his financial goal.

Finally, my life is going right!

Upon Arthur's registration for his three AD-Levels of mathematics, mechanical engineering and physical education, he felt a sense of relief and excitement until he remembered the hours of studying that would be required; he was driven purely by his end goal but not the intrigue of his chosen subjects. He had never taken a great deal of interest in science or maths, meaning that he had to immediately begin work on learning the bases of his subject content.

Furthermore, he was plagued with the knowledge that he would be forced to study far more than he ever had if he was to achieve his qualifications quickly. Returning to his flat, he took time to ruminate on his tireless future that felt as if it would last indefinitely, knowing his full-time job and constant studying would be a sharp contrast to his preferred schedule of relaxing as much as possible.

On the next work day, Arthur requested a reduction in hours at work starting in September, which was approved; he would spend the majority of his time studying to fully grasp the subject content since it was not an area he was familiar with.

Taking his first online class in mathematics, he was immediately greeted with the face of an elderly woman, who quickly stood up and began explaining the foreign symbols that Arthur did not recognise. While his attention drifted, he feigned interest to ensure she would not call him out, as he had come to expect due to the many teachers that had done so while he was at school and his first boss had continued to do throughout his short career at Cakecut Bakery.

Five minutes before the conclusion, the teacher informed Arthur that weekly congregations were hosted across the country and attendance was encouraged, as a portion of the course would require him to work with another student to complete an assignment. Letting out a groan once the lesson had concluded, he marked the date in his schedule and began to procrastinate on further study.

Saturday soon arrived; it was the day of the student congregation. Arthur reluctantly attended and saw numerous people talking in groups. He walked into the field and was approached by a man, similar in age.

"Alright?" the man asked Arthur, who stared and nodded uncomfortably. The man stared back, as if expecting him to speak.

"Alright," Arthur said. "I'm Arthur."

"I'm Alex; Nice to meet you. I'm guessing you're new here."

Arthur muttered in agreement and followed Alex around the field, introducing himself to the people faced with a similar academic experience. Afterwards, they stood away from the others and conversed.

"I'm studying maths to get into engineering. What about you?"

"Mathematic...sorry, mechanical engineering," Arthur told him, fighting the urge to escape the conversation.

"Lush. Are you from Yorkshire?"

"Yeah, moved here a couple of years ago," Arthur told him. *I thought my accent had changed since I was sixteen.*

They stood in silence for a few moments,

unsure what to say to each other, until Alex broke the silence. "I've got something to do, but I'll see you later."

"Really?" Arthur asked. *Of course not, it's a phrase.*

"Just a phrase," Alex responded, pulling out his phone and encouraging Arthur to do the same. "Is that your dog?"

Arthur looked down at his lock screen, seeing the image of Shadow that had appeared. "Yeah, his name's Shadow."

"Great name," Alex told him. "If you give me your number, we can help each other out; I failed an AD-Level in engineering."

Arthur laughed awkwardly and exchanged phone numbers with him. Alex waved and left, leaving Arthur to interact with the other students. He approached a woman, who turned to reveal a discontent expression. They spoke for a minute, clearly having different personalities.

"You gotta do something you like," she told him.

"I am, it's just complicated," he quickly retorted, desperate to leave.

"I don't know what you expected from AD-Levels," she said, walking away.

Arthur slipped away from the gathering and headed home with the desire to avoid human interaction until it was necessary. As future congregations approached, he made the decision to avoid them, if possible; he would only attend if it was required for the course and would instead spend his time earning an income.

His dreams had become more vivid as he painted, since his imagination had had little stimulation in the past; he now knew his passion, which had awoken his creative mind and allowed him to see the two figures he regularly visualised; the two figures he hoped to find.

Despite this, Arthur struggled to revise regularly to achieve this goal. He had never taken a great interest in studying and instead found himself to be distracted by anything available, as he had always found during school. He still attended lessons and had even attempted to study in shorter periods to maintain focus but would instantly move to check any device in the flat, or to play with Shadow.

Three nights after he failed a mock exam, he dreamt of one of the figures, viciously attacking Arthur for his failures. His vision was blurred and he struggled to make out his surroundings, focusing more on protecting himself.

"You know what will happen. You know what will happen," it taunted continuously as it delivered blows to Arthur's entire body.

"Stop it! Stop!" he called out, defending his head from the sudden attack. He eventually weakened and allowed his body to suffer injuries, feeling helpless.

Looking to the side, he saw horses galloping towards him, each falling to the ground before they could reach him. He suddenly pushed up against his attacker and awoke before he could see the figure's face.

Sitting up in bed, he reached for his phone and began reading his online textbook, knowing the consequences for giving up on his goals.

His work quickly improved, with Arthur pushing himself to his limits. He became stressed, as he was unable to maintain high grades and quickly wore himself out. As the end of the academic year closed in, he was faced with yet another dream, where he saw a woman walking thorough a field, picking flowers. She seemed to be at peace with herself, studying the intricate plants as she went. Arthur sat down as she placed the flowers onto the ground and disappeared in a debris storm.

His progress slowed and his quality of work improved; working within an equilibrium of effort, he managed to reach the day of his first exam with little stress.

Why did you guide me so closely? How did you... Arthur's thoughts trailed off as he rushed towards the city hall. He felt his fears, his doubts, his uncertainty lingering in his mind as he paused at the door of the great building.

"I can't, I can't, I can't," Arthur repeated under his breath, grabbing his keys out of his pocket and running back to his flat.

Shadow was as excited as always to see him, albeit slightly confused as to why he had left for such a short period. Arthur ignored Shadow's greeting and rushed past, collapsing on the sofa.

I can't, I can't.

His phone began to vibrate in his pocket. Taking it out, he answered to hear a familiar voice

"Arthur? I wanted to wish you luck before you go in," Rose told him. "I hope I'm not disrupting the exams."

"I'm at home," Arthur answered. "I can't do it."

"What? Of course you can! You've waited your whole life for this," she replied, "or, at least, the last few months."

"It's too much. It's not worth it,"

"You have absolutely no chance if you don't go. Your dreams will be dead."

After a moment of silence, Arthur stood up, weighing the two outcomes of his predicament.

"Just go," Rose told him. "Don't worry about anyone or anything else. Just go."

Arthur sighed and began to walk out of his flat with his phone in hand, locking the door and walking down the stairs onto the street.

"Thank you," Arthur said weakly.

"No problem," she replied.

"You've saved me more than once; I can't repay you."

"You saved my job."

"You could find any job you wanted," he said. "I genuinely want to repay you somehow."

"Just let me know how the exam goes. I'm curious!" she said to him.

Arthur agreed and they exchanged farewells before hanging up. He rushed back to the hall where the exams were taking place, stealthily making his way to his seat. He was fuelled by ambition and determination as he began to write complex equations that would soon leave his mind, never to return.

Placing his pen onto the table at the end of the exam gave him a relief greater than any he had felt before. He walked confidently out of the exam hall, immediately calling Rose.

"I did it!" he excitedly told her, much to the confusion of those around him who were focused on their next exam.

"That's great!" she said with a distant tone, followed by the rustling of paper.

He rushed home and pushed open the door to his flat with the intention of celebrating for the rest of the evening.

Throwing his stationery onto the entryway table and inviting his only two friends over, he threw himself onto the sofa and stared out of the window.

"Just two left," Arthur said, relieved, yet

feeling a creeping nervousness infiltrating his thoughts. Snapping back to reality, he began setting up for his guests.

Over the next week, he revised studiously, with the knowledge that he could relax once he was finished. When the day of each exam came, he suffered a panic attack before venturing out, hiding his fears once reaching the hall.

Over the duration of two weeks, he completed his subjects with an air of mild confidence, although the doubts of his future began to weigh on him as the exams concluded and results day neared.

"Those numbers will affect my whole life," Arthur said to Shadow on the day that would determine his future. He struggled to build up the courage to check his results. Forcing himself to open his e-mails, he tapped on the only one that was unread.

"I…I passed," Arthur stammered. "I…I can do it! I can go to university!"

He spent a moment enjoying the adrenaline rush from his success, a success he never expected to achieve. As he reached for his phone to call Rose and Alex and inform them of the great news, the device began to buzz regardless.

"Hi Rose!" Arthur said, unable to contain his euphoria.

"I take it you passed, then," she said laughing.

"Even better," he said. "They're good grades

as well. I can go to university with these."

"Then come to mine," Rose said. "I want to show you something but I need your help to find it."

CHAPTER 7

"I see," Kol said, following his sister's finger to the city, where a blanket of sand was draped over the tall buildings.

"Do you think it's abandoned?" she asked.

"I can't tell," he replied, "but I wouldn't want to stay if I had to clean up that much sand."

They approached the entrance, from which two long marble walls extended into the distance, wrapping around the towers and skyscrapers that contained no light or life at a first glance. The broken hologram beside the door flickered and welcomed the siblings to the "City of Modspi."

The entrance was blocked by a thick sheet of metal and was indestructible to the ancient spear that was pummelled against it.

"We need to get inside—we're near the first key," Kol said, checking the map in his bag and feeling for a switch on the wall that could grant them entry.

Kretai hovered above the ground, eyeing a crack within the black wall, which was covered by the darkness of night; it was almost indistinguishable from the indents that lay within the long barrier.

She dug her claws into the crack and pressed down, causing the siblings to hear a click and rumbling as the door slid up into the thin frame. The archway that welcomed the siblings revealed the empty, dusty streets with broken glass and lamps. They entered the forsaken city warily, looking for signs of life.

"It looks deserted, yet someone must've been here," Vekk said, making note of the flickering lights whose power had not yet drained.

"What if the people are asleep?" Kol suggested, allowing Kretai to perch on his shoulder.

"With their windows broken and the city gathering dust? Anyway, there are usually at least a few people outside at night," replied Vekk.

Kol entered a neglected hotel lobby but failed to find any lifeforms inside; he noticed that some lights were broken and others had been intentionally switched off.

Vekk looked towards the city centre and saw a man slumped over a fountain rail, the fountain itself devoid of water and the geometric pattern beneath visible. She walked towards the man, concerned for his wellbeing as he lay stagnant.

"Hello?" she said with a wavering tone,

reaching for the body.

Kol sought for signs within the lobby to explain the apocalyptic scene, finding nothing. The doors upstairs were locked and gave no indication of what may have happened.

He walked out to hear a short yelp from his sister who was staring at the body of a man.

"He's dead!" she shouted to Kol, who rushed to her position.

"More!" he said, pointing to multiple figures in the distance, all slumped over on paths and steps. The people were of many different species; the siblings did not recognise them all.

"They look as if something happened all at once. People just going about their lives when something struck," Vekk said, attempting to block out the image of the lifeless corpses.

"But they don't seem to have any injuries," Kol noted, looking over the body in front of him.

Vekk looked around, realising that the bodies were surrounding her; they all appeared to have been struck at once with whatever weapon had been used.

"I'll check that shrine-like structure," Kol said, struggling to stand as he stared into the eyes of the person that lay in front of him, quickly looking towards the largest building in the city to redirect his focus.

"It's like Zrelyar, but with many, many more

people—who are dead," Vekk said.

"And more disturbing—we don't know what this is," Kol replied, cautiously walking towards the great structure. He reached the grand entrance and entered, seeing that the building was devoid of life in spite of the fresh offerings that had been laid.

Stepping over the dying flowers on the ground, Kol saw a staircase leading to an area below; it showed few signs of being intentionally concealed as it was covered by a thin cloth that had fallen onto the steps below. He made his way downstairs and walked into a small room where only one slim passage was available to him.

Catacombs? Kol wondered, seeing openings in the walls that resembled shelving.

He walked through, quickly realising that it was a sort of labyrinth that failed to provide a way to mark his path—Kol wandered into complete oblivion.

Vekk walked around the city with Arkriat and Kretai, looking for any signs of life or notes about what had taken place. Both creatures remained close to Vekk, disliking the sight and smell of the bodies.

"It's like a massacre…but was it purposeful or accidental?" Vekk said to herself quietly.

She walked into a home to see people with their heads to the table, still sat in their seats.

"It must've been instant," she said, trying to

fill the void of silence.

She reached into her pouch and took the Floruna that Kol had given her; she grabbed the hand of one of the bodies, placing it upon the rare flora.

"What happened to you?" she said as calmly as she could.

Vekk saw a family, joined by a couple of friends discussing the state of Quelliare. The atmosphere was calm and joyful, every light switched on to combat the darkness outside.

One of the people at the table stood up and opened a window, before quickly turning around to head back to the table, despite the people in the street falling in front of their home. As she sat down and breathed the air believed to be fresh, she suddenly clutched her throat and her head fell to the table immediately, much to the surprise of the others.

However, they all soon fell too. Each one dropped with little time to comprehend the situation. Vekk heard someone drop to the floor upstairs, before the flashback showed her no more.

"It...it's as if someone poisoned the air," Vekk said. "But only advanced civilisations would be able to acquire technology like that."

She ran out the door, determined to update Kol about her findings.

Kol walked around the dark maze, unable to

see where the floor met the walls or where the next corridor would be. Lights began to flicker unexpectedly and he followed, hoping to be led to some sort of life form. He managed to find a door, distinguishable by the unique shape and handle. Opening it, he found a small room, devoid of life.

"Hello?" he called out, looking at the bed and bags covering the majority of the floor. As he began to search the room, quiet footsteps approached from behind. Kol turned and was immediately struck in the face, causing him to fall back into the room as the lock was activated.

"Who is that?!" Kol called out as he fell to the ground.

"Me," a voice said calmly, handing him a drink through the bars. "Drink up."

Vekk ran into the shrine and rushed down the cloaked stairs to find herself at the start of a complex maze. Not willing to risk losing Arkriat or Kretai, she commanded them to stay until she returned, before running into the darkness. She soon encountered flickering lights, which began to switch off as she approached.

Kol could've activated these, she thought, running into the darkness while repressing doubts for her own safety as she worried about Kol's, being uncomfortable with her brother's absence. Vekk soon reached a lit area where a figure was heard speaking in a calm manner to a metal door.

"The spear?" he asked in a monotone voice.

"I don't have it," Kol's clear voice said. "You'll never find it."

The figure opened the door and immediately attacked Kol. Vekk ran towards them and grabbed the spear from her back, taking advantage of her unheard arrival. She stabbed the familiar Kerrilas, who staggered away in shock and pain.

"Stay away from him!" she shouted, exasperated from protecting Kol. She then plunged the spear into Kol without hesitation, immediately healing him. Vekk walked menacingly towards the figure, who was now visible enough to identify as Yarsnael.

"Leave us alone!" she yelled at him, before jabbing the spear into the ground near his feet. He pulled himself away from the incoming strikes, fearing Vekk's proneness to violence against him.

Kol stood behind his sister, more aggravated than their last encounter and seeking revenge.

"What happened in this city?" he asked in a serious voice.

"Death," Yarsnael said with a smug grin for the first time. "Poison from the mistress of potions."

"Where is she?" Vekk asked, slowing her attack.

No more questions," he said, quickly moving away and standing up, grabbing Vekk's spear. He sent the blunt end of the spear into Vekk's face, causing her to fall onto Kol; he quickly escaped by a staircase that had revealed itself directly opposite them. Kol quickly stood up and grabbed the spear off the floor, clutching it fiercely.

"Trust me," he told his sister, before running off to confront his attacker.

Vekk stood up, delivering her concerns for him while he was still in her line of sight and slowly followed, seeing Kol in pursuit after Yarsnael; the Kerrilas ran away from the maze and Kol chased after him. Vekk ran towards the shrine to find both Arkriat and Kretai waiting at the entrance, appearing concerned.

"This place is horrible. Come on Arkriat, Kretai," Vekk said with a disgusted tone as she took one more glance at the shrine. The large number of corpses had affected her.

Vekk walked around, noting the cleaner air that no longer held the poison, which had caused the massacre. She sat down on a vacant bench, feeling defeated.

"I can't fight off soldiers, find the keys and protect Kol," she said, head in her hands. "I promised that I would take care of him until he was old enough to do it himself. We have to learn how to survive like people twice our age."

Arkriat, sensing her sadness, sat beside her in an attempt to relieve her pain. Kretai sat on top of the bench beside her owner, seeing that something was wrong.

"I'll have to leave him at times to save Zrelyar," Vekk said to her pets, who had no understanding of the situation but recognised her distress, "but last time I left him alone, it ended horribly. I don't ever want to experience that again."

She stood up, understanding that she could help more by finding the poisoner. Vekk walked towards the concealed staircase inside the shrine, seeing the dark depths below.

"There must be something down here. Why else would this maze have been built?" Vekk said, walking down.

They were quick to find the small room that Kol had been locked in, as it had now lit up and the door remained open. Vekk walked inside to see a bed that appeared to have been recently used and various brown pouches on the floor. She picked one of the pouches up and found various gems inside.

"These may be important to Yarsnael," she muttered to herself, taking them for later use.

A locket lay on the ground containing a single small gem with little meaning to those who did not own it.

A family heirloom? Vekk wondered. Arkriat

and Kretai were waiting outside; the room was small.

Vekk checked under the bed and the pouches but found nothing of obvious value.

Until she opened a small wooden box, hidden in the corner of the room.

Vekk took out a holographic note that appeared to be recently typed and received.

"Agent," Vekk read aloud. "Zavroon expects the mixture to be completed in ten days. If you fail to deliver by this point, the fugitives will escape and you will be punished. Neither your potions nor your hidden laboratory will be enough to escape us. They defied the rule of the great Queen Lasapra and they will pay the price, a price that you will be instrumental in collecting. Ensure that you stay as our ally by carrying out your role, otherwise you will be terminated—permanently."

She read the bottom of the note to find its source, finally understanding Yarsnael's involvement in Modspi to its full extent.

"A real poet," she said to herself as she placed the note in a pouch and clipped it to her pocket. "I don't even know how he arrived so quickly. He must've had air support prepared for him, or something."

Kol watched Yarsnael run in fear of the ancient spear; he felt a sadistic satisfaction in the moment, finally able to take revenge on the man who almost caused his death more than once. Kol threw the spear into the Kerrilas' shoulder, piercing it and causing him to fall.

"Drink up," Kol said, removing the spear from his captive's shoulder to prevent it from healing him.

"As you did?" Yarsnael asked, his eyes scanning for a route of escape.

"I'm in control," Kol told him. "It feels good."

"It does feel good," Yarsnael replied. "The military enjoys such a dominant stance."

Kol froze as he saw the military's forcefulness in himself, providing Yarsnael with an opportunity to escape. Kol soon recovered and chased him down, hoping to prevent the spy from alerting Zavroon.

He saw Vekk running across the street with Arkriat and Kretai behind her, expectedly seeking more answers about the massacre of Modspi; Yarsnael had been uncooperative and this was clear to her. Kol managed to catch up to him as the Kerrilas slipped and fell on the broken steps that led to the fountain while Vekk watched from a distance. Yarsnael laughed, defeated, and persisted in seeking an escape route.

"Who killed these people?" Kol asked before his captive could evade questions once again.

"Here. Below," Yarsnael cryptically told him, searching the area for other obstacles to his escape. Vekk began to walk towards them as Yarsnael began to move carefully away from Kol, slow enough that he did not notice.

"I guess Kerrilas don't suffer too much from a stab wound," Vekk said. "He looks fine."

Expecting few answers from their captive, Vekk once again walked away and searched the city for the source of the poisonous release; this quickly became a difficult task as there were no obvious signs of leakage or damage, regardless of how far, or carefully, Vekk searched. The city appeared to have a lack of sewer or pipe access, making it difficult to discreetly infect individual homes or spread toxic gases quickly. There were no canisters of gas in the deserted streets, the poisoner clearly having left few clues.

Kol interrogated Yarsnael, who confidently rejected his captor's threats and pleas. He was well trained; he told Kol how the majority of his life had been spent in classes and simulations to perfect his skills against rebellious subjects or armed forces.

"An overconfident child who is unable to save his city," he told Kol.

"I have the spear here," Kol reminded him.

"I have the upper hand," Yarsnael responded as both heard a seal open on the fountain's base, which began to emanate a visible, gaseous substance.

Kol pushed the Kerrilas away and ran, urgently searching for his sister. Yarsnael took the opportunity to flee from the siblings and chose to observe them from afar.

Kol saw Vekk directing Arkriat and Kretai towards a hotel and warned her of the new incoming danger.

"Vekk! Someone's rereleased the gas!" he said.

"How do you know—"

"We need to seal ourselves away!" Kol yelled as he pushed her into the hotel, followed by Arkriat and Kretai.

They locked the doors and closed the windows, hoping to reduce the possibility of a gas leak. From what they could see, the gas appeared to erode parts of the buildings and flow inside, pushing its way past the security measures that had been set up long ago.

"How did you know it was gas that killed everyone the first time?" Vekk asked her brother, who was turning away from the window to explore their surroundings.

"I figured it out quickly when someone, or something, released it," Kol told her. "How did you know?"

"I searched the memories of a victim and saw them drop, as well as reading a message sent by the spy," Vekk said, staring vacantly in the distance.

"Our parents always said you would need your powers at some point," Kol reminded her.

"And our father said he wanted to see your

art when he returned," Vekk said. "But we haven't even seen him since. He...he doesn't know—"

"I'm sure both our parents will return, just not while we're trapped in here," Kol replied, attempting to break through the hotel doors into the apartments.

"How do you suggest that we solve that?" Vekk asked doubtfully.

"We—" Kol began as the sound of a laser sizzling was heard above, followed by a click.

A laser smashed into the skyscraper, destabilising its structure and sending it toppling onto itself and other buildings.

The four fugitives were quickly crushed by the incoming debris, sealing them from the gas that hunted them. Metal plating and glass shards flew across the district, causing damage to other buildings, which were shadowed by the source of the laser.

A large military force flew over the city, recharging its weaponry and passing the damaged site to eliminate another source of resistance elsewhere. The sonic engines glowed brightly enough that the siblings could see them from below the rubble.

Footsteps could be heard soon after; the agent believed his work to be complete as he avoided the collapsed district to make his exit —a cough was heard soon after that he was unable to detect.

The cough persisted in defiance of death, wavering as dirt and dust filled the lungs of the survivor. A long, golden arm clawed at the debris and pushed it away with little success. A foot broke through the remains of the hotel a few metres away, allowing more rubble to crush the leg below.

Vekk pushed herself through the cement coffin she had been trapped inside, breathing at last. She looked upon the relatively flat remnants of the hotel and feared for Kol, quickly scanning the area with her eyes and soon identifying the singular foot coated in dust.

"Kol!" she yelled, pulling herself out and crawling over to the body part; Kol managed to free himself and Vekk pulled him free from the last pieces of debris. They began removing the concrete chunks from the ground, desperately seeking Arkriat and Kretai while forgetting the poisonous air that had infiltrated the district.

However, it had subsided and almost vanished, allowing the skies above them to be engulfed by dust and smoke. Vekk and Kol pulled away some balanced debris to find both creatures, lying together and injured.

"Arkriat!" Vekk yelled as she pulled him out, while Kol picked up Kretai and lifted her into the air.

"That was horrible," Kol said, before choking on the suffocating air.

Vekk, disregarding her brother's statement,

asked, "Is there a veterinary hospital nearby for Arkriat and Kretai?"

"It won't be staffed."

They rushed through the collapsed district, both siblings carrying Arkriat in their arms and with Kretai laying on the Alpha Garisal's stomach. Soon reaching a distant section of the city, they found a veterinary practice that would care for the two creatures; running inside, they were surprised to find it staffed by robots.

"They were just crushed in a building collapse," Vekk said, breathing heavily, Arkriat laying partially in her arms.

"What is your animal's species?" the robot asked with an enthusiastic tone, clearly oblivious to the dramatic events of the city.

"We have a Garisal and a Ukrifar," she told them.

A robot hovered out from a door and took Arkriat and Kretai, appearing to be pleased with the sight of new customers.

"You are our first visitors in months!" The receptionist robot noted.

"Everyone's dead," Kol said bluntly, still processing the events that had happened since their arrival and struggling to reclaim his breath.

"Oh my!" the receptionist said. "Have you alerted the appropriate law enforcement? I'm sure they would be happy to assist."

Vekk and Kol looked at them in disbelief and sat down without response.

"We can't wait here," Vekk said. "We should come back for them."

"The spy probably thinks we're dead. We'll be fine."

A bot entered a few moments later, informing the siblings that the recovery would require at least one day for Arkriat and Kretai to be fully healed; both had sustained heavy injuries and would receive maximum attention.

Morning was beginning to surface and Vekk and Kol ultimately elected to leave the veterinary hospital until they had discovered the source of the gas release.

"We need to find out what happened before the perpetrator leaves," Vekk told Kol.

"Yes, and find a hospital for ourselves," he replied.

They sought out a hospital and found one closer to the city centre, fortunately also operated by robots.

They remained there for several hours but were soon able to leave, their injuries quickly healed. They left the building and gazed upon the apocalyptic site of the collapse that had crushed them.

"This isn't something I ever expected to see in real life," Kol noted.

"It must've been caused by the military vehicles that flew over," Vekk replied. "Those giant engines are hard to miss."

"The spy must've targeted us….Yarsnael."

"I can't see him anywhere. We should check the fountain where you said the gas was released from."

They walked towards the city centre, climbing over rubble and displaced objects, where they saw the empty fountain that killed every citizen in Modspi.

"Careful, in case it activates again," said Kol.

"It's a risk I'm willing to take. Stay back," Vekk told him, and was promptly ignored as Kol stepped forward. They analysed the geometric octagons that decorated the base of the fountain, unable to find anything out of place.

As Vekk stepped into the centre, the octagons began to shift downwards, forming steps around the barrier of the fountain and then dropping altogether, preventing Vekk from climbing back out and falling to an unknown fate.

"Vekk!" Kol yelled in panic, leaping over the meagre barrier and descending behind her.

They both fell into a large glass tube, only suited for one person. They could see the underground laboratory around them, filled with various medical instruments and test tubes.

"Quarailians. This'll be interesting," an elderly woman said, dressed in a grey-collared coat meant for biohazard protection, as she walked across the room to analyse them. She had a respirator sealed to her face; it moved freely when she spoke, as if it were a natural extension of her face.

The large test tube the siblings had fallen into was filled with a red liquid, keeping them suspended but allowing them to breathe. However, it was not designed for multiple life forms and pressure started to mount, pushing against the glass.

"Studying, studying, observing! I can't wait to observe you, rebels," she said to them, placing a frail hand on a table and suddenly striking a small test tube, which smashed on the ground.

I don't want to die here, Vekk thought, unable to speak without swallowing any of the liquid. Both Vekk and Kol attempted to hit the glass but were wholly unsuccessful.

"Let's test...this one," the woman said, selecting an orange-coloured potion and walking towards them.

Their panic intensified and they began to hit harder and more frequently, creating miniature waves within the tank, which splashed against the glass. Kol grabbed the spear from his back but dropped it, watching it sink below him.

"You're unlike the others," the scientist noted as she observed Vekk. "This will be a fun experiment!"

Both Vekk and Kol were paralysed in fear. Vekk involuntarily froze and descended to the bottom of the tube, as the spear had. As she reached out for it, she was lifted by the liquid but managed to reclaim the weapon, although unable to use it.

Kol saw what she had done and slowed his movements, carefully dropping lower and taking the spear from Vekk. He pummelled the glass, with the butt of the spear, reducing its structural integrity and finally creating a small crack, which the suspension liquid seeped through.

The scientist placed the potion into a tray attached to the tube, unaware of the siblings' resistance. As the orange liquid emptied from the glass tube and entered the tank, Kol thrusted the spear through the crack, shattering the glass through the force of the liquid.

"No!" the scientist yelled. "No! You're perfect for my tests! Stay there! Stay!"

As the stress appeared to further destabilise the scientist, Kol shakily held the spear in her direction while Vekk searched the room.

"Why would you voluntarily stay in a place like this?" she asked, before knocking a shelf onto the ground in panic after hearing growling.

Kol brought the point of his spear closer to the scientist, who fearlessly grabbed onto it and threw it to the ground. Kol backed away, hurriedly grabbing a bright blue potion from one of the metal test tube racks.

"Stay where you are!" he commanded.

She charged at him and he threw the potion, causing her to fall to the floor in agony. She let out an ear-splitting scream at him as he reclaimed his spear and began to destroy the potions with it, taking out multiple in one sweep.

"My potions! They'll jump out and eat you all!"

The deranged woman picked herself up and stood as the siblings began to destroy her laboratory. She pressed a button beside her, opening concealed large test tubes and releasing deformed creatures of her own creation.

"I can't deal with that!" Kol told his sister.

"We can't let her keep these potions," she reminded him.

She grabbed the spear from her brother's hands and began to jab it at the creatures, attempting to keep them away. Kol knocked more of the potions off the shelves with his arm, jumping away to avoid the spill of its contents.

Vekk hit one of the creatures in the eye, before dodging its hulking claws as they swung at her. She ran around one of the counters and stabbed it through its brain, causing it to fall to the ground. She placed her foot to climb over it but was grabbed by one of the other creatures and smashed into a cabinet, the spear sliding across a nearby countertop and falling onto the other side.

"This is too much; we need to go!" Kol shouted across the room as the scientist positioned herself between the creatures, one of which dashed at Vekk as she reclaimed the spear.

"What are you doing?!" Kol yelled as his sister leapt at him in an attempt to escape.

"Sorry," she responded, after both had fallen to the ground. "We've got to make sure they don't get out."

Vekk narrowed her gaze as the creatures, with their owner, walked towards her and her brother, determined to kill with their deformed claws and abnormal hands.

"Eat them! Have a snack!" the elderly woman commanded the creatures, who did not understand her but remained under her control. They stood ahead of her as Vekk aimed the ancient spear at their owner's head.

"L...let's hope this works," she muttered, repositioning herself so that the scientist was in sight.

"I'm sure Zavroon could use two mutated Quarailians as guards!"

Vekk threw the spear as the words were uttered, horrified at the disturbed woman's ideas. It passed between the creatures and stabbed the scientist cleanly through her chest, killing her on impact.

The creatures became enraged as she fell to

the ground, leaping at the siblings. Vekk and Kol slid over the counter to avoid the liquid spills, with Vekk recollecting the spear from the bloodied remains.

"I'll find a way out!" Kol said as he began searching the laboratory for a button or lever while Vekk faced off the creatures. He bent down and began searching the floor, soon noticing a loose panel and pulling it away to reveal a weapon stash. He took out a gun and threw it onto the counter behind him; Vekk heard the impact of the weapon and backed away from her attackers to claim it.

She used both of her weapons to distract and dodge the large creature's swipes and leaps while Kol removed the flimsy plate below the weapon stash to find a lever. He pulled it with difficulty but soon succeeded, opening a door that began filling the room with dirt.

A crack reached across the white metal ceiling and began to bend under unseen pressure. Vekk and Kol ran for the door and pushed their way through the mounds of dirt rushing into the laboratory. They rushed up the hidden steps and reappeared beside an office building, hearing the crushing of the creatures below.

"I...can't believe...we made it," Kol said as he and Vekk struggled to reclaim their breath.

"It happened again; someone else is dead at my hands," Vekk said as they began to walk towards the veterinary hospital to reunite with

Arkriat and Kretai. They quickly stopped at a store, where Kol took a small amount of food so that they could later stave off hunger.

"We would be mutants if you didn't," Kol reminded her. "I killed the creatures—we've both done it."

"I still don't think we should continue doing it!" she snapped, struggling to deal with the overwhelming emotions that engulfed her.

"It's horrible, I don't understand how people like Yarsnael do it for a living," he replied, attempting to calm her down. "At least we're alive and those...monsters...didn't get out."

"That's true—we should've freed that woman, though."

"What?!"

"I doubt being trapped in an underground laboratory was good for her."

Kol remained silent, taken aback by his sister's sympathy for a murderer, until they arrived at the veterinary hospital and questioned the receptionist about the state of Arkriat and Kretai.

"They have mostly recovered. They will be ready in a couple of hours!" the robot cheerfully replied.

"Oh...ok," Vekk replied, desperate to leave the desert behind her.

They sat down and waited, trying to understand the events of the city.

"Do you think this place'll ever be populated

again," Kol asked his sister, wondering about her thoughts.

"I hope so," Vekk said. "It would be a beautiful city if it was restored."

"I'm not willing to return to find out," Kol muttered, unable to forget the images of death that he saw upon arrival.

Several hours later, a robot led Arkriat, whose back was being used as a viewpoint by Kretai, towards their owners.

"Arkriat, Kretai!" Kol said in awe; they appeared to have been perfectly healed. Vekk profusely thanked the robots and they left, determined to avoid Modspi for as long as possible as they exited through the gates of the city.

"We should've stayed in Zrelyar," Kol muttered.

"And given ourselves over to the General of the Royal Guard?"

"We shouldn't have rebelled; we wouldn't have had to see Modspi."

"Kol, we're past it now."

"You saw it too! How do you not understand what it felt like?!"

"I do! I saw the bodies! But it's best for everyone if we move on!"

"Why can't you—" Kol asked her, before looking at her blank face. "You're thinking about it right now."

"I need to sleep before we set off again."

They reached a hill and climbed it, seeing

endless sand dunes ahead of them that filled them with dread and determination continue their odyssey. The siblings laid down and slept, finally free from the fear of attack.

As morning arrived once again, they awoke quickly and immediately prepared to set off, eating the small amount of food that Kol had taken from Modspi. After ensuring everyone was well fed, Vekk directed the group to their next location: the endless desert.

CHAPTER 8

A sandstorm brewed around them. The desert gave no immediate indication of salvation for the siblings, who were beginning to tire against adversity and sought more pleasant surroundings.

"This is my first encounter with sand, and I never want to see it again," Kol muttered.

"I'm holding onto hope that something friendly lays beyond all of this sand," replied Vekk, forcing her draining positivity to the surface. They were walking towards the great rock formations that rivalled Modspi's skyscrapers in both height and width; the natural mesas had created a wall that would take weeks to walk around, forcing the siblings to consider how they would climb them.

However, their focus was redirected while en route by the platinum white spires protruding out of the ground, culminating in a spike that barely surfaced above the clouds. Upon further analysis, the siblings noticed that the four metal legs of the spires ran deep into the ground, connecting with nature and intertwining with the roots and rocks underneath, which were used by many animals to survive.

They continued to stride towards the mesas, hoping to find something other than sand; nothing more than rock awaited them upon arrival. They began to slowly climb the rock face, carrying Arkriat as they ascended. Kretai stood beside the crevices in the rock, allowing Vekk and Kol to locate them easily.

Pulling themselves and Arkriat onto the flat top of the formation, they were greeted by a panoramic view of more sand dunes. The landscape was dotted with peach-coloured rocks.

"I can't keep going," Kol remarked upon seeing what faced them.

"Then let's use this time wisely," Vekk said, holding out the spear.

Kol took the weapon and walked towards the edge of the plateau, holding the spear over the ledge. "Take a break."

"Kol..."

He threw it onto the ground beside him and sat on the ground. Vekk dropped the gun and joined him, watching Kretai fly around them.

"Do you know the danger we're in?" she asked, staring at his blank face.

"Well aware."

Vekk sighed and lowered herself onto the hard ground, staring at the grey-blue sky above. She heard Kol begin to rest but little other movement, as if he had fallen asleep immediately. She turned her head to see that he was staring at the sky with uncertainty—as she felt like doing.

She forced her eyes shut and repressed the thoughts of Modspi.

Thrakalir, my brother, I wish you could guide me now.

They slept until the following morning, surprised to find that they had not been discovered.

Kol stood up and saw his sister laying quietly, unwilling to continue their journey. He smiled at her and looked at the desert below, admiring the quietude of an uncivilised place for the first time.

He looked to his side, picked up the spear and began to mimic fighting a soldier. He continued for a few minutes before he heard a laugh.

"Shut up, Vekk," he said, walking towards her.

"I'm sure Zavroon will be shaking next time you two meet," she said with a smirk as she stood up and grabbed the gun laying near her foot. "We do need to practise, through."

Kol looked at her incredulously, watching as she aimed her gun at non-existent targets. He walked away and swung the spear, feeling his hands adjust themselves to fit the wooden shaft.

He envisioned soldiers and superior generals standing in front of him as he attacked, quickly becoming more comfortable with the weapon, while continuing to lack the training to fully wield its power.

"Remember killing is a last resort," he heard Vekk shout behind him.

"I know!" he called back, sighing as he repositioned himself.

Vekk relaxed her shoulders, realising the futility of shooting the air. She began to fire at nearby rocks, discovering tactics that would improve her aim.

She tried to visualise the stances that her adversaries had used against her but struggled to replicate the years of training that Zavroon and Yarsnael had received. She sighed, deciding to use the distinct maroon markings on the blood red cliffs as targets.

She shot without mercy, feeling satisfaction as stones were thrown into the sand far below. Behind, she listened as Kol allowed his mind to take control and stabbed the invisible foes ahead of him.

Vekk soon clipped the gun to her belt and allowed Kol to swing the spear at her, stepping away to avoid being hit; this continued for several more hours as they became comfortable with combat.

"We need to keep going," she said as she backed away from Kol, who slowly lowered his weapon.

"We need real training," Kol said, walking towards the edge of the plateau. He sheathed his spear and sat on the ground.

"I don't think we'll ever get it." Vekk knelt down beside the edge of the cliff, watching the sun set over the endless desert. She then turned around and began to climb down, encouraging Kol to follow her.

He grabbed Arkriat and they slid down to a lower section of the cliff, sitting on a flat rock surface. Vekk gestured to Kretai to fly beside them as she joined her brother, before beginning to continue the descent.

They reached the pale sands after an hour through a mixture of sliding and climbing. They walked, exhausted from their inadequate training, towards a colourful oasis accompanied by a teal forest in the distance. They rushed towards the body of water to find that it was filled with various aquatic organisms.

"I'm surprised that there is life near this dead desert," Vekk said, sitting beside the water with Kol.

The daylight had faded as the trees began to radiate warmth and light reached over the oasis like a group of suns. The moons of Vennirein and Jarelin casted light over the entire planet, except for the thick smog that surrounded Zrelyar; Vekk and Kol were determined to eliminate it. They soon slept after a day of climbing and training, hoping to be prepared for the next series of events.

When they awoke the next day, the sun had reappeared and the trees had lost their warmth. The brightness had forced the siblings awake, along with Arkriat and Kretai.

"I guess we should get going again," said Kol, disgruntled and starving.

They were in desperate need of supplies, particularly fresh food and filtered liquids. They walked slowly towards the forest, exhausted by the physical and mental toll of their grand task. Leaping over a river, they approached the remnants of a forest, characterised by the leafless trees; the only other sign of its existence were the shells and skulls of ancient wildlife that lay dead and ready to be forgotten.

"This doesn't fit with the lively-looking forest ahead of us," Kol noted.

"But it's perfect for the desert," Vekk replied, stepping over the skeletal body of a small animal.

They reached the forest after several minutes of walking through its lifeless counterpart, noticing the diverse wildlife that resided in the new biome. The birds, bugs and insects graced the land as they walked upon its teal surface; many hid under trees that consisted of a shell of spiralling blue wood and purple leaves.

The siblings smelt fresh air for the first time in their lives, noticing the dense flora surrounding them. They were taken aback by the strength of the smells, almost overwhelmed by the natural scents that reminded them of new life.

"I didn't know nature could exist like this on Quelliare," Kol said.

"Maybe this is normal outside of Zrelyar," Vekk said, feeling the deep lines on a tree's warm bark. "Strange how it's next to a desert, though."

"Hopefully the keys are in places like this," Kol remarked, looking at the red and white birds flying away into the clear sky.

Vekk looked down, quickly noticing the grass that had decayed beneath her feet and had faded from a bright purple to a simple grey, harbouring no life. "I disagree."

"Why?" Kol asked while admiring the scenery, until he turned to see the corruption that lay at his own feet. The flowers rotted and were drained of life simply through contact with Arkriat and the siblings' feet. Insects witnessed the area become devoid of life and ran. Most of the insects failed to escape and decayed until they reached an early death.

"We're killing everything; we need to leave!"

Vekk said as she watched herself unintentionally massacre a part of the forest's ecosystem. She attempted to step away, only to corrupt the ground behind her.

"We can't," Kol said. "We'll just keep spreading...this...until we get out."

"Then we need to find someone," Vekk suggested as she searched for sentient life in the area; the siblings began to run through the forest in an attempt to minimise the damage they caused. Despite this, they instinctively slowed at the sight of a figure atop a hill, appearing to emit a radiant blue light that was almost blinding.

"Is that a lamp?" Kol asked his sister as they approached.

"Lamps aren't usually shaped like that," Vekk responded as they slowly walked up the hill to analyse the glowing figure.

"Greetings," the female figure said to them, her face now visible and clearly humanoid.

"Can you help us?" Vekk asked in desperation as she marvelled at the spirit-like figure that spoke to them.

"I see that you are not yet pure," the figure queried. "I assume your progress has stagnated?"

"Progress?" Kol asked.

"To complete your trials," the figure said, almost surprised that they did not understand her.

"We've just arrived," Kol said.

"Ah, I see," the figure told them. "Then I shall help you."

She directed them through the forest, ignoring the damage the siblings and Arkriat caused to the ground while Kretai flew above.

"I am a spirit," the figure said. "I am a guide, a teacher, a protector."

"What's your name?" Kol asked.

"I do not have one," she said. "What do others designate you?"

Vekk took a moment to understand the question. "I am Vekk and his name is Kol."

"Those are unusual names," the spirit replied.

"Officially, we're called Vekkilar and Kolansar," Kol interjected. "We need a key."

"Kol!" Vekk hissed, concerned for their safety.

"I have no contact with anyone beyond these lands; do not fear," the spirit told her.

They approached a village, specifically walking towards an animal sanctuary. Farmers worked nearby, unreactive to their presence.

"These are the first people we've met that don't reject us," Kol mentioned to his sister, who was in awe at the many forms of plant life that the villagers were growing.

"That's a good point," Vekk said. "Let's just hope we can keep it that way."

"Follow our rules and peace will remain,"

the spirit told them.

They entered into a circular room inside the animal sanctuary to find many small, injured animals being cared for by their older counterparts.

"Is this a sanctuary or a vet?" Vekk asked, alarmed by the number of injured animals.

"Your first task is to heal these animals," the spirit told them vaguely.

"How?" Kol asked, instinctively looking towards his sister.

"There is a rebuilt chamber at the end of the left corridor," the spirit said. "The method is clear."

"I've never healed anything in my life!" Vekk protested.

"Your unwillingness to learn is…disappointing," the spirit said, suddenly fading away. "This is why you will always fail."

"Wait!" Kol said. Despite this, the spirit did not return.

The siblings stared at the animals, desperate for love and care from any willing participants.

"I expect she's still watching, only disappearing so we feel abandoned," Vekk told Kol, unable to ignore her feeling of guilt. "Otherwise, it doesn't make sense why she left so abruptly."

"Well we need her back now," said Kol, looking down at the various infant animals.

He realised that they the spirit had abandoned them as the animals watched to see what he would do next. "We'll have to separate them first."

They pulled the young animals away from their carers with great difficulty, aided by the intervention of Arkriat, who forced the older animals into a corner. Kol watched the animals as Vekk searched the rebuilt chamber, soon calling her brother over.

He walked inside to find various pieces of medical equipment unique to the village, unseen anywhere else on Quelliare. They began to read the vague instructions left for them and called Arkriat to guide the animals forwards. He ensured that they remained in line as Kretai drew them towards Kol, knowing the strange creatures would be attracted to a flying animal.

Kol placed each individual animal onto one of the counters, using the lasers situated above to sedate them. He then passed each one to Vekk, who healed the animals with unexpected ease by utilising the equipment, each of which refused to function if incorrectly utilised.

Within three hours, they had completed their task and stepped outside, seeking further guidance. The villagers paid no attention to them as the siblings walked along the paths to explore the mysterious existences of the people.

Before they could walk further, the spirit returned and approached them.

"You were selfless and those animals will live fulfilling lives," the spirit told them, despite having pushed them to complete their goal. "You are ready for the next trial."

Vekk watched the spirit with disfavour as she directed them back into the forest, without giving them indication of where they were being led.

They reached a marble temple, far from the village. The sun held itself in the centre of the sky, its rays reflecting off the polished roof of the sacred place.

"Welcome to my temple," the spirit said to them. She gestured for them to enter and they found a small fire pit in the centre of the main room accompanied by a golden throne at the back. Two portals hung by the throne, one on each side.

"Which future do you desire?" the spirit asked, pointing to the portals which offered a glimpse of potential futures conjured by the temple's owner.

The left portal showed a throne room, the walls covered in black panelling with gold lining the top and bottom. A black throne was at its centre, with two trees curving to encompass it and a glass panel was fitted in the floor ahead, revealing various purple wires leading to separate areas of the room. People stood beside the throne, waiting for their ruler's next orders.

The right portal showed a hellish landscape of ash and dust, the sun barely visible. The familiar houses were eternally burning and had lost their colour long ago. Soot-stained chimneys billowed out smoke alongside the fires that danced upon the roofs. Barely detectable traces of life were heard screaming, as they had no choice but to embrace the suffering that awaited them.

Vekk walked briskly towards the left portal, having an obvious preference to the throne room.

"Wait," said the spirit.

Vekk turned around to listen, fearing that she was being deceived.

"If you pass through The Ideal portal," the spirit said. "Your brother will be forced to experience The Dystopian future. Your creatures will not be allowed to join you; they are not part of this."

"The four of us should be allowed to enter one together," Said Kol in a distressed tone, "and how did you know we're siblings?"

"One of you must enter The Ideal portal, and the other must enter The Dystopian portal," she said, disregarding his question.

Vekk thought hard. She was trusted with a responsibility to keep her younger brother safe, yet she would be faced with some of the most horrible sights in existence if she were to allow him to enter The Ideal portal.

"I'm not opposed to entering The Dystopian portal," Kol said. "I would rather not, though."

"Make your decision, Vekkilar," the spirit told her, "or the responsibility will be passed to Kolansar."

"I...I would prefer to enter The Ideal," Vekk said, her mind amounting with guilt.

"And do you accept this decision?" the spirit asked, turning to face Kol.

"Doesn't sound like I have a choice—I accept," Kol agreed, after taking a moment to consider the request with apprehension.

"I'm sorry Kol!" Vekk told him.

"This better be quick," he said to the spirit in an irritated tone. "Arkriat, Kretai, stay here."

They both entered the portals, Vekk feeling concern for Kol, despite having made the decision.

"Queen Vekkilar," a man said to her, bowing.

Vekk was standing in front of the black throne, watching as multiple people from her city bowed before her. She sat down, curious as to what lay outside of the palace.

"We have captured spies from our neighbouring cities," a man before her said, followed by a woman showing her a hologram of the spies.

Vekk was overwhelmed; she had not been blessed with the powers of a Queen upon entering the portal and assumed her actions were of little consequence in the real world.

"Orders?" the man asked, appearing visibly confused by her silence.

"Oh, sorry," Vekk said. "Question them for information."

"No need to apologise, Queen Vekkilar. It will be done," he said, walking out with his entourage.

"Your royal address is now," one of her guards told her.

"Grea—good," Vekk responded, attempting to fit the role of a Queen.

She approached the throne room doors and was greeted by a curved balcony holding her above the crowds that had amassed beneath her.

"What do you want for your subjects?" the guard said to her.

"You're the spirit!" Vekk whispered to her, knowing that a guard would not ask her such a random question.

The guard stayed silent as Vekk approached the crowds, looking at the thousands of people waiting for her speech. She had only a few moments to prepare something and simply said what she had wanted since she escaped Zrelyar.

"People of Zrelyar," she announced to the crowd. "Ever since I escaped this place with my brother, Kol…Kolansar, we have worked tirelessly to improve the lives of everyone here. It has been difficult, we have become exhausted and without direction—yet we persist!"

The crowd gave a scattered cheer, waiting for her to say something that was directly relevant to their lives.

"Lasapra poisoned this city, our planet, even us!" Vekk told the people of Zrelyar. "I will do everything in my power to shut down those which allow that. It doesn't matter who rules; a leader should care for their subjects. Kolansar and I will ensure that happens whether I am Queen or not!"

The crowd began to cheer. They understood her.

She knew what she was fighting for.

Her guards guided her back to her throne, where she sat waiting for her next task.

"Where is Kolansar?" she asked the spirit disguised as a guard.

"I cannot say. You alone know his whereabouts," she was told.

"Oh...yes, of course," replied Vekk.

Another man walked into the throne room, a corridor having appeared behind the doors.

"Your Majesty," he said, bowing. "The construction on your family's museum is complete. Would you like me to give you a tour?"

"Yes," Vekk said. "I'm intrigued."

He guided her through the palace and out of the front door, where she was exposed to the beauty of a utopian version of Zrelyar. The air was entirely clear and there was a beautiful, fresh smell. Birds and butterflies were visible in the skies; they could survive and thrive in the clean atmosphere.

As she followed the man, she noticed the beam had disappeared and the factories had been replaced with other buildings that were covered in grass and moss.

She even recognised the road she was being led to; the houses had not changed.

It was the street she was born and raised on.

"I can't wait to make this reality," she said aloud to herself, earning her a confused look from her guards.

Their home had been replaced with another building, marked by a rotating glass ceiling in the ground and an influx of tourists walking inside.

"Excuse us, Queen Vekkilar is passing through," the man told the people. They immediately moved for her to pass through.

They had retained the living room and kitchen of her house before being attacked by Zavroon, but the back of the building opened up into a grand room, displaying various pieces of artwork from their home, excluding Kol's work. Vekk was awed at the precision of the main section of her home despite the fact that it had likely been destroyed in reality.

As they walked through, Vekk saw the number of people interested in her and Kol's history. They moved away to make space for her to pass through as she was led into a side room containing all of Kol's pieces of art, all considered a masterpiece by the viewers.

"Your brother is an incredible artist," a man told her, "surely he could have brought you art like this for your palace if you had not banished him."

" 'Banished him'?" Vekk said, stunned.

"It's well-known that you stole the throne from your brother—but we trust in your decision, my Queen," he said.

This is because I chose to send him to The Dystopian future, Vekk thought.

A piece of artwork in the centre of the room, titled *The Spirit Desires Return* hung, calling out to her. The man nodded to her as she realised that the vision was over; she had to go back to reality despite the enjoyment she felt.

Vekk climbed into the painting, being thrown onto the temple floor.

Kol had fallen unconscious as he entered the portal, waking up on a barren cliff, built of grey rocks and covered in ash. The world around him was unfamiliar but it was clear that everything was dying or dead.

Fires raged below him on the rooftops of houses, leaving him little other choice visible. Kol jumped into the chaos to find himself facing a Quarailian home.

"Zrelyar..."

He rushed inside the house, seeing a father with his child, covering her from the onslaught of flames. They surrounded the small family, making it difficult for him to approach them.

Kol placed his hand onto a charred pillar, which collapsed upon contact, much to the horror of the father and daughter. He managed to escape before the roof fell and was forced to watch the building crush the small family. However, their fates were impossible to discover as Kol did not see their bodies—yet he knew there was little chance they could have escaped.

Kol stared in shock until he was forced to escape the falling meteorite fragments that smashed into the ground, displacing the paths and setting fire to its surroundings.

The heat was spontaneously starting fires as if the atmosphere was aflame and purposefully killing all life on Quelliare. The dust that had been pushed into the air made for little visibility but Kol could discern densely populated areas based on the number of fires.

Kol stepped over a rocky hill that had come from the ground to see Lasapra's palace was falling apart due to the meteorites and earthquakes breaking through the east side of the city and reaching the centre; Kol faced it, fortunate to have appeared in the slightly less damaged area.

He began to recognise the nearby buildings

and managed to discern his location, moving towards his own home but arriving in time to watch a chunk of fiery metal throw itself into the room, causing an electrical explosion and sending Kol flying backwards, through the glass of Leritri's door.

The inside was dusty and dark due to a shortage of electricity. He walked around and found no sign of life or movement, including the elderly woman who usually resided there. He felt around the room, noting the books missing from her bookshelf shortly before stepping on them by accident.

He quickly escaped out of the deserted home, unwilling to find any unpleasant surprises.

He walked up to the surface to find his family's former home replaced with a pit in the ground, the remaining walls covered in dirt and burning.

"What is this...?" Kol began, before running to find any other trace of life.

As he ran across the street, the ground rapidly raised in front of him, blocking his escape. He ran in the opposite direction and was faced with a collapsing wall. He elected to run between them, escaping narrowly and barely with his life.

He unsheathed his spear and smashed away at the sealant in the wall of a house, running through before it collapsed.

He saw people screaming, before being crushed by boulders and debris. Their homes were rapidly destroyed by the various natural disasters that occupied the city and the ground was quickly reclaiming itself from the oppressive stone and metal pathing that was being broken up.

Kol ran towards Lasapra's burning palace, assuming he would be able to find a reinforced bunker or vault, despite not having any keys or authorisation.

The entrance was protected by two royal guards, covered in purple-hooded robes and held spears, with each unflinching to the chaos that surrounding them, including the burning of the building that they were sworn to protect.

"Access is currently unavailable," one of the guards bluntly told Kol.

"Quelliare is being destroyed!" Kol said. "I need protection."

The guards drew their sharp staffs and began to jab at Kol, who rapidly moved to dodge. They positioned themselves either side of him, preventing him from escaping the fight unscathed. Kol stabbed his spear into a guard but it appeared to cause little injury to him.

They're wearing armour, Kol thought, realising his mistake.

He grabbed the head of a guard and thrust him at the other incoming attacker, both guards noticing his tactic and evading injury.

Kol jabbed his spear at one of the guard's faces and managed to create a minor scar. The guard showed no reaction to the injury and persisted his attack.

Kol was successfully dodging their staffs until he backed into a wall and the scarred guard knocked him to the ground with the blunt weapon. He knelt down to mock him when Kol stabbed his spear between a gap in the guard's exposed armour.

He staggered back and Kol stood up, preparing himself to hold off the other guard. He thrusted his spear at his trained opponent, who knocked it away with his own weapon and shoved Kol through the palace doors. Kol scrambled and grabbed his weapon before retreating into the palace and listening as the doors closed behind him. As he turned away from the doors, he heard unnatural, loud screaming and crying as several giant fists banged on the door, desperate to get inside.

Kol rushed through the grand halls of the palace, oddly devoid of people while remaining in pristine condition. Gold was a clear feature of the palace, a likely display of wealth by its owner to emphasise her power to potential usurpers.

Kol ran upstairs, finally being exposed to damage inside the fortified building; he managed to find two metal doors, which slid apart upon detecting his presence. He walked into a vault full of the city's riches, including the rarest metals on Quelliare.

"This part is certainly not dystopian," Kol remarked, awed by the amount of wealth that surrounded him.

He heard a click behind him, noticing that the doors had lock and sealed him away from the disaster that was occurring outside.

The lights began to flicker but Kol was still safe. The vault was seemingly secure, but he felt no enjoyment at the hordes of wealth, as they were seemingly part of the illusion of The Dystopian. He sat atop a block composed of various metals and waited for a chance for the environment to calm and the vault door to open.

His wait was over as his expectations were partially fulfilled, the vault doors being blown in by a chain reaction in the palace's private power system. He escaped onto the street to find the palace almost destroyed and the guards nowhere to be seen.

A monstrous creature stood in front of him, seemingly out of nowhere but ready to attack Kol, its multiple arms moving from its chest to reveal a portal. Its face looked as if it had recently bled yet it still acted as if it was at full strength.

That must be the way out, Kol thought, preparing to charge.

The creature began to charge, attempting to

grab him with its many arms but Kol slipped out of the way, as he knew that he would not survive the encounter if he tried to fight.

Kol gripped the edge of the portal but was grabbed by the creature, its strength surpassing his own.

He clawed at the creature's chest, weakening its grasp on him and allowing Kol to throw himself through, escaping the horrific possibilities of his future.

CHAPTER 9

"Vekk!" Kol said, picking himself up off the floor after being thrown down and greeting Arkriat, appreciating the company.

"It was incredible!" Vekk told him as she stood up, feeling enthusiastic about what she had seen.

"You forced me through that!" he accused, jabbing his finger at his sister.

"I'm sorry Kol," she said. "But that's what we're fighting to stop."

"You're not intellectually superior," Kol sneered, frustrated by his sister's obliviousness.

"Congratulations," the spirit said. "You survived, Kolansar, you will be stronger for this."

"I better be," Kol responded.

"We're ready for the next trial," Vekk told her.

"I'm not!" Kol told them, trying to take a moment to process the future he had seen. "The Dystopian was horrible!"

"Surpassing The Dystopian means that you can survive the next task," the spirit told him.

"That's reassuring!" he sarcastically told her.

"You must—" the spirit began, before being interrupted by the distant sounds of bombing. "We are under attack."

"Is this the trial?" Vekk asked her, preparing to grab her weapon.

"It is not," the spirit said, looking into the distance to try to find the source of the disturbance. Yelling could be heard, which confirmed that the sound of bombing was real and approaching.

"Your final task was supposed to be to fight an enemy," the spirit told them, slowly exiting the temple. "This was not the enemy I had in mind, however."

"Do you know who it is?" Vekk asked her, following behind with her brother.

"It is likely bandits. Heavily armed bandits with powerful weaponry capable of destroying all life here," the spirit said.

"We'll fight them off," Kol said. "I have a lot of frustration to release."

"More importantly, you have embraced experience and learning," the spirit reminded him, clearly detached from the emotions of mortal beings.

They ran out of the temple, noticing the ground beneath them now surviving as they ran. They sprinted towards the village to see the precious trees burning to the ground, surrounded by bloodthirsty bandits of an unknown species.

"Eliminate them!" the spirit commanded everyone nearby, including the civilians who immediately reached for their weapons.

Arkriat stood in front of the siblings, ready to take down any that opposed them. Kretai was perched on Kol's shoulder, ready to face the attackers.

Kol led the attack, wielding his spear and viciously attacking while Arkriat lunged at the bandits. Bullets flew past them, clearly having come from Vekk's gun.

"Are they allied with Zavroon?" Kol yelled to his sister, who was struggling to fire without hitting him. *You think you know everything else; you should know this.*

"They think we're dead!" Vekk reminded him.

The spirit levitated in the centre of the village, dissuading nearby animals from approaching and filling the farmer's minds with positive reinforcement.

"Kol, to your left!" Vekk shouted as Kol stabbed a raider ahead of him and rapidly turned to face the bandit, hitting him across the face with his spear.

Arkriat jumped between the attackers; the terror of being mauled by a Garisal was enough to slow them down, regardless of whether he attacked or not. Kretai flew at them, landing on their arms and affecting their aim as they struggled to push her off.

Kol was surprisingly quick with his spear after having practised on the guards in The Dystopian and was only improving after fighting the bandits; he was prone to being injured by the enemy's attacks but continued regardless, fuelled by anger.

Vekk was constantly moving towards their enemies as Kol cleared the way, attempting to dispatch any bandits who would try to sneak up on him from behind. His leadership surprised her as she was used to protecting him; his experience through the portal had hardened him for the journey to come, from her point of view.

In reality, Kol was attempting to escape the images of suffering that he was forced to experience and found it easier to channel that suffering into another person. He was also determined to avoid Vekk due to her selfish decision; the thought of her irritated him greatly.

As if leaving a trance, Kol knocked out the final bandit—of that wave.

"More will come!" the spirit announced from afar as firebombs echoed in the distance and the forest lit with flames.

They came with greater numbers and strength, proving to be a challenge to Kol and forcing Vekk to locate weak spots before firing. She aimed at their limbs, hoping to reduce their endurance before they reached Kol.

Kol continued to fight valiantly alongside Arkriat and Kretai, the bandits being slowed so Kol could take them down despite his lack of training or physical strength.

However, Kol was not prepared for the corpse that walked towards him, passing through the organised army of bandits that moved aside to allow it to approach him. It corrupted the ground beneath its feet, before stopping ahead of Kol. Both stood with the dead grass beneath them, staring into each other's eyes with anger.

Kol prepared to thrust his spear into the animated corpse, before being shoved into the ground. He quickly backed away as Vekk shot over his head, causing little injury to the undead attacker.

"That is my body. Destroy it," the spirit said from afar.

"What?" Vekk asked as she ran to Kol and began pulling him away. She listened for an explanation but one did not come.

Arkriat tore into the corpse's leg but was swiftly grabbed by the neck and held in the air, the attacker's strength apparently unlimited. He wriggled to escape but could not, listening as his owners panicked nearby.

Kol stood up and charged at the corpse, thrusting his spear through its throat. It dropped Arkriat and grabbed the weapon, forcing the blunt end into Kol's face.

Vekk shot at its face and watched as it charged at her. Kretai swooped past but was grabbed out of the air, struggled to escape the corpse's tightening fist.

Kol appeared from behind and placed his arm around its neck, before wrapping his legs around the corpse, placing all his weight on its thin bones.

It collapsed to the ground, bringing Kol down with it. He felt his body slam into the soft soil and release his opponent, allowing it to stand back up and charge at Vekk. He slowly stood back up and picked up Kretai, ensuring she was relatively uninjured.

Vekk shot rapidly but did not cause any noticeable injuries to the corpse, which now had extended its arms towards her. She shot its face and broke through the burnt flesh to see a hole in its skull, revealing a brain.

As it reached out to grab her, Arkriat sunk his teeth into its leg and held it back, allowing Vekk to shoot through the skull and pierce the brain. It frowned at the spirit and fell to the ground, imprinting in the dirt.

The army of bandits began to approach but the spirit created an earthquake beneath their feet, disorientating them and causing them to scatter.

"Why didn't you do that before?" Vekk asked as she shot at the bandits, who tried to escape. She watched Kol and Arkriat run forwards to finish off the invaders.

"I could not," the spirit told her as it watched Kol stab several bandits and Arkriat assist him in ensuring they did not rise again.

Once the attackers had fled, Kol and Arkriat returned and stared at the corpse on the ground, lying face down in the dirt. "That was you?" Kol asked.

"No. It was the body of the traitor who led to my departure from a mortal existence," he was told. "The bandits utilised it to weaken my abilities. I hoped to own it so I could destroy it."

"Alright."

"Thank you for helping us, despite it being of little gain to you," she told them. "I would like to reward you with one of the keys you seek."

I forgot about the keys, Kol thought as he forced himself to relax after the high of battle.

"However," the spirit said, "only one can collect it."

"Vekk," Kol said, "I'm not doing it. You're going in this time."

"Fair enough," Vekk said, reflecting on Kol's bloodthirsty performance with the bandits. "I'll need the spear."

Kol handed her his weapon and she turned to the spirit, eager to follow.

"This way," the spirit said, leading her to a cave approximately a mile away from the village where Kol had chosen to rest.

They approached a cave marked with glowing lines across the walls; the spirit gestured to Vekk to enter but chose not to follow.

Vekk entered, noticing the walls morphing into a metallic corridor while the illuminated markings remained. She approached the main room quickly, passing through a short corridor leading to it. She walked in to find a tomb with a metal coffin laying in the centre, with no sign of the key. She inspected the stone room, analysing the symbols on the back wall that appeared to be ancient, in a language that she did not understand.

She approached the metal coffin, expecting the key to be among whatever corpse lay inside. She pushed the stone lid off to find it empty of a mortal body.

A spirit lay inside—identical to her.

Vekk's spirit sat up, before climbing out and standing face to face, copying her emotion.

"What is this?!" Vekk questioned, stepping away in shock.

The spirit began to attack with a spear-like, ethereal dagger. Vekk's spirit lunged at her, causing Vekk to stagger back in surprise before grabbing Kol's spear and beginning to attack back, finding that she could indeed cause the spirit pain.

It began to scream at her and its attacks became more frantic and violent as Vekk became increasingly tense, forcing her to become accustomed with the spear that only Kol had trained with. She clashed with the spirit, spear on dagger. It then laughed at her and ran away into the darkness. Vekk began to acknowledge the small, stabbing pain she felt every time she hurt the spirit, assuming both of them to be connected.

"Stay away!" she shouted to the unrelenting ghost who was determined to prevent her from acquiring the key.

"Crawl away," it sneered, slowly stepping towards her with its weapon drawn.

Vekk grabbed her gun and fired at the exposed foundations of a pillar, causing the spirit to move swiftly to avoid certain death; it became aggravated and charged at Vekk relentlessly, causing her to dash around the room and struggle to defend herself.

"You would kill Kol for a seat of power," the erratic spirit told her, watching as she nervously clutched the spear. It suddenly slowed, clumsily approaching Vekk.

Vekk managed to ram it into the side of the metal coffin and stabbed it through the chest, causing it to scream in agony and attempt to bite her arm. She stepped away as it stood up, hanging its head in defeat.

"In my grave," it told her as it dissipated and Vekk looked inside the metal coffin to find a glowing gem enclosed in a skeleton's ribcage.

She pushed her hand through the spaces and pulled out the pentagonal, diamond key hidden inside.

"I just need to remember that I'm doing this for others," she said in exhaustion, walking out towards the cave entrance where she met up with the spirit that led her there.

"You retrieved the key," the spirit pointed out. "I will escort you to the village."

They arrived to find Kol waiting for them both and showing weak enthusiasm when they returned with the glowing gem.

"I thought that would take longer."

"Not hard to find, hard to claim," she told him.

Arkriat and Kretai left the home that they had stayed in temporarily to greet Vekk, grateful that she had returned.

"You are pure," the spirit reminded them as they turned to face her. "You may leave knowing you can return at any time as we are grateful for your assistance."

They thanked her and turned to leave, Vekk handing the spear back to Kol.

"I have one last request," the spirit told them.

"I'm desperate to leave," Kol said, the images of The Dystopian trapped in his mind.

"Deter any unwelcome visitors from these lands," she told the siblings. "We will take time to recover from this intrusion."

"We will do our best to do that," Vekk reassured her, edging towards the exit.

"Save this world," the spirit said, beginning to disappear into the air. "Farewell."

"Thank you!" a villager shouted from afar, hoping to show his gratitude before their heroes left.

The siblings walked with Arkriat, who was transporting Kretai on his back, towards the uncorrupted lands, searching for an escape. They had become accustomed to the colourful biome and searched for a new location, seeking a place where they would be accepted and supported.

However, they finally had time to appreciate the genuine beauty of the lands, all of which appeared to be entirely natural and unspoiled by civilisation.

"I won't return here ever again," Kol muttered.

"Are you alright, Kol?" Vekk asked. "That Dystopian portal changed you."

"You're right!" he responded in a sarcastic tone, before a quiver emerged in his voice. "I saw families being crushed and our home being ripped apart by disasters that I couldn't prevent while you lived like a Queen or something."

"But we're preventing the destruction of Zrelyar now," Vekk said, not entirely understanding the situation while admiring the bright trees.

"You didn't see it! It doesn't matter if it hasn't happened yet, I know what it looks like—I've lived it! Seeing something like that doesn't leave your mind." Kol vented, hoping his sister could comprehend the horrors he had experienced.

"I didn't think the spirit would force us to experience anything extreme," she told him. "I wouldn't have entered The Ideal if I had known how much you'd suffer."

"So what did you see?"

"Well…the opposite," she told him. "Zrelyar, a city ruled by me…I mean us, where the sky was clear and we were respected by all."

"Sounds like you had a good time."

They continued through the forest in silence, Kol taking the time to gather his thoughts and prepare himself for the next challenge. Vekk admired the glowing trees, housing many birds and reminding her of her own connection to the plant life of Quelliare. Feeling the key on her belt, she passed it to Kol, who analysed it and confirmed that it was one of the keys they sought.

A cool breeze passed by them, causing them to realise the perfection of the weather throughout their trials and wondering about the inner workings of the planet.

"How did those people meet inside that room in the sewer?" Kol asked his sister, hoping to redirect his focus.

"I...have no idea," she told him. "Perhaps they have a way of bypassing the lock, or a secret entrance."

"So we could've searched for that instead?"

"How are we going to search several officials and highly protected places for access without being arrested or killed?"

"I don't know!"

"Somehow, it's easier for us to cross the planet to gain access."

"Lasapra's too powerful for us," Kol muttered as he looked to the ground.

"She won't be forever," Vekk said.

"We should hurry if we want to stop her," her brother replied, desperate to escape the forest.

"We've already gone further than anyone else I know of," Vekk said, crossing her arms in an attempt to conserve heat as she walked. "It's beyond anything we would've done otherwise."

"True," her brother said, rushing over to Kretai to pull her away from a flock of birds that were watching her in eager anticipation of their next meal.

"Look!" Kol said eagerly, pointing towards what lay ahead of them.

"Another forest?" Vekk asked with an equivalent amount of dread and exhaustion.

Kol nodded. "Hopefully with a better adventure ahead."

They entered, stepping onto the green grass and looking up to the red leaves that hung above. There were fewer animals than the teal forest, and a cool, constant breeze filtered its way through the thin trees surrounding them.

There were minimal signs of civilisation, the small depressions in the ground marking the footsteps of ancient travellers but providing the siblings with little direction.

"These trees are...surprisingly thin," Vekk noted, visually analysing the weak bark and broad leaves that provided a roof over the forest. The light was sliced into thin lines in order for it to pass through and stimulate growth within the plants below.

"I thought this forest would be warm... I'm...freezing," Kol said as he began to walk slower and search for a heat source.

"It doesn't look...inhabited," Vekk communicated with great difficulty, watching as Kol held onto Kretai to ensure the Ukrifar's safety.

"The forest's animals have gone into hiding," Kol said, using his eyes to scan the area for danger.

Arkriat was adapted to lush jungle environments and had short fur, reducing the amount of heat that he was able to conserve. Kretai had thicker fur and a smaller body, allowing her to keep warm. Snow started to fly at them, piling upon branches and plants and giving the siblings a sign of what was to come as they were gradually losing vision of what was ahead.

"I can't see anything!" Vekk shouted in desperation as she looked at the tree towering above, its body bending under the weight of the snow.

"Vekk!" Kol yelled back, hoping to avoid being separated from her once again. Both of them began to run through the snowstorm in desperation, struggling to find Arkriat and Kretai. Vekk grabbed onto trees as she ran to ensure that she remained within the forest as Kol disappeared from sight. She kept running until she felt sand grains underneath her feet, wedging themselves in the soft lines on the underside of her foot.

"Sand?" she said aloud, before hearing someone running nearby. The snowstorm appeared to be too weak to reach her now.

"Kol?"

Arkriat ran out from the blizzard, providing a sense of both relief and fear for Vekk as she greeted him and watched for Kol and Kretai. Several minutes later, they were reunited as her brother stumbled out of the inhospitable forest, holding the Ukrifar in his hands.

"Kol!" Vekk shouted, running towards him with Arkriat behind her.

"We've found our next location," Kol pointed out, struggling to catch his breath as he glanced at the icy-blue sand beneath them and the snowy trees that surrounded the area.

The biome was covered in snow and populated by tall, dark trees which offset the brightness created by the biome's other features. The ground was covered in deep sand yet the trees grew through, appearing significantly shorter than they actually were.

"We need to find warmth," Vekk suggested, looking desperately for signs of life.

"The last village was in the middle of the forest," Kol said. "Maybe that's the best place to start."

They walked through one of the smaller sections of the forest and came across another clearing. However, it was much smaller and had many animal dens situated nearby. Arkriat became tense and stood close to his owners, evidently waiting for danger. Kol noticed and began to survey the area for any obvious dangers.

"Are we under attack?" he asked as he backed towards the centre of the clearing. Vekk followed behind him and grabbing her weapon after seeing Arkriat's vigilance against the darkness.

Growling was heard. The smell of dripping blood was emphasised by the heat of the sun above them, beaming on the exposed ground.

The sun revealed a pack of Garisals, coated in white fur with icy backs, approaching them eagerly. Kol grabbed his spear while Vekk aimed at the approaching predators, waiting for them to strike.

"Not again!"

Arkriat stood ahead of the siblings and Kretai, barking furiously as his necklace began to glow radiantly; the Garisals became more vicious, seeking to remove him as the pack leader.

Kol slashed the feral Alpha Garisal with his spear as the others leapt at Vekk and Arkriat, who struggled to hold them off. Kretai stood atop Kol's shoulder, hoping to avoid the incoming danger as she scanned for an escape.

One of the Snow Garisals leapt and ran off with Kol's spear, leaving him to fight off the attackers with his hands and feet; he threw one Garisal into another and reached for Vekk's attacker, but was pulled to the ground by two of the pack members.

Arkriat grabbed his attacker by the neck and threw him across the sandy ground, causing enough of an injury that it began to back away. He then ran to Vekk and rammed the Garisal that was attacking her, struggling to keep it back as Vekk fired her gun at the ground in an attempt to scare them off. Kol saw the Garisal running with his spear and chased after it, hoping to reclaim it before the creature reached the deep forest.

Vekk managed to shoot it from a short distance, slowing it enough so that Kol could grab his spear and return to his sister. They managed to fend them off and the pack retreated into the forest, waiting for easier prey to hunt.

"I hope we don't have to fight any more Garisals," said Vekk. "They're too unpredictable."

"I doubt Arkriat wants to fight his own species," Kol said, surveying the darkness to ensure that the predators had fully retreated.

Vekk stepped back onto hidden ice as she looked around. Feeling her grip on the ground loosen, she attempted to move but instead slipped and hit the ground. Kol turned around to hear the sound of cracking, followed by his sister falling below the ground.

"Vekk!" Kol shouted, running over to her.

CHAPTER 10

At last, progress, he thought, packing various bags containing various items.

Arthur had applied for, and had been accepted into, university. He had browsed the different undergraduate degrees available to him and studied in preparation; he would be completing a Mechanical Engineering degree at Mirren University, located on the other side of Bristol.

"I've got a lot more stuff than I thought," he told Shadow, who was standing over him as he packed his bags on the hard wooden floor.

He filled one bag with art supplies, planning to paint while studying in order to cover the student debt that would arise, and another with drawings and notes so that he could continue to build a picture of the figures in his mind.

Why do I need this much stuff just to paint?! Arthur thought as he zipped up his bags and ensured his flat was prepared for his return.

It'll be nice to return with a degree, he thought, imagining his life in his ideal workplace away from civilisation.

Clipping Shadow's lead onto his collar, he led him out of the door onto the nearest bus; he had no choice as he could not afford to pay someone to look after his dog for three years —he did not want anyone else to look after Shadow except for him.

The bus was full; students from all over the world had been accepted into the university and would undergo their first experience along with Arthur and his dog.

They watched as the overcrowded vehicle arrived at the grand campus; the university was clearly a new construction. Every building was incredibly modern and many featured grand glass windows that displayed the classrooms inside, waiting for the prospective students' entry.

"You'll normalise it," a voice said to Arthur, walking over. He quickly turned to recognise the familiar face of Rose.

"I never imagined I would ever see you here," she told him, leading him to his accommodations.

"It's a shame that we're not studying for the same degree," Arthur said.

"Yeah," Rose responded, "but I would argue that my degree is more useful."

"English literature won't get you to space," Arthur countered, laughing.

"It'll get me across the planet!"

"The universe is larger than Earth."

"I'm glad those courses taught you something!" Rose said jokingly.

"You wanted to tell me something?" he asked.

"I...I'm engaged!" she told him with uncertainty.

"Engaged? To who?" Arthur asked, unaware of her dating life.

"I'll show you when we get to your student accommodations," Rose replied cryptically.

They reached his new dorm and Arthur was surprised to see multiple people he had already made acquaintances with.

"Isn't this your dorm?" he asked.

"It's yours as well, now," she told him. "Are you alright with that?"

"Yeah, that's fine."

He had already met several of Rose's roommates through video calls, although he was not familiar with all of their names or their living habits.

"Hello," one of the roommates said to him with a thick French accent. "You must be Arthur."

"Hi," he said uncomfortably, unsure of her name.

"That's Isabelle," Rose interjected, taking note of his facial expression.

"Hi," he repeated to her.

"That's Amy, who is also new," Rose said,

pointing to a woman preparing food. "There's Sarah and Steven on the sofa."

"Hello," Arthur said to his flatmates, uncomfortable with the amount of attention on him. "I'm Arthur and this is my dog, Shadow."

"He looks very nice," Isabelle said to him.

"Thank you," Arthur said as she removed Shadow's lead and allowed him to wander.

Everyone sat down on the two sofas ahead of the small television to acquaint themselves with their new roommates. Shadow walked around everyone in the room, eager to greet them.

"Sorry, I couldn't just leave her at home for three years," Arthur said, watching Shadow closely as he was greeted by his roommates.

"That's fine. We love dogs!" Sarah said as she and Steven stroked their new fluffy roommate. Arthur was able to recognise her American accent from the background of the phone calls that Rose had made to him.

"You've both got a few days before courses start," Rose told Amy and Arthur, hoping to smooth the transition back into full-time education.

"Who are you engaged to?" Arthur asked her.

"You're with someone?" Sarah asked her loudly, in shock.

"Come with me," Rose said to Arthur, leading him to one of the bedrooms containing twin beds opposite a drawer.

"I'm not engaged. I just didn't want you to ask me questions in front of everyone," she told him. "Stay here a second while I tell everyone that I'm not getting married anytime soon."

She left Arthur, who sat on a bed and wondered what he was about to be told.

She wouldn't tell me about any medical problems unless they were serious, he thought, thinking over their friendship.

Rose returned and sat on the bed opposite him.

"This is your room to share with Amy, by the way," she told him.

"Right," he said. *I was hoping for a room to myself.*

"One night Isabelle and I were staying late to grab some textbooks, but we wondered off and found an…interesting discovery," Rose said, lowering her voice. "There's a vault under one of the buildings, likely part of a demolished building, and it's been rumoured that there's some sort of ancient secret within. It looked frozen shut but we didn't have a lot of time to analyse it as someone began to approach us."

"Did they ask any questions?" Arthur asked, matching her volume.

"No. We left before they saw us," Rose told him, maintaining a serious glare.

"What do you want me to do? Crack it open?" Arthur asked jokingly, knowing that he would prefer the ancient secrets to stay hidden during his studies.

"Yes, exactly," Rose told him.

"Oh, right," he said, clearly having misinterpreted her tone.

Several weeks later, Arthur was accustomed to university life and knew the names of his roommates and classmates without prompt; he had avoided mentioning the vault to them but constantly thought of it in the back of his mind, imagining a dark interior with brick walls that held an extraterrestrial secret. He had made the decision to help Rose open it and planned to notify her of his choice—after his lectures.

He entered his first class of the day, preparing his pre-made notes and continuing to familiarise himself with the room he would spend many more hours inside.

The elderly lecturer walked in, his bionic legs smoothly taking him to his desk where he introduced the day's focus. Arthur was listening attentively; he doubted that his enthusiasm would last much longer than a few more weeks but hoped to learn as much information as he could before he lost interest.

He began to make notes on his old laptop, knowing that they could be crucial to his exams that would determine his future. *If I fail this, I'll have a load of student debt and no chance of escaping it.*

He attended multiple lectures that day and explored the university campus alone. He enjoyed the freedom, knowing he had no financial responsibilities for the moment and could spend his free time however he wanted until exam season came.

While exploring, he saw Amy looking lost and tightly holding onto her laptop. He approached her, planning to help.

"Hey Amy," he said. "Are you alright?"

"I can't find my class," she said. "Do you take English Literature?"

"No, sorry, but maybe Rose can help you," Arthur told her.

"Thanks," she said quietly, walking away to find someone she recognised.

Arthur walked back to the dorm, hoping to deliver his decision to Rose before his next lesson begun. Walking up the stairs and into the dorm, he only found Isabelle and Amy conversing.

"You got here fast," he said to Amy, who looked panicked. "I thought you had English Literature?"

"It's…cancelled," she said uncomfortably.

He did not believe her but decided to ignore it, seeing no benefit from the situation. He was informed that Rose was currently in a lecture and unavailable.

I'll have to wait a few more hours then, he

thought, walking to his next lecture.

He sat inside the lecture hall, only to be greeted by another elderly lecturer; Arthur had a strong respect for all his teachers, knowing that they understood their subjects well and were far more knowledgeable than him. He was still unfamiliar with the other students, and he did not mind—he was more focused on becoming friendly with those he lived with.

After listening to a presentation on electricity for fifty minutes, Arthur rushed home, hoping to finally meet with Rose.

To his luck, she was lying on the sofa as Sarah and Steven were preparing healthy meals for everyone without waiting for Isabelle and Amy, who were absent.

"Rose, can I talk to you?" he asked, walking towards the bedroom he shared with Amy.

"Sure," she said, following behind him.

They shut the door, cutting off Steven's plea for them to be quick as to not miss their meal.

"I've made a decision," Arthur told her, both of them sitting down. "I want to help."

"That's great, because Isabelle has disappeared," she said to him, staring with a deep concern.

"Disappeared?"

"I've tried to contact her all day but she won't respond."

"I saw her hanging out with Amy when I came to find you earlier," he told her.

Rose stared at him, clearly processing the new information she had just learnt that went against what she already knew.

"I was hoping to get in the vault as soon as possible but I would've preferred to have the three of us," she finally said. "I can show you the area now so you know where we'll be going —tonight."

"Tonight?" Arthur asked, surprised at her short notice.

"Yes," she said, getting up to leave "Don't tell the others, just in case."

They reunited with Sarah and Steven, who were laying out their meals.

"Fresh ingredients," Steven told them. "Amy and Isabelle better be back soon. They told me they wouldn't be in lessons right now."

He's actually a good cook, Arthur thought, attempting to distract himself from the vault— and where his other roommates were.

"That was great, thanks," he said as he finished his meal a couple of minutes later, standing up with Rose to leave abruptly.

"You're not staying for dessert?" Sarah asked as they closed the door behind them.

They snuck down to the oldest building on the campus, still considered new by many university's standards. Rose walked in, greeting the professor and introducing Arthur.

They pretended to search the room for missing equipment until the professor left;

they waited a couple more minutes to ensure he would not return for the rest of the night.

"Right. Let's go," Rose said quietly, leading Arthur behind the professor's desk and moving some broken bricks to reveal a hole in the floor. They climbed down and were greeted by a stone trapdoor in the middle of a small room.

"Wait, are we doing this now?" Arthur asked in bewilderment.

"Yes."

"Your plan?" he asked.

"I hoped you would have one," she said, searching for a switch. Arthur knelt down to the door crack, noting the ice that held it shut.

"It's a shame we don't learn how to make flamethrowers in engineering," he joked as he began to hit the ice with his elbow. Rose dusted the wall to reveal that part of it was missing and a switch remained in its place. She pulled it, Arthur backing away as the doors slid out of sight.

They climbed down a rusty ladder into an embellished rounded room, with four giant cages embedded in the walls. Behind them lay statues of people they did not recognise. The vault appeared to have been owned by a wealthy being, based on the blue and white walls and ceiling of the domed room.

"How could they cover something like this up?" Rose asked in awe.

"Maybe there was a good reason," he said,

looking through the bars of the cages to check for any living beings.

A grand door was situated across from the hatch they had used to enter. Rose and Arthur began to search for a switch, desperate to know what lay beyond.

Arthur managed to squeeze himself between two of the bars and found a button on the base of one of the statues. He pressed it, returning to the centre of the room as the door opened to reveal a stone hallway.

"Why is this here?" Arthur said as they began to explore deeper into the ancient building. Upon further examination, it appeared to be some sort of temple, potentially to worship the figures in the statues.

The hallway opened up into a larger hall, which led to two rooms on either side.

"I'll check the left, you check the right," Rose said, hoping to find what they were looking for and leave as quickly as possible. Arthur initially protested, preferring to stay together, but soon relented upon realising that they could cover more ground and leave sooner.

They checked each room, only finding bedrooms likely for students or worshippers. Each bedroom contained a bed, a statue and a container, which opened to reveal weaponry that was far more advanced than anything currently available. Both of them took a gun and a sword, each weapon having glowing outlines.

"I'm worried about what we'll need these for," Arthur said as he returned to the hall. Rose mumbled in agreement, looking ahead.

They passed into another large room, more ovoid-shaped than the first. In the centre stood a massive stone statue of a man wielding a double-bladed sword, having a similar design to the ones found in the bedrooms.

Rose walked up to it and pressed a button on its base, expecting a door to open. Instead, the stone statue began to disintegrate, revealing a living giant with a dangerous weapon. It jumped off the base and stared angrily at the two humans below.

"Who are you?!" it shouted deafeningly at them.

"Humans?" Rose timidly suggested.

"Wrong answer," it said loudly, the loud voice echoing across the room. It swung its sword at the two of them, both managing to dodge.

"What the—" Arthur yelled, having expected his university experience to be uneventful—or at least normal.

The giant swung again, this time walking through a couple of cables dangling through the roof; the ancient being seemed to be more aggravated, unable to escape.

"Someone must've stopped him before!" Rose yelled to Arthur, stepping closer towards the centre so she had more room to retreat.

Arthur backed away, standing against the wall, to avoid being hit. However, the giant began to slash around him and Arthur was forced to run towards his attacker's feet.

Rose quickly figured out the mechanisms of the gun and began to fire at the giant's eyes, distracting it from Arthur's brave dash and caused his attention to turn to her. Shooting it appeared to do little damage but allowed Arthur to stab him in his foot with his blade.

The giant howled and moved its hand up, ready to strike again. It became tangled in the roof's wires, shocking it as it tried to break free; Rose realised that the cables were not part of the university and were likely designed to restrain it.

"Arthur! Find a switch!" she yelled to him across the room.

Arthur ran around the stone statue base in the centre of the room, seeing two levers on each side.

"I need your help here!" he called to her and she began to run for the base as well, trying to avoid the giant's great hands.

"I'm not athletic," she said, preparing to pull the lever.

"Neither am I," Arthur responded. "Pull the same time as me."

He counted down and they successfully activated the levers, causing a power surge through the cables. The giant unexpectedly shook off the electricity pulsating through his body and glared at Arthur, who stood still and relaxed his facial features. Rose stared in fear, before running towards the nearby exit. Arthur then turned, his face flushed with blood and his eyes narrowing while his arms shook involuntarily.

"No!" Arthur commanded as he held his hands out on either side of him.

What is this? What am I doing?!

His hands slowly turned gold, travelling from his wrist to his fingertips. He felt the sensation of thousands of daggers piercing his hands but was involuntarily frozen—he did not know if it was the magic or fear that prevented his escape.

He watched as an innumerable amount of miniature metaphysical daggers appeared from his hands and were launched at the giant, forcing it to the ground. Arthur also fell as the creature shrieked, with his uncontrolled powers reactivating the wires a second time as they finally brought the weakened creature to the ground.

Rose moved close to the door, fearful of what she had seen.

"What...what did you just do?" she asked him as he struggled to stand.

"I don't know...I thought I did this once, when I was younger but assumed it was in a dream or something," he said, stumbling towards the door. Rose held her sword in a defensive position and he backed away. She timidly pressed a button beside the door and the ground began to lower unexpectedly, leaving the door unreachable.

They walked through a small archway to an empty room, lacking statues or any other form of decoration. A stone door stood half-open, looking as if it broke long ago. They walked through and down another hall.

"Isabelle's really missing out," Rose said, wondering about her whereabouts.

"Clearly whatever she's doing now is much more exciting—and probably safer," Arthur responded, struggling to recover from his previous encounter. *How did I do that? What if I do it again accidentally?*

"I wish she had seen this because there's no way I can recount this in a believable way."

"I'd rather you didn't recount it at all," Arthur muttered as they entered a small room with three separate corridors leading to other rooms.

"Which one then?"

"It's not usually the main one," Rose said, looking behind her to ensure Arthur was not unleashing his powers once again. "Let's try the other two."

Arthur walked down the left corridor to find a small room, with a stone statue of an alien woman against the back wall.

The alien woman had long, light hair and the chipped paint showed that she had blue eyes, although the rest of her was reduced to grey stone.

Arthur did not trust the statue as he held his sword in fear, although he felt a sense of safety as the figure appeared to be recognisable. She resembled one of the figures he had seen in his dreams.

Maybe this is their resting place, Arthur thought, looking around the otherwise empty room for any hidden treasure, but found nothing.

In the opposite room, Rose saw a statue of a middle-aged human man with pale skin, short hair and a beard. Most of the paint had worn away and she was unable to find out any more details about him. She turned to walk out, only to find the door shut behind her. The wall above opened and the ghost of a dog jumped out, ready to attack. She was helpless against it and struggled to find an escape, silently wishing that she could utilise the display of power she had just seen.

Arthur walked down the corridor, his head throbbing from the use of magic combined with his past head operation, to hear the commotion. He rushed down the corridor and unsealed the door by ramming his sword into it, with the ghost disappearing before he could see. He ran to Rose, who had fallen to the ground in unexplained pain.

"Are you alright?" he asked in panic, despite the answer being clear. He helped her to stand and they walked into the central room, seeing a shrine surrounded by candles. Rose, reliant on Arthur's shoulder for support, clutched harder to avoid falling to a fiery death. Arthur had slowly recovered, enough to function without medical attention and was more interested in the secrets of the vault.

Arthur distanced himself but allowed her to use his arm, not wanting his friend to miss the rewards after finding the temple in the first place, and used his free hand to open a small ornate box.

Inside was nothing but a relic with a primitive tooth-shaped space, likely to cause some sort of activation.

"I have no idea how to use this," Arthur said, taking the relic and giving it to Rose to hold so she could analyse it while he sought an exit. He discovered a crack in the wall and slipped his fingers through, activating a switch and revealing a dark passage that led to the surface.

Upon reaching the professor's room and walking out, they noticed Amy and Steven standing nearby.

"What are they doing?" Rose asked.

"Kissing, I think," Arthur told her, tilting his head as he struggled to identify them in the dark. Rose's foot slipped as they walked outside and onto the path, causing both Amy and Steven to turn around to see them, running off immediately once they identified her.

Rose fell to the ground and Arthur tried to help her stand; she could not force her legs to work. She handed him the relic, grasping her ribcage with her other hands.

"If the ambulance gets here, they can't see that," she told Arthur as he accepted the artefact.

"What?" he responded, before seeing the blood that stained her shirt. He immediately grabbed his phone from his pocket and called an ambulance, struggling to stop the bleeding before they arrived.

"What happened here?" one of the paramedics asked as they stepped out of the vehicle.

Arthur stayed silent for a moment before responding. "She...she...slipped while... climbing over a fence with decorative spikes."

The paramedic regarded him with suspicion as Rose held back laughter at his unusual lie. However, she agreed with him and was rapidly lifted onto a stretcher, before being carried into an ambulance.

Arthur swiftly walked back to his dorm to find his roommates sitting around and casually conversing.

"They're back! Hey!" Sarah said with her back to him although she quickly turned around to see that he was alone.

"Where is Rose?" Isabelle asked suspiciously.

"She fell over," Arthur told them, "and….smashed her head on a desk while cleaning."

"You two are left alone and she gets hurt?" she asked with a tone of distrust.

"If you didn't leave us alone to go through that vault then she wouldn't have!" he snapped at her, shocking the others in the room, the other three roommates oblivious to the temple's existence.

Isabelle quietly sat down, wondering what they discovered. Arthur walked over and sat down, only to find Steven with his arm around Sarah.

"Are…are you a couple?" he asked them.

"Of course!" Sarah told him, unaware of what he had seen.

"Right," Arthur said quietly, feeling uncomfortable. Amy and Steven looked similarly worried yet stayed in the room to avoid further suspicion.

"So what's this vault?" Steven asked, changing the subject.

"It's a room below the university," Isabelle told him. "It's just some old ruins."

"Oh okay," he said. "I doubt Rose would've gotten hurt in some 'old ruins' though."

They soon went to bed, Amy and Arthur feeling extremely uncomfortable having to sleep in the same room.

Arthur awoke in the morning to find himself alone. He sat up and got dressed, before walking out into the living room to find his roommates relaxing and ignoring the previous night's events.

Arthur left and headed off to his classes, trying to take his mind off the events of the previous night. He later returned to his dorm, compiled his notes and revised the new content he had learnt, knowing that he could not risk failing the exam.

After a rigorous, revision-orientated hour, he noticed that he was alone. Searching in each room, he found Steven on his laptop.

"Hey," he said without looking up, writing something down on paper and looking back to the screen in front of him.

"Would you like...to go...for a walk around the campus?" Arthur said. "It can be quick."

"Sure," Steven said, closing his laptop and following Arthur out.

They began the walk mostly in silence except for exchanging a few brief comments, both unwilling to talk about what Arthur had seen with Steven and Amy.

"What...degree are you studying for?" Arthur asked.

"Fine arts," Steven said bluntly.

"Cool."

They walked past the building, which hid

the underground temple, and they saw Amy standing in the same place she was on the night that she was caught with Steven. However, she did not see Arthur immediately.

"Steven!" she called out to him.

He looked incredibly uncomfortable as Arthur came into view and Amy looked at him, horrified.

They walked past, no one interacting and attempting to ignore the situation in front of them. They then saw Sarah switching classes in the distance. Arthur felt obligated to resolve the situation, but he had little experience with relationships and he did not know how to approach the subject.

After they were far away from Amy, Steven tried to reignite the conversation, asking about Rose's condition.

"It's probably too early to check on her," Arthur told him, struggling to maintain focus on their walk.

"Right," he responded.

They made their way back to the apartment to find Sarah and Isabelle talking. Steven joined them, speaking in a surprisingly enthusiastic tone.

Arthur went to his room, followed by Shadow while everyone spoke, most of them having no awareness of the current situation. He sat in silence, stroking Shadow who was blissfully unaware of his owner's problems.

I'll feel awful if I say nothing, he thought, *but I'm not a relationship expert.*

He usually had the backup of his friends but they were not present.

Wait.

He immediately called Alex, knowing that he had been in many relationships before.

"Hello?" he asked.

"Please help me," Arthur asked quietly, hoping not to draw the attention of any of his roommates.

Alex agreed and Arthur explained the situation, unable to gauge Alex's reaction to what he was saying.

"You have to tell her," he finally advised. "Let her heal as soon as possible."

"Thanks mate" Arthur told him, hanging up the call. He remained conflicted about how to act, silently wishing he could escape the situation.

Rose will be back soon. She could tell them, he thought, leaving the room to join the others.

Rose returned home after a couple of weeks and was settled within a month. She had refused to inform Sarah about what she and Arthur had seen and insisted that he should tell her, knowing he knew more about the situation than Rose did. He promised that he would do so but instead went to study.

One day, he woke up to shouting and arguing in the main room.

Not today, Amy. Go shout somewhere else, Arthur thought, getting up and walking out only to find Sarah yelling at Steven, barely intelligible.

"You disgust me!" she shouted at him as he tried to speak but only came out with fragmented sentences. Their other roommates began to walk out to see the commotion, including Amy, who was terrified.

"Is it because she's young?!" Sarah asked angrily, "or is she smarter? Do you think she's smart because she studies old words?!"

Amy joined Steven as both attempted to defend their actions. Isabelle watched from her bedroom doorway and Rose lay confined to her bed but could still see the fight.

"How come no one saw you two?!" Sarah demanded.

"Well..." Steven said, glancing at Arthur. Arthur quickly looked at the other people in the room to gauge their reactions as he felt his face becoming warmer. The last face he glanced at was Sarah's, who had her gaze fixed on him.

"I thought we were friends or at least...acquaintances!" she yelled at him, clearly feeling betrayed. She continued to yell at the three of them, making Arthur feel as if he had cheated on her as well.

As she began to advance towards him, Shadow barked at her, sensing her hostility and trying to protect his owner. Sarah backed off and stormed out of the door, fed up with all of her roommates.

Arthur turned to shut himself in his bedroom, but Amy rushed inside first and forced Arthur to take himself and Shadow outside to escape the situation. After approximately ten minutes, Isabelle met him outside and sat beside him and his dog.

"Why didn't you tell her?" she asked, despite knowing that it was an obviously sensitive question.

"I didn't want to upset everyone," he said, feeling like crying and shouting simultaneously, "but I've clearly failed at that!"

"I overheard them talking about the details," she said. "I know Rose saw it too."

"She refused to tell her as well. Sarah probably wouldn't have been so angry if Rose had told her since she's injured."

"I didn't join you on the vault tour because I was talking to my family," she told Arthur. "You can move past this. You weren't the one who kissed her boyfriend. Although, Amy may have given herself a bad reputation now."

"Your English is very good," he told her, which she thanked him in return and gave him the details on the English degree, even telling him about her dream to teach languages across the world.

"Maybe you should learn a language as

well," she suggested.

"Maybe," he replied, thinking over the amount of languages available to him and hoping to redirect his focus onto something else.

They walked back inside and Arthur sat beside Shadow on one of the sofas, staring blankly and hoping to avoid contact with anyone else. He began to browse his phone and found several suitable apps to teach him a second language.

He began a course in French, hoping to be able to converse with Isabelle in her first language.

"What's this?" he suddenly heard from his shared bedroom.

He suddenly remembered the ancient weapons and relic he had left inside.

Oh no.

CHAPTER 11

"Vekk!" Kol shouted, yet hearing no answer. He climbed into the hole that his sister had fallen into, followed by Arkriat and Kretai.

They were in a frozen metallic corridor, showing signs of weapon damage that had likely originated from an ancient battle. Vekk stood up quickly, realising she was lying on the body of an ancient Kerrilas.

"How has that not decomposed?!" she asked.

"Well I'm glad you're alright," he said. "Maybe the cold has kept it fresh."

"I wouldn't call it 'fresh'," Vekk muttered, quickly moving away.

They walked further inside to find many broken or sealed doors, with the buttons to open them damaged beyond repair.

"Maybe they have some sort of medical room?" Kol wondered, hoping to recuperate after the last battle.

"Do you really want to be using ancient medical supplies?" Vekk asked, feeling disturbed by the cold atmosphere of the abandoned building.

"I suppose not."

They found one door that had previously been blown open and looked around, seeing bunkbeds against the walls and boxes spread across the floor.

"It must've been raided," Vekk said, looking at the body beneath her feet.

Kol walked back into the corridor to see that the building was much larger than he initially believed.

"I think it's a military base!" Vekk shouted from the other room, looking through the boxes and reflecting on the metal corridors of which they had passed through.

"That would make sense," Kol said.

Kol managed to pry one of the doors open with his spear, using his arm to increase the pressure. Shoving the door open, he found yet another bedroom, although it was sparser than the last and contained a single bed with a smashed laptop on the desk beside it. A locker had its doors hanging off, which revealed the military uniform inside.

"Definitely a military base," Kol said to himself as he heard Vekk walk past him to explore the rest of the area.

He pulled back the duvet on the bed to see a dead body, bent unnaturally so that it would fit beneath the cover.

"Ergh!" Kol said, stepping away. Regardless, he could not take his eyes off the corpse and noticed that it was holding a glowing tablet. He hesitantly took it from the corpse's hands and realised that it was a report of the battle, up until the captain's death.

"Let's hope something will go right, for once," he said, walking out to catch up with his sister, who was already looking around another room.

She searched through a temporary jail, filled with tubes that appeared to have once been used for containment; Vekk looked up to the ceiling to see rays of light breaking through the cracks, shining through the ice above. She felt around the walls and managed to find a red switch, activating it and igniting emergency lighting for the base. She then moved to a computer terminal and stared at the screen, looking for a password.

As she searched for the password, Kol entered and effortlessly tapped the keys on the screen after reading from the tablet he held, granting them access. Despite the lack of power, the computer terminal hummed and displayed a prisoner list.

"I'm assuming they died long ago," Vekk said, staring at names she had never heard of.

"Probably," Kol responded, looking at the computer for more details on their location. He handed the captain's log to Vekk, who began to read through to understand their situation.

"There was a battle," Vekk said. "This was a base of rebellious Quarailians, Kerrilas and others who were overrun by Cristrial soldiers."

"I guess Leritri was right," Kol muttered, focused on the computer.

"I forgot about that story," Vekk said, intrigued at the details of the battle.

They left the room and walked into the final area of the base, into a command room where the majority of the technology had been destroyed.

"Doesn't look like there's much left," Kol said, trying to use a computer with a broken keyboard. Vekk pulled a panel off a piece of machinery, only to find that it was completely empty.

"Someone took the components from the computers," Vekk told Kol as she walked over to a table in the centre of the room.

Kol also turned around and a device activated a hologram, showing a Cristrial officer, likely having been dead for centuries prior. It flickered and began to hum, finally emitting audio.

"Greetings to whoever receives this recording," It told them. "However, it also means that you've activated the Engine."

Vekk and Kol were stunned, despite having no knowledge on what the officer was referring to.

It continued, "The superweapon will activate in one day starting from the conclusion of this message. However, this recording has the details to shut it down. It is too complex to try figuring it out yourself."

"We need to go!" Kol said loudly as he ran out of the door, followed by Arkriat and Kretai. Vekk stayed, transfixed on the hologram.

"You must destroy four pylons and locate the Engine control room to deactivate it," she was told. "When that is complete, your planet will be safe."

Vekk pursued her brother and they found winter clothing in a storage room, allowing them to brave the harsh snow and sandstorms that would likely arise. They quickly searched for a way out, not knowing how much time they would need to disable the weapon. Vekk briefed Kol on the details that he had missed.

"Don't we need a map or something?" Kol suggested.

"We have the map for the five keys," Vekk reminded him, pointing to his belt pocket.

"That's not for pylons, though," he replied, running back to check the command centre. Vekk managed to find an exit to the base and opened the door, only to be immediately faced with oncoming sand and snow. She jumped back as it slid in, digging her way outside.

Kol ran back with a tablet and a crate he had

taken from the hologram projector and they quickly dressed for the unpredictable weather. They exited the base and walked towards one of the pylons that was conveniently stood nearby, unknowing of any defences deployed to protect the weapon.

They ran into one of the pylons, having moved fast to avoid predators and the power of the snowstorm that had begun. As they approached, they took notice of five robots that rose from the ground on pedestals, turrets mounted on their heads; the siblings held onto their weapons and hid in the dense bushes nearby, hoping to isolate one of them.

One of the robots charged into the forest, unaware that Kol had emerged from hiding and was following behind. He drove his spear through its back, which caused a delayed reaction long enough for Vekk to shoot it. It fell to the ground and electricity bounced off its broken parts. Four other robots remained and suddenly positioned themselves, waiting for attackers as if their lost soldier had given them some sort of notification.

Kol moved to the left of the pylon with Arkriat, failing to remain hidden as one of the guards moved to face them but remained passive. He revealed himself slightly so he was visible to his sister and silently commanded Arkriat to attack; he followed directly behind the robot and was quickly pursued by Vekk.

Vekk shot one robot; Kol impaled another. Vekk looked upon the broken body as she was tackled to the ground and held face down, forced to permit the cold to grasp her face and travel down her spine while Kol directed his attention to the other robot. He was quickly slammed into the ground and unable to break the robot's grasp on his neck.

They listened to the footsteps hurriedly approaching, soon breaking into a sprint, as Arkriat threw his weight onto Kol's captor. It stumbled away, breaking its grip on the weak flesh of Kol's neck and stabilised its metallic frame. Vekk wrapped the back of her legs around the robot and pulled it down on top of her.

Kretai soon came to her assistance, scratching its sensors and rendering it blind. They soon broke its chassis and caused it to collapse to the ground as Arkriat tore the head off the final robot.

Vekk ran over to the terminal beside the pylon and struggled to activate its self-destruct sequence, the blinding sun's glare dominating the screen. She managed to shield the screen with her hand and saw a singular button. Pressing it, the four of them escaped the snow and sand being thrown in the air from the explosion of the pylon.

They retreated beneath a tree and analysed the functions of the tablet that they had procured earlier, managing to find a map that displayed the precise location of each pylon.

"Finally," Kol said, pointing to the location closest to them. "We know exactly where we're going."

They ran towards the next pylon, watching the robots rise from the ground on small pedestals. They fought from the shadows, managing to disable four of the five robots before charging into the clearing and impaling the last metallic guard. Vekk quickly disabled the nearby terminal and called Kol, Arkriat and Kretai to follow her, leading them to the next pylon.

The layout of the third pylon was identical. They successfully destroyed one of the patrolling guards and Kol moved, ready to command Arkriat. When he charged, the robot instead self-destructed, causing no damage to the other guards.

Kol was thrown back and Vekk began to shoot with little thought to prevent them self-destructing on her. They ran to her and she was forced to move, running to the pylon terminal and hurriedly attempting to disable it. She struggled as the robots approached her and elected to run as one of her attackers began its own self-destruct sequence.

It caught both Vekk and the pylon in the blast; Kol ran over to her and they walked towards the final pylon, resting in the cover of the forest before striking again.

Kol ordered Arkriat and Kretai to remain

passive as he healed Vekk with the ancient spear. She soon recovered and the four of them approached their objective, eyeing the pylon terminal.

Efficiently removing the guards, Vekk ran to the terminal and was taken aback at the layout of the screen; it was unlike the others and the text was completely incomprehensible.

"I can't figure this out—I can't disable it," she said, staring at the terminal screen.

"Let me try," Kol responded, taking her place at the screen. The screen was difficult to navigate, with an entirely grey layout under the blazing sun. The text was in white and impossible to read in the bright biome.

He tried to familiarise himself with the layout but failed. He stared at the screen for a few moments; the pylon suddenly shut itself down without his intervention.

"Odd," Kol said, checking the map of the pylons once again. An icon depicting the superweapon control centre had appeared—it was hidden underground, beside the third pylon. The siblings and Arkriat ran towards their next objective, hoping that they had enough time to shut down the superweapon.

The storm had worsened considerably under the clear sky, which darkened significantly with each hour that passed. Vekk and Kol were forced to stop and sit down on the sand, ruminating on their goal.

"We'll…we'll die if we don't destroy the Engine," Kol said as he held onto Arkriat for warmth.

"We'll die in this cold regardless," Vekk responded, feeling cynical about their options. They forced themselves to continue on, with Kol sheltering Kretai in his hands, as they were unwilling to risk their lives waiting for the superweapon to fire.

Running into the nearest clearing, they found a giant grey dome built into the ground that aligned with the co-ordinates on the map. Looking around the immediate area for access, they found nothing and were forced to search further out, Kol leaving with Arkriat to search the bushes.

Vekk remained by the dome and attempted to break it open with her bare hands while Kretai analysed the metallic surface of the object for weaknesses. She stared at it, feeling anger in her mind and tension in her hands.

How long will this take us?

Kretai attempted to pull a metal panel from the hot surface but was unsuccessful. Vekk kicked the dome and tried to dig beneath it, finding nothing. She sank into a sitting position and stared at Kol in the distance, enthusiastically digging through the snow and sand with Arkriat.

We're going to die.

"This reminds me of our experience in the

jungle!" Kol shouted to his sister as he returned to her. "I've found a hatch."

"Show me," Vekk said as he approached, before following him to a hidden trapdoor in the ground. She pulled it open, revealing a freely hanging metal ladder for them to climb; they descended into a dark room, clinging desperately to each rung.

The ladder swung back and forth as they climbed, with Vekk yelling at Arkriat to wait for their return. They dropped onto the ground and looked across a giant pit filled with an unknown sizzling liquid; large platforms moved back and forth, clearly having been built out of scrapped parts.

Kretai flew across; beneath her, the siblings leapt over the large spaces between the platforms while eyeing the depths warily. Vekk managed to reach the other side of the pit while Kol struggled amidst the chaotic movements of the ground around him.

Do something! he thought to himself as he stared at Vekk and Kretai, who were both watching him. His sister fiddled with the controls into the next room, instead activating a defence mechanism that involved lowering the roof.

Kol threw his spear onto the ground beside Vekk and leapt after it, managing to cling onto the edge of the ground that loomed over the pit and pull himself up.

"I really appreciated your help back there," he said as he walked past his sister to decipher the control panel.

"What else could I have done? You should've followed me when we first stepped on!" Vekk retorted as she pushed passed him and managed to unlock the door.

The siblings entered to find the super-weapon control room, surrounded by computers and terminals, which were being automated by robots who paid no attention to the visitors.

Vekk slowly approached the giant machine in the centre of the room, setting it to shut down when a hologram appeared and blocked her attempt.

"You were sent by the military, weren't you?" the figure, some variant of Quarailian, said to them. "You've been deceived."

"How do we know if that's true?" Kol asked the figure, his eyebrows arched defensively.

"How do you know if the one who sent you was telling the truth?" the figure asked them, laughing. "The weapon was originally built here but it was quickly moved once they were in control of a new outpost. It was then used against, and almost destroyed, us."

The figure continued, "If you shut this place down, you will have no protection against the Engine. If you want to stop it, I suggest you go back to the instigator."

"Stay here," Vekk said to Kol, who handed her the map. "In case he's lying."

"Be quick!" Kol shouted as she left the room, exiting by a ramp that had been revealed by the hologram.

Vekk ran back to the abandoned military base, moving towards the direction stated on the map and arrived to see turrets inside. She hid behind the door and held onto her gun, trying to avoid detection.

She quickly turned into the doorway and began to fire, destroying two turrets as four more fired at her. Escaping into a storage room, she managed to jam the door shut and began to search for supplies, finding only rotten rations stored under dirty duvets. She sat upon a bed stripped of comfort and took a moment of respite, ruminating about the outcome of the situation.

How would Kol know if I died? Where would he go?

She stood up, breathing heavily, and pushed the door open as far as it would go, then proceeding to shove a broken box into the space to ensure it would not automatically close. She slid her hands into the open spaces on either side of the box and began to push on the edge of the door, requiring the strength of her whole body.

She successfully opened the door, standing ahead of the flickering lights as the box fell to the ground. Stepping over it, she destroyed one of the turrets ahead of her with one shot and quickly ducked behind a wall.

She began to fire without direction and mostly missed her shots. The emotionless turrets pummelled gunfire into the wall and left Vekk with a slim possibility of escape. She tried to move her gun around the corner but almost lost her hand, forcing her to remain in cover.

She sighed and began to walk forward, facing away from the wall she had cowered behind. The turrets did not calculate her move and took several seconds to readjust. Vekk suddenly turned and ran towards them, shooting frantically. Two of the turrets incidentally fired on each other as she destroyed another, leaving one turret remaining.

Vekk backed away as it fired at her repetitively and she managed to dash from one corner to another, soon reaching the command centre. Walking in, the Cristrial officer reappeared and began to laugh.

"You're back," he said. "I wonder why."

A few of the walls of the command centre began to disintegrate and revealed a giant room, resembling the one Kol was waiting at. The Engine was clearly there; a superweapon ready to activate when given the command; it was a giant hexagonal device with glowing edges and sparks flying out of the glass ceiling atop of it.

"Welcome to the Engine," the officer said to her, holding out his hand towards the great weapon.

"Do you really think you can destroy it in one hour?" he asked as she began to search for a terminal to access it.

"You told me we had a day to shut you down!" she protested, finding a terminal and trying to shut it down.

"I lied," the officer told her, smirking.

Vekk looked up to see that there was a skylight in the ceiling, covered with a blanket of snow.

It won't be for much longer if this weapon activates.

"Are you ready to lose all to save your family?" the officer asked, noticing Vekk was unable to find a way to deactivate it.

"I won't lose anyone else, including myself," she told him and stepped away from the terminal, grabbing her gun and firing it at the screen.

The release of the gun caused the weapon to rupture. Vekk hastily escaped the room as her old weapon began to fire rogue shots, which turned nearby objects to stone as it hit, despite not having done so before.

The officer attempted to stop her but had little power as a holoprojection and was ultimately destroyed by the rogue shots and rubble. Some of the plating flew at Vekk, forcing her to shield herself with the map and ultimately destroying the large tablet.

Vekk ran past the turret she had previously spared and grabbed its gun, dislodging it and rendering the machine useless. She escaped to the back of the base, watching debris spread across the ground above and through the corridors, which ensured that the base could never be used again.

After bracing herself, the explosions ceased and the area was no longer erupting with chaos. She cautiously began to make her way back to the ruined command centre and saw random parts of the corridors covered in stone. She ran through the base, managing to stumble across an armoury; she scavenged some explosive munitions and improved weapons. She took a handgun, modified beyond recognition of its original weapon.

She once again approached the corridor leading to the command centre and set several explosives in place before stepping away, taking cover behind a terminal in a nearby room. She fired at one of the explosives with her new weapon, setting off a chain reaction and granting her access to the remains of the room.

She walked over to inspect the wreckage of the superweapon and saw a glowing object in its centre. She began to hear voices as she approached.

"Haha…"

"The key!"

"Everyone used you…"

"You'll never know!"

Vekk walked briskly into the remnants of the Engine and pulled out a glowing dagger purposefully stabbed into a pure black box. She clipped it to her belt and opened the box to find wires, cables and a glow emanating from the bottom.

She reached through and unscrewed the mystery object. She held another key in her hand; a square-shaped key created from cobalt and glowed a dark blue upon contact. She held it in her hand and walked out of the base, trying to ignore the persistent voices around her.

She ran back to the superweapon construction facility and reunited with Kol, who was sat on the large holograph emitter in the centre of the room.

"You're back!" he said, standing up and walking over to her. She could see that Arkriat had joined him and had been waiting patiently for her.

"I have gifts," she said, taking out her dagger and the key, handing the latter to her brother. He verified that it was one they needed and they departed the facility, hoping to escape the cold and deceit.

They travelled past the thin trees and began to see remnants of walls; they were clearly visible under the sun as the black stones stood out from the white sands in which they were buried. The entire area appeared to be fragile despite remaining for hundreds, possibly thousands of years and was destitute; there appeared to be no signs of life.

They walked through the remains of a long-destroyed village or town; outlines of buildings were made clear by the raised snow and black stone walls marked the area as once being a centre of life. Arkriat felt the broken paving beneath his feet and looked up at the damaged walls that had not provided warmth for centuries.

The ruins led up to a large building at the back of the remnants, appearing untouched. It had no signs of abandonment; the windows were clear and movement could be seen inside. Nothing had been covered up on the exterior although a quick glance could not see any technology inside.

The siblings passed through the desolate streets, noting the stale smell in the air as they approached the building. As they walked up to the grand metal doors, they opened automatically to reveal many figures walking around what was now clearly a library or archive.

The books were placed in sleek modern shelving, despite appearing to be incredibly old, most volumes lacking a technological edge from what the siblings could immediately tell. The library appeared to consist of many levels, which did not seem to fit inside the building that they had seen outside.

The occupants floated around and paid little attention to their visitors, constantly reorganising books and researching ancient knowledge. As Vekk and Kol walked through the library, some of the figures were seen waving their hand to summon computers from the ground, which were accompanied by both a desk and a chair.

To the far right was a staircase, presumably leading to the other levels. To the left was a floating desk with one of the figures behind it, taller than the others. The siblings walked towards the desk and heard a voice echoing, speaking to them.

"We are Archivists," it echoed. "How may we help you?"

The figure from the desk approached them, revealing its six glowing arms, which were half-covered by the white cloak that engulfed the rest of its body, distinguishing it from the other Archivists who wore grey cloaks. The face resembled an abstract painting but was oddly comforting, consisting of various hues of various colours and having a paint-like facial texturing.

"I am One," the Archivist said. "What are you?"

The siblings introduced themselves, hoping to gain the Archivist's trust and learn about the library.

"The archive is open," One told them. "Any information you need can be found by asking the other Archivists. I am simply here to observe."

The siblings cautiously walked away and approached another Archivist, who introduced themselves without prompt.

"I am Five," the Archivist said to them in a similar echoic voice. "How may I help you?"

"What...what happens here?" Vekk asked, glancing at the ruins outside.

Five responded, "Our Archive was constructed approximately fifty-thousand and twenty-five years ago. It has since existed as a place of knowledge and has been maintained by us since its construction."

"Who else has visited this place?" Kol interjected, hoping to link it with any historical knowledge he already had.

"We have had many different species visit, many peoples. This once included this town's inhabitants and past rulers of Karadestar," Five told them.

"Karadestar?" Vekk asked.

"This is the name of the planet we are on. Based on your confusion, I assume there is a need to update our records—we've been almost isolated for approximately nine hundred years," Five responded.

"You've been alone for all that time?!" Vekk

asked, surprised the Archivists could survive for that length of time without imported supplies or interaction. "The planet is called Quelliare now."

"We have not been entirely without contact; three other groups have visited us in that time. Regardless, we do not require basic organic necessities; our purpose is to compile information on Kar...I mean Quelliare, and its neighbouring planets and moons."

"Do you know anything about Zrelyar, the city?" Vekk asked, taking her family's map from Kol's possession and pointing to their home city. The Archivist stared at it for a moment and recalled its basic information.

"The city has a different name from our records, but we know that it was founded by the survivors of a crash approximately fifteen million years ago. They were the ancestors of various species, including your own."

"There is a green beam powered by a building within the city, trapping pollution. Do you know anything like that?" Kol asked, the Archivist taking a few moments to understand the question.

"Yes," Five finally said. "The Beam of...Zrelyar was built by the founders of the city as an attempt to raise the planet's temperature. The conditions were initially too cold to survive but the founders used the wreckage of their space ship and harnessed its power to create a barrier to keep themselves warm. It should have been dismantled by now as it is no longer needed."

"That's why we're here," Kol said, walking away. "Thank you."

The siblings requested the use of two computers by an Archivist named Six, who complied and allowed the siblings to research anything that they desired to know and was available.

They spent several hours researching, causing Arkriat and Kretai to become impatient. However, the Archivists were intrigued by their species and began to play with them as a distraction.

Once the siblings were satisfied with their knowledge, they recalled Arkriat and Kretai and one of the Archivists approached them.

"I am Eight," the Archivist told them. "We are fascinated by your creatures."

"Thank…you?" Kol said as Vekk walked on, unsure how to react. He quickly rejoined his sister and they approached One for more information.

"Are you able to help us with the Beam of Zrelyar? It may have gone by a different name," Vekk asked, hoping that they would be able to simplify their journey.

"Five has just updated me," One said. "The Beam of Zrelyar requires five keys for non-military personnel, each a piece created by the five survivors who began creation on this world."

"We have three," Kol said, laying them out on the desk. "Is there an easier way to find the other two?"

"I may be able to help," One said. "Follow me to the depths."

CHAPTER 12

The library had concealed its sub-levels well, hiding them within the wall behind One's desk. Kol masked his concern as they walked down the brown stone steps, wondering about the artefacts contained inside.

The wide halls of the sub-levels appeared to be ancient and did not radiate with light or show any signs of being technological, something Vekk and Kol were surprised to see.

"Most of the rooms in our archive's sub-level contain valuables stored by our town's residents to avoid damage from the Engine, a powerful superweapon used approximately five hundred and eighty-five years ago on the planet," One told them.

"It's been that long since the weapon was activated and the area still hasn't recovered?" Vekk asked, remembering the thin trees and decaying signs of life.

"We do not have extensive information on the Engine, I apologise," One said to them, before noticing Vekk's dagger. "I do recognise the dagger you have claimed as originating from the Engine. It is an ancient tool and we have many guides on how to utilise its power. However, we are not able to release information based on rumours or from unconfirmed sources."

"Please," said Vekk. "I need full access to my weapon, for the sake of our planet."

One stayed silent for a minute before replying. "The weapon comes from one of the survivors, according to rumours. It adapts itself to the user's hand and can kill a target in one hit."

"How?"

"It should activate when you are calm; your grip will adjust and activate it."

They walked in silence for several more minutes until Vekk asked. "Who are the other groups that visited in the last nine hundred years?"

"The first group was an independent team, the second set of visitors were warriors who tried to burn down our Archive and the third was a pair who sought knowledge on a hidden cabal."

"A cabal?"

"The pair were suspicious of those around them and left everything behind to keep their families safe."

"Our parents left us abruptly—did the pair visit in the last eighteen years, approximately?" Vekk asked.

"I do not remember. I apologise."

Kol nudged Vekk before she spoke again and thanked One for answering their questions, alarmed by the Archivist's sudden inability to remember specific details.

"Maybe we shouldn't barrage them with questions," he whispered to Vekk, who quickly remembered that the Archivists were strangers to them.

One told them that they existed to provide information, although the Archives desperately needed to be updated. As they passed rooms in the sub-levels, One occasionally opened doors, showing the valuables left behind by residents of the ruined town, destined never to be reclaimed.

Vekk and Kol updated the Archivist on the current state of Quelliare as they walked, allowing the knowledge to be passed on to other Archivists telepathically.

One led them to a room covered in ancient symbols and drawings. The history of conflict throughout Quelliare was revealed and was usually split between two or three factions. Lasapra's rule was relatively peaceful compared to many of her ancestors, one being a powerful commander who led many armies to victory. The siblings were also shown a proper guide on how to use their ancient weapons to their full potential.

Kol informed One about the existence of Leritri, a silent rebel whose home contained great historical knowledge. One was apprehensive about visiting her; the Archivists had never left the Archive.

They were finally led to a room containing many scrolls, maps and messages left behind several decades ago.

One, and several other Archivists who were inside, searched through the documents to find the precise location of the last two keys. The Archivists were able to process multiple sources of information at once, utilising their many hands to find it. Vekk passed the map of the keys to an Archivist so that they could update their planetary map and find information directly relevant to the keys.

One of the Archivists found an ancient tablet after several minutes and gave it to the siblings; neither of them were able to decipher the language the map was written in and had to be led to another room where One was able to translate it for them using ancient scripture.

They discovered the location of one of the keys, but One was unable to decipher the other as it had multiple co-ordinates listed and names of carriers, none of which they recognised. The possible locations ranged from Zrelyar to a forest on the other side of the planet.

"The keys may have been moved from their original locations," One told them. "None of them have ever been officially documented within your city of Zrelyar."

"So why should we even follow that map?" Kol asked.

"If any of your keys are in a city, which is something you would only know with the map, it may have been moved during construction; I would suggest searching quarries or vaults nearby the original locations. However, it is likely that you would need permission from a high ranking official," One suggested.

"Thank you for all of your help," Vekk said.

"We are here to provide information," the Archivist responded, guiding them back to the staircase in order to reach the surface.

As they walked down the many halls, the torches lighting the room extinguished simultaneously, with no apparent cause. One's thin, almost skeletal body glowed underneath its robes.

"I will leave you here so I can understand the cause," the Archivist told the siblings, leaving them in the darkness.

"We can't just wait here. We don't know how long it'll be," Vekk said, beginning to panic. She heard Arkriat's fearful whining and began to comfort him.

"I'll look for an exit," Kol said, leaving Kretai with Vekk and quickly departing. He ran down a dark hallway and dived into the nearest room in which the torches continued to glow. The door slid shut behind him, sealing him inside.

He blinked for a fraction of a second and he

suddenly found himself surrounded by ghosts, shackled and clearly seeking freedom.

"I doubt you're supposed to be in here!" one of them sneered at Kol.

"No, I don't think so," he replied, rapidly moving towards the door. He tried to open it but it was automatic and refused to shift.

"Free us!" they began to chant without order or rhythm, with some demands overlapping others as they heard the fear in Kol's rapid breath.

"Break our chains or we will break you," one threatened, followed by several more ghosts repeating him.

Kol was throwing himself at the door, smashing it with his hands but it would not open. He knew weapons would have no effect on the ghosts and directed his energy into a futile escape.

One of the ghosts held a pair of chains, preparing to bind Kol to the group of tortured spirits. They surrounded him as he screamed for anyone within earshot.

"Vekk! Vekk!" Kol shouted as loudly as possible, fearing for his life and finding no other methods of escape. "Help me!"

The ghost grabbed onto his shoulder and placed a chain atop Kol's arm, who was still calling out in despair. The door suddenly opened and One, flanked by several Archivists, entered and lifted their arms, chaining the ghosts to the wall and allowing Kol to escape. They called out in agony but they were left to suffer as the door closed upon them.

Kol was breathing heavily and on his knees, reflecting on the fear he had felt upon expecting to face death.

"Thank you," he managed to say, scarred by the fear and helplessness he had felt. Vekk ran over and comforted him, feeling guilty about leaving her brother to explore alone. She had alerted One that he had left; knowing the dangers inside the Archive, the Archivist had gone to investigate.

"That is a room containing the ghosts of those who have died here. They have descended into insanity and are incredibly dangerous," One told them, the torches relighting around them.

"I'm...sorry," Kol said, struggling to focus.

"I will take you to the surface immediately," it replied, hoping to spare them both further concern. They were swiftly led to the surface and One apologised for the shock and suffering.

"How do I get into these situations every time?!" Kol asked himself aloud, hoping to leave and move on to their next location to search.

"I'm really sorry, Kol. We'll leave now," Vekk said, mentally emulating the fear she believed him to have faced as an attempt to empathise with him. They quickly left the Archive and stood in the thick snow outside, analysing the map.

"I feel awful about what I've let you go through," Vekk said, looking at her brother who was still shaken from the many incidents he had experienced.

"I can't deal with any more of this mental torture, Vekk," he told her. "The Dystopian was enough—I'm not trying to build an archive of distressing memories!"

"I know," Vekk said. "I want to actually protect you—I want to protect you from that suffering."

"Let's hope you don't have to any more," Kol muttered, walking ahead slightly.

Vekk began to discuss the new knowledge they had acquired, although neither of them knew enough about the history of Quelliare to sustain a full conversation.

"Over there," Kol said just before they left the ruined town, pointing to a group of vehicles that appeared to be untouched since the Engine's last activation.

They ran over to the small, sleek vehicles, which were still functioning and mounted them, Kretai gripping to Kol's arm and Arkriat sitting on Vekk's lap.

They sped into the distance, hoping to leave the Archive behind for as long as possible. They did not speak as the wind became deafening and gave them an opportunity for some separation. Furthermore, piloting the vehicles required their full attention due to high speeds and the many obstructions ahead such as trees and foliage.

Evening quickly arrived, the two moons being the only visible sights as the area became difficult to navigate and small details became invisible; their lack of skill in piloting became apparent.

Despite this, they were able to stop at a large object and looked up to see a small mountain, with many vehicles flying around its peak and landing or taking off.

They dismounted and looked up, seeing no roads or tracks leading up which would aid them in their climb. They began to grab at the rock with their bare hands, discarding the gloves from their winter attire.

They scaled the rock face and Kol looked up to see a cave entrance, verbally alerting his sister. They climbed inside, Kretai flying above them, to find a cave filled with stunning crystals and the powerful sounds of machinery in the distance.

They cautiously walked through the cave, unsure if it concealed any hidden predators. The crystals provided sufficient light but the dust had dimmed their glow and created great shadows.

They tried to pass through quickly, trying

to avoid the giant drills that occasionally broke through the walls of the cave and almost deafened the siblings, forcing them to walk faster.

Vekk, Kol and Arkriat suddenly slowed their walking speed as their vision blurred slightly and the hum of the crystals rapidly grew louder. Drills smashed into the ground behind them as they struggled to maintain their balance.

Kol struggled to stride forward as his hands and feet became numb, soon followed by his arms and legs. He looked to the left to see Vekk and Arkriat suffering the same fate, although his sister was able to kneel on the ground for several seconds until she similarly lost control of her limbs.

"Kol...I...it—"

She looked at her brother, who had been stunned and now lay unconscious. She looked up to see Kretai's absence in the air; she scanned the area with her eyes for their pet, before fainting several seconds later.

Vekk awoke in a constricted prison cell, unable to stand due to the effects of the crystals. She could see Kol conscious in a similar cell and Arkriat and Kretai in small cages powered by electricity.

She stared into the cameras, which adjusted themselves to watch her futile struggle to get off the ground to reach them. She turned her head to hear Kol grunt as he stretched his arm towards the flames that covered the door, before quickly withdrawing from the heat.

Vekk finally managed to bring herself to her feet and looked out of the window behind her. Kol also stood up and tore the head off the camera in his cell, looking for a power source.

Vekk slid her fingers into a small broken panel beside the flames and managed to pull an exposed wire from its original position. She rapidly withdrew her hand as she received an electric shock and watched the flames disappear from both cells.

Kol stepped out and smashed the camera head into Kretai's cell, deactivating it and freeing her; he proceeded to free Arkriat as Vekk grabbed the broken cages and threw them at the large cell windows, shattering them.

"That was surprisingly easy," Kol said as he looked for a safe route of escape.

"Suspiciously easy," Vekk responded as they both grabbed onto jutted rocks, Kol holding Arkriat between his legs until the Garisal could comfortably fall onto a ledge, and began to climb to the summit of the mountain in search for their weaponry.

They held onto a raised area of rock upon reaching the summit in an attempt to conceal themselves from the soldiers, who appeared to be unaware of their escape.

Kol gestured to a small building that occupied a quarter of the plateau, with a decorated soldier standing in the centre of the area. The siblings and Arkriat slid into the area, with Kol swiftly removing the one camera watching their arrival.

"Hello commander," Vekk said aloud as they approached the centre, followed by Kol throwing the camera head to the ground. The commander turned around and smirked at them.

"I didn't expect you to return," he said, emotionlessly staring at the camera head. "I predicted that you would escape those weak prison cells and provide me with the fair challenge of tracking you down."

"There's too many guards for us to retrieve our weapons," Vekk said. "How about you remove some—to make it 'fair'?"

"I don't think that will be happening," he said, amused and looking past both of their heads. Several guards had congregated behind them and one grabbed onto Arkriat, who yelped and drew the attention of the siblings.

"Get off him!" Vekk said with a raised voice and moved to an offensive position. The guard let go of the Garisal and another used the distraction to grab onto Kretai, almost crushing her.

"Let her go!" Kol commanded, sneering at the commander.

"I would like to take this opportunity to make you pay for the damage you've caused to Queen Lasapra's glorious reign," the commander said as one of the guards ran off.

"Don't touch her," Vekk said with fire in her eyes. The guard quickly returned and placed Kretai in a cage, causing her to scratch at the bars.

"Such a crude device, but it does its job," the commander said. "Now you will do yours."

The commander led them into one of the mines below, flanked by guards who were prepared to counter any escape attempts the siblings made. They walked through the machines and labourers towards a platform built on the side of the mountain.

"Where are you taking us?" Vekk asked the commander.

"To your first task," he said sternly. They walked onto the platform and the siblings were introduced to a truck containing captives and supplies.

"You will drive these to a nearby outpost and immediately return," he said. "These guards will join you for your guaranteed cooperation." The guards climbed onto the truck, standing beside the holding cells. The siblings began to walk towards the vehicle as they heard a yelp and turned around to see the commander holding Arkriat back.

"Once you return," he said, smiling maliciously.

"I will kill you for this!" Kol said loudly, struggling to hold himself back; he knew they had little other choice but to climb onto the truck and begin the supply drop.

They drove in silence, feeling the anger and the desire to rebel rapidly rising within them. However, they were held back by fear for the lives of Arkriat and Kretai, along with the daunting appearance of the armed guards surrounding them.

Vekk drove while Kol looked over the controls, trying to relieve his boredom. He kept moving towards certain buttons and switches, only to be given a stern glance from his sister, who tried to focus on arriving at their destination.

Vekk soon relaxed once Kol held back his curiosity, giving him an opportunity to strike suddenly. Upon pressing a button beneath her arm, the back of the vehicle detached and deactivated the holding cells. The prisoners immediately escaped from the collapsing cells and fought the guards off, before running into the forest with a guard escort in pursuit.

"No!" Kol shouted with feigned surprise. The guards stopped the rolling vehicle and re-attached the two parts of the truck together, before seizing control and leaving the siblings under supervision in the back seats.

I expect our return won't be too well received, Vekk thought as the truck fumes infiltrated her nostrils and reminded her of Zrelyar.

"Where are the other supplies?" the outpost captain asked upon their arrival as the siblings unpacked the supplies.

"Escaped thanks to the two unwilling pilots," one of the guards told him and gestured to the siblings.

"You chose rebels to transport rebels?" the captain asked, surprised.

"It wasn't my choice," the guard said with a tone of irritation, who then turned around and ordered the siblings to collect the next supplies.

Once the truck had been loaded up with food rations, Vekk and Kol were ordered to return to the mining base, with no other options. They drove in silence, fearing the commander's response to Kol's actions.

They drove onto the platform to find the commander waiting for them with a beast beside him. It had black fur and black eyes, its back covered in fire that did not burn out.

"I heard about the diversion," the commander told them as they dismounted the truck.

"What is that?" Vekk asked, unable to take her eyes off the mutated creature in front of her.

"This is a Garisal we acquired from the forest," he said. "Remarkable creature, isn't it? Biotechnology can do some wonder things."

"That's horrific," Kol said, also staring at the

mutated Garisal and fighting off the anger in his mind.

They were led back into the mine, where the commander announced their next task.

"Supply delivery is clearly not your strong point, particularly when you are together," he said to them. "So I will give you separate tasks."

Vekk felt frustration building, remembering her pledge to protect her brother. "Why would you assume that we're weaker alone?"

"Because you will have no accomplices and you cannot cause as much harm to our operations," he said as he silently signalled orders to two workers.

"You," he said, pointing to Vekk and pulling back his Garisal, "will come with me while your brother will collect medical supplies."

"You just said you don't want us to do that," Kol reminded him.

"I don't think you're a very careful person," the commander told him, walking closer. "If you make a mistake, no one will be there to hide it for you."

Kol was surprised; he had never realised how Vekk had always covered for him and how he would have to watch his movements carefully. He was lead to the armoury, where he was allowed to reclaim his spear.

Two guards then led Kol to the makeshift medical centre while Vekk remained with the commander, thinking of ways of silent rebellion without endangering her brother or pets. The commander sent his other guards away and faced Vekk.

"I'm taking you to dinner," he told her.

"Absolutely not," she snapped. "This is a hostage situation, not a first date!"

"I'm not taking you on a date!" he snapped back. "I need someone to take to a formal event and I can't just leave you here with little supervision."

"If this is a trap, I'll come for you first," she told him.

"With what, a dinner plate?" he asked her in a mocking tone.

She glared at him as he detailed the task, wishing she could help Kol instead of deal with an enemy commander over a formal meal.

Kol walked into the medical room to see many Quarailian soldiers, with most suffering severe wounding.

"I see your army is ready to take us on," Kol said, walking past the beds to a computer. He checked the inventory to find that most of their supplies were almost depleted or entirely gone. He made a note of what they were missing and turned back around, tempted to tamper with the medical controls but was dissuaded by moral guilt.

He climbed into the supply vehicle outside, followed by several guards as he sat in the driver's seat. He was given directions and had little choice but to follow them as there was nothing to release—nothing was being delivered yet.

The journey was rough, lacking a smooth road for him to drive over and instead forcing him to plough through the foliage and almost into trees. The darkness surrounding the vehicle obscured the trees ahead, causing Kol to make several sudden turns that angered the guards around him.

I need Vekk. I'll die if I'm left alone, he thought as he braced in case another tree appeared ahead of him.

Upon arrival at the outpost, Kol parked and paused after the uncomfortable drive until the guards insisted he got out. He climbed out of the vehicle and began loading up medical supplies. He realised that the guards in the outpost were also severely injured and that there was a shortage.

"Thanks," he muttered as he was handed the last of the supplies and loaded them back onto the vehicle. The drive back was quiet but Kol feared what task had been set for Vekk; despite claiming to be his protector, he knew she needed his help to survive.

The journey back was even rougher and Kol drove over a large object, causing the vehicle to fall at an angle and throw the supplies onto the ground. The guards were irritated at Kol and forced him onto the snow, before stepping out themselves to help reclaim the packages.

"Drive slower to the base," the guard told at him as they pushed the vehicle upright.

"Give me a better route," he responded as he placed one of the packages back into the vehicle. The guard shoved him into a fragile tree, which broke away from the ground and smashed into the supply vehicle.

The vehicle was surprisingly damaged by the thin trees, which had destroyed the controls and ruined the metal plating, covering it in scratches and dents.

One of the guards swore, before calling the mining base for a replacement truck as he knew the journey would be too arduous on foot; he watched as the remaining guards surrounded Kol to ensure that he would not escape.

It had turned to night, the moons giving them the little light that could shine through the air pollution. The vehicle delivery was taking longer than anticipated and the guard escort grew impatient.

The supplies were laid out beside the vehicle, which turned out to be a mistake as shouts were heard, followed by Garisals running through and grabbing the packages; they escaped into the forest before anyone could stop them.

"Oh, great!" one of the guards exclaimed,

running after them with little luck. Everyone, including Kol, were instructed to follow him and they did so, tired of waiting for their vehicle to arrive.

Suddenly an arrow impaled a guard's head, instantly killing him and causing the group to panic; Kol considered escaping but he knew who was at stake if he were to do so. He remained with the group of guards, who chased after the Garisals with the supplies.

They arrived at the edge of the forest, the snow and sand changing to green grass. Nearby was a large hill with a cave inside, likely a den.

"We're getting those supplies," one of the guards said, eyeing the cave entrance.

"No, it's too dangerous. Just tell the commander that they were lost," another responded, preferring punishment over death.

"My brother is waiting for treatment! We're getting them," the other guard told him, determined to help.

I forgot they were people with families and feelings, Kol thought as he eyed the look of concern on the face of the guard beside him.

"Send the prisoner in first," another guard suggested.

"No—" Kol interjected.

"He won't bring the supplies back to us," one of them said over him, assuming Kol to be some sort of trained criminal.

"We go together," the first guard told them,

preparing to utilise their extensive training. One of them grabbed Kol's arm and they collectively walked towards the den.

As soon as they walked inside, a Garisal jumped from the shadows and mauled the soldier holding Kol. The other soldiers jumped and began to attack the Garisal, killing it after the soldier had bled out.

"Let's keep going. Weapons out," one of the soldiers said, ignoring that their captive was no longer restrained, but Kol followed regardless as he still worried about Arkriat and Kretai's safety.

Four soldiers remained, all of their weapons drawn and Kol holding his spear; the guards were too preoccupied to watch him.

The cave got progressively darker and the soldiers switched on the various lights on their armour and weapons. The stalactites on the ceiling hung lower than expected and were a constant source of surprise for the soldiers walking through, who tended to walk directly into them.

Garisals continued to leap out, managing to kill three of the soldiers and leaving very few people to reclaim the medical supplies. With the loss of soldiers, light decreased and there was little left to show the way.

Approaching the main cavern, one guard and Kol remained and both were on edge, weapons drawn. Kol was constantly doubting himself as he was still helping his own captors but he remembered the soldiers suffering in the mining base and continued on.

They entered to see several Garisals sleeping on the rocks and an Alpha Garisal in the middle, eyeing their new guests. It stood up and began to walk towards them. They readied themselves and Kol began to run at it, slashing it with his spear. The soldier began shooting at the smaller Garisals, mostly trying to protect himself.

Kol was able to take down the Alpha Garisal surprisingly swiftly and dashed to the medical supplies, finding some torn open and others mostly untouched. He gathered them while the soldier fought the rest of the beasts off, the majority of the creatures retreating into the corners of the cave. He then joined Kol and took the rest of the supplies, carrying them outside.

They ran to the damaged supply vehicle to find a new vehicle waiting for them with drivers inside. They loaded the supplies and the soldier turned to Kol, taking his helmet off.

"Thanks for your help," he said, "but I'm not letting the commander know of your contribution." He proceeded to hit Kol across the face with his reinforced gloves, throwing him to the floor.

"I'm sure he'll be happy to have one less person to track down after your sister walks into his trap," the soldier told Kol. Kol stared back, knowing he had no way of alerting his sister.

"Vekk," he whispered, before the soldier approached him once again, delivering blow after blow.

CHAPTER 13

Vekk dressed into the long black skirt and jacket laid out on the commander's bed, appearing to be new and expensive. White crystals lined the black sleeves and trouser legs, suggested it was a high-quality piece of clothing. A chain of multi-coloured crystals lay atop the pillow while a pair of black, toeless shoes were placed under the bed. At the top of the bed sat a small metal headpiece that would cover the back of her head.

She checked for cameras and then changed, taking her dagger from an unlocked chest and securing it to her waist by ramming it between her hip and the inside of the suit.
I haven't dressed well for a long time, she thought as she placed the circlet on her head and opened the door to allow the commander to change into his formalwear.

After several minutes, he walked out wearing grey trousers with a sleeveless long jacket, also grey but with a golden lining that extended down to his black boots. His medium-length hair appeared to have been styled, showing Vekk that he was dedicated to this event.

"Let's go," he said. "Avoid the dust from the minerals; that outfit was expensive."

"I don't want to do this," she told him, keeping a slight distance between them. "You've spent way too much on me."

"I aim to impress," he told her as he grabbed the crystals from her hand and attached them to her circlet, allowing them to hang down.

"I thought they were a bribe or something," Vekk remarked while making no attempt to force him away.

"I thought you would be able to dress yourself," he muttered in response as he led her to the military vehicle waiting for them.

"I guess all of the money went on the clothes, then," she said upon sight of the vehicle. He ignored her and led her inside. The driver wearing similarly formal clothing and clearly had instructions prior as once they were settled in, she immediately drove off.

The drive was silent and Vekk tried to ignore the commander. However, she noticed a growing feeling of comfort around him. She had to remind herself that it was a hostage situation with the expensive clothing, paid drivers and formal events that she was receiving for free.

"How…much did all of this cost?" she asked him, hoping to fill the void-like silence.

"A lot," he said. "More than I would've liked."

They spoke little for the rest of the journey, which lasted approximately an hour. Once they arrived, the commander offered her his hand, which she hesitantly accepted after seeing the other couples in the building. It was far from the mining base, even from the forest.

The building was grand and was clearly built for events hosted by the richest of Quelliare. Everyone appeared to come from great wealth and was in incredible shape, making Vekk feel uncomfortable, as she had never been one to work out. However, both she and Kol had lost weight from the lack of food and sleep of their journey, making it difficult to ignore the constant feeling of hunger.

They entered into a grand ballroom, with many couples talking and having drinks. The commander offered Vekk a drink but she refused, eyeing the drink suspiciously. They soon approached and spoke to another couple, who were seemingly unaware about the false couple's real identities.

"I...work in accounting," the commander told them as he smiled weakly. Vekk nodded in agreement, hoping to avoid conversation, as she had never been among a group of high-class citizens.

They walked around, both feeling oddly relaxed with each other yet still limiting themselves to their thoughts and the occasional couple who would speak to them.

The room was loud and the music playing faintly in the background was mostly unheard by anyone except for Vekk, who was trying to ignore the conversations around her as she had no interest for them. The suit she was wearing was quite tight, clearly not intended for her, which made her wonder who it had initially been bought for. She began to feel sympathy for the commander, suspecting he may have recently broken up with someone.

He's threatening the lives of your family, she reminded herself, wondering how her brother was faring.

The room itself was quite hot, likely due to the number of guests inside. It differed from the base that they had come from, characterised by the relentless snow and sandstorms.

They walked into a side room, where a buffet had been laid out beside a blank wall that clearly set up for a photoshoot.

"Take a hologram to remember this day!" a woman announced to the room, which was divided as some took up her offer while others ignored her completely.

As she said this, the commander looked to Vekk, who rolled her eyes and walked forwards towards the woman, who was clearly enthusiastic about another customer.

If only she knew the circumstances, Vekk thought as she smiled, the pain hidden behind her joyful facade. The commander paid for two holograms and Vekk quickly walked away, feeling frustration and guilt boil inside her as she considered the comfort of the event compared to the danger of the wilderness.

The commander left her for a moment and spoke to the couples nearby, not wanting to cause a public outburst or to ruin the event by conversing with Vekk. She stood by the buffet, eating more than she had in months and trying to forget severity of the situation she was in.

This is a hostage situation, she thought as she took another handful of a biscuit-like food, distinguished by its black and blue colouring. After several minutes, she walked back over to the commander, giving him a sarcastic smile as they linked arms and walked back into the ballroom.

Vekk had forgotten that she stood out; her unique skin colour stood out among the other Quarailians, yet no one had commented on it.

Probably politeness, she thought, unsure what to expect from the people at the event. Regardless, she enjoyed the lack of attention as the commander stared at those who stared at her.

"I see that you really enjoyed that buffet," he said quietly to her, much to her surprise.

"I see that you like getting young people to do work you're too old to do," she whispered harshly.

"I'm not old," he sneered, instinctively moving his hand to briefly conceal his forehead.

"You are unlike the other people here," one elderly woman told Vekk as she walked through the building.

"Because I'm not snobby?" she responded, causing the commander to glare at her and usher her away, apologising.

"Be polite! These aren't soldiers!" he told her in a hushed tone, gripping her thin arms.

"What benefit do I get from being polite to these people? They aren't soldiers. They don't control my brother's fate," she whispered back, becoming annoyed.

"But I do," he told her, "so it's in your best interests to at least pretend that you fit in."

Vekk tried to be polite, holding back comebacks to a few people's slightly insulting comments; she did not want to lose her brother and pets over an insult with an elderly couple who were unaware about her situation.

A bell rung somewhere within the building and everyone began to congregate in a separate room, to which the commander and Vekk followed.

They entered a large dining room with all of the tables reserved for a variety of people. The commander led Vekk to their table and they sat across from each other in an attempt to keep their distance. They looked at the holographic menus, neither of them being accustomed to the unique dishes available.

"Would you like to order sarcasm with some apathy? It's discounted," he asked her quietly, taking the unique opportunity to mock her.

Vekk stifled a laugh as she was surprised by his wit, making the commander smile, as he knew he was breaking down her barriers. She glared at him while repressing her smile.

They looked to the waiter while ordering, before awkwardly turning to face each other.

"I hope I have provided a change from the other times you've been captured," he said to her aloud.

"You've been the first," she countered, trying to resist the urge to open up to him, as she knew it would allow him to control her better.

They sat in silence for several minutes, admiring the room and the upper-class people inside in an attempt to avoid focusing on each other.

"What do they call you?" the commander asked her, looking at her hands fidgeting on the table.

"You know my name," she said calmly, turning her head to face him. "You must've seen some alerts or something."

"I just wanted to follow the conversational procedure."

"Fine then," she said. "I'm Vekkilar. And you are?"

"Reqilar," he told her, writing it down on his holographic tablet and showing her for full clarity.

"It's easier than calling you 'the commander'—or nothing at all," she said to him, secretly noting how she had never heard of the name, yet liked it.

He told her of his journey into his service in the military, how his parents had encouraged him to enlist but his extended family had disagreed. He had followed his aspirations and reached his current post, far from Zrelyar—far from opportunity.

Vekk also detailed the adventure with her brother, avoiding the military forces and meeting new people to achieve their goals; these descriptions were vague as she did not want to give everything away to him—he was still her captor.

She looked around the room as he spoke to her. The people inside were predominantly Quarailians but many other species were present. Vekk saw several Kerrilas, which immediately reminded her of Zavroon's agent, Yarsnael.

"Do you usually go to formal events?" Vekk asked, seeing Reqilar's body tense at the question.

"No...not usually," he said, clearly having other thoughts on his mind.

"So why this one?" she asked.

"Captives don't ask questions," he said quietly yet sternly, trying to steer the conversation away from that specific topic.

There was a long silence until their meals arrived, Reqilar soon relaxing once he began to eat.

"What do you hope to achieve?" he asked her in a low voice as he stabbed his knife into a cooked animal corpse.

"What?" she replied, confused and surprised by his question.

"What do you think your rebellion will do to our society in Zrelyar?" he asked her.

"It will free the people," she told him. "The Queen is killing their freedom—and their respiratory systems."

"Elaborate," he said bluntly.

"Have you breathed the air of Zrelyar? Compare that to the forest air," she said, having another mouthful of food. "Something in the city is preventing that pollution from escaping. That's what we're trying to sort out."

"Do you know what you're doing, though?" he said. "Have you considered that the populace in Zrelyar don't see it that way? Your plan is weak—it is based on assumptions."

"It's not an assumption, the Beam of Zrelyar is holding it in," she told him.

"How do you know its name?!" he asked, unable to hide his surprised expression.

"You can't hide all of your secrets," she said,

biting into the mysterious creature lying dead and roasted on her levitating plate.

They ate quietly for several more minutes, Reqilar adjusting his initial assumptions of his captive as he learnt more about her.

"Don't you want more in life? Directing miners doesn't seem particularly aspirational," Vekk asked.

"It is a temporary posting, Vekkilar," he told her.

"Temporary? How long is it?" she asked, under the impression that he had become accustomed to the atmosphere of the mining base.

"One year," he said quietly. "It's been five months."

"Ah," Vekk responded, testing the various foods laid out on the table, placed with the intention of being shared.

"This is a consequence of chaos: I'm starving," she told him, noting the stare he had given her.

"So you see that order is preferable to chaos," he told her in a strict tone.

"But if that order is oppressive, a little chaos may bring a greater rule in the future," she countered.

"But what if it doesn't?" he responded with a smirk.

"What if it does?" she responded as she finished off a dessert.

"If we had no order, we'd still be using technology from the time of the first settlers of Zrelyar."

Vekk looked away from his face as she took time to respond. "If we hadn't had any chaos, every creation would have been made with intent of being efficient."

"Inventions tend to maximise efficiency," he said with a smirk, leaning back in his chair slightly. "Name one invention that did not."

"Paint colours," Vekk swiftly answered as she looked at the food on the table beside them, thinking about her starving brother in the forest. "The colour only adds an aesthetic edge."

"Have you heard of a piece of art called 'Survive'?"

Vekk's face visibly expressed disappointment as she looked up at the ceiling. *The most famous piece in Zrelyar. Painted without any tools to reflect the primitive technology of the survivors.*

"Queen Lasapra asked for that one to hang in her gallery. Do you think our Queen, who has access to any art in Zrelyar, would choose a cheap piece of art?"

"I don't care about Lasapra," Vekk told him, ignoring his stern glare. "She's an oppressive tyrant."

"So you think you can do better?"

"With some help, yes."

"You think you can run every aspect of

Quelliare? That includes foreign relations, the management of Zrelyar and the protection of the people who live in it."

"If Lasapra can do it, I can as well."

Reqilar laughed at her. "Your ego is as grand as her palace!"

"Unlike her, I will use chaos to cement a semi-orderly society."

"If you can create order from the chaos of usurping a Queen, I will personally congratulate you."

"Your confidence is as extensive as this meal ever was," Vekk told him as her eyes scanned the empty plates on the table.

"Your insults are weak imitations of my retorts. Order has allowed me to master verbal ripostes."

"'Order' led you to work in a mine for five months," Vekk told Reqilar.

"So? Do you think someone like me should be in a better position in society?" he replied, clearly amused. "Someone like you shouldn't be running around, working against the rightful ruler of Quelliare."

"No one else will do it," she said

"I'm surprised you didn't just loot a guard to get to the Beam of Zrelyar."

"Only Zavroon would have them," she said, "but we're not strong enough to take him down."

"I've noticed," he said, finishing his drink.

"We've both been wronged by him," she said with a sigh. "Both chased away from Zrelyar."

Reqilar said nothing and glanced at the empty plates surrounding them both. He then looked up at Vekk as her bright blue eyes darted around the room curiously and quickly. She tapped the table with her slim fingers, which created a rhythmic metallic thud that persisted until she stretched her long arms and rested them on the cold table.

Vekk soon turned and matched Reqilar's gaze, causing him to look away. She looked at his bony face and visibly muscular arms, the latter laying comfortably on the table. His eyebrows showed tension as they gradually narrowed, yet the rest of his face remained relaxed.

"I've...had...doubts about the military since I was first assigned to the mining base," Reqilar said as he and Vekk stood up and watched as the other guests convened in the centre of the room, preparing to dance.

"I would too if I had dedicated my life to them, only to be sent far away," Vekk responded as they both walked over to join the rest of the guests and stood facing each other.

Reqilar held both of Vekk's hands and looked at her. She nodded and he began to move slowly with her, enjoying the moment.

"If you're wondering about the expensive suit...the last woman who was going to wear it decided she wouldn't come with me," he told her, silently admiring her slim figure.

"I guess I should thank her then," she said, smiling at him.

"You're enthusiastic for a hostage," he told her, slyly looking out of the window behind them. His face turned to show grave concern.

"What is it?" Vekk asked, the reality of the situation returning to her.

"I…must apologise," he said, trying to maintain his composure in front of the crowds. "This has all been a trap."

Vekk was visibly shocked but he reassured her, saying the attackers were not due to arrive for several more minutes, and provided her with codes that would allow her to access the entire military base.

"I want to help you," he said. "I'm enthralled by your efforts…and you."

"You've been a worthy enemy—and hopefully a better ally," she told him.

"Go! Before the general comes!" he told her as he let her hands go.

"Come with me!" she shouted, drawing the attention of the crowd. He shook his head and gestured towards the window. Vekk was visibly saddened but began to run as fast as she could, impaired by her small shoes.

As she reached the main room of the building, she heard the shattering of glass, followed by a squad of soldiers calling for her. Her breath accelerated and she froze, listening sharply.

As she prepared to run again, she heard footsteps and a familiar voice.

"Vekkilar," he said. "You're a surprisingly hard woman to track down."

She turned to see Zavroon, standing on a balcony and watching her.

"Chasing ghosts?" she asked.

"I'm chasing a liar," he said as he jumped onto the ballroom floor, walking up to her.

"Your presumed deaths were surprisingly well-planned. It's a shame you revealed yourself to the commander and fell into his trap," he told her.

"It wasn't planned," she said. "You're just easy to deceive."

"The commander's betrayal wasn't planned either, Vekkilar, yet it happened. You're more of a risk than I first anticipated," Zavroon said, readying his rifle.

"Where has the commander gone?" she asked.

"Probably to a rebel group," he told her. "Everyone assumes that you're associated with them; I know they're wrong."

"Why do you see me and Kol as a risk? Two average people shouldn't be a concern for you."

"You defy expectations; you have succeeded where you should have failed—until now."

He walked up to her, close to her face and aiming his rifle.

"The curse of clothes without compartments," he said, watching her hands carefully and expecting her to reach for her nonexistent weapon. "I give you a chance to surrender."

Vekk tactically placed her hand on her waist to push the dagger hidden by her waist, concealed to the general. She managed to loosen it and catch it with her other hand as it slipped out of her jacket, immediately thrusting it into Zavroon's torso, who was overcome with shock.

Vekk panicked and began to sprint, being cursed by the general while she ran to one of the transports outside and climbed inside, commandeering it along the thin road that she had arrived over.

She drove frantically in the large vehicle, destroying trees and animal dens during her escape. Once the battered vehicle reached the mountain, it struggled to ascend the rock face and forced Vekk to abandon it, removing her shoes and circlet as she haphazardly grabbed onto the rocks above.

She climbed to the top of the mountain base, watching the soldiers work as usual, although noticing that they were less efficient in Reqilar's absence. She slid into the base and the workers gave her a quick glance before turning back to their work, assuming that an official had sent her due to her calm demeanour.

Vekk rushed into the armoury and took a belt adorned with small bags, filling one of them with the three keys that they had already found. She also reclaimed her handgun, using it to dispatch the guards outside as they turned against her.

She heard the bellowing engines above the base and ran outside to see several airborne warships above her. They soon began firing and Vekk ran into the deep mines, finding Arkriat and Kretai in cages that hung from the ceiling. She unlocked the two metal plates beneath them and they ran to the back entrance of the base, finding it under heavy surveillance.

They climbed the tracks inside the mine and reached the surface, walking out to see the warships landing. Zavroon climbed out one of the vehicles, supported by a medic but looking well considering he had just been stabbed. Soldiers surrounded Vekk, Arkriat and Kretai and blocked all routes of escape.

"I can't wait to find your brother," Zavroon told Vekk as a soldier approached her from behind and handcuffed her.

Kol blocked his face from the incoming blows from the guard and managed to push him away and stand back up, ready to fight properly. He grabbed onto the soldier's head and pushed him into their damaged vehicle, causing him to shout in frustration and pain.

Kol ran for the replacement vehicle, which had just arrived, climbing inside. As he looked at the controls, the guard grabbed him from behind and pulled him to the ground, grabbing Kol's spear. Kol managed to wrest control of his weapon and hit his attacker with the blunt end, doing little more than disorientating him.

Kol took the opportunity to stand up, positioning himself behind the soldier and hitting him with the sharp end of the spear. The soldier fell to the ground unconscious and Kol quickly climbed back into the replacement vehicle with the medical supplies, familiarising himself with the controls enough to get him back to the mining base.

He drove back to the mining base to see various flying military ships landing outside; Kol rapidly dismounted and walked inside as workers unloaded the supplies. He walked into the medical centre and looked at the soldiers, resting in unimaginable pain.

"Thank you," one of the soldiers said to him with a strained voice. Kol smiled back, becoming accustomed to the emotions of the soldiers hidden behind their stern military might. The medical staff left for a moment to take emergency orders and an injured soldier called Kol over.

"Where…can I join your rebellion?" she asked him quietly as she looked around for surveillance.

"I…I don't run a rebel group," he said. "But I've seen a lot of them in the forests."

"Thank you," she said. "The commander wouldn't have tried that hard to heal his enemies."

Kol smiled and walked towards the door, opening it to see staff rushing around and many soldiers guarding the perimeter. He merged with the groups of miners running outside, sensing eyes glaring at him for several moments before disappearing.

Kol walked briskly towards the platform, now guarded with soldiers. He unsheathed his spear and was surprised when he felt a force preventing its movement. He turned to see Zavroon gripping the handle, grinning a malicious smile. Kol pushed all of his strength into freeing the spear, but Zavroon was stronger and pulled it from his hands and held it away.

"You're coming with me," he said, clutching Kol's arm. Kol pulled away and ran through the guards, jumping over the edge of the base and sliding down the small mountain. Zavroon snarled and ordered the guards to send out all available vehicles to hunt him down.

Kol ran through the forest, chased by several Hovercles flying over and the vehicles that he had first seen in the desert that produced lasers; Zavroon was aboard one of the flying vehicles, watching down.

'Hoveroon-Z' Kol read from the side of it, seeing the resemblance to Zavroon in the name.

They fired at him through the trees and blasted the snow and sand into the air, their target difficult to detect through the trees. However, these were swiftly mowed down by the various vehicles chasing Kol.

Vekk watched from behind Zavroon, hardly breathing out of fear for her brother.

"You have no chance of catching him," she told Zavroon, who was eagerly watching the spectacle.

"Oh, I think I do," he said. "He has no reinforcements and no one to save him."

Kol was breathing rapidly, leaping over fallen trees and rolling out of the way of turret fire. *Apparently they're not concerned with taking me alive.*

He suddenly dashed to the left and jumped off a hill, becoming invisible to the enemy's scanners. He then reappeared and the military forces pushed their attack, trying to cut him off.

Zavroon realised Kol's weakness and grabbed Vekk, pushing her to the edge of the vehicle where she wrestled to escape. Her struggle was heard by Kol, who stopped and turned to see Zavroon smiling back at him. He turned to see Hoverengths surrounding him and Vekk staring in shock as she realised what had been done.

Kol tried to run but the vehicles began unloading soldiers, which blocked his escape.

"Family's always a weakness," Zavroon said in a raised voice as the siblings were taken into Zavroon's personal Hoveroon, where they were both locked in cells. The siblings were placed individually but Arkriat and Kretai were locked together.

"I'm surprised you would put us in the same vehicle," Kol snarled as Zavroon stepped inside.

"Oh, usually I wouldn't. But this time, it will cause more suffering than I could do single-handedly." he told them as he walked into the cockpit and left the siblings to dread what was to come.

CHAPTER 14

Arthur ran into his bedroom to find Amy opening the box under his bed.

"Don't touch that!" he warned as she ignored him and opened it regardless.

"Why do you have weapons in your room?!" she asked, gasping and backing away.

"Do not mention this," he told her sternly as he closed the box lid.

"Why? Because you didn't tell Sarah about me and Steven?" she asked sarcastically.

"Shut up and get out," he told her, feeling anger rising within him. She left and he moved the weapons into a bag, away from the box. He ran into Rose's room to find her conversing with Isabelle.

"Rose, I need to talk to you," he said.

"I can't leave," she said, tapping the side of her bed. "Isabelle, would you give us a moment please?"

Isabelle nodded and walked out, leaving them alone.

"Amy found the weapons I took from the temple," he told her, struggling to sit down as fear clutched his body.

"If she reports you, tell them she's been stealing university property," Rose advised.

"What? I can't prove that."

"Yes you can," she said, using her one able hand to grab her phone from her bedside table. He soon received several videos of her taking various items from public spaces on campus.

"Wait, she actually did this?" he said. "What if she looks for your weapons too?"

"Isabelle agreed to keep it quiet in exchange for one of them. I'm here to look after them anyway."

"I better stay on Isabelle's good side, then," he joked and thanked his friend, leaving her to rest.

Arthur walked into his room and gathered his coursework, knowing that his professor would not extend deadlines due to his personal issues. He worked in the living room, hoping to draw attention away from his bed. Isabelle sat on the sofa adjacent to him and began to read a novel, quickly turning the pages.

Arthur worked on a presentation for several hours until someone knocked on the door. He opened it to find a woman, seemingly a member of staff, who told him to follow her.

"What is this about?" Arthur asked.

"We've been alerted to suspicious activity in your dorm," she said with little further explanation.

He was led to an office, where Amy was waiting with a smug grin. She had given them several images of the weapons, despite only having just seen them.

She's seen them before, he immediately thought as he sat down.

The staff showed him the images and he denied them, citing how their unique designs were non-existent in known human history.

"How about these?" he said as he took his phone out and showed them the photos of Amy's own crimes, much to her horror.

"This is insufficient evidence to take any sort of action," they told him.

"It's the same as what she gave you," he countered.

The staff deliberated for a few moments and told them both that they were free to go. Arthur smiled slyly at Amy, who appeared irritated.

I'm going to show them what you've done, he thought as he looked at her deceitful face. They walked out and took separate routes back to the dorm, hoping to avoid each other as best as they could.

Unfortunately, they both reached the door at the same time and opened it to see Steven telling a humorous joke to Isabelle and Rose, with the latter laying on one of the sofas. He soon silenced himself when he saw Amy and Arthur walk into the room.

Arthur slowly lowered himself onto a sofa, sitting opposite Steven, and continued with his coursework while Amy locked herself in her shared room.

The next day, Arthur sat down in the lecture hall and e-mailed his coursework to his professor while ignoring the introduction to the lecture. Hearing a break in his professor's speech, Arthur looked up and listened as the next part of the lecture began; he had become intrigued by the intricacies of Mechanical Engineering, something he had never even considered before.

He listened intently as the professor explained hydrostatic pressure. Drawing quick diagrams and making brief notes, he constantly checked the time. *Not yet. The videos were taken later.*

Once the lecture had ended, he rushed out and saw Amy entering her next class.

Off to steal supplies? He thought to himself as he walked back to his dorm. He walked in to find Sarah and Steven talking to each other about their relationship issues; he swiftly passed by to avoid intruding on their privacy. He sat and watched videos on his laptop for several hours. Once the device had died, he stood up and checked the time.

Seven, he thought. *Perfect.*

He left his room and walked to the door,

politely refusing a meal from Steven. Running down the stairs and towards the building housing the vault, he saw no activity. He walked slowly to minimise noise as he approached an empty classroom.

Where is she?!

Then he heard a click. Turning around, he saw Amy photographing him in the doorway. She began to flee but Arthur managed to outrun her, knocking her to the ground and causing the camera to slide into a nearby bush outside. She tried to stand up and escape but Arthur pulled her back down.

"Help me!" she screamed, causing people nearby to turn towards them.

"Why do you have a camera?!" he whispered angrily to her.

"To prove a point," she said softly, and tried to stand up again.

Arthur stood up and ran to the bush, fighting her off for the camera. She said nothing and instead pointed to a surveillance camera on a building that was recording the whole situation.

She smiled and Arthur stood stunned, unsure how he would justify his act with evidence. Amy slowly took the camera from his hands and ran; he thought about catching back up to her to reclaim the camera but knew it would make him look worse if he failed.

Arthur walked back to his dorm to find a

meal laid out for him, despite his earlier refusal. *Steven mustn't hate me then*, he thought as he sat down to eat.

Isabelle sat beside him with a book. She read and occasionally spoke to Arthur as he ate, discussing general topics such as the weather and studies.

"The weather's been bad recently," Arthur said, wondering how long his food had been cooked for.

"Sometimes it's *trop chaud pour moi*," she said, providing no explanation for the change in language. Arthur turned to see that Amy had walked in as she was speaking.

"*C'est trois bien, je pense*," Arthur replied in a heavily anglicised French accent.

Amy stared for a few moments in confusion but tried to ignore it and went to bed, visibly concerned.

"*Très bien*," Isabelle corrected. *Very good*.

"Thanks!" Arthur responded as he pushed his plate aside.

"That girl will be scared of French for the next few weeks," Isabelle joked, skipping through her book. Arthur laughed and finished his meal, heading to his room. He found Amy lying on her bed and eyeing him suspiciously. He smiled at her and lay on his bed, taking out his phone. She watched him dial a number and begin speaking to them in French. She was monolingual and could only recognise her name, which was frequently mentioned.

"What are you saying?" she whispered to him.

"*Excusez-moi*," he said softly to her, in a mocking tone, before returning to his 'conversation'; he had typed a random number into his calculator app and had spoken random phrases due to his limited vocabulary.

Amy looked irritated and worried; she tried to ignore it, even trying to sleep despite the man speaking in an unknown language near her.

He eventually put his phone away went to sleep.

Amy lay awake, fearing what he was planning.

Over several months, Arthur continued developing his knowledge of French and began to hold fairly accurate conversations with Isabelle.

Within a year, he had passed numerous exams and failed others; his confidence weakened with every piece of negative feedback, with the difficulty of the course leading Arthur to doubt his abilities. He had also considered giving up the course several times to focus on painting instead but he saw no reason to cut his journey short after all of the effort he had put in.

However, money became a concern as his

paintings did little to boost his income and he instead had to work a part-time job in a restaurant, which paid the minimum wage. He found little time to walk Shadow yet refused to cut down the number of walks; Sarah and Steven had offered to take him out for one of his walks so they could talk away from the dorm.

On one morning, Arthur was working on his French and Rose sat beside him, having fully recovered. He heard Isabelle walk past and turned his head to face her.

"Why do you want to help me?" he asked her with no warning.

"Because...I find Amy irritating and you're the only one who has tried to learn my language," she said, slightly taken aback by the question. She walked into her room and Arthur turned back to his laptop, surprised.

"She holds grudges," Rose said.

"So do I," Arthur said with a malicious smile.

"Well I've got to get ready for work," Rose said, grabbing her crutches and standing up.

"What?" Arthur asked as he stared at her injured legs.

"I can stand behind a counter," she said. "That's good enough for Reese and his failing business."

Arthur took a moment to understand and stayed silent as she walked off to her room. He had called her boss "King Cut" for so long he had forgotten his real name.

She's still working there? he thought as he continued practising his French colours.

Sarah suddenly rushed in and sat on the sofa adjacent to Arthur. "I'll help you."

"With what?" he asked, closing his laptop as he knew he would be unable to focus.

"Amy," she said as she breathed heavily. "She just mocked my accent."

"Do you have evidence?"

"Right here."

Sarah handed him her phone and showed him a video of the insult.

"This is perfect," he said in awe as he placed his laptop beside him, his eyes fixated on the screen of her phone. He felt her eyes glaring at him and he immediately looked up, "not because she insulted him, but we it'll help me get her kicked out."

Someone suddenly knocked on the door and Arthur opened it to see a member of staff, a woman he recognised.

"Follow me," she bluntly told him.

He walked behind her and she took him to a building he had seen before. Inside was one other staff member, yet Amy was not present this time.

They showed Arthur the video evidence of him looking into the English classroom and the minor struggle with Amy after.

"Do you have an excuse for your actions?"

the woman asked.

Arthur wanted to show them the evidence he had collected so far, including proof from other people but he had not yet compiled it or even brought it with him.

"Am I allowed to go and get it?" he asked, expecting the answer.

"No," the other person said sternly.

"Then I can't show you my defence."

"Then you will take ten weeks of classes in discipline."

He felt extremely anxious, as he was more concerned about the people he would meet than the satisfaction Amy would feel. It would also likely impact his studies, reducing his study and relaxation time.

"Is there any way to get out of them?" he asked quickly.

"No. If you miss a session, another one will be set up."

Arthur quietly stood up and walked out without saying a word.

He returned to the living room to tell his roommates but found only Amy waiting for him.

"How did it go?" she asked innocently.

"You snake!" he sneered viciously, before walking off to his room to vent.

About half an hour later, he saw that she had left for classes and Steven was sat in the living room, watching something on his phone.

Arthur sighed and walked outside to try and calm down. His phone vibrated in his pocket and he took it out to see that he had been sent a schedule of his new classes. He texted it to Alex, who advised him to take the discipline classes regardless as further refusal would not help his case.

Later in the evening, he saw Sarah and Steven sat together on the sofa, watching a programme on celebrity relationships. He decided to paint alone in his room to make up for the time he would miss and to generate a greater income.

Over the next few weeks, he began the disciplinary classes with a variety of people he would rather not associate with, further dreading any partner or group activities—he was out of place. Some of them had tried to become friends with him but he politely pushed them away.

After the fourth class, Arthur ran home with a deep desire to compile his building evidence and present his case, preferably forcing Amy to deal with the consequences of her actions.

He called Sarah and Isabelle, who sent him all the evidence that they had, which he put into a folder on his phone. He had photos, videos and text message evidence, mostly from Sarah who was eager to help him.

He checked his timetable to see that he was free for another two hours and ran down to the office where he had been sent twice, determined to correct his mistakes.

He approached the receptionist, who told him he would have to book an appointment, fortunately offering an open slot in one hour. He sat outside, checking his evidence and ensuring it was sufficient. He heard someone walking down the corridor and saw Sarah and Amy happily conversing. He stared at them as they turned to see his face.

Sarah was mortified and ran, hoping to avoid Arthur for as long as she could. Amy stubbornly sat down and waited to join Arthur's meeting in hopes she could pursue further action against him.

The woman welcomed them inside and they sat down, as far from each other as possible.

"I have all of the evidence that you need to expel her," Arthur told them, handing them his phone and directing them through the videos, choosing not to tell them of Sarah's deceit.

"I'm friends with Sarah!" Amy blurted out.

"You weren't 'friends' when you told me she yelled at you," the man at the desk countered. She went silent, unable to explain.

I don't think 'we're friends' would work in front of a judge, Arthur thought.

After a while analysing the evidence, the

man asked Amy to add to her own defence and she had a few photos, many of them copies of previous evidence. She then began to defend herself with words, utilising the full range of her vocabulary.

I wonder if she studies Jekyll and Hyde.

The man and the woman walked out and privately discussed their verdict and the steps that would be taken. Amy smiled maliciously as she felt assured of victory, knowing that she had already moulded a negative image of Arthur in their minds.

They walked back in and sat down, not showing any preference towards the two.

"In light of the actions that we have seen," the woman said authoritatively. "We have sided with Mr Brookes."

Arthur was visibly shocked. He had expected the outcome but not the euphoric feeling that followed. Amy was similarly surprised and bewildered as her tactics were not as sufficient as she believed.

"The use of bigotry and malicious acts has led us to this decision, which we did not take lightly," the woman said, turning to Amy. "We will contact you with the details of your departure soon."

Arthur quietly thanked them and walked out. However, he also saw how miserable Amy looked as her future would not be as bright as she once believed.

She tried to do the same to you, he reminded himself, walking to his dorm. He saw Isabelle waiting for him by the front door.

"How did it go?" she asked upon his arrival, eager for the results.

"She's been expelled," he said quietly.

"Well then," she replied, walking into the dorm beside him. "Congratulations."

Rose and Steven were sat around, waiting for the news and Arthur delivered. The room was quiet as everyone realised that her future career growth had likely been stunted.

"She's facing the consequences of her actions," Rose said with a smirk.

Two months later, a new term had begun and new university students had flooded the campus. Arthur and his roommates watched from their living room, seeing most of them visibly intrigued by the new surroundings.

"Wait until they get used to this place," Sarah said, sipping her coffee. "Hope we don't get any here."

"I doubt we will," Rose said. "I doubt they want any new students anywhere near us."

Isabelle sighed and said. "I'll miss this place."

"You're leaving?!" Arthur asked in disbelief.

"Next year is my last year," she said. "I thought I told you."

"Nope."

"That year, you'll have Sarah, Steven and anyone else who moves in!" Rose reminded him, already having told him when she would complete her degree.

They spoke for approximately another hour until someone knocked on the door. Isabelle stood up and opened it. A man quietly spoke to her and she let him in, allowing Arthur to identify him easily.

"Alex?!"

"Hi," he said weakly to the strangers in front of him.

"He is our new roommate," Isabelle told everyone.

"I thought you weren't going to uni," Arthur reminded him.

"I wasn't, until I got a job," he explained. "I want more opportunities than that place."

Rose invited him to sit beside her and he formally introduced himself to everyone.

"From what Arthur told me, it looks like nearly everyone is here," he said, causing confusion in the rest of the room.

"What do you mean?" Sarah asked.

"Well everyone except Amy," he said, becoming confused himself. "Is she not a real person or something?"

"No she's real," Steven said, before lowering his voice. "Definitely real."

"She got kicked out," Arthur told him in a flat tone.

"Ah," he said, before electing to change the subject. "Is there somewhere I can store my suitcase?"

Arthur realised that there was only one available bed and eagerly showed Alex to their room, which he had become accustomed to being solely his.

He began moving bags and boxes while explaining everything inside the bedroom. Alex nodded and pushed his suitcase beside his bed while Arthur moved his own belongings out of the way.

"I've been looking forward to this," Alex said as he unpacked his bag.

"So what degree are you studying for?" Arthur asked as he relocated his bags.

"Mathematics," Alex told him as he put his clothes into one of the drawers.

They spoke while they organised their belongings, Arthur inquiring the details as to why his friend had suddenly changed his life plans.

As the weeks progressed, Alex helped him with his coursework, explaining measurements and sizes to help scale diagrams accurately while Arthur helped him to settle into life at university.

Life had become generally easier for Arthur after his conflict with Amy and the exploration of the temple; he had gained one of his only friends as a roommate, someone who would not search through his personal possessions. Arthur occasionally visualised the two figures before he slept, both wielding weapons like the one hidden under his bed.

Throughout the next year, he studied hard and increased his linguistic abilities, managing to speak to Isabelle in French with some fluency. He struggled to maintain his mediocre grades, although his knowledge of engineering had risen exponentially and had given him the opportunity to study the mechanics of a rocket that could deliver him to space.

The academic year passed by more rapidly than the last, being less eventful than his first year. He attended the graduation of Isabelle and Rose, who were both elated yet saddened to move into a new part of their lives. Arthur was even able to meet Rose's family and Isabelle's brother, although their conversation was brief.

He later returned to find the dorm empty, everyone having left to attend the ceremony. He sat in his room, stroking Shadow.

"We're getting there," he said, beginning to smile. "I'm just glad you're here to experience it with me."

"Where are you going?"

Arthur looked at Shadow with an alarmed expression, before turning to see Rose standing in the doorway.

"To…space. It's been my plan for the last four years."

"What happened at twenty-two that made you want to become an astronaut?!"

"I...I—I keep seeing these...alien figures in—in my mind. I kn-know that probably sounds weird. I believe—not believe as in a god, but—I think they exist but I don't know, m—much, actually anything about them. It's—"

Rose stayed silent as Arthur struggled to produce any more sentences, processing the information. "Is this something you choose to do, or is it hallucinogenic, or...?"

"It's...involuntary but it's nothing to worry about. I think they're communicating with me—it's strong enough that I want to seek them out."

"Do you want me to call a doctor...or a therapist?"

Arthur shook his head and stood up, directly facing her.

"I—I shouldn't have said anything. It's nothing serious," he told her, noting the concern in her expression.

"You might have some sort of mental condition," she responded. "You can't uproot your life for something in your head!"

"It's not in my head! Something tells me it's real."

"Well, I saw you unleash something in that vault building so clearly things aren't as they seem. I'll hold off, but let me know if it gets worse," she told him, placing a hand on his shoulder before turning around and walking out.

He sat back on his bed, silently doubting himself as the alien figures drifted back into his head.

If they are real, how will I communicate with them?

His final academic year began several months later, with Rose and Isabelle replaced by a student who largely kept to himself. Arthur struggled with doubts about his mission to find the figures, feeling that his efforts were futile and that the figures were nothing more than creative thoughts.

His progress declined as he focused on his social life; parties were prioritised as a method of distracting himself from his stressful situation and he focused on other people's problems. Sarah confided in him, providing reasons as to why she was in contact with Amy and diving into her deeper relationship issues.

His roommates soon reciprocated the support and began to offer solutions to his doubts, despite his vague explanations of the issue. Rebuilt with assurance, he was able to take control of his life and reach the end of the academic year with fewer concerns about his future.

The exams soon passed and graduation approached. Arthur was quick to invite his family and friends to visit, the former being unaware that he had even attended university. The calmer atmosphere improved his mood and took his mind away from the figures and the relics that ordinarily surrounded his thoughts.

He woke up tired, yet excited for the day to come. Dressing into his robes, he arrived early to the hall and bid farewell to some of the other students, avoiding any interaction other than a friendly wave.

The ceremony began and the university's chancellor gave a speech to congratulate the graduates and expressing his hope for their futures.

This sounds like the same speech from Rose's graduation, Arthur thought.

Upon its conclusion, Arthur rushed to see his parents, who were talking to Sarah and Steven. He smiled at them both before greeting his parents.

"When did this happen?!" his mother asked with thinly-veiled surprise.

"When I realised I didn't want to become a baker," he replied, hugging her.

"So when do you get your degree?" his father asked him. "I didn't go to university—I don't know how it works."

"It gets mailed to me," he told them, glancing around the room for his closer friends.

They spoke for several more minutes, discussing how he came into the situation and what he had been studying. He had not spoken to his parents in a long time and was elated to be able to discuss his future plans, much brighter than they had previously believed.

"I think your friend's over there," his mother said, pointing behind him. She was correct as Alex walked up to him and hugged him.

"Congrats," he told Arthur, before releasing him.

"Thanks," he said, introducing him to his parents.

"Hello Ruth, Damian," Alex said respectfully.

Arthur then surprised Rose, who was facing away from him and had begun speaking to other graduates in the room.

"So, you did it!" she said.

"You doubted me," he reminded her.

"I'm sorry about that," she said, "but I'll support you when I can from now on."

"Okay, thanks," he struggled to say. *This feels too formal.*

The event lasted an hour and a half, giving everyone time to say their farewells and reflect.

Arthur walked outside with Rose, looking around.

"I can't believe I did it," he said, close to tears.

"Neither can I," she said, putting her arm around him, "I can't believe you did it either to be honest."

They sat down on a bench and Arthur was pushing himself to repress his tears.

"I can't believe it," he managed to say. "Thank you, thank Alex, thank Isabelle, thank everyone anyone else."

"Maybe not everyone," Rose said, laughing.

"Well, no," he said, stifling a laugh.

"I've become a news journalist and you'll become an astronaut," she said.

"We've succeeded—well, succeeding. I haven't got the job yet," he said, smiling at her.

"Life will be good," she said. "Let's go and get Shadow."

They entered the dorm to find the newest roommate cooking food; he was unaware of the graduation ceremony and appeared to relax at the sight of Arthur's robe.

Arthur packed his items and clothes, including the weapons, and clipped a lead onto Shadow. He walked out with Rose, seeking greater gain.

CHAPTER 15

"I'm curious as to what you have learnt in Quelliare's wilderness," said Zavroon, sharpening his knife.

"I thought I already showed you," Vekk taunted.

"That was impressive," he said. "But perhaps it's my turn."

He wielded his knife and instead of walking to Vekk, turned to Arkriat.

"No, don't you dare!" Vekk yelled at him.

He slashed the laser bars of the cage, scaring them.

"Imagine if the people knew you were torturing young people!" Kol said.

"'Young'? You are not children, although your behaviour may prove otherwise," Zavroon said, walking up to Kol's cage.

"When we're finished, you won't be taking such risks," Kol threatened. Zavroon laughed at him.

"What's a winter warrior and a high-class lady going to do to me, the General of the Royal Guard?" he said mockingly, in a raised voice when referring to them.

The siblings said nothing but looked at him with distaste and anger. They wanted to attack and escape, but the power was with their captor.

"It's a shame that you're not actually associated with the rebels. They could've freed you," he said, turning away from them.

He suddenly walked up to Vekk's cage, trying to scare her into submission.

"Which one of you has the keys?" he asked in a malicious tone.

"Why would we have the keys? We knew the risks of this happening," Kol countered.

"You're on the run. You have nowhere else to store them but on yourselves," he said. "You've also confirmed that you are indeed searching for the keys."

He deactivated Vekk's holding cell and pulled her out, putting his knife to her neck.

"So where are they?" he asked again, now looking at Kol.

Kol said nothing, conflicted by the risk to his sister's life and the potential to lose all of their progress.

Vekk managed to knock the knife out of his hand and he quickly pushed her to the ground, before throwing her back into her cell and activating the bars. Reclaiming his knife, he put it back on his belt.

"I don't have time to play," he sneered.

"Your taunts don't scare me," Vekk said to him. "Your authority wasn't enough to stop the commander from deserting the military."

"The commander will die, as will you if you don't answer me!" Zavroon said, becoming irritated and angered with their lack of co-operation. After several minutes of their silence, Zavroon walked over to a crate and took out a robot. He pressed two buttons on top on it and it hummed to life.

"You don't want to know what it can do," he said.

He deactivated Kol's cell and held him against the wall, allowing the robot to walk towards him.

"Tell me what I want to know," Zavroon said. Kol tried to punch him but Zavroon held him down and the robot stabbed Kol with something that made him fall to the ground in agony.

"Causes pain with no scarring," he told them.

"You're disgusting," she told him.

"Apologies, I didn't expect royalty," he said, a sarcastic smile forming on his face.

Vekk began to threaten Zavroon verbally through the bars of the cage and he gladly accepted her challenge. He deactivated the cell and slammed her into the wall, then threw her on the ground, clutching her arm until the robot could inject her as it had done with her brother.

"Pathetic," the general said, standing over them.

Arkriat began barking at him, angered at the suffering caused to his owners.

"Shut up!" he shouted at Arkriat, who was unrelenting.

Kol was finally able to stand up and was immediately thrown back in his cell, as was Vekk despite her pain continuing.

"This is what happens when you don't answer my questions," he said as he gestured to the robot, as if threatening to do it again.

"You're almost worse than Lasapra!" Kol told him.

"I am worse than Queen Lasapra," he said. "Now, will you give me the information I ask for, or will I have to inflict pain once again?"

"We've destroyed tanks...we'll destroy you," Vekk said as she struggled, and failed, to stand, still recovering from the pain.

"I must admit I've been impressed by your exploits," he told them, forcing them back into their cells. "However, they have crossed the line. I will not tolerate attacks against my Queen."

"Why do you help her? I would've thought that you'd have taken her place by now," Vekk said as she pushed her body to stand, with little success.

"I respect my superiors and the effort of my

foes. You wou—" Zavroon suddenly coughed and fell to one knee, grimacing in pain and clutching his stab wound. He lifted his hand to his ear and muttered something, before opening the doors of the Hoveroon and clambering into another vehicle, closing both doors behind him.

Vekk looked towards a box in the corner of the room, beside Kol and diagonal to her. They had no way of reaching it without being caught —unless the pilot moved from his station.

She gestured to the crate when Kol looked at her and then pointed to the cockpit. He clearly understood and stayed silent before shouting loudly in a deep voice, mimicking their torturer.

"Intruders!" he shouted as he jumped on the ground of his cell and managed to kick the box beside him, his foot reaching through the bars. Vekk began to slam her fists and feet into her cell and the pilot rushed down to find the room as it should be.

"Who was that?" he asked as he stormed towards Kol's cage.

"Give us some weapons," Kol commanded, pointing to a nearby locker.

The pilot laughed and refused, turning to walk back to the cockpit to reactivate the cameras. Vekk kneeled in her cell and began digging her fingers through the damaged metal floor, locating a wire and severing it on the sharp metal edges of the plating beneath her feet.

The cell soon shut off as the cockpit door closed behind the pilot. Vekk quietly walked towards the locker on the wall and opened it, retrieving her weapons while Kol's spear remained on the back of Zavroon, who was elsewhere.

"I expected a lock," she said as she approached Kol, and reached towards the cage controls.

"Take out the pilots!" Kol whispered as engines hummed nearby. Vekk ran for the cockpit and quickly dispatched the guards, taking control of the vehicle as she heard the Hoveroon doors open and Zavroon return to see that she had escaped.

"She used her own brother as bait," he said, staring at Kol in his cell.

He quickly walked towards Kol, unsheathed his knife and deactivated the cell. The general held him with his knife to Kol's neck. Vekk watched on a screen in horror as she mentally decided on a course of action.

"You could have taken the keys by now!" Kol muttered as he struggled to escape Zavroon's grasp.

"Oh, I know. I wanted to see you hand them over willingly."

The lights suddenly shut off and the vehicle moved unpredictably. Narrowly missing obstacles, it flew out of formation and distanced itself from the military escort.

"Ah, that's where she is," Zavroon said to himself as the cockpit door opened and Vekk approached him, wielding her dagger and handgun. Kol was thrown to the floor as Zavroon sheathed his dagger and brandished a sword; he waved it unpredictably before lunging at Vekk, who ran in fear.

She managed to avoid the swinging blade and began firing at him from a distance. Kol released Arkriat and Kretai and crept up behind Zavroon. He took his spear from the general's back, earning him the attention of Zavroon as Vekk struggled to hit the general with his flawless evasion.

The spear did not break when it was hit by the sword and Kol thrusted it towards his attacker. Vekk ran at Zavroon from behind and failed to pierce his back plating. They attacked from multiple angles, before electing to escape.

Kretai pressed the button to unlock the ship doors and the siblings watched as the military escort continued to follow them. A Hovercle flew in front of the door and fired inside, causing the roof to collapse on them and ignite the fuel stored inside; everyone inside was thrown out of the door as the ship exploded and the remnants plummeted into the forested terrain below.

They awoke to find that they were once again

locked in cells, inside of a large prison block with other prisoners. The siblings had been separated and Arkriat and Kretai were out of sight.

Vekk stood up and looked around to find her brother but she could not identify him. She looked at the tile on the ground in front of her cell; it only required someone to step on it to unlock the cell. Guards patrolled the room but consciously avoided stepping on the tiles.

Kol was situated by the door of the prison room and watched guards walk in and out, waiting for someone to interrogate him but no one came. He sat for hours, waiting for something and hoping food would come as he had only eaten leftover rations from the mining base between tasks.

Servants soon approached the cells and pushed meagre bowls of food through the bars. Kol took the bowl but felt guilty about keeping it after staring at the servants' skeletal frames as they moved on.

Vekk watched the food come to her and quickly planned her escape. She sat patiently while other prisoners quickly grabbed whatever was available.

As a silent servant walked towards her and held out her food. Vekk whispered, pointing to the tile in front of her. "You can keep the food if you open this cell."

The servant stood still for a moment, before gesturing to the cameras that surrounded them. Vekk promised to destroy them and he complied, disabling multiple cells and freeing around three other prisoners. Vekk ran past the other cells, successfully freeing Kol and informing him on her plan to disable the cameras.

"I'll find our weapons—and Arkriat and Kretai," Kol told Vekk as she chose to honour her promise and began searching for a security centre. She watched as a female soldier patrolled the corridors, sensitive to the quietest sounds. Vekk sprinted past and the soldier pursued, following her into a storage room.

Vekk crouched behind an armour stand and watched as the soldier walked past. Vekk jumped out from the shadows and punched her, knocking her unconscious. Vekk stole her gear and weapon and began to search the storage room, locating the map that had been confiscated from the siblings; it had been damaged and required repair.

She hid the guard behind an ancient wall that was being transported inside and walked out, wearing the armour and attempting to act naturally. She saw a soldier walking down the corridor and asked him for directions to the security centre, which he provided.

Walking at a moderate pace, she approached the centre and reached towards the door, hesitating before pressing the button beside it.

Kol was running down corridors, several guards following behind him and firing. Several doors automatically opened by his passing and he chose not to enter any until he heard the sounds of various creatures. He dived through the door, knowing he would be followed.

He hid behind an animal cage as the soldiers opened the door and activated the lights; he saw Arkriat and Kretai packed in small cages, watching nervously. Kol crawled around the room, evading the guards' sight and reaching his companions. Opening their cages, they followed him quietly as he knocked over cages and released feral creatures that attacked the soldiers, who began firing randomly, accidentally freeing more animals and killing others.

Kol pushed a soldier away from the door and made his escape with his companions, the corridors now empty as the soldiers had left their posts. He ran in search of his weapons, checking every room while attempting to avoid detection.

Vekk entered the control room to see a man standing in front of many screens, his back turned to the door. As she approached him silently, he turned around, picked her up by her waist and threw her to the ground in front of him with no warning. She looked up into Zavroon's eyes. He stared back at her; he appeared as surprised as she was.

She suddenly dashed past him and grabbed his knife. He ducked behind a computer terminal and drew his sword, soon re-emerging and beginning to swing at her. She fell to the ground and dropped the knife as he unholstered his gun, aiming at her head for a quick kill.

She scrambled for the small black knife and threw it at Zavroon's legs to distract him. He was stunned for a moment as the knife sliced through his armour and fell to the ground, which allowed her to stand up and run to the opposite side of the room.

Kol ordered Arkriat to find the weapon room and he complied. The Garisal ran as if he knew the location thoroughly and led Kol to an armoury, containing purely military-grade weaponry but with no sign of Vekk and Kol's weapons.

"This is the wrong room," Kol told Arkriat, who simply looked at him in confusion. Kol sighed and looked for a suitable weapon to help him escape. He noticed the back wall was oddly devoid of weapon racks or any sort of inventory. Kretai stood on the wall, showing Kol that there had to be something to grab onto. He felt around the wall and found the minuscule outline of a door.

Arkriat nudged all of the weapons off the racks against the other walls, prompting Kol to urge him to be quieter as he did not want to draw attention. As the last weapon fell, the wall slid open to reveal a vault full of weapons, including his spear in the centre, which was floating above a pedestal. He reclaimed both his and Vekk's weapons, before running back out to search for his sister.

Vekk stood against the wall, knowing she could not fight him without support as his combat training extended far beyond her own.

"Every time you escape, I will find you," Zavroon told her as he approached her, his gun drawn and aimed at her. They heard footsteps outside and disregarded them as patrolling soldiers until someone opened the door.

Kol quickly recognised Vekk through her armour and jabbed his spear at Zavroon, who moved to dodge. Vekk ran to Kol, who rearmed her with her weapons. She fired at Zavroon, who dived behind the surveillance screen and Kol moved to escape.

"Wait," Vekk said as she aimed at Zavroon, who slowly stood up.

"I thought—" Kol began to say, before turning to see Zavroon throw a grenade at his head. He dodged and watched as it rolled into a corner of the room; it exploded several seconds later as the siblings escaped, destroying the terminals that stood against the walls and shutting off the security system throughout the ship.

"Alright then," he said once they were a safe distance away and began to run. They did not know the layout of a Quarailian prison ship and had hoped that they would not need to in the future.

"Walk in front of me," Vekk said quietly to Kol, who complied and continued to move while Vekk held a weapon to his back.

"I assume this isn't a trap," he said.

"It's good to know you still trust me," she sarcastically whispered behind him.

They saw a passing soldier and Vekk asked for directions to the hanger, implying she needed to transport her 'rebellious prisoner.' The soldier quickly gave directions and offered backup to control the animals beside her, to which Vekk declined.

They walked quickly down a flight of stairs, through many more corridors and levels until they found a large door that opened to show the plethora of vehicles available. Kol was about to run to the nearest ship until he brushed his hand against his bag.

"The keys are gone," he said quietly.

"What?!" Vekk said in shock.

"Zavroon probably has them," Kol responded, knowing it was unlikely he survived the blast.

Alarms suddenly began to ring and people began to rush to the nearest vehicles. A voice was heard over the intercom warning that the ship's engines had taken critical damage and commanding all crew members to evacuate.

"Someone must've messed with the engines," Vekk said.

"Should we save the keys or our lives?" Kol asked, running towards a ship.

Vekk heard someone stumbling behind her and turned to see Zavroon once again, this time with damaged armour and unseen injuries that were visible by his stance. Instead of attacking her, he pushed past and limped towards a vehicle with the intention of escape.

Vekk walked behind him and grabbed his arm. He turned and she heard the sound of gems hitting each other somewhere on his armour. He suddenly punched her, causing Vekk to release her grip and fall to her knees, her helmet falling from her head and rolling down the hangar floor. Kol ran over and helped her up, with Arkriat barking furiously to keep enemy soldiers away.

Kol escorted her to a free ship and they took off, following Vekk's advice to pursue Zavroon. Kol chased after him, struggling to familiarise himself with the controls while his target used his many years of experience to escape—the hilly biome below that they flew through provided many obstructions that Kol was forced to make sharp turns around.

He followed Zavroon's vehicle as it flew around mountains and through trees, although their ship was larger and could not fit into the same spaces that their target could. He flew through the flames of the burning prison ship and Kol fired randomly, hearing their impact on metal and seeing the sudden turn of their target into the ground.

The crash sent burning metal plates into the trees, starting a jungle fire and making any nearby landing difficult; the night sky was illuminated only by the crash and forced them to land at a distance.

Kol landed beside the flames, opening the door and leading Vekk out into the new jungle. He ran through the burning wreck, his sister behind him with Arkriat and Kretai to prevent Zavroon from escaping. They approached the vehicle and saw that it had already been abandoned.

"He's gone," Vekk said, pointing to the open hatch. They heard rustling and followed the sounds to see someone running.

"That's him," Kol said as he ran after Zavroon, determined to stop the General. Other military ships flew above, searching for their leader.

Vekk began to shoot at him as he limped over bushes and fallen trees, through the flames and gunfire incoming. He retreated into a clearing and looked up as he pressed the device in his ear and watched one of the military ships prepare to land at his position.

The siblings reached him and Kol pulled out his spear, expecting Zavroon to also aim with a weapon.

"You only make me more determined," he told them, attempting to conceal his defencelessness. The vehicle suddenly exploded, leaving Zavroon concerned for his escape.

"Come with us," Vekk ordered as the ship landed.

"We're not all like your commander, Vekkilar," he said to her as he ran into the jungle.

"You have a commander? Where?" Kol asked, oblivious to her previous encounter.

"Not...like that," she responded awkwardly. Kol quickly understood and stared at her as he realised who she was referring to. They then began to run after Zavroon to ensure he did not escape.

"You weren't there," Vekk told her brother. "You would've liked Reqi...I mean the commander in that setting."

"I don't think so," Kol replied. "Did you see what he did to us?"

Vekk insisted that they should drop the issue and so he did, instead ordering Arkriat to chase the general down. The siblings followed him and he led them through the foreign jungle, forcing them to avoid the many creatures laying in the bushes and in the short grass that appeared to sprout from everywhere. Thin, red sticks grew out of the branches and occasionally fell, providing a meal for the animals and distracting them from the running prey.

"How are we unable to catch an injured man?" Vekk asked, beginning to feel exhausted.

"Because he's a General of the Royal Guard," Kol reminded her.

They began to lose track of him but Arkriat was determined and began to run faster, despite knowing he would eventually tire. Kretai flew quicker than they ran, targeting the man she knew to be a threat to her family. However, due to her speed she quickly flew into another flying creature, causing them both to fall to the ground. Kol stopped to attend to them both as Vekk and Arkriat continued the hunt.

Arkriat leapt over rocks and foliage while Vekk followed the fading path, focusing her energy into a sprint. They managed to corner him at the edge of a small cliff with several jagged rocks preventing him from climbing over.

"Surrender Zavroon, you're too weak to escape," Vekk ordered him, yet he did not move.

"I will not be given an ultimatum by a runaway!" he yelled at her despite being too weak to fight back. He braced himself as Vekk charged at him with her dagger, losing it as he pulled it from her hands and held it in front of him, pointing towards her.

"Hand over the keys," Vekk demanded, aiming her handgun at him.

"How you've become the greatest target of my career is beyond my knowledge."

"That's exactly how. We're unsuspecting," Vekk said as she walked closer to him, levelling her gun with Zavroon's chest.

He suddenly stepped off the hill, the keys bashing together as he moved. He gripped the edge while Vekk took a moment to realise what he had done. Zavroon then climbed down the cliff, into the jungle below, breathily heavily as he descended. Vekk sighed and ran back to Kol, who had removed the bulkiest parts of his winter clothing and was tending to Kretai.

Upon inspection, he had noticed that the animal that Kretai had collided with was another Ukrifar, a surprise, as they had never met another of her kind. She had been given to them as a gift and her origins had not been known until now.

"He escaped," Vekk told Kol, who simply nodded as she gave them to him and he finished inspecting Kretai for injury. "I couldn't get the keys."

"I think Kretai's well enough to travel," he said, clearly having accepted their loss. "I'm not too knowledgeable on biology, though."

"It's better than nothing," Vekk said as she picked up Kretai and allowed her to regain her senses. She retrieved her equipment from Kol and watched him open the map detailing the locations of the keys.

"The fourth key is nearby. I think we should get it now and recover the rest of the keys later," he said as he pointed to the nearby marker.

"I agree," Vekk muttered as she checked her equipment for damage.

"I have no idea where we are," Kol said as Zavroon's escape vehicle could be heard in the distance. The siblings stood up and looked to see the red treetops, which sliced the moonlight as it shone through and weakly illuminated the jungle.

They heard rustling nearby and chose to move quickly through the jungle, looking for their ship. They ran back through the flames to find a burning wreckage and their ship broken in half by a charred tree trunk.

"There goes our escape," Vekk said, after a swift inspection, and walked away.

"Where are you going?" he asked, rushing to catch up to her.

"To find someone. Anyone." she told him.

Ancient dirt pathing remained underneath the foliage, although it had been covered by centuries of glowing flora. Kretai flew above, occasionally stopping on the tree branches and eating the mysterious red sticks that grew from them; they appeared to have no adverse effects on her. As night approached, these sticks began to glow a faint red light, allowing the siblings to make their way through the bushes.

They encountered a giant hill that was almost the size of a small mountain; they walked into the cave entrance at its base, encouraged by the sudden enthusiasm of Kretai. The interior was lit with small orbs that lay in the cave walls and marked the way for the siblings as they ventured deeper inside.

It took them several minutes to find the main chamber, given away by the hive-like structure that was not present elsewhere in the cave. Thousands of Ukrifars were contained inside, sleeping in slots constructed in the wall and paying no attention to their visitors.

The siblings walked into the centre and heard nothing. The deafening silence was surprising as thousands of beings were alive inside yet none made a single noise or sound. Walking through in awe, Kol looked at the many Ukrifars and was intrigued to learn more.

Ahead of them was a golden orb on a pedestal in the centre of the room, resembling the ones that had lit the passage but was larger, and its purpose was unknown. The room was lit by the hive structure and gave a sense of comfort.

"What is this place, Kretai?" Kol asked without expecting an answer and searching the room.

"It's the Ukrihive," a voice responded. Kol's eyes darted from Kretai to the humming orb ahead of him.

"Who was that?" Vekk asked, looking around at the sleeping Ukrifars.

"Greetings," the voice repeated.

Vekk and Kol turned to look at the orb, which began to hum a tune.

"Are you talking...orb?" Vekk said.

"I've been called worse," it told them.

"What is the Ukrihive?" Kol asked, enthralled by the chamber.

"The hub for Ukrifars, of course!" it responded.

"Makes sense," Vekk said as she wandered the giant room.

CHAPTER 16

"Do you know if there is any other sentient life in this jungle?" Vekk asked the orb, who had finished its hum.

"No," it bluntly told her.

"Do you know the location of any...keys?" Kol questioned as he stared at the strange patterns on the orb's glassy surface.

"No," it repeated.

Kretai flew up to an open space in the Ukrihive and sat inside, awaking the Ukrifars around her who responded positively to her presence.

"The Ukrifar would like to stay here until you are ready to leave the jungle," the orb told the siblings.

Kol was about to protest but then realised that Kretai was content inside the Ukrihive, more so than she was during their journey.

"We'll see her when we return," Kol said as the siblings turned to leave the chamber, with Vekk scoffing at the orb's lack of knowledge.

"I can teach you more about your Ukrifar companion!" it said in a raised voice as the siblings and Arkriat walked out in silence, worrying about any military forces remaining in the jungle that would be searching for them. They reached the entrance of the cave and crossed into the thick jungle, its colour scheme being darker than the first that they had visited.

"Where are we going?" Vekk asked, despite neither of them having any knowledge about where they were.

"I think we should find a way to repair the map," Kol said. "It'll make finding the fourth key easier."

They walked where the faded path remained, assuming that it had been made for a purpose. They soon began to run through the jungle and saw the many creatures watching them from their dens and the thick bushes that engulfed the ground.

They entered the deep jungle, characterised by the dimmed light and the ferocity of the creatures heard nearby. The rising sun was still visible enough to shine over an open pit on the ground, clearly designed to serve a purpose.

"It looks like a quarry," Kol said as he saw the other sides of the pit, roughly forming a rectangle.

"It must be old," Vekk said as she circled the quarry. "Grass and trees have grown around it."

They walked down the decaying stairs, into the stone pit, and noticed a corridor covered by a thick wooden pole. Arkriat became alert at the sense of another being in the area.

"What makes you think there'll be someone here to repair the map?" Kol asked as he looked inside various crates.

"I don't know...but something must be here," Vekk responded, pointing to the corridor. "That pole would've rotted by now if it was undisturbed."

"Good point," Kol said he as knocked the pole onto the ground; the siblings entered, led by Arkriat.

The corridor was well-decorated and oddly clean, making it clear that it was in use. The walls were built from green marble and held up the silver roof above. They walked through the straight corridor, down to the single door opposite the opening.

Vekk cautiously opened it to find a Quarailian woman bashing two pieces of metal together. She had not noticed her visitors until Vekk greeted her.

She was alarmed, clearly having lacked visitors for several years.

"Who are you?" she asked, staring her down.

"I am Vekk and this is my brother Kol," Vekk told her, being careful not to make any sudden moves.

"What do you want?" she asked quickly, evidently distrustful of them.

"We need this map fixed," Vekk said, taking

it from Kol and showing it to the woman. "We mean no harm—I'm not a soldier, despite wearing the gear."

"I see," she said, taking the map. "I am Leterar and I can help you."

Vekk inquired about payment and Leterar agreed that she would be compensated in tasks.

"Hands can't fix this mess alone," she said, placing the map on her desk and analysing the breakages. "I can find stone and metals to begin repairs, but that's not all I need."

"What else?" Kol asked in frustration, wanting to escape the jungle as soon as possible.

"Wood. I need wood!" she said. "And some food. The trees are ripe this time of the year."

"We'll get those," Vekk said, quickly leading her brother and Arkriat outside.

"Where are we supposed to get food?" Vekk asked her brother as they left the quarry. Kol pointed to the red sticks protruding from the branches of the trees.

"We'll get them later," Vekk said, concerned as to whether the sticks were actually edible.

They searched for hours to find a source of wood or a tool that would allow them to cut down trees; Kol's spear proved to be too weak to topple the great trees and nothing Vekk possessed was strong enough to make a mark.

They came across a sudden stockpile of wood and stone, surrounding a door within the hill behind them. No one was nearby, yet the supplies appeared to have been strapped together recently; Vekk walked up to the door and called out to see if anyone lived nearby. A woman opened the door, having many of the features of the woman in the quarry, yet younger and clearly a different person.

"We need some of your wood," Vekk told her.

"How would you rather pay? Floras or a task?" she asked.

"Is there a third option?" Kol questioned, hoping to avoid complicating the mission further.

"No," she said. "Either find my sister or pay up."

"What's her name?" Vekk asked, feeling increasingly disconcerted by the woman.

"Leterar. She usually hides underground, just like her mother," the woman said bitterly.

"Is this a game?" Vekk muttered under her breath, hoping Leterar's sister did not hear her. The siblings decided that they would split up and Vekk would wait with the woman while Kol retrieved her sister.

The sun was firmly in the sky when Kol and Leterar reappeared, with the latter less than happy to see her sister; they began to argue and Vekk, Kol and Arkriat stood away.

"Give me the wood!" Leterar shouted at her sister, who vehemently refused, citing her sister's rage. They argued for several minutes, the repetitiveness of their words confusing Vekk and Kol.

Vekk soon intervened and demanded for the wood to be given over.

"You don't need wood to fix a map, you fool!" the woman told her, causing Vekk to back down.

"She's right," Kol said over her shoulder.

"I know, shut up," Vekk sneered as she impatiently waited for the sisters to finish their argument.

"Just fix our map so we can leave!" Kol shouted at Leterar, causing Arkriat to begin to bark.

"Get me food," Leterar said bluntly. In response, Kol walked over to a tree and threw his spear at one of the branches, causing the red sticks to fall onto the ground. He picked them up and handed them to her, surprising even Vekk with his boldness.

They walked quietly back to the quarry and Leterar spent several minutes finding materials while the siblings and Leterar's sister waited in silence.

"Let, I—" her sister began once she walked back in.

"No, Kessrar, I don't care. You abandoned our mother when she was dying," Leterar responded.

"Leritri was hardly my mother!" she snapped back.

Leritri? Vekk thought, *but she's not dead—at least, since we last saw her.*

"Did your mother live in Zrelyar?" Kol asked, clearly making a similar connection.

"Yes, she did. She's the reason we were exiled from the city," Kessrar replied. "The witch must be dead by now."

Kol began to describe the Leritri he knew and soon came to realise that they were referring to the same person.

"Leritri's alive," Kol told them. "We used to see her every day."

"She is a liar and a deceiver," Kessrar told them, having calmed slightly.

"Be glad that she's alive!" Leterar told her, slamming her hand on a table as she spoke.

Kessrar said nothing and instead turned to Vekk and Kol. "Never see that woman again. She's trouble."

"She can barely stand!" Vekk said.

"She's a good faker," Kessrar responded, laughing to herself.

They discussed Leritri and the state of Zrelyar for several minutes, until the sisters managed to come to a weak agreement on their views. Both Kessrar and Leterar began to calm down and spoke to the siblings in a calmer tone.

"I guess it was for the best that we were exiled, if the military are getting tougher on criminals," Kessrar said, as she checked on the map that Leterar was busy repairing.

"I've repaired most of the map, although the locations aren't showing," Leterar told them, handing it to Kol.

"So what are we supposed to use it for then?" Kol asked, seeing the broken technology behind her on the desk.

"We know one's probably in a city," Vekk said.

"There are many cities," Kol countered.

There was a short pause until Kessrar interrupted.

"I have made a decision," she told everyone.

"For what?" her sister asked.

"I want to join you," she told the siblings.

"Oh, we're not part of a group or anything," Vekk told her, with Kol reinforcing his sister behind her.

"Then we will seek one out," she said. "Do you have a ship?"

Kol told them of the burning wreckage and led them to the site of the crash so that they could scavenge materials.

"I've never built a ship before," Leterar told them as she pulled the window off Zavroon's burnt escape ship.

"That's reassuring," Vekk replied.

"Will you be joining me in our escape to find the rebels?" Kessrar asked the siblings, who politely declined her offer.

"I will," Leterar told her, surprising Vekk

and Kol.

"Thank...thank you," Kessrar replied, stealing a control panel from inside the ship.

"We'll need wood," Leterar said as she analysed the wreckage. Vekk and Kol agreed to collect it and ran off to Kessrar's former home. They arrived to revisit the giant tree trunks, which were piled atop each other.

"We're going to need to cut these down," Vekk said as she walked towards the home to find a cutting device or tool. As she entered, Kol tried to remove the straps with Arkriat and was eventually successful—too successful.

The tree trunks rolled out, causing Kol to dash out of the way and hide behind another load of logs.

"Kol?!" Vekk shouted as she heard the sound and rushed out of the house, only to see her brother missing and Arkriat appearing concerned.

Kol slowly exited from behind the stable logs to see his sister looking worried.

"I'm alright!" he shouted back. She sighed and walked back inside to find a weapon. Kol stepped over the fallen logs and walked inside to help his sister.

They found several axes, with the blades igniting on fire at rhythmic intervals before sizzling out. They carried them out on a mat that was laying on the floor and placed them beside the trunks.

"Cut them before the axe reignites—we don't want to burn the wood," Vekk told Kol as she poised herself to run.

As the axe in front of her extinguished its flames, she grabbed the handle and smashed it into the middle of one of the tree trunks, splitting it in half. Kol did the same and they both threw the axes back onto the mat before they ignited again.

Kol was too slow on one attempt and threw the axe at the trunk with little effort; it burnt the trunk and split the logs with precision. He pointed it out to his sister, who began to use the axe when ignited. They quickly collected the logs and met the sisters at the quarry.

They collectively worked for approximately one day to create a ship that was operational, albeit weak. The sisters thanked them and climbed inside, sitting on the metal stools that had been hastily made and prepared to take off. Vekk and Kol stood at the access ramp, which had not been yet closed, and spoke with the sisters.

"Are you sure you don't want to join us?" Kessrar asked them.

"No, we have business here," Kol said, despite Vekk's willingness to join them.

"I see," Kessrar responded. "We'll see you again."

The access ramp closed and the ship took off once Vekk and Kol were at a safe distance. Fire attacked the surrounding flora as the engines finally generated enough power and launched the ship into the sky, searching for the nearest town or city, as it would not hold together for long.

"What else do we have to do here?!" Vekk asked in frustration. "Why can't we leave?! The map is mostly fixed."

"We need to get Kretai," Kol told her with concern. Vekk immediately went silent and they walked towards the Ukrihive.

They entered to find the Ukrifars awake and socialising through a high-pitched humming sound, similar to the hum of the orb that had been previously heard.

"Hello," the orb cheerfully greeted as the siblings walked inside.

"Hello," Vekk said. "We're here for Kretai—our Ukrifar."

The other Ukrifars became silent and Kretai began to hum loudly to the orb, making short, aggressive sounds.

"The Ukrifar wishes you to state the meaning of your visit," the orb told the siblings, who both looked confused for several moments.

"We're...here to collect her and leave to find a city," Vekk told it, wondering if the orb had mistranslated. The orb hummed back to Kretai, who communicated with it once more.

"By context, I assume Kretai is the name of the Ukrifar," the orb said. "If so, she is curious as to why you are here."

"We're trying to find a key," Kol told it, appearing as confused as his sister. "It's under a city...we think."

"Try this!" The orb said as the walls at the back of chamber began to shift and fold back, revealing a hidden door and trapping many of the Ukrifars.

"You just crushed those Ukrifars!" Vekk said, pointing to the wall.

"They're in their pods," the orb told them. "They didn't want to go anywhere anyway."

Vekk, Kol and Arkriat cautiously walked to the door, taking note of the golden stone pillars that marked the entrance, which blended in with the hive walls. The corridor split into two different routes, with the siblings choosing to split up and Vekk leaving with Arkriat.

She walked through the left passage, curving around until she reached a large, square room that was heavily decorated with statues. She could hear muttering and whispering around her.

"Hello?!" she called out, listening intently for the whispered words.

"Destroyer..."

"She wants peace...to die."

"Murderer!"

"Please," she said loudly. "I need your help!"

"A con artist..."

"Falsifier..."

"...twisting the truth."

The voices continued, hardly acknowledging her confusion; they surrounded Vekk and Arkriat, giving the impression that they were spoken by the statues. Vekk saw two stone doors, both closed and requiring some sort of stimulus to open.

As Vekk searched for a switch, the doors suddenly opened by themselves and two large, robotic guardians entered the room, weapons drawn. They appeared to have been built centuries ago but were as active as if they had been recently created. They slowly ran towards Vekk and Arkriat, who quickly moved back to the exit but found that the door had locked. Vekk stood by the door as Arkriat ran towards one of the guardians, but was quickly swatted away. Vekk began to fire at their faces, having little success as they were much taller and stronger than she was; wires were visible under the transparent plastic covering that engulfed the robots' bodies.

"Liar!" Vekk heard in a deep, robotic voice from another room, followed by smashing and tearing.

Kol heard the sound from another room, looking behind him before realising he would not be able to intervene.

She has Arkriat with her, he thought to comfort himself.

He walked into a round room, filled with many orbs, slotted into carved out spaces in the wall that perfectly held them in place.

"Hello!" they all said simultaneously.

Kol walked around the room, looking confused.

"What are you?" he finally asked.

"Replacement orbs," they said. "But we can still answer your questions!"

"Where...where is the key I seek?" Kol asked them, still hearing a commotion in the other room.

Vekk was trying to escape, being pursued by the two giant guardians who refused to relent. She hid behind a statue, which was quickly knocked over and broken. Roaring was coming from a nearby room, which suddenly became louder with the sounds of cracking nearby.

She ran at one of the guardians, digging her dagger into its foot and causing it to malfunction for a second before it became more violent.

Help me! Vekk thought as the two guardians cornered her.

A crack became visible on the wall, quickly breaking and shattering as a giant leapt through, destroying most of the room; the ceiling began to crack and collapse upon them, killing the guardians and the giant. Vekk dashed out of the way but was trapped by a falling statue base, managing to cling onto Arkriat so that he could avoid the other toppled statues.

Kol was struggling to explain the key that he needed but was finally able to convey his message through explaining its use.

"One is in a city, another is in—" the orbs began, until the wall behind Kol burst open with rubble and destroyed the glass spheres. Kol managed to avoid the worst of the damage but glass littered the floor and the orbs appeared irreparable.

Kol quickly climbed up the rubble in an attempt to find his sister, who was nowhere to be seen. He dug through with his bare hands and the blunt end of the spear but found little.

He held back tears as he climbed up to the surface and re-entered the Ukrihive in search of help.

"My sister and my Garisal are trapped inside!" he told the original orb.

The orb hummed and the Ukrifars rose up, flying towards the temple entrance. They tore through the bricks and rock, breaking down the rubble and allowing Kol to follow behind to find his missing family. The Ukrifars quickly found Vekk and Arkriat, who were unconscious from the injuries they had received; Kol was forced to carry them individually to the Ukrihive, seeking further support from the orb.

"Please," he said. "Can you help them?"

"No," the orb told him.

"They'll die!" Kol said in response, not knowing of any nearby medical centres.

"I don't have the ability to do so," it replied, lacking sympathy for him. It began to close the entrance and freed the Ukrifars who were previously trapped behind the doors.

"Your spear?" the orb suggested.

Kol stared at his sister in silence as he unsheathed his spear and plunged it into her chest, followed by Arkriat's, an ability he had learnt from observing Vekk. They both awoke and Vekk grunted, before being embraced by Kol.

He helped his sister up and thanked the orb for its support.

"No," the orb replied.

"What do you mean?" Kol asked, backing towards the exit.

The walls shifted and blocked all routes of escape and the orb let out a high-pitched hum. The Ukrifars turned to them and repeated the hum, creating a chorus of unbearable noise. Kretai was the exception and flew towards her owners with an intention.

The orb split into four and began to emit light, progressively becoming brighter. The siblings stepped away and ran towards the blocked exit, jabbing it with any weapons they had. Kretai flew atop one of the orb fragments and dug her feet into it, eventually causing it to crack and crumble and damage the other sections of the orb as it fell.

The orb's light weakened and caused the Ukrifars to become louder. Kretai managed to locate a tiny crack in the wall and unlocked the door, allowing her and her owners to escape alongside Arkriat. The orb shattered but the Ukrihive was intact, drawing its inhabitants back inside to await a new leader.

"All of the replacement orbs are gone as well," Kol muttered, climbing back inside the main chamber to see what would happen to the Ukrihive. He could hear rumbling in the roof and called Vekk to join him. He instructed her to fire at the roof and she did so, dislodging another orb in the process, which fell onto the pedestal. The siblings began to turn towards the exit, fearing the actions of the new ruler of the Ukrifars.

"Wait!" it said, once adjusted into its new position.

The siblings turned around and listened as the orb apologised and spoke of a new threat.

"The Ukrifars are in danger of becoming extinct!" it told them while surrounded by the thousands of Ukrifars who seemed perfectly content.

"Are you trying to stall us?!" Vekk asked, evidently expecting further betrayal.

"The last orb sought revenge for the destruction of the underground temple," the orb said. "It failed and I shall not pursue this."

It began to detail the hunters who regularly patrolled the forest and shot many Ukrifars on sight, along with other animals who were completely defenceless. They tended to hunt for hour-long periods and then return to their camp, with the bodies left to rot or be eaten.

"Fine," Vekk said. "We'll help."

The siblings sat within the darkness and watched the larger animals fight for food and chase prey, while minuscule insects scattered away to avoid a quick death.

"How do we prepare for a battle?" Kol asked, laying with his spear beside him.

"We don't," Vekk said, watching a group of Ukrifars tear a larger animal apart. The Ukrihive had given her a teal set of armour as the soldier uniform she had been wearing had begun to break apart. Kol was given some light plating to provide minimal protection against attackers as only one full set of armour was available.

They lay in the thick bushes beside the cliff entrance and watched as several hunters entered, weapons drawn. They began to slash and shoot everything that moved, leaving the corpses and moving on to their next target. The siblings followed undetected and watched as they destroyed as many animal dens as possible and marched through the forest, disappearing into obscurity.

They conferred with the orb, who offered them sanctuary for the night inside the Ukrihive. They slept throughout the night and awoke in the day, where they began to make preparations such as marking positions and entry locations.

Once night arrived again, the siblings waited in the jungle foliage, facing the attacker's usual attack point. They watched as the armoured hunters entered as usual and aimed their weapons at everything nearby, almost perfect in precision. They shot all of the nearby animals and aimed towards the bushes, exactly where the siblings lay in wait. They were forced to run in opposite directions and began to face the group who had begun to fire rapidly.

Vekk fired at the hunters and ran with her dagger ready. She shot one of the hunters and an electrical explosion blasted from the helmet.

Robots? Vekk thought as she continued her approach.

Kol threw his spear at one hunter and ran to collect his weapon. He had come to the same conclusion as Vekk and knew the robots would be more dangerous than a living target.

Vekk slashed one of the hunters with her dagger and shot another while Kol impaled one hunter and threw its body onto the ground. Electrical explosions littered the area as Arkriat dragged dangerous robotic corpses away to clear space for the siblings to fight. Kretai scratched the sensors of each hunter, impairing their ability to detect their enemies.

As they took out the patrol, they saw one of the robots flashing and looked up to see an army approaching.

"Take the trees down," Vekk said.

Vekk fired at the incoming wave of hunters while Kol moved out of sight to cut the trees that lay aside the overwhelming forces. Arkriat ran at the robots with incredible speed, accompanied by Kretai who flew above him at an equal pace.

Kretai began to disable their sensors once again while Arkriat tore into them, giving Vekk time to catch up, as her aim required further practice. However, her armour naturally steadied her arm and helped her to hit her targets. Her speed was also accelerated by the armour, helping her move beyond her natural velocity.

Kol began stabbing into a tree left of the army with a flaming axe he had kept, creating a mark which he exploited to reach the core of the tree, taking many minutes to do so as the unbroken trees were large and incredibly difficult to cut. He then watched as Ukrifars flew towards the battle, with many aiming for the army while others headed for the trees.

They sped through several trees, causing them to split from the pressure and collapsed onto several rows of the army. Nearby, the collapse of the robots damaged their fellow soldiers and Vekk was able to clear out the rest of the army near her.

She helped Kol to place electrical charges on the trees and detonated them, slowing the next wave of soldiers. She aimed her handgun at the incoming wave and an electrical impulse travelled through her arm, which caused the gun to glow and pulse with electricity. Vekk fired repetitively at the soldiers, destroying many without sustaining any injuries.

Kol dashed to the right side of the battlefield, behind his sister. Ukrifars assisted him in destabilising the trees, which fell into the oncoming forces, allowing Vekk to continue her attack with a lower risk of being injured.

As Kol began to hack away at the next tree, the Ukrifars flew through before he was ready and broke through the right side of the tree, causing it to crack and fall towards Kol. He ran and leapt away as it fell, struggling to compose himself after his near death.

He thrusted his spear towards the Ukrifars, who were clenching the fallen tree, before he ran towards the soldiers; unlike his sister, he was lacking armour and was wearing little more than a thick underlay which offered him little defence from the collapsing trees. He smashed through the robots with his spear and they quickly eliminated the rest of the wave, despite Kol and Arkriat receiving several injuries.

"More are coming!" Vekk shouted as more robots approached from the thick jungle and into the open space, stepping over their fallen friends.

Arkriat and Kretai sped ahead of the siblings and began to tear through the enemy wave. Vekk ran to the nearest tree and tore through it with her dagger, bringing it down on the soldiers.

"Vekk!" Kol shouted as he narrowly avoided shots from the robots and missed his opponent with his spear, with his attacker then punching him in the face and causing Kol to fall to the ground, placing his hand over his face to protect it from more blows.

Vekk toppled another tree and ran into the enemy forces, fighting her way to Kol and ignoring all of the soldiers shooting at her. One successfully injured her arm but she fought through the pain and tore through the remaining soldiers to come to the aid of her brother. She continued to fire at the hunters as she laid her brother down and protected him.

The soldiers became harder to destroy as her attention was divided; she knew she had to make a choice.

"Arkriat, let's move."

She left Kol and ran for the soldiers, supercharging her handgun and taking down as many robots as she could. The Ukrifars began to collapse the trees once again upon the enemies and they quickly defeated the second wave. Vekk ran back to her brother and saw that he was struggling to move; she tried to help him up but he pulled away.

"You left me," he muttered as he used his arms to support his body in sitting upright. "You're lucky I'm not dead."

"I'm sorry, but I won't again," she told him, trying to reach out to him again. "Let's get going."

"You're not my protector," he said as she began to walk off. She stood still, without turning around.

"What?" she asked in shock.

"You're an awful protector," he snapped, standing up. "I've taken most of the pain on this journey and you've done nothing to alleviate that!"

"I've tried to defend you, but when we're split up it's hard to do that!" she responded with an irritated tone.

"You're shifting the blame to me!" Kol said. "You just told me to walk as if nothing happened a moment ago!"

"We need to get going!" Vekk said, beginning to walk away from him.

"No," he replied. "My health is more important than some keys."

"The health of an entire city is more important than just yours!" she snapped back, before going silent in shock of her own words.

Kol responded by walking off towards the distant army approaching, ignoring his sister as Arkriat and Kretai followed beside him.

"Kol, please!" Vekk said, hesitating before running after him. "I'm sorry!"

He kept walking, spear ready, towards the endless waves of soldiers.

CHAPTER 17

"Kol!" Vekk shouted, running and grabbing his shoulder.

"What is it?" he asked bluntly.

"I'm taking the lead," she said, "and Arkriat will protect you."

"You should've done that before," he replied as he ran into battle. They were now in an open field at the edge of the jungle and the soldiers were marching over the hills from their base—much larger than first imagined.

"A city!" Vekk said, pointing to the skyscraper in the distance.

"I see it," Kol muttered as he repositioned his spear to face the army ahead.

Vekk shot at the first row of soldiers, with Kol following behind Arkriat and destroying the remaining robots.

Vekk fired a shot that ricocheted off several soldiers and killed many more. She ran in with her dagger and took out most of the soldiers, while having to retreat as she opened the way for more to shoot at her.

They managed to thin the number of robots

approaching, despite the lack of trees to collapse on their opponents. Arkriat was tearing through the soldiers while Kretai and Kol held their focus.

It took longer to defeat the final wave but they were eventually successful and ran over the hills to the city, which was open for visitors.

They approached one of the few robot guards, who simply let them inside without any checks or queries; the city itself was grand and beautiful but lacked life. It was pristine but had no plants or people around—it was purely populated by robots. The road they were standing on was surrounded with stores; each building was plain, lacking the traditional need of attracting customers.

"I'm going to look for someone who can make me some gear—so I can defend myself," Kol said, looking through the doorways to see if he could locate a store that sold clothing or armour.

The glass skyscrapers were felt cold to touch, despite the rising sun shining directly at it. They were impressively tall and were packed with robots who were busily working to ensure the continued operations of the city.

As Vekk walked away from the marketplace, Kol sighed loudly and accompanied her. She glanced back at him but he continued facing ahead, fixated on their objective.

They passed through the marble streets and found a robot advising a group of other robots. It was painted differently to the others, likely to indicate a higher ranking. The siblings approached it and were welcomed by a blunt greeting. Vekk asked about the location of the fourth key but it did not understand and suggested that they should speak to a royal guard.

"Is your leader unavailable?" Vekk asked.

"It is likely," the information robot replied, before turning to assist another advice seeker.

They asked another robot for directions and it pointed them towards a lower level of the city, distinguished by the guards guarding the staircases that led lower. They ran over to the steps and explained their situation to the soldiers.

"We need to find a key," Vekk said. "It's for Zrelyar."

"What business is it of yours?" A robot asked, walking up the steps towards them.

"We're trying to shut down the beam that's destroying the planet," Kol said with little emotion.

"Help the residents of our city, the city of Drixav, and I shall provide what you seek," the robot told them.

"How do we know you have it?" Kol asked, hoping to avoid pointless expeditions.

The robot removed its necklace that contained oval-shaped amber key and held it out to the siblings.

"Ask for the prince when you are done," it told them, clearly referring to itself as the other guards bowed as the robot walked towards them.

"How will you know if we've completed the tasks?" Kol asked, staring at the key.

"Any citizen of Drixav can contact me," the prince said as it walked back down into the palace. The guards urged them to leave and they did so, looking around until they found a bot hovering by a doorway and emitting crying sounds.

"What's wrong?" Vekk asked as she approached cautiously.

"My creation has disappeared!" The robot said, looking over its shoulder.

"What does it look like?" Kol said. "We'll find it."

"He is small and has red markings," it told them. "He has been gone for two hours."

"Are you talking about your son?" Vekk asked her.

"No, he is my creation. The sun is in the sky," it said with a tone that indicated confusion.

"We'll look for him."

Vekk turned to Kol, who walked off with Kretai. She looked down at Arkriat, who followed her as she began to navigate the city.

Kol searched the pathways and found minuscule pieces of metal, clearly broken off something. He collected as much as he could in his hand and approached the nearest bot. "Can you tell me what these are parts of?"

"That's from someone's head!" it told him; Kol thanked it and searched the path for more broken pieces. He found more but they were in smaller quantities and gave him no clear direction. He stepped into a nearby store and asked about the incident, but none of the robots could help him. They watched him with distrust as he left, eyeing the metal pieces in his hand.

He searched in and under objects, finding nothing. He turned to Kretai, who flew towards the city centre as if she knew what she was searching for. Kol pursued, glaring at the metal box in the middle of the area that supported a beam similar to the one in Zrelyar.

He ran towards it to see that the door required identical keys, which suggested that the beams they had the same effect. However, the city of Drixav was less polluted and the door was in plain sight, without guards.

"We can't shut this down yet, unfortunately," said Kol, who had taken out his camera and verified the similarity of the key holes. He walked away and saw a small bot laying on the ground, which appeared to have red markings on its head. Running over, Kol dropped the metal chips he was holding and picked the bot up, seeing that it was missing a small part of the metal covering on its face.

"Pick me up," it said emotionlessly.

Kol complied and stabilised the robot so it would be able to answer his questions.

"What is that beam for?" he asked.

"I do not know."

Kol sighed, knowing it had likely experienced memory loss. "I think your creator's looking for you," he told the small bot.

"Thank you," it said in the same tone as before, hovering away to its home.

Kol and Kretai hurried towards the home and found Vekk discussing potential clues with its creator.

"We found him," Kol told them. "He's on his way back."

"Thank you so much," the robot said. "I'll let the prince know."

They walked away and searched for more people in need of assistance, with Kol walking at a distance from his sister to avoid conversation.

"You found him fast," Vekk remarked, ignoring Kol staring in the opposite direction to her.

"Yes—and another beam," Kol said.

"Like the Beam of Zrelyar?"

"Yes—this time it's the Beam of Drixav."

Vekk went silent for a moment before asking more questions about it so she could fully understand. As the conversation ceased, they saw two robots with similar features discussing something with a distressed tone throughout.

"Can we help?" Vekk interjected.

"Someone attacked our soldiers outside of the city. We need to fight against those brutes!" one of them said, as if recruiting for a war.

"I don't think that's necessary," Vekk replied, walking away to find a more favourable task.

They approached another robot, selling various items of clothing despite them not wearing anything aside from plating.

"Who are these clothes for?" Kol asked.

"Visitors, such as you!" The robot replied.

"Do you have anything...stronger?" Kol said. "I need something like my sister has."

"I can offer you something strong...if you can get the final piece for me to complete it," the robot told them.

"Do you have any clues as to where it is?"

"Try one of the governor's homes," the robot whispered.

"Which?" Vekk asked in a low voice.

"If I knew, I would not have asked you to get it," it said, moving away to sort merchandise.

Kol approached a bot and asked for directions, but was quickly ignored. As they walked around, they came across a grand marble villa with gold plating decorating each side; they saw two guards protecting the building. Kol ordered Arkriat to attack them and stood behind a corner as the Garisal caused a distraction. They climbed onto the balcony and ran inside, finding the house devoid of any robots or any other beings.

"How do we know this is the right place?" Vekk asked as she searched for the armour piece.

"Why do you expect me to know?" Kol said as he ran into the kitchen.

He looked inside the cabinets and food dispensers, feeling around for a secret door or hidden key. He looked under the dining slab and found a device attached to it. Pulling it off the magnetised table, he looked and saw that it showed a code that could be randomised easily. He continued to search the room for the hidden door but struggled to find anything.

I wish I had Kretai right now, he thought.

Vekk and Kretai searched a room containing a luxurious charging station, expecting to find the greatest secrets there. However, they were unsuccessful, even with Kretai's incredible identification abilities.

"Go and help Kol," Vekk ordered as she searched through a chest of valuables; Kretai flew out and down the slim halls to find her other owner.

Vekk left the bedroom and walked downstairs to find two large doors sealed shut.

Now I need a key card or...something, Vekk thought, dropping her handgun so she would know where to return once she found a key.

Kol saw Kretai fly inside the kitchen and he greeted her, before ordering her to find a vault door. They found nothing until Vekk walked in and told them of her discovery.

"You could've told me earlier!" Kol said as he followed her to the vault and entered the passcode. The doors shuddered and sank into the wall, revealing a vault full of the governor's riches and the greaves from a set of gear.

"That must be it," Kol said, walking towards it as Vekk reclaimed her handgun.

"It must be quite dusty," a robotic voice said behind him. He turned to see a robot, painted with dark colours and standing authoritatively.

"I assume you're the governor," Vekk said, grabbing Kretai and backing into the vault beside her brother.

"Yes," the robot replied, standing before the grand doors and locking them inside before the siblings and Kretai could escape.

"It's locked," Vekk said as she tried to open the doors, with little success.

"Really?" Kol asked in a sarcastic tone as he deactivated the security measures around the treasure and carefully lifted the greaves from the pedestal; He held them while Vekk and Kretai searched for an exit.

"Wait for the guards to come." Kol said calmly as he leant on the pedestal and waited.

Several robotic guardsmen soon opened the vault and ran inside, all aiming their weapons at the siblings. Vekk held her handgun and aimed it at the guards while Kol stood firm behind her, holding his spear unsteadily.

Vekk suddenly fired and ran at the guards with her dagger while Kol ran at, and impaled, one of the guards calling for backup; Kretai broke the robots' sensors and blinded them to the onslaught of the siblings. Once they had defeated the guardsmen, they escaped the vault and ran through the cold corridors.

Approaching a nearby window on the ground floor, the siblings climbed outside and ran past the guards into the city's crowds. Vekk, Kol and Kretai ran behind a wall to avoid detection and were soon joined by Arkriat, who was unable to distract the soldiers for any longer.

The armour shop stood out with the hologram that displayed atop its roof. Entering the shop, the robot was delighted to see the siblings.

Kol threw the stolen pair of greaves on the counter and the robot made a delighted noise before quickly taking them and going into a back room, shrouded in darkness. It returned and called out to the siblings, who quickly followed it inside. It shut the door and switched on a light, revealing a machine that held the rest of the armour set.

The robot inserted the greaves into the machine and pointed to an opening.

"Step inside."

Kol entered and stood still, allowing the machine to take hold of his body and resize the armour to his bodily specifications. He emerged with a jet-black set of armour that had the potential to rival the abilities of his sister's gear.

"I like this!" he said, testing the flexibility of the tunic beneath by swinging the spear ahead of him.

"Now test it properly," the robot said, taking a gun from a hidden compartment and aiming at him. "Attack me. I've already sent my thanks to the prince."

"Oh, I don't think that's—"

The robot fired at him and Kol dodged. He moved swiftly through the air and smashed his spear into the bot's central core, rendering it irreparable. A light flashed on the wall and sent an electrical signal into a deactivated bot, which began to radiate with light.

"Now that's done," Vekk said, "I guess we're equal now."

"We were equal to begin with," Kol said, swiftly walking out.

They exited to find a guard checking out the

shop front and eyeing the siblings with suspicion.

"We were just helping out," Vekk said as they walked behind another building to break the guard's gaze. A meat vendor called out to them, displaying many animal corpses for sale.

"That's disgusting," Vekk said, looking at the butchered Ukrifars.

"I bet you've killed worse," the vendor quipped. Vekk was shocked but kept walking.

"He's not wr—" Kol began as he held Kretai firmly in his hands, before she climbed onto his shoulder.

"I know."

They ran over to two policebots, who were repeating low, beeping sounds.

"Do you need help?" Kol asked them.

"We have lost a prisoner," one of the robots told them. "It is a danger to society."

"Do you have any clues as to where he's gone?" Vekk asked. "We don't even know what he looks like."

"It has black patterns, mostly circular," they were told. "It hovers and is very violent. It "It has probably gone to a populated area."

Vekk and Kol searched the area but failed to find any chaos in the regimented city. Kretai flew above, attempting to locate the bot with her superior sight while Arkriat searched the ground, his senses useless to find his inorganic target.

They approached the city centre, where a bot had electrocuted several innocent robots and was in the process of disabling another victim. Vekk pulled out her handgun and fired, causing the bot to become aware of their presence and rapidly hover away.

Kol leapt over a small wall and took out his spear, shouting to bystanders to slow the criminal down. Instead, they left the siblings to do their task alone.

Kretai sped towards the escaping robot and identified a crack in its plating. She pulled on its exposed wires and causing it to malfunction for a second, giving time for Vekk and Kol to reach it.

Vekk shot the robot's back and disabled its holographic lower body. Kol thrust his spear through the robot's arms and they carried it back to the policebots to receive their virtual payment.

"That's the wrong bot," the bots told them.

"He was attacking robots in a populated area," Kol countered.

"No, it looks like this," the policebot said, showing them a hologram of the robot. It was half the size of the average bot and was missing an arm and a portion of its head. "We will take the remains of the murderer you destroyed."

Why didn't you just show us that earlier? Vekk thought as Kol led them through the streets to once again search for the target. They quickly located the bot on a street corner conversing with a hooded man, who turned to look at them and ran off. The robot saw the siblings and began to fire at them; the crowd dispersed as Vekk began firing back at the robot. It then activated a holo-shield and produced a high-pitched buzzing sound that attracted several more criminals, who surrounded them.

Vekk supercharged her armour, sliding her fingers across the centre of her torso, and ran at the guards with her dagger and her handgun, firing rapidly and stabbing the bots as quickly as possible. Kol ran at their target and swung his spear at the short robot, who easily dodged him and knocked the spear out of his hands.

He grabbed the robot's gun and placed it through the shield, firing into the exposed wiring and disabling it. He assisted Vekk in destroying the remaining attackers after reclaiming his spear and turned to see that the target was attempting to escape, despite missing a head.

Vekk knelt down in front of it and attempted to drive her dagger through it, only for it to twist its remaining arm and pull her weapon from her hands. It then reactivated its shield and stood up, newly rearmed.

"I thought it was disabled," Kol said as he readied his spear.

"It will be, soon."

Vekk fired at the shield, causing it to flicker

for a few seconds as the robot lunged at her. Kol knocked the dagger from its hands using his spear and Arkriat tore its arm off. Kol inserted his spear through its chest and it began to lose functionality.

"It's...too...late," it said, collapsing to the ground. "He's...got it."

"Who?" Kol asked but the bot simply began to shut down. Vekk picked up her dagger and placed it onto her belt before they dragged the bot back to the authorities, who were horrified.

"We wanted it functioning!" the policebot told them.

"Aren't you able to extract something from it?" Vekk asked, looking down at the damaged bot.

"It was scheduled for punishment, not execution."

Kol attempted to justify their actions but the policebots were still irritated, as the task had not been completed properly. After evaluating the outcome, the bots begrudgingly agreed to send their appreciation to the prince.

"They are more than bots to each other," Vekk said. "These are their people."

"I've noticed that," Kol responded, searching for yet another person to aid. They instead saw the hooded figure that the robot had been conversing with. The figure was moving through the crowds, clearly unaware of Vekk and Kol's nearby presence.

The siblings agreed unanimously to chase them down and took different routes. Vekk ran through a crowd with Arkriat and Kretai and pushed the bots out of the way, which encouraged the target to retreat. Kol ran through alleys and jumped over low walls, managing to climb onto a balcony and watch the target from above.

He saw the figure beside a large sculpture watching warily as Vekk stealthily approached through the large crowd. Kol shivered with the expectation that he would witness Vekk impale another person, despite knowing they had both killed soldiers in the past.

I've become numb to death—the fights were so quick that I didn't even consider the people that I—we killed as actual people! he thought as he grasped the metal balcony rail and his body seized up.

Vekk and Arkriat suddenly sprinted towards the figure as Kretai flew above the crowds towards Kol to protect him. Vekk attempted to decapitate her target but the man grabbed her arm and twisted it behind her back; he threw his cloak onto Arkriat and stood behind Vekk, who had been pushed to the ground.

Not again, Kol thought, barely identifying the figure and ignoring the sensation of Kretai digging his claws into his shoulder.

"I guess it's fitting we're in a city again,"

Yarsnael said, aiming a gun at Vekk's head and grabbing a small bag, overfilled with powder.

"Why are you here?" she muttered as she fell unconscious. She caught a glimpse of Kol descending the building he had been watching from and saw him draw his spear.

Kol held his spear defensively as Yarsnael drew a sword and began an assault. The spear remained unwavering upon contact with the sharp weapon but Kol struggled to fight back; Yarsnael hit Kol in the face with his arm and knocked his opponent unconscious, leaving Arkriat and Kretai to flee.

They both awoke in a home that was within the city of Drixav, upon inspection of the architecture. Kol looked around and saw a robot preparing food. It turned to them after several minutes and gave them bowls of mysterious hard fruits.

"I am the only one in the city of Drixav that is specialised in the healing of living organisms," the robot told them in a soft voice.

"Where's the cloaked man?" Vekk asked, sitting up beside her brother.

"The medics did not see one," it said as it organised a medicinal meal.

"Thank you for helping us but we need to go," Kol said, moving to stand up. The robot instead walked over and slowly pushed him back down.

"The medicines are not working yet," it said. "I'm preparing more in case they are not effective."

Are you working for Yarsnael? Kol thought as the robot tried to comfort Vekk, who was becoming restless. Arkriat and Kretai were sat in the corner, watching the siblings and occasionally wandering over to check on their health.

"Let us help you with something to show our gratitude," Vekk said, hoping to leave as soon as possible.

"You're not in a particularly fit state to do so, but I understand the gesture," the robot said as it looked at the various bottles laid out on her desk.

Approximately an hour later, Vekk appealed to help once again and was granted the opportunity to leave; they had been tasked with finding a rare herb in the jungle so that the robot could stockpile supplies for future healing. The siblings, Arkriat and Kretai walked swiftly to the city's edge, knowing the jungle hosted a variety of plant life.

"Should we look for Yarsnael?" Kol said to his sister, the tension in his shoulders still present.

"He probably left a while ago to alert Zavroon," she replied.

They were given permission to leave the city and stepped over the destroyed hunter robots remains, back into the jungle. They had been given a hologram of the specific herb needed and began to search through the bushes, with Kretai squeaking to warn them away from dangerous fungi and fruit.

She suddenly let out a hum and summoned a group of Ukrifars from the Ukrihive nearby. Vekk watched in confusion, subconsciously expecting them to attack. She explained their objective using simple wording and the hologram and they soon assisted, picking through bushes and trees. They soon supplied the herb and the siblings thanked them, returning to the city as the Ukrifars returned to the Ukrihive.

The siblings entered the medic's home, with Arkriat and Kretai running in. They handed over the herb to the robot, who thanked them and sent its regards to the prince. The siblings sought out the royal robot and found it patrolling the palace grounds, missing the necklace that contained the key.

"Have we earnt the necklace yet?" Vekk asked, exhausted yet energised from the number of tasks they had completed.

"Yes, but it is too late," he said. "Another has won my gratitude."

"Who?!" Kol asked.

"A cloaked—"

"Thanks, we need to go."

Kol led Vekk away from the palace and they began to search for Yarsnael, whose location was entirely unknown.

"Kretai, find that spy, the Kerrilas." Kol ordered as he checked underneath a bin.

Vekk knelt down to study some broken pathing when gunfire burnt through the building beside them. They looked up to see a cloaked figure, who turned and ran.

"Arkriat! Chase him down!" Vekk yelled as she stood up and produced her dagger from her belt.

I just want a simple task for once, Kol thought to himself as he followed his sister, his spear in hand.

Bystanders parted to allow Vekk, Kol and Arkriat to pass through and pursue their target. Yarsnael fired the occasional shot behind him but missed the siblings every time.

Vekk continued to chase after him while Kol alerted a group of policebots, who refused to help, as Yarsnael had done nothing illegal from their perspective.

"He spoke to the criminal that I helped to arrest earlier!" Kol protested.

"We have no evidence of that," one of the bots told him, forcing Kol to abandon his plea and try to reach Yarsnael himself.

"You do not know the extent of my influence!" Yarsnael shouted, climbing over a high wall. The siblings managed to pursue but were significantly slowed by their inexperience in climbing and Arkriat was left behind the wall, forcing the Garisal to find another route while

Kretai simply flew over.

She flew ahead of the siblings and pulled Yarsnael's cloak onto the ground but he paid no attention and ignored the Ukrifar as she tried to distract him with high-pitched screams and by flying in front of his face.

Vekk managed to shoot Yarsnael in the back of the knee, causing him to stumble and clutch the key around his neck to ensure it was still in his possession. She sprinted towards him but he suddenly turned and shot her in the chest, creating a deep dent in her armour. She was surprised by the sudden retaliation and slowed, allowing him to escape further into the city.

They saw a military ship landing and people standing on the flat roofs, likely waiting to stop Vekk and Kol. However, Yarsnael moved away from them, searching for a different route to his destination.

The area was unlike the rest of the city; it was characterised by small buildings that were connected together and did not resemble the skyscrapers of the city centre. Vekk and Kol climbed onto one building and jumped onto the roofs of others, avoiding the people watching them intently.

Yarsnael slipped off a roof and fell onto a balcony, with Vekk and Kol jumping down to surround him.

"Your second defeat in our second city encounter," Kol said as he held his spear close to Yarsnael's neck.

"General Zavroon would like a rematch with both of you; I will ensure he has the opportunity to do so," Yarsnael said, his eyes darting around the area in search of an escape route.

"I don't think he'll be too keen after our last meeting," Vekk said sharply.

Yarsnael suddenly dashed for the railing beside Kol and kicked him in the face before jumping over.

"Stop him!" Vekk said as she leapt over the railing and followed him to the landing pad nearby. Kol quickly followed behind and watched as his target broke a window and ran through the other end of a house, terrifying a robot family who were receiving tunings by another bot.

He shot both Vekk and Kol in the legs, causing them to stumble for a moment as their amour absorbed the damage. Yarsnael was able to reach the landing pad, running onto the access ramp of the ship. Something prevented him from entering as he looked inside and immediately leapt back onto the landing pad, before the ship exploded and sent debris into the buildings nearby.

Vekk and Kol dashed into the house beside them and swiftly climbed onto the roof to catch Yarsnael. They saw him running through the large paths between the houses and stores and the siblings moved in opposing directions in order to corner him. They were slowed by their injuries but Kretai was able to keep track of him and alerted the siblings when he began to create significant distance between them.

Yarsnael was soon forced to slow down due to the streets becoming narrower and the siblings managed to corner him in a courtyard, with the only exit blocked by an exhausted Arkriat who had just managed to catch up.

"I see that your friends have prepared for this fight," Yarsnael said as the siblings approached him cautiously and Arkriat joined them.

"We don't have any friends," Vekk said.

As Yarsnael attempted to climb the wall behind him, an unidentified Quarailian jumped down and slashed him across the chest.

"You sure about that?" she said as she stood up to face the siblings and handed Kol the key from Yarsnael's neck.

CHAPTER 18

The journey back to the flat was quiet but filled with thoughts of ambition. He was temporarily returning to his flat to collect any leftover belongings as he was moving to York to apply to be an Astronaut at YAATO (York Aerodynamics and Astronaut Training Organisation). Fortunately for him, it was his birthplace and his parents still resided there; they had invited him to live with them.

He sat in the front of a self-driving taxi with Shadow and a couple of his personal belongings, staring at the renovated buildings in the area and the golden lights that illuminated them.

Ten years ago, in 2018, I started working for King Cut—now, I have a degree and am heading for goals beyond Earth; I couldn't have fathomed this five-ish years ago.

The taxi suddenly stopped itself and Arthur looked out to his old flat, now under renovation. He left Shadow outside walked up the familiar metal stairs, unlocking the door to his flat and walking inside.

It was untouched, albeit dusty from three years of disuse. He ran his fingers over the soft fabric of his sofa that had been worn down and was beginning to tear.

This is where I thought I would stay forever, He thought as he gazed onto the street below. *My darkest moment led me here and my greatest aspiration leads me away.*

He picked up Shadow's bowl and dusted it off, throwing it into the box he had placed beside the door. The dust in the air caused Arthur to sneeze repeatedly and he was glad that Shadow had not been forced to share the adverse effects.

He packed up all of Shadow's items and then took his electronics, even the broken devices for which he had little use. He took anything he could carry from his bedroom, as well as the canvas that hung above his desk in the living room. The cardboard boxes he was using were close to breaking but had saved him money—something he desperately needed to pay off his university debt.

He left the keys for the landlady and picked up Shadow's lead, which he had tied to a streetlamp to prevent Shadow from escaping. Arthur quickly dropped the lead but Shadow walked beside him without prompt as Arthur struggled to balance the many boxes of miscellaneous items.

A car soon pulled up and the driver waved to

him.

"I'm not doing this again," the driver said. "I'm supposed to be at work."

"I only need to move in once, Mum," Arthur said as he put his boxes in the back of the car and got in with Shadow.

The journey was silent but it gave Arthur time to think about his old flat, where he had lived for several years; he also had time to doubt himself on whether he was making a good decision.

That weird magic I used in the temple doesn't prove that those figures exist—what if they're not even linked?!

Shadow became restless as he wanted to leave the car, prolonging the journey, as they had to stop twice to walk him. By 7pm, they arrived at the house and Arthur walked up to the door with his mother. Arthur smiled awkwardly at his father and rushed inside, placing the box on the table and running back out to get Shadow.

As soon as they returned, Shadow was left to roam the house while Arthur picked up a letter that was lying on the dining room table.

Finally, he thought, confirming that the letter was his before tearing into the envelope.

Yes!

He looked at his new degree in Mechanical Engineering and stared at his name printed on the paper, confirming that he had achieved the qualification.

He quickly unpacked his bags and sat on his bed for a few moments. The sunlight had abandoned the view outside of his window and the light in his room had automatically activated.

Arthur, a voice whispered in his mind—a voice that was not his own.

He heard the howl of an animal outside, eerily similar to a wolf.

Arth—

A fox barked and ran through the bushes beside the house.

A—

A hum was heard beneath his bed.

Aaargh!

The man's voice ceased in Arthur's head. Arthur immediately stood up and left his room, his mind vacant of thoughts. Walking into the living room, he noticed that both his father and Shadow was missing.

"Where are Shadow and Dad?!" he asked his mother, who was laying on a sofa watching a nature documentary.

"They've gone out for a walk," she said. "He thought you would be too tired to do it."

"We took him out on the way here," he told her.

"Well, another walk won't hurt," she said, sitting up and pausing the TV. "Come and tell me about your journey to university again."

He provided her with the brief details of

his struggles, from the bakery to finding his degree. They spoke until Shadow returned and Arthur retreated to his room to apply to YAATO. He updated his CV and typed in the website's address; he had admired the website enough times to commit the address to muscle memory.

He joyfully browsed the job openings and felt a surge of adrenaline as he clicked to apply. He entered his details and attached his CV, sending his application off to his potential fellow employees or employer.

I'm glad they've softened the requirements—I don't have time to find experience.

"We never thought you'd get this far!" his father told him once Arthur had returned to the living room.

"Okay, thanks…" Arthur replied.

"Ruth, get our dinner ready, we need to celebrate!" his father said to his mother, whose face quickly turned from a smile to frustration.

"Cook it yourself! What've you done all day?" she said, sitting down to continue watching her programme.

"Right," Arthur said, awkwardly backing away. "I'll be in my room if you need me."

He spent some time updating his friends and acquaintances from university about his current work and completed unpacking his boxes and bags.

This better work out.

Several weeks later, he returned to his laptop once again and checked his e-mails. He was relieved to find a message sent from YAATO and opened it swiftly.

How was I...rejected?! He thought as he read through. He quickly e-mailed them back with a passionate plea, requesting another chance to prove himself.

He sat alone while he waited for a response, ruminating about his future and what other options remained.

I'm not working in a bakery again.

The darkness comforted him; it was a shield from the light outside which had rejected him and his aspirations. Shadow later barged inside and knocked the laptop to the ground, jumping onto the bed and comforting his owner.

"My life doesn't need to revolve around my job," Arthur said to him, stroking the dog's warm head.

His hand stilled as he turned his head to the window behind him, hearing a butterfly hit the glass due to the violent winds. He watched the blood run down the window and into the darkness.

He turned back to see Shadow's head glowing faintly as Arthur's skull and arms began to ache. Arthur purposely fell back and watched the ethereal daggers destroy his phone. Shadow yelped as broken metal scattered across the room; Arthur managed to slowly bring himself to his feet, fighting off the pain that had extended through his body.

Death. Death—or the fear of death—causes it.

Arthur grabbed his coat and ran out of the house, leaving Shadow behind. He wandered behind the building and located his bedroom window where the blood stained the glass.

Signs? Magic? Aliens? What's next, telepathy?!

He heard the birds chirping from the adjacent field and ran towards them. He climbed over a gate designed to prevent trespassers and walked into the long grass to find it vacant.

I've been watching too many TV shows, why am I expecting something supernatural?! This is real life!

A butterfly flew towards him and the chirping birds raised the volume of their songs.

Or is it? Is it real life or is it a dream? Arthur thought as the butterfly landed on his finger and he felt the pain drain away.

This isn't normal—I've never seen butterflies, or heard birds, at night. I must be hallucinating.

An adder approached him in the long grass. Arthur did not feel threatened by it, despite having a fear of snakes, and he watched as it wrapped itself around his leg; it tightened its grasp and Arthur's pain was revitalised in its assault on his body.

Arthur began to panic and unleashed an innumerable amount of ethereal daggers towards the creature, leaving it bleeding over the grass. The stench of fresh blood caused him to cover his nose as he moved away, walking through the long grass and relishing the dissipating pain.

What draws me to this place?

He began to hear a woman's voice in his mind, as if she was talking to him.

Wh—who is that? What are you doing? she said softly.

Who...are you? he thought, bewildered by the conversation contained within his head.

He heard a door slide open and an unintelligible voice that caused Arthur to fall to his knees.

My name is...wait— Arthur heard her say, until he passed out among the long grass.

Arthur was blinded by the sunlight that shone through his window. He turned to see Shadow sat on the bed opposite his, sleeping and unaware of his owner's return to consciousness. Once Arthur removed the duvet that held him down like a coffin lid, he stepped onto the floor and awoke Shadow to see his elated reaction.

His sudden movements alerted his parents, who threw open the door and stared in shock.

"We thought you were dead!" his mother said, visibly confused by his reawakening.

"We found you in a field—we thought you'd been murdered or something," his father told him.

"I thought I saw something outside," he told them as he reached for his laptop and looked through his e-mail inbox once more to find a reply from YAATO.

I know there's more to this world than jobs, but I need this job to meet that woman, Arthur thought as he located the e-mail and opened it. He read the message quickly, scanning for his final answer and seeking acceptance, knowing both his career and personal growth would be stunted by a second rejection.

"Yes!" he shouted once he found his response, which was worded as if it was a reluctant acceptance. They wanted to gauge his enthusiasm in an interview but informed him that he would be the first to be kicked from the programme if he was not performing according to expectations.

He began to exercise with vigour in the weeks before his job began as the fitness requirements were expectedly demanding. Formal interviews were scheduled to begin two weeks prior to the start of the job.

He had practised his answers for the first interview up until the anticipated day, which came quickly. He rehearsed his answers to a variety of questions while walking to YAATO headquarters and upon arrival he confidently walked inside the complex.

He sat among potential teammates for

a few minutes, before being called and led through the wide corridors to a room that was indistinguishable from the others that he had seen.

"Hi—hello," he said, as he was welcomed inside.

"Hello," the interviewer said. "Come sit down."

Arthur obliged and sat down, forcing his body to relax as he was spoken to. His grades were lower than the other candidates but Arthur explained his sharp lifestyle change, surprising the interviewer as it was clear that he was speaking honestly—or, at least, was an incredible liar.

"Lastly, do you have any questions?" the interviewer asked him.

"Is there an opportunity…to visit a planet out of this solar system?" he said, hoping to achieve his prime desire.

"No, you'll probably just visit one of the space stations above Earth or the other astronauts on Mars," he said. "You'd need extraterrestrial help to do so anyway."

"Okay, thanks," Arthur said, followed by a deep sigh.

"We'll call you soon for your next interview," he said, shaking hands with him.

"Thank you," he responded, calmly walking out.

Maybe I've already had extraterrestrial help,

he thought.

He returned home, immediately walking into his room where he began a video call with Rose and Alex.

"I can interview you when you return from space," Rose joked, "or look after your dog while you're gone."

"I hadn't thought about Shadow," Arthur said as he made notes on his laptop.

"I bet the work you do in space is nothing compared to my coursework," Alex said as he glared at the person who had just entered his room.

"I need to work out to prepare for the military training they'll give me," Arthur said. "I wonder if alien civilisations have to do the same."

"What if they don't have a military?" Alex said.

"If they do, it could be a militaristic regime," Rose suggested, "but who knows?"

"I will, hopefully," Arthur replied as he invited Shadow to sit beside him.

After their conversation was complete, Arthur updated his parents about his next steps and called Shadow to take him for a walk.

His next interviews turned out surprisingly well each time, giving Arthur confidence and allowing him to learn all of the information he required for his potential career.

He was determined not to be rejected again.

As time passed after his final interview, he waited anxiously for his final answer and finally received it. A confirmation of his willpower, Arthur knew he was finally en route to becoming an astronaut—assuming he would be able to pass the training.

On the day of the first training session, Arthur was given the opportunity to see who he would be working with. A variety of people were present, but he had never met any of them.

"Today you will begin your training," the instructor said. "Some of you have had military training and for those of you that haven't, you learn it soon enough."

He seems like a fun guy, Arthur thought, showing no emotion externally.

"But first, psychological testing," he said, approaching Arthur and another candidate. "If you follow Amy here, she'll lead you to the rooms."

Why does she have to be called Amy? Is this the psychological test? Arthur thought as he followed behind her and walked into a small room with another person.

He was asked about his skills in communication and working with others. He admitted his lack of communicative abilities and the woman was visibly concerned.

"I'm working on it," he told her. "I'll do whatever I must if it means I can succeed."

"Let's hope your eagerness persists," she said as she began questioning him on his other weaknesses. After ten minutes, she gave him a list of the skills that he needed to work on and explained solutions for each.

I'm glad I'm being paid for this, he thought as he thanked her and left the room.

He returned to the lobby and tried to converse with the other trainees but was unsuccessful.

"He'll be our greatest astronaut if he can get through all that," he heard from the woman behind him; she had been present with him when Amy had listed his flaws. He lashed out in his mind but externally acted as if nothing was wrong.

The rest of the day was filled with further psychological tests and checks to ensure they would be able to endure the difficult training that lay ahead. When Arthur was finished, he was mentally exhausted and spent the rest of the day alone.

In the following months, he managed to familiarise himself with those he worked and trained with in order to succeed in communication tasks. He also enjoyed the opportunity to interact with people who understood the struggles of training as Alex and Rose could only listen and talk about their own work.

Once the bulk of the psychological training concluded, the candidates' physical activity rapidly increased as they were placed in simulations that adjusted them to low-gravity environments; Arthur came to enjoy these training sessions as they provided a moment of discovery and intrigue amongst his monotonous schedule of exercise and lectures, the latter required for the technical aspect of training.

Arthur watched as many candidates became stressed and exhausted from the rigorous schedule, causing some to quit and be replaced by more experienced astronauts.

One morning he woke up to see his father standing uncomfortably close beside him; Arthur yelled upon seeing the shadow across his bed.

"What are you doing?!" he shouted in panic.

"We need to tell you something now. Your mother's waiting in the dining room."

Arthur grabbed his nearest clothes and quickly changed into them. He followed his father to find his mother glaring at his exhausted face.

"Your grandmother has a terminal illness," she said, barely giving Arthur time to sit down.

"What?" Arthur said in disbelief, staring at her. "I...I..."

I expected today to be difficult, but not like this.

"We've also adopted a child—Patrick," his father told him several seconds later.

"Wait, what? Wh—"

"Your uncle is unable to look after him anymore."

Arthur chose not to interrupt as they began telling him about his new brother, hoping that the conversation would end as quickly as possible.

"He's behind you," his mother told him. Arthur quickly turned in surprise and weakly smiled at Patrick, before turning back to his mother.

"You can't look after a child now!" Arthur said, before turning back to the boy behind him. "No offence, lad."

"We just wanted to relive a beautiful experience once more—but instead of you, it'll be with Patrick," she told him.

"He's a living being!" Arthur told his parents. "He's not just an 'experience' that you can have when you're bored!"

"What if you loo—"

"I'm going to space!" Arthur told them. "I don't have time to look after a child, especially if I need to check on my gran in the hospital!"

He saw that his father was about to speak, until he saw Arthur's pained expression and chose to hold back. Arthur silently stood up and walked towards his parent's house phone. Slowly picking it up and calling his instructor, he gave a vague explanation and requested a break for the day to solve all of his problems.

The instructor refused, instead recommending that he speak to an onsite mental health specialist.

No one's on my side today, he thought, as he got ready for work. He quickly left and tried to clear his head during the long walk to YAATO's training facilities. He arrived on time but was the final one inside and slipped into the briefing that was being given by the instructor.

The instructor detailed the day's activities, briefly describing the difficulties that awaited the candidates. Once they were vaguely aware of what to expect, they were led out of the building and taken to a large lake fully clothed, and told to reach the other side; the lake was incredibly deep and they were expected to carry heavy survival gear.

Are they trying to drown us? Arthur thought as he grabbed his backpack with one hand and placed it over his shoulder prepared to jump in.

"You can do this," a deep voice said behind him. Arthur turned to see an instructor looking back at him with a kind smile.

"Thank you, sir," he responded in a nervous tone, before forcing himself into the body of water; he struggled to remain afloat while dragging his bag through the murky water and chose to carry it on his back after a few seconds.

Many of his peers swam past him without diving and the instructors began yelling at him to move faster. The backpack routinely pushed him beneath the water and he would surface for a few seconds and move a couple of metres before being pulled back down.

I don't know if I want to do this, he thought as he removed his backpack again and placed one of the straps around his right leg.

He managed to swim for a few more seconds without sinking but continued to fear the death that would come for him if he sunk to the bottom of the lake.

Would the instructors save me?

As he struggled to keep afloat, he was suddenly reminded of his incident at the pool many years ago.

No, no! Not again!

He fought to keep his head above the water and pushed himself forward, trying to reach the middle of the lake while the others were almost at the end.

Why did I do this? Is it worth it?!

He elected to remove his jacket, boots and several other items that were weighing him down, excluding his backpack, and began to swim with more ease. He had a few of his survival items attached to his jacket but had decided that they were worth dropping if it meant he would not drown.

Panic had begun to form in his mind as his body began to ache and he was tempted to drop the backpack to make the journey much easier. He felt the eyes of his peers watching from the other side and embarrassment clutched his mind, with his career at risk due to his struggle.

Either I'm unemployed or I die—I really don't want to die.

He eventually reached the other side and collapsed to the ground, exhausted and suppressing the thoughts of death. One of the instructors looked down at him in disdain, before walking towards the other candidates.

"Now we will meet at the summit of this hill," she said, pointing to the giant mound beside her.

This is my old life, he thought, *my boss is cruel and I almost died.*

Regardless, he picked his bag up and followed behind the other candidates, trying to ignore his soaking clothes. Despite struggling to keep up with the other astronauts, he relished the opportunity to calm down without being watched.

They jumped across a missing section of the path and eventually reached the peak, being gifted a beautiful view of the surrounding fields and lakes.

Is this the life I want? Arthur thought as he looked at the facility to his right, *is it worth it?*

He gazed across the open fields and reflected on his supernatural experience that had occurred in the weeks prior to his acceptance to

YAATO.

You had better be out there, aliens. I'm not doing this for nothing.

Soon after, they walked back down the hill and crossed over a bridge that had extended over the lake that they had swam across. One of his peers attempted to push him back in, but he managed to remain steady and resisted the urge to return the gesture.

Back inside the main building, Arthur was led away from the rest of the group to a psychologist's office. He sat back down with the woman he had spoken to previously and she began to read the details of his performance off a small screen; the notes had been created by one of the instructors who had stayed behind to observe.

"The truth is…we don't know if you're ready to take on the intense training that comes with being an astronaut," she said. "You were previously told that you were the mostly likely to be removed from the programme."

"It was one mistake," Arthur told her, his voice becoming louder. "I'll do better in the future."

"Statistics and studies show that someone like you will most likely not complete their training," she told him.

"I've overcome a lot," he said. "I'm not ready to throw that away!"

"There's a lot of other jobs you can get with

your qualifications," she said in an attempt to reassure him.

So? I got them so I could become an astronaut! Just let me stay!

Arthur knew that becoming upset or angry would make the situation much worse and tried to keep his tone calm, summoning every example or promise he could think of to allow him to stay.

"What if you reapplied in a few years?" she suggested.

"Give me another chance," he said. "I want to get through this; this meeting has given me the encouragement to push through."

They sat in silence for several minutes as the psychologist debated her final decision. She ultimately chose to allow him to remain in the programme but warned him that he would have to perform consistently well.

Arthur thanked her profusely and left the room, rejoining his group of trainees. The day soon concluded and he returned home to isolate himself, hoping to find effective solutions to his weaknesses.

What am I doing wrong? he thought as he overthought his mistakes and imperfections. He analysed the list that he had been given by Amy the instructor but found many of the suggestions to be too generic.

Six days later, he returned home from training to find his parents sat on the sofa with

Patrick. They all suddenly stood up and Arthur saw that they were all wearing coats.

"Are you all okay?" he said, knowing he had become distant throughout the week.

"We need to see your grandmother now," his mother told him. "It's serious."

"What?" he replied, before being rushed out of the door.

As much as he wanted to be alone, he knew that he had to appreciate any moment he had left with his grandmother; his career would be forced to wait for this, if necessary.

They rushed through the hospital and found the correct ward after much confusion. Arthur felt uncomfortable around all of the elderly people surrounding him, each of them likely awaiting their final moments.

He came across his grandmother, who had become incredibly pale and thin. She no longer had the joyful spirit that Arthur remembered and he rushed to comfort her. She showed him a false smile and he smiled back, feeling sympathetic to her pain. Arthur's parents spoke to her for a while until she turned back to him.

"How's the bakery?" she asked cheerfully.

"Oh, I haven't worked there for a long time now," he said. "I've been to college and I'm currently doing astronaut training."

She laughed, thinking he had made a joke, but his parents confirmed that he was correct and her eyes widened.

"Oh, I'm so proud of you!" she said as she reached out to him with her bony fingers.

I wish I was proud of myself, he thought as he held her frail hand.

He felt a chill as he realised how close to death she really was; a life was disappearing in front of him. Suddenly a group of nurses and doctors came in, pushing themselves past the family.

"Vital signs are dropping quickly," one of the nurses said. Arthur's father suddenly became visibly tense and asked for clarification, which was quickly given—she was dying.

The medical staff quickly left them in peace as Arthur's grandmother expressed her love for her family and her hopes for them.

"I hope you go to space one day," she said to Arthur, clutching his hand tightly and laughing slightly. "You always spoke about being an astronaut when you were younger."

Arthur began to cry as she spoke to his parents and eventually began to lay down. Her eyes began to close, despite her attempts to keep them open, and her body relaxed, leaving her hand in Arthur's. He slowly let go and walked into the bathroom to regain his composure.

He failed to compose himself; he instead cried relentlessly as he replayed his grandmother's final words as many times as he possibly could. After half an hour, his parents came to see him, empathising with his emotive state and walking with him towards their car. Shadow was waiting in the back seat and immediately greeted Arthur once he opened the door. He got inside and sat with his dog, who licked the tears from Arthur's face. He clutched his dog, having reflected on the inevitability of death.

What if Shadow dies and I'm not able to be with him?

Once they returned home, Arthur sat in his room with Shadow and his parents drove off to deliver the news to his grandfather.

"I have no choice," Arthur said, laying on his bed. "I have to keep going."

The funeral was a month later, held in a church due to his grandmother's religious roots. He managed not to burst into tears at the sight of her coffin and tried to be strong for his family, despite never having met most of the relatives that were present in the church.

Her memory became a source of happiness to him—she believed in him in her final moments and he knew he could not betray her request. His instructors were surprised at his sudden increase in endurance despite what had happened.

He was no longer working for ruthless instructors—he was working for himself and his loved ones.

CHAPTER 19

"Is that better?" the medical bot asked Zavroon as he lay above the scattered robot parts.

"It will have to do," he said, struggling to stand up.

"You need rest," the bot told him.

"You need to know your place," he told the bot, who quickly apologised and left the room.

He looked at his weapons laying on the table beside him and reached out for one but was too weak to clutch its hilt. He sighed and returned to his bed, calling the robot to return to him.

The wait was long but it finally returned and injected him with a bubbling liquid that immediately restored his strength. The robot helped him to stand, despite his resistance, and Zavroon began to walk towards the door until he fell to the floor. The robot helped him back to his feet and he shoved it into the wall, taking a weapon and walking into the adjoined ward.

I hope Yarsnael has completed his task, he thought as he walked past the injured soldiers in disgust.

He made his way up a flight of stairs and to

the landing pad, where his Hoveroon awaited him. He quickly took control and flew to the palace—a place he only visited when necessary.

He was granted permission to land and docked his personal vehicle on a golden landing pad. He clambered out of the ship, trying to hide his limp, and approached the guards protecting the doors into the palace. The two guards bowed to him as the automatic doors opened to reveal the grand halls.

I will be gifted a home the size of this once I destroy the rebel group, he thought, *and those siblings.*

It took him longer than usual to make his way to the throne room but persisted nonetheless and alerted Lasapra's assistant to his desire for an audience with her. Zavroon stood to attention at the throne room doors and listened as the assistant announced his presence.

Once his name was heard, he entered to find Queen Lasapra waiting on her throne, regarding him with suspicion. He struggled to maintain his formal posture and his injuries began to reveal themselves.

"I see you have had some...trouble with the rebels," she said as he stumbled towards her.

"It's nothing, my Queen," he said, bowing to her. "I will destroy them as soon as I am able to."

"Who did this to you?" Lasapra asked, tapping her fingers on the arm of her throne and gesturing for him to stand.

"The rebel siblings," he told her as he stood up. "They will pay soon enough."

"And if they do not?"

"Then I will personally answer for my failures." Zavroon said.

"I will see that you do," she said. "What will you do to ensure my city's safety against these...misguided siblings?"

"I will target the keys that they search for and bring them to you," he said. "I have an agent who is currently retrieving one of them."

"You have learnt not to underestimate them," Lasapra said, raising her hands in the air and throwing them back down. "Adapt accordingly."

"They are nothing but children rebelling against their parents."

"That is your weakness. Overconfidence."

"I know I can kill them—I killed their brother!" Zavroon said passionately.

"I'm surprised you remember young Thrakalir's death—he was the only one who knew about their parent's fates."

"I have researched their family enough to know that Vekkilar and Kolansar were blind to the information that both their parents and Thrakalir knew."

"You managed to kill the boy without even noticing the threat that he posed—ensure that his siblings' deaths are as quick as his was and that the Beam of Zrelyar cannot ever be accessed by a civilian."

"My agent will be successful and I will retrieve the keys for you, my Queen," he promised with absolute confidence.

"I believe those siblings to be the greatest threat that my rule has ever faced," Lasapra told him. "See that you do."

"Hello," Kol said awkwardly, accepting the amber necklace and placing it around his neck. "Thank you."

"We're getting you out of here," the woman said, gesturing to the fellow Quarailians on the roof of the building. The five of them leapt to the ground, began to run through the narrow streets, and escorted the siblings, Arkriat and Kretai into the centre of the city of Drixav, followed by the woman who had saved them.

"I assume it was you who destroyed Yarsnael's ship," Vekk said.

"One of our better plans," she said.

Once they had left the area, they began to walk, instead of run, through the streets to avoid drawing attention. The Quarailian woman stayed with Vekk and Kol while the other Quarailians walked separately, at different paces and pretending to admire buildings and peruse stores so that they were not simply wandering around. The exception was two of the people, who were dragging Yarsnael through the streets; he was clearly visible as they did not have a box or crate to hide him inside.

"Where are we going?" Vekk asked quietly to avoid drawing attention.

"To our leader, who organised this mission," the woman said. "I think he'll be glad to see you safe."

Do you mean Zavroon? Why would he want us to be safe? Vekk thought. She looked at Kol with a great concern and he quickly interjected.

"Who are we meeting with?" Kol asked.

"Trust me. We've all been inspired by your rebellion and this is what you need to complete your objective," the woman vaguely told them as quietly as she could.

They walked far from the city, into a jungle clearing where a ship awaited them. It appeared to be a heavily modified Hoveroon with greater space; the main frame of the original vehicle was still visible, but compartments had been added on, including an additional room, which provided extra seating and storage.

The journey was much more comfortable than their last and the siblings began to learn cryptic pieces of information from the mysterious woman; she soon told the siblings that her name was Psykier and was second-in-command to the leader of their rebel group, who they were being taken to.

"Is that your real name?" Kol asked her.

"I don't...know my real name," she said without turning around. They stayed silent until they arrived at a city—one they recognised well.

"Why are we here?" Vekk asked with great concern.

"It's our base of operations," Psykier said. "We've been working on it since you were last here."

The ship gently touched down onto the landing pad and the rebels climbed out of the redesigned vehicle; they had landed in the centre, where the fountain used to be.

"Welcome to Modspi," Psykier said. "Now the most alive place in the entire desert."

The desert city that they had remembered was now full of people working and talking to each other. Two of them offered to take care of Arkriat and Kretai during their stay, to which the siblings agreed.

At least it's not full of corpses anymore, Kol thought.

"What did you do with the dead?" Kol asked as they wandered down a large road.

"We've buried them outside the city and dedicated one of the buildings here to a remembrance centre."

"Incredible," Vekk said as she saw the clean streets where she once ran down for help.

"I don't know if we should've taken Yarsnael here," Kol said quietly.

"He'll be under tight security, don't worry," Psykier said.

They entered one of the main skyscrapers and took a lift to the top floor. Once the doors opened, the three of them walked into a white room that was decorated with plants and seating areas. Four doors branched off the room and were constantly opened by rebels as they went about their daily business.

"Feel free to explore," Psykier said, before pointing to a door. "The boss is in the room to your left."

Kol walked through one of the doorways on the right, seeing a few people inside and hoping to learn more about the operation.

Vekk approached the door on the left and opened it. She walked down a corridor and opened a door to see a man standing at a glass window that curved from the floor to the roof. Vekk saw the beautiful view of the city that it provided but quickly turned her attention to the rebel leader, recognising his rigid stance and short hair.

"Reqilar?!" Vekk said, her body full of tension and thrill.

He looked shocked to hear her voice and turned to see her face.

"Vekkilar," he said, overwhelmed by emotion. "You're here!"

She walked quickly towards him and threw

her arms over his neck, hugging him with some tension in her arms. She slowly let go and looked into his eyes as the door closed behind them.

"I can't believe Psykier found you," he said. "She's incredible."

"She even captured Zavroon's top agent—Yarsnael," Vekk said as she stood beside the window with him and they looked out together. "Also, you can call me Vekk."

"I thought I'd never see you again, Vekk," he said, turning to her.

"I wanted to look for you but I didn't have time," she said.

"It's fine," he said. "I knew you were busy so I sent a specialised group to find you."

"You probably saved my life by warning me about Zavroon, back at that event," Vekk said.

"What happened to the suit I gave you?" he asked, admiring her new armour.

"It got lost in my escape from Zavroon, sorry," she said with a smile.

"It's fine," he told her." Helping the rebels… it's been even greater than I originally expected."

"They just let you lead them?" Vekk asked with hint of surprise.

"I had to prove my loyalty by killing a Zrelyarian governor or two, but that's essentially what happened," he said. "I lead, along with a Kerrilas named Sydrilla—but she works behind the scenes."

"How do the rebels know that they can trust you?" she asked.

"I've attacked many military targets and supported Psykier's decision to renovate Modspi," he said.

"Well, I trust you," she repeated with a smile. They embraced as Kol walked around the building, completely unaware of Reqilar's presence.

"So what exactly do you do?" Kol asked a group of rebels, while he eyed a list of room codes that one of them was holding.

"Steal from military bases—or destroy them," one said, taking a grenade from her belt, throwing it in the air and catching it.

"We're glad to have celebrities fighting by our side," another joked.

"Maybe I'll get a decent price for some of my artwork, then," Kol quipped.

"You paint?" he asked in surprise.

"Well, not recently," he responded. "Travelling the planet takes up a lot of my time—or all of it."

He waved awkwardly and walked away, making his way through the rooms on the lefthand side on the floor he was currently on. He located a door that required security clearance and approached the keypad, hearing talking and laughing through the thick metal doors.

Vekk must be in here, Kol thought as he entered the passcode he had memorised from the rebels that he had spoken with. As the two doors slid into the wall, he glared at Vekk and a tall man looking out at the city of Modspi, while they spoke as if they had known each other for years.

"Vekk?" Kol said, as Reqilar turned around to reveal himself. "Is that—that the commander? I thought…he was still at the mining base."

Vekk nodded in agreement as Kol backed towards the door, his ocular muscles tightening. "Don't worry he's not a threat—to us."

"I'll let the rebel boss know, just in case," Kol said with false confidence, quickly glancing at the Survivor's Last Hand sitting on a shelf behind Reqilar.

"I am the boss," Reqilar told him.

"No—that's not—why would they—" Kol stuttered as he exited Reqilar's quarters. He walked through the corridors and made his way outside to admire the changes to Modspi and to distract himself from Reqilar's presence. He visited Arkriat and Kretai, who were being cared for in a renovated building designed for animals.

Vekk smiled awkwardly at Reqilar as she approached the door.

"I guess I'll wait for your orders since I'm

under your command," she said.

"It doesn't work that way. You're like unpaid mercenaries," he said, smiling back. "You don't need to follow our hierarchy,"

"I still need to know what we're doing," she said as she disappeared around the corner. She met up with Kol and toured the city with him, remarking on the changes and the number of people within the rebellion. They had a quick meal in a nearby restaurant and continued their stroll surrounded by their temporary new home city.

"How old is the commander?" Kol asked, looking back at the main skyscraper.

"He's about fifty; I'm forty-one—we're only a couple years into adulthood in terms of Quarailian ages. You know that," she said quietly, "also, his name is Reqilar."

"It'll take a while for me to trust him," he said. "Did he tell you if we have to attend any meetings?"

"We're outside of the usual ranks," Vekk told him, "but we still need to know what to do."

"We're looking for the last key, that's what we're doing," Kol said fiercely, pointing to the amber key around his neck.

"Of course, but we can't use them without the rebels to help us get to them," she responded.

A messenger ran up to them and relayed a request from Reqilar to interrogate a prisoner, something they had little expertise in.

"We don't know how to do that!" Vekk protested.

"We should try," Kol said as they followed the messenger to the prisons.

They reached the skyscraper, its marble structure hiding the true purpose of the building. They spoke to the woman sat at the desk, who then led them to the top of the building; Yarsnael sat in a cell that was surrounded by guards. The siblings were given several devices, along with access to his prison cell.

"Neither of us imagined this would ever happen when we first met," Kol said, struggling to activate the devices.

"You won't learn anything here," the agent said defiantly.

"Oh, really?" Vekk said, throwing a round device at him. He allowed it to hit his arm and made no attempt to pick it up.

"A grenade?" he said emotionlessly. "Are you trying to kill us all?"

Vekk scrambled to reclaim the grenade while Kol began asking questions about Zavroon's current plans. He stayed silent despite Kol's attempts to reason or threaten.

"What will make you talk?" Vekk asked him.

"An invitation into your rebel group," he said.

"That's not happening," Kol said. "You've already deceived us more than once."

"Our last encounter ended with you claiming your key and meeting your rebel friends," he reminded them. "I technically brought you here."

"We're certainly not letting you join us," Vekk told him sternly.

"My blunt speech is simply the way that all Kerrilas' speak," he told them. "Is that why you detest me?"

"No, it's because you're a liar who has shown no desire to join us until you were captured!" she responded.

"Clever," he said. "Doesn't that remind you of the commander?"

"He was not at any risk before helping us!" Vekk said sharply.

"That's what you choose to believe," he said.

Kol grabbed Vekk's dagger from her belt and pushed Yarsnael into the wall.

"What is Zavroon planning next?" he asked.

Yarsnael laughed and refused to answer.

"Your only hope is torturing me. When will you bring yourself to do it?" he said to Kol.

"I don't think it is," Kol said. "In fact, we already know what he's doing."

"No, you don't," Yarsnael said with confidence.

"Is it something to do with this?" Kol said, gently pushing his amber necklace back and forth.

"It's clear that that was my goal," Yarsnael

responded, eyeing the key.

"He wants access to the Beam of Zrelyar for himself!" Vekk blurted out as she watched Yarsnael relax in spite of the knife to his neck.

"Exactly," Kol said, trying to hide his surprise. "So all your suffering was for nothing."

Yarsnael looked at him menacingly as he was released from the strong grip. "I know nothing of what he wants."

"Tell us how he will find the keys."

"You will lead him to them!" Yarsnael told them, before proceeding to laugh.

"Where is he now?" Vekk asked.

"I do not know," he responded. "I have lost contact with him."

"Another agent has already told us," Kol said. "We just want to see you confess."

"I am not lying to you," he said.

Vekk and Kol tried to break Yarsnael for several hours but were unsuccessful and began to believe that he was truly disconnected from Zavroon.

They left and reported to Reqilar, who called a meeting to plot their next move. He stood at the back of the room and explained the next aspect of their mission.

"Our overall goal is to storm Zrelyar and overthrow Queen Lasapra!" he said. "But first, we need to increase our own resources by stealing tanks and ships."

"I've heard that there are other rebel groups

across the planet," Kol said. "Shouldn't we unite them first?"

"Psykier and her elite forces are focused on doing so at this very moment," Reqilar said.

"You know what you're doing then," Kol said.

"Of course," he replied, typing something into the computer terminal behind him. "Although I thought you and Vekk—I mean Vekkilar, may be able to help with that later."

"We will," Vekk said.

"Our current objective is to build our military. Everyone here will be tasked with scouting a vehicle factory, before contacting me; I will send reinforcements to support you so can you steal the vehicles and escape mostly unharmed, preferably with the schematics in case anything needs to be fixed," Reqilar explained, showing a hologram of one of the factories.

He concluded the meeting and provided coordinates to the rebels, who quickly left to arm themselves. Reqilar turned to Vekk and kissed her while Kol turned away and called for her.

"Be safe," Reqilar said as he stepped away and began typing on a nearby computer.

"That'll be difficult when we're diving into enemy territory," Kol said.

"We'll try," Vekk said as she led Kol into the corridor outside. They exited the skyscraper and were immediately greeted by Leterar and Kessrar, who were flanked by Arkriat and Kretai.

"I was surprised when I was asked to deliver these animals to you," Leterar told them. "I didn't think I'd see either of you here."

"Didn't you say that we'd see each other again?" Kol asked as he greeted Arkriat and Kretai, placing the latter on his shoulder.

"I did." Kessrar said.

"We'll have to catch up another time, we've been assigned a high priority mission," Vekk said.

"It's not high pri—" Kol began, before being interrupted by Kessrar.

"We don't want to interrupt you, we'll speak before your next task," she said, leading her sister away.

Vekk and Kol managed to locate the hangar and boarded a stolen military vehicle that had been marked out for them.

Upon boarding, they were greeted by complex controls and little space to move.

"I don't know how to fly this," Vekk said as she sat in front of the controls.

"I hope you learn quickly," Kol replied, pulling Arkriat inside. "Our mission is to steal vehicles."

He sat beside her and tried to help her determine the purpose of the ten buttons that lay in front of Vekk. They struggled for several minutes and eventually managed to find the basic controls needed to take off.

The vehicle departed the city of Modspi and they flew to a warm forest, populated by thin trees that rose to meet them in the sky. The area was devoid of sentient life and the ashy industrial complex stood out amongst the natural beauty of Quelliare.

They landed on a nearby hill and watched as smoke billowed out of the metal grids on the roof while vehicles left the central factory, awaiting pickup. They watched the guards from afar, their regimented formation deterring the siblings from approaching without backup.

Vekk contacted Reqilar, exchanging greetings before she began to explain what they were able to see. Kol occasionally interjected but was mostly watching to ensure that they remained undiscovered.

He noticed a hovering camera moving towards them, its head emitting a high-pitched noise. Kol quickly notified Vekk, who was relaying information to Reqilar; the camera detected Kol's voice and sent a patrol towards the siblings.

"The other rebels could be in the same situation," Kol said. "Don't send all of your soldiers towards us."

"They are not in trouble right now," Reqilar said. "We have many more forces waiting if they are faced with resistance."

He said farewell to Vekk and disconnected,

leaving them to fight off the guards that were approaching quickly.

The siblings drew their weapons and Arkriat stood in a defensive position as the soldiers drew their guns and swords. The commander of the patrol ordered his subordinates to wait for him as he approached the siblings alone. Vekk aimed her handgun at his head as he walked closer.

"Surrender, rebels," he said, failing to recognise the siblings.

Another soldier walked up and notified the commander to the siblings' real identities. Vekk immediately began firing at them, Arkriat running into the patrol and taking down as many soldiers as he could without being shot.

The siblings slid down the hill on their backs and ran towards the soldiers, distracting them from Arkriat's attack while Kol ordered Kretai to fly inside the industrial complex.

They managed to dispatch the patrol but noticed that their fight had been watched; a soldier had monitored them from afar and was holding his hand to his ear to call reinforcements.

"I hope your partner hurries up!" Kol said as he watched for vehicles to angle towards them.

"We're not partners, and the rebels will be here as soon as they possibly can!" Vekk responded.

"Well, at least we have company while we

wait," Kol said as he pointed at the flying Hovercles speeding towards them at maximum velocity. They began to shoot at the siblings, who scattered and attempted to climb back up the hill behind them.

One of the Hovercles began to fire ahead of the siblings, creating large craters and blocking off escape routes. They ran into the middle of the field, watching the soldiers approaching them.

"Hurry up, Reqilar," Vekk muttered as soldiers began to surround their position.

"We've failed the only mission we were given," Kol told her as they stood closer together.

"We found the factory," Vekk said. "That was our mission."

"Part of our mission," he reminded her.

The incoming vehicles began to explode as several bombers flew over them and began to head for the factory.

Vekk, Kol and Arkriat managed to fight off the nearby soldiers who had become distracted by Reqilar's reinforcements.

"That was a lot sooner than I expected!" Kol shouted from the other side of the battle.

"They were likely already en route," Vekk said, running to shoot an enemy beside Arkriat.

They were able to clear the incoming attackers with the support of the rebels and moved onto the factory, now lacking full security. A stolen tank blasted through the tough walls and they entered the courtyard, which contained giant vehicles that appeared to be experimental. They began to activate but took time to reach their full potential.

Bombers attempted to destroy the factory, but its defences were seemingly impenetrable. However, they provided a distraction that allowed the rebels to airdrop several tanks and position them for an assault.

They began to weaken the external walls of the industrial complex as the siblings and rebel soldiers attacked the experimental vehicles before they could fully activate.

Despite their best efforts, the vehicles soon came to life, crushing as many soldiers as possible with the hulking feet that had been hidden underneath its heavy chassis. The siblings ran from the vehicles while Arkriat ran through enemy lines for an unclear goal.

Vekk and Kol began to climb the legs of separate vehicles and the rebel soldiers fired at the windows of the vehicles, causing the pilots to step away and leave the vehicle inactive. The siblings successfully reached the pilot's stations and self-destructed two of the vehicles, quickly climbing down before they collapsed onto the concrete floor.

The rebels managed to commandeer the remaining experimental vehicles and used them to blast through the factory doors. Rebels rushed inside and dispatched the security forces, while allowing the innocent workers to escape through a back entrance.

Vekk and Kol began to raid the factory, taking plans, tools, equipment—whatever they could carry. They ran across the grand assembly floor, ignoring the machines slowly shutting down from disuse and falling into a death-like state as electricity was cut from the building.

The rebels ran for the nearest ships in the adjoining hangar, familiarising themselves with the controls while still docked as the siblings sought the controls to open the roof so that they could escape.

"We need to find a button or something!" Kol said as he stole a pair of goggles from an unattended workbench and took command of a ship.

Vekk scanned the walls and managed to locate a control panel. She pulled a blue lever and watched as the hangar ceiling slid away and their allies fled.

As they departed, several rebels were suddenly shot down and the remaining ships turned to see the large number of military forces behind, pursuing the rogue vehicles.

That's impossible—they couldn't have expected us! Kol thought as he flew in front of the base to avoid damage.

Vekk ran back into the factory, hoping to find a hidden ship that had not been hijacked by the rebels. She could hear the trampling of the tanks coming towards her and resorted to taking cover behind a metal table, as she knew she could not escape.

Kol and the rebels destroyed some of the military forces that were advancing on the factory but soon retreated and returned to Modspi, expecting Vekk to be behind them.

Vekk hunkered behind a wall as the vehicles came to a halt and the soldiers piled out of them, running into the factory.

Wait for the rebels to clear a path, she thought, unaware that they had already left.

She had discarded her stolen items beside her and waited with her handgun drawn as she heard people approach. She moved silently and hid behind a workbench, its thick structure concealing her.

Authoritative footsteps approached and Vekk grabbed her knife from her belt. A commanding officer stood beside the workbench as Vekk's breathing ceased in crippling fear.

The officer stared at the top of her gun barrel and walked in front of her. He looked at her still figure and lifted her by the neck. She immediately dropped both weapons and was held against a wall.

"It's a shame they disposed of you in such a

dark place," the officer said, ensuring that she could not escape.

"They're just waiting to strike," Vekk said as her breath was choked from her.

"They've left," he replied. "I don't believe that they'll be coming back."

Vekk was overcome with shock and was unable to break the officer's hold on her. He tased her and allowed her to fall onto the cold concrete floor while the soldiers watched her with neutral expressions.

She felt her muscles seize and her body shake violently. She cried out before losing all control and laying limp on the floor, where she thought of her abandonment by Kol.

The officer ordered soldiers to drag her stunned body to a Hoverength and they complied, expecting no resistance from the infamous rebel.

Kol returned to Modspi and saw the pilots exiting their ships. He looked around for Vekk, Arkriat and Kretai, quickly becoming tense as he realised they were not present. He asked a pilot about their locations as fear entered his mind and forced him to consider the possibility that they were trapped inside.

"Your sister didn't have a vehicle when we left, and none of us picked up the animals," the pilot said. "You'll need a lot of ships to get back in there."

Kol immediately ran to the command centre and took the lift, knowing that the rebel leader would assist him. He knocked and entered the meeting room, where Reqilar was planning the next phase of the plan.

"How did the mission go?" Reqilar asked, focused on a hologram and only aware of Kol's presence from the sound of the doors.

"Vekk's still trapped inside," Kol said. "Soldiers have already swarmed the place."

"She's still inside?!" Reqilar asked, immediately looking up at Kol.

"We need some soldiers to—"

Reqilar passed some notes to the person beside him and headed for the lift, pursued by Kol. As they exited the building, Kol began to eye Reqilar as he ran for the hangar.

"I'll get her myself if I have to," Reqilar said.

"What about the traitor?" Kol asked.

"Traitor?"

"The military arrived far too quickly in order to stop us."

Reqilar ran to his personal ship but was held back by Kol, who glared at the former commander.

"We need to find who betrayed our group," Kol said calmly.

"You suspect me," Reqilar said knowingly.

"You're ex-military!" Kol said.

Reqilar pulled away from Kol and dashed to his ship's controls, closing the ramp as quickly as possible. Kol was still able to climb aboard, forcing him to join Reqilar on his mission.

"I imagine you have a lot of military contacts," Kol said, sitting down beside him.

"I do not speak to anyone in the military," he responded. "My betrayal is well-known."

"What if it's a ruse? Yarsnael tried to join us, why not you?" Kol countered.

"Yarsnael works for the General of the Royal Guard." Reqilar said. "I worked in a forgotten mine and Vekk offered me the chance to do something worthwhile."

"This isn't about Vekk," Kol told him. "I just don't believe that you changed over one dinner with her."

"If you feel so apathetic about your sister, why are you even here?"

"I was the one who told you that she got left behind—"

"And who left her behind?"

"I thought she was behind me! Vekk has protected me ever since we lost our brother and I would do anything to repay her!"

"There was a third sibling?" Reqilar asked in an attempt to elicit information from Kol, but he refused to divulge the sensitive information.

They remained in silence until they arrived at the factory, landing outside of the factory to conceal themselves from the military forces inside. Reqilar stepped through a gaping hole in the wall and watched the soldiers patrol the area, despite the valuables already having been stolen. He retreated to his ship and informed Kol, before flying inside the complex and landing on the factory roof.

They debarked and crossed over to the hangar, where the roof had been left open. They slid onto the walkway below and looked down to see Vekk in a special containment chamber that was flanked by six soldiers and an officer.

Kol and Reqilar lay down to avoid detection and watched as the officer taunted Vekk, who was unconscious. Soldiers patrolled the walkways beneath Kol and Reqilar but failed to spot them under the night sky as the moonlight favoured the nearby forest.

"Get back in the ship and support me," Reqilar told Kol, who quietly left after being given the order.

Reqilar listened as the ship engines hummed behind him. He watched the guards turn away from the centre of the room and he leapt over the rail, falling onto the walkway below. He felt the guards take notice of him and he jumped onto the hangar floor.

The guards began calling for support as Kol fired the ship's turrets at the walkways while Reqilar ran into the centre of the room and shot the officer at point-blank range, immediately killing him.

"You will pay for this," Reqilar told the soldiers as his ship destroyed another ship, sending debris across the hangar and forcing him to hide. Once it had subsided, he deactivated the containment chamber and freed Vekk as Kol landed Reqilar's ship outside.

"Vekk, Vekk!" Reqilar called as he shook her violently. She soon awoke and held onto him as he helped her onto his ship, with Kol assisting her onto a metal bed and Reqilar piloting the ship back to Modpsi.

"Wait," Kol said as he entered the cockpit. "Arkriat and Kretai!"

Reqilar sighed. "I doubt you will find them in that wreckage."

CHAPTER 20

Kretai lay in between the paws of Arkriat as she struggled for breath. A soldier had shot her mid-flight and she had lain inside the factory complex until Arkriat had detected the scent of blood and sought her out. He had carried her in his mouth and rescued her from the conflict by taking her into a nearby field.

Arkriat looked up at the full moons of Vennirein and Jarelin and grumbled with satisfaction as he felt warmth from the glowing necklace around his neck. He then turned to Kretai as she squealed in pain from her injuries.

They listened as military vehicles swarmed the factory, unaware of the two animals bathing in the moonlight. Searchlights were activated and Arkriat quickly stood up. He gently picked up Kretai and allowed her to rest in his mouth as he ran into the nearby forest that trembled due to mining activity in the area.

The smell of decaying carcasses overwhelmed Arkriat's senses as he navigated the deadly undergrowth and scanned the area for predators. While he was unfamiliar to the forest, he was able to identify dangerous features from his travels with his owners.

Arkriat's heavy feet crushed the insects beneath him and he soon began to sprint, as he tasted Kretai's blood on his tongue. Roughly a minute after he began to run, he felt the warmth of his necklace fade. He turned around and began searching the forest for its link to his necklace.

He rammed his nose through bushes as explosions were heard around him. He closed his eyes and opened his mouth to allow Kretai to breathe fresh air while the Garisal carefully sniffed the air to find the source of his intrigue. A familiar smell struck his nose, one that he had associated with Kol—it was not him, but something he owned.

Arkriat located a damaged ornate box filled with mint green sludge. He opened his mouth to taste it and accidentally realised his mistake as Kretai fell from his jaws and into the box. The Ukrifar suddenly relaxed as she felt her pain dissipate and relief from the wounds that once promised death.

She spent several minutes bathing in the sludge while Arkriat patrolled the area for predators, his necklace having regained its warmth and preventing Arkriat from freezing in the chilled forest air. Once Kretai was able to fly again, she stood on Arkriat's back as he sprinted through the thick bushes and grass that littered the forest floor.

They came across a pack of Garisals hunting for easy prey, mercilessly tearing apart anything that came close. Arkriat and Kretai lay in the thick flora and watched them act aggressively to a predator, who quickly retreated when the pack refused to back down.

Arkriat watched in confusion, knowing that Garisals were naturally fearful of predators. Kretai involuntarily squealed and gripped Arkriat's back as she expected a retaliation from the bloodthirsty creatures.

They did not hear her and turned away, likely to compile their animal corpses for a grand meal. Arkriat hesitantly emerged from the bushes and watched them walk away, the trees swaying gently and distorting the moonlight that illuminated portions of the forest.

Arkriat looked around for Vekk and Kol, in case they were present. However, he saw no sign of civilised life and continued to explore the forest in hope of finding his way back to his owners.

Kretai scanned the area for predators as Arkriat ran through the forest. She struggled to search the shadows as Arkriat was running fast enough that her sight was little more than a blur. She looked ahead, panicked as the Garisal almost ran into several obstructions, and slid underneath fallen trees.

She looked around at the strange surroundings and squealed in fear, knowing that Vekk and Kol were not present to protect her from potential threats. Shadows slid over the ground and rock formations stood in a way that resembled predators; Arkriat was not disconcerted by their surroundings and focused on finding shelter, knowing Kretai was vulnerable to attack.

Arkriat felt a thrill from running free, knowing that his owners were elsewhere. His natural instincts were unlocking themselves and increasing his awareness of nearby threats while Kretai struggled to adapt to the natural environment that surrounded her.

Kretai heard a growl and squealed to alert Arkriat. He slowed and studied the shadows with his piercing green eyes, sensing the Garisals that watched him. The growling grew louder and Arkriat suddenly broke into a sprint towards his observers.

The Garisals emerged from various obstructions and ran at Arkriat and Kretai. Kretai lifted herself off Arkriat's back and flew out of reach so that she was not a liability. Arkriat sensed the predators surrounding him and he quickly darted away from them.

Kretai flew to keep up with Arkriat, who was running at speeds, which the Garisals struggled to match. The forest's fauna parted to avoid being savaged and were surprised to see Kretai actively attempting to catch up to them.

The moons watched with an active interest, with both Arkriat and the predatory Garisals choosing to run through the moonlight to avoid any creatures that used the cover of the trees to their advantage.

Kretai soon began to tire and watched as Arkriat struggled to lose his pursuers, forcing him to stop running and growl aggressively at the other Garisals.

They huffed at him and disregarded his necklace, despite knowing it was a symbol of leadership. Arkriat suddenly howled at the moons and he began to pace defensively.

He did not expect the Garisals to respect the fact that he was an Alpha Garisal; if they were willing to attack deadly predators, they would not be concerned about a Garisal that had grown to be slightly larger than they were.

Kretai managed to reach them but chose to perch on a nearby rock formation, watching the encounter from afar.

Arkriat sought an escape route but saw no other option other than trying to outrun them. He expected them to suddenly attack, surprised that they had not already torn him apart.

"Stop!" a voice called out, speaking a dialect of the Quarailian language that Arkriat and Kretai recognised from Vekk and Kol. The Garisals immediately kneeled as a Quarailian woman stepped out of the bushes and approached Arkriat, who cowered in her presence.

Kretai watched, expecting the woman to harm Arkriat in some way. Instead, she commanded him to follow her and he did so, knowing he could not escape her Garisals. Kretai maintained her distance and studied her for something he could recognise, such as a uniform or a weapon.

She wore tattered green robes and a sheath, which was occupied by a sword. She walked with authority and her Garisals obediently followed behind her at identical speeds. Arkriat stood in between the woman and the Garisals, hoping that the woman would lead him and Kretai back to their owners.

Kretai recalled a similar woman from the beginning of their travels outside of Zrelyar, but did not know what the Quarailian had said to Vekk and Kol; the status of her morality was unknown.

They approached a giant rock that stood in the ground but instead of walking around, the woman tilted her head down and muttered something. The rock immediately disintegrated and she walked over the remaining pieces of stone with confidence.

"Hold!" she suddenly called out. She turned to Arkriat, knelt down and slid her hand under the tooth-shaped object that hung from his necklace. She suddenly tugged on it but Arkriat snapped at her and began barking, triggering the Garisals behind him to become aggressive.

"I'll get it later," she told him, waving her hand and causing the Garisals to become passive. Arkriat continued to follow her as she walked, feeling uncertain about her intentions.

The woman effortlessly cleared any obstructions that lay in her way and ordered her Garisals to hunt down any creatures that stood ahead of her. After ten minutes of walking, the ground around them lay barren and the decaying trees held out purple lanterns on their thin branches to light the way.

Kretai landed on one of the branches behind the group and escaped the woman's notice. The Ukrifar studied the lantern, before knocking it onto the ground and allowing it to smash. She escaped the scene as purple liquid spilled onto the ground and the woman turned around to study the broken object.

Her Garisals surrounded Arkriat while she knelt down and lifted up a piece of the broken glass. She looked around the area for the perpetrator, who watched from the shadows in fear of retaliation. The woman dropped the glass after several seconds and stood up to rejoin her pack.

Kretai emerged from the shadows and flew over them as they walked, observing Arkriat to ensure his wellbeing as he nervously followed behind the woman who led them to an unknown destination.

Kretai further studied her appearance; her back was straight and her arms swung with the small degree of freedom that she permitted them. She paid no attention to the stones she stepped over and faced forwards, expecting her Garisals to ward off threats. Her maroon hair was in a bun, held in place by a metal object shaped like a proud bird.

The group maintained a fast walk as they approached a small village of Quarailians and Kerrilas, working together to survive in the desolate area. Trees obscured the moonlight and covered the brick houses from aerial sightings while lanterns were hung nearby to deter predators.

The woman waved to an elderly Kerrilas, who nodded in response. The villagers seemed comforted by her presence as she walked past them, despite the pack of aggressive creatures behind her.

She led them into her brick home and locked the door behind her without looking back. Avoiding detection, Kretai managed to fly inside and hide behind an ornate box as the woman sat on one of the many padded metal seats in her living room.

"Hold!" she called out as her Garisals approached, causing them to sit simultaneously. Arkriat lingered by the door, fearing whatever power forced them into submission. The woman mumbled to herself, speaking words that neither Arkriat nor Kretai could interpret.

Kretai looked around the room but remained behind the box; she studied the marble tiles on the floor and noticed the absence of dirt, despite the ground outside being covered in dirt. The wooden panelling on the walls and the rustic furniture reminded Kretai of the simple homes of the Cristrials.

The woman spent an hour studying her holographic tablet and occasionally glancing at Arkriat's necklace. He watched her carefully and maintained an angered expression to mask his fear of her.

"Sleep!" she suddenly called out, and her Garisals immediately dropped to the floor and slept. Arkriat became startled and backed further towards the door he had entered through. The woman stared at him for several seconds as she stood up from her chair, before turning away and entering a room on her left.

The lights immediately switched off and Kretai quietly squealed, alerting Arkriat to her presence. He sat beside her as she began to scratch at the ornate box, her superior night vision providing her with clarity in the darkness.

She tried to open the box out of curiosity but Arkriat began to hit the floor repeatedly with his paw in an attempt to discourage her, hearing the frantic noises of the Ukrifar. Despite his attempts, he inadvertently nudged the lid of the box and revealed the mint green sludge inside.

Arkriat growled quietly and Kretai suppressed her intrigue, knowing Arkriat was warning her of the dangers of exploration. She flew behind a shelf and hid behind a large discarded camera to descend into a slumber, her head visible enough that she could clearly see Arkriat placing his head on the ground.

They awoke the next morning to see the woman staring out of one of the windows at the back of the house. Arkriat felt his necklace caught on the back of his ears, despite being hung around his neck the night before. He quickly shook his head and allowed it to fall into its correct place, knowing it had been deliberately moved.

The Garisals were sat in a line with their noses in the air. Kretai watched their eyes narrow as they stared at the camera in front of her. She remained hidden and waited for the woman to issue another command.

"Follow!" she ordered as she unlocked the door to her house and stepped outside, pursued by the domesticated animals. Arkriat huffed and walked behind them while Kretai remained in the house and sought a second, more secure hiding place.

Arkriat obediently followed the woman into the forest, watching as she cleared the natural obstructions that stood in her way. He glanced back at the house and attempted to discern Kretai's location but was unsuccessful. He turned back towards the woman and her Garisals and enjoyed the brisk walk in spite of the ambiguity of their goal.

Seeing the sunlight expose the hiding places of nocturnal animals brought Arkriat some relief, as he knew that they could not catch him by surprise. He sniffed the air and knew that nothing had laid claim to the area; the absence of predators was unusual but not alarming.

They entered a clearing where the woman began to wave her hands frantically. The Garisals watched calmly while Arkriat tensed his feet and arched his back, expecting her to attack someone or something.

"How do they work?!" she yelled, before destroying the nearby rock formations with words under her breath. The Garisals approached to support her but she waved her hand in front of her and they immediately backed away.

"You. Here," she said to Arkriat, pointing at the ground in front of her. He hesitantly approached and watched as she closed her eyes and crossed her arms. She spoke to him, using language he could not understand; her tone insinuated confusion and anger, despite the words being unintelligible by Arkriat.

She finally waved her hand and commanded him to step away, to which he complied. She stepped towards a tree and watched as it rapidly rotted away due to her presence. She placed a leaf under her hand and ran her finger over its rough surface and around the holes left by miniscule creatures, visibly excited as the green pigmentation drained and was replaced by a dark purple tint that now covered the rest of the leaves in the area.

"Find me prey!" she called out as she turned around, a large grin breaking across her face. "I must learn more!"

Arkriat remained in the clearing as the Garisals sprinted in various directions to fulfil their master's command. He watched them run with an unnatural lack of fear and determination; the woman had done something that Arkriat wanted to correct.

He watched her kill the wildlife around her by simply walking around. Her eyes narrowed as one of the Garisals returned and dropped a dead snake on the ground. She kicked its corpse and began shouting at it, as if it had been expected to answer all of her questions.

The Garisal that had returned observed her violent act with sadness; it knew the snake could have become food for a predator instead of a wasted object for the woman to exert her anger.

The other Garisals soon returned with prey and sat in a regimented line as the woman stared down at the corpses in front of her. Arkriat began to bark at her before she could interact with them, and she responded by approaching him and rotting the grass around him.

"I will make you see," she told him, grasping his head and causing him to enter a brief trance that lasted a few seconds; he saw flashes of himself where he was as large as a mountain and could trample enemies with ease. He relaxed as his mind told him that he was destined to be a protector—one that was incredibly successful at his role.

In the present, she spoke more words that could not be interpreted, before extending her hand towards him; he backed away in fear and she pursued him into the forest. She suddenly stopped and turned around, leaving him alone; Arkriat sat several metres away from the clearing and watched her redirect her attention to the corpses in front of her.

She tilted her head down to look at the animals in front of her and muttered a few words that brought about no change. As she brought her head back up, she stared into the eyes of Arkriat and frowned at him.

She lifted the head of a small canine animal and stared at its bloodied neck, before placing its head back on the ground. She paced around the clearing and suddenly stopped to face Arkriat, who was unsure why she had even visited the clearing in the first place.

"Follow!" she commanded. The Garisals moved into formation behind her and she marched through the decayed wildlife, back to the village. Arkriat looked into the forest but chose not to escape, fearing for the safety of Kretai.

At the moment that the woman and her Garisals left the house, Kretai had emerged from behind the discarded camera and began searching the room. She eyed the window to ensure that the woman did not turn back, as even Arkriat would be unable to defend the Ukrifar from the pack of Garisals that protected the woman with their lives.

Kretai hovered by the electronic fireplace and felt its warmth, remembering a time where her life was less chaotic. She suddenly remembered the threat that would return and hesitantly abandoned her comfort in favour of exploration.

She flew towards a metal door and rammed her head into a button beside it. The door remained shut, despite her attempts, as her weak body could not muster enough strength to open it. She hovered in front of it and frowned as she turned to see that the other doors were impenetrable by a Ukrifar.

She grumbled while searching for a window from which to escape. One of the back windows had been left open, so she slid through the gap and entered the locked room through a crack on the exterior wall.

The room was lit by candles and differed from the living room; instead of wooden walls and a tiled floor, the entire room was adorned with metal plating. Judging by the glowing stones and other relics inside, Kretai suspected that the material was chosen deliberately to prevent the room from being destroyed.

Kretai let out involuntarily squeaks as she hovered over the burning candles that offered her a slow death. She navigated her way towards a shelf that contained a golden orb in a transparent box—it had been taken from the Ukrihive and showed signs of damage, particularly scratches and cracks.

She managed to remove the lid of the box and attempted to pull the orb out. She dug her claws into the cracks and managed to roll it to the front of the box, which was hanging off the shelf. The weight of the orb caused it to fall into the mint green liquid below and Kretai squealed, as she feared that it had been broken.

The orb hit the ground and a large crack broke across its surface, although it did not shatter due to the liquid beneath it. Kretai flew down to it and it lit up as she approached it.

"What? Why am I not on the pedestal?!" the orb asked in a frightened tone, using a language that could only be heard and understood by Ukrifars. Kretai glanced around the room but could not see anything to place the orb atop of; even if she had found a pedestal, she was too weak to pick up the orb.

"You! You there! Ukrifar! Please help!" it called out. Kretai stared at it out of curiosity but was unable to comply with its request. It began to hum as it waited for rescue, unaware that she could not provide it.

"I wonder how long it's been since I was taken from the Ukrihive," it said as it watched Kretai search the room for something to carry it upon, "and I want to know who took me in the first place!"

Kretai soon returned, as she knew she could not get it outside on her own. She sat beside the orb as it mumbled and provided useless knowledge, hoping to find some support amongst the ramblings.

"I'm just glad you're not that woman who always comes in!" it told her. "She likes to use magic on me—I'm too fragile for that." Kretai immediately began to pay attention, as she knew nothing about the mysterious woman.

"I don't know her name, or her family, or anything like that," the orb told her, "but I know that she can defy the laws of nature to do her bidding—she has already proven that with her pack of mindless Garisals."

Kretai worried for Arkriat, knowing he could not resist her power; the Ukrifar relied on him and feared her own fate if she lost her last protector.

"Despite being young, she has a vast knowledge of ancient myths and beliefs. She knows they may aid her in developing her magic."

Kretai thought about the powers wielded by one of her owners; she had witnessed Vekk place a Floruna in a person's hand and conjure up emotional imagery that left both her and the other person in shock. Kretai had always watched in wonderment and wondered what else Quarailians were capable of.

"The magic-wielding woman has lived here since adolescence, I think," the orb continued. "I have concluded that she may be someone of importance, but I haven't received any new information for several years now so I can't check if that's true."

The orb was unable to provide any more information and pleaded for assistance once again but Kretai ignored it, choosing to search for more stolen treasures. She opened anything she could but did not find anything that she could recognise. However, one of the items that caught her attention was a mini statue inscribed with words that could not be read under the candlelight. She soon moved on as Ukrifars were not intelligent enough to read, regardless of the light level.

As she removed a tiny lock from a small metal box, she heard a slam and the pattering of many feet. She immediately assumed that the woman had returned and Kretai immediately escaped through the narrow crack in the wall.

Arkriat entered the house and lay beside the front door. He attempted to locate Kretai, who was hovering outside of the window but out of sight; he suddenly noticed a great discomfort from sitting beside the door and moved himself to sit behind the Garisals. Kretai watched from afar, eyeing the woman as she sat beside the fireplace.

"Where is that relic?!" the woman shouted, dropping her holographic tablet. She stood up and locked herself inside her treasury, forcing the Garisals to sit outside the door and wait for her return.

Kretai approached the house and grasped the outer windowsill with her claws, listening for the woman's return. The Ukrifar heard her pick up the orb and place it back onto the shelf, before extinguishing all of the candles. She re-entered the living room several minutes later and turned to Arkriat, her eyes narrowed as if she wanted to conceal her rage.

"I can't wait any longer. Give me the necklace," she told him. Arkriat did not oblige but did not back away, allowing her to approach and kneel in front of him. She reached over his head and Arkriat swiftly sunk his teeth into her hand, drawing blood.

The woman quickly rose to her feet in shock and struggled to comprehend the situation. Arkriat was similarly surprised by his instinctual response and immediately turned to the Garisals, who had stood up and began growling.

"Don't kill him, he's needed alive," she told the Garisals who surrounded Arkriat. Kretai flew into the house, taking advantage of Arkriat's unintentional diversion. She saw that the treasury door had been left open and entered, flying towards the orb.

"You're back!" the orb exclaimed. The woman turned her attention towards the room and walked inside with her eyes closed. The candles suddenly reignited with a dark blue flame and Kretai could see that she had begun sweating, despite the cold temperature of the room.

"Please, no flame magic!" the orb called out. Kretai sped across the room and caught the attention of the woman. She stepped over the candles and unsheathed her sword, waving it unpredictably in a vicious rage. She struggled to see Kretai, making her more dangerous with her sudden swings.

Kretai knocked the orb off the shelf once again and glass flew from its cracked surface, sending shards into four of the candles and slicing them through the centre. The wax slid onto the floor and forced the woman to retreat into the living room, as she feared stepping into the fire.

The Garisals leapt at Arkriat and he backed into a bookshelf, causing it to topple over. He managed to slide away and turned to face the woman, who was staring back at him and swinging her sword.

"I'll cut that necklace from your neck if I have to," she whispered as she pursued him. Kretai hovered in the air and watched, knowing she could not stop the woman.

Arkriat lunged at her legs and caused the sword to fall from the woman's hand. She attempted to grab his necklace but he backed away and turned to the front door. The Garisals ran at him and forced him into the corner of the room as the woman chuckled to herself.

"Just a few more minutes, now," she said, quickly turning to face Kretai. Kretai immediately squealed and returned to the treasury where the woman could not reach her, the flammable relics alight from the candle flames.

"Your necklace is a key," the woman said as she returned to Arkriat, "but not the type of key your owners are looking for—it's a key for a relic." Arkriat was confused by her words and focused on the Garisals who sought to tear him apart.

Kretai landed on the orb that lay amongst the flames and began to dig her claws into the cracks. It was already fragile and easily broke apart, causing a small explosion that burned a hole through the wall and allowed the fire to enter the living room.

Kretai flew towards the door but noticed a set of glowing stones beside her; she had seen them before. She darted towards them and managed to carry two, but one still remained that she could not pick up.

The treasury began to collapse on Kretai and she tried to swoop through the flames, her wing catching fire. She hit the marble tiles in the living room, which extinguished the flames but left her battered.

The fire caused an item from the fallen bookshelf to explode, causing the building to become unstable. The woman rushed towards the wall and pulled a switch, listening as a loud rumbling began and coincided with the collapse of the walls. "We'll all die, then."

The woman tried to break the wall behind Arkriat to collapse the roof on him but she could not, her powers affected by the injury on the palm of her hand. The Garisals were hesitant to attack Arkriat after seeing her wound, knowing that she was no longer strong enough to maintain control of them.

Arkriat noticed Kretai laying on the floor behind the woman and immediately barged through the Garisals to reach her. He picked the Ukrifar up with his teeth and placed her in his mouth, turning to face his opponents. He turned to see a glowing stone on the ground, similar to the ones that Kretai was clutching. He slowly moved and picked it up in his mouth as the woman watched in a stance that suggested she was ready to attack.

The living room had partially collapsed but provided enough space for Arkriat to run through the debris. He rammed his head into the front door and broke the lock, causing the door to open. The woman fought her way through the remains of her home and stepped outside, watching them run.

Arkriat was alarmed by the humming of engines above and stopped to search for the source, hoping it was someone they knew. The sound soon turned out to be two Hovercles and a Hoveroon, landing around them.

As a military general stepped out of the Hoveroon, he was immediately impaled by a dagger and fell to the ground. A woman stepped over his corpse and turned to face the one other Hoveroon that had opened. She lunged at the soldiers and quickly dispatched them, turning to face Arkriat.

"You're those creatures that travel with the siblings," she said as she approached. "What are you doing here?"

Arkriat opened his mouth to show Kretai's burnt wing and the woman looked at it, her expression conveying confusion and slight disgust.

"I can't do much about that—I'm a rebel, by the way," she said as she led them to the deceased general's Hoveroon. The military's vehicles were soundproof and the soldiers inside the Hovercles were unaware of what had happened.

As the doors closed, the rebel noticed the magic-wielding woman running at their vehicle, clearly angered that her plan had been foiled.

"Did she abduct you? No wonder you looked scared when I approached you," the rebel said as she entered the cockpit. Arkriat and Kretai sat in the adjacent room and tried to ease their tension, listening to the hum of the engines and hoping the woman controlling the ship could be trusted.

The hijacked Hoveroon departed the forest; Arkriat and Kretai became more relaxed and became excited at the concept of reuniting with Vekk and Kol, despite being unsure as to whether it would actually happen. The rebel was surprisingly relaxed, despite flying a stolen vehicle, and hummed to herself between the occasional question that she directed at Arkriat and Kretai.

"I am a rebel, I promise. I know Reqilar, Psykier, Kyyrarr, Vanr—why am I talking to animals, you probably don't know any of them," the rebel told them, choosing to remain silent for the duration of the flight.

Arkriat allowed Kretai to lay on the ground of the Hoveroon but remained beside her in case the rebel was deceiving them; their trust for strangers had eroded. The smell of Kretai's burnt wing infiltrated Arkriat's nostrils and caused him to shake his head violently to remove the stench, despite preferring cooked animals.

Arkriat slapped his paw on top of Kretai as they descended in order to prevent her from sliding across the ground. She squealed but was unable to break Arkriat's grip as the Hoveroon descended unsteadily; the rebel was clearly unaccustomed to piloting.

They soon landed and the rebel led them out of the vehicle, into the streets of Modspi. Arkriat carried Kretai in his mouth as they were taken to the command centre. The rebel approached Kol, who was looking out of a window with great concern in his eyes.

"Uh, I think these are yours," she told him. Kol turned around and his expression quickly changed to relief as he knelt on the ground and placed his arms around Arkriat. The Garisal allowed Kretai and the keys to drop from his mouth and Kol immediately scooped Kretai into his hands.

"What happened to her?" he asked, picking up the keys with his other hand and rushing towards the lift. Arkriat pursued him and the rebel watched as the doors closed.

"Thanks, by the way!" Kol called out as the doors sealed. They ran towards the nearest veterinary clinic and admitted Kretai. Knowing Reqilar was with Vekk at the hospital, Kol walked towards the building and bathed in the relief that had washed over him.

"I know you can't tell me what happened, I'm just glad you're both back," Kol told Arkriat; the Garisal huffed and walked at a slight distance out of distrust—he saw the lives of the Garisals under the magic-wielding woman and did not want to fall into a similar trap.

CHAPTER 21

"You'll be alright," Reqilar told Vekk, smiling at her, as she lay in a hospital bed, almost immobile; she weakly returned the smile as he left for his next meeting.

Vekk stared at the medical bot who was tending to her injuries as it focused on analysing the extent of the damage. It attempted to remove the bag from her belt and a decayed Floruna dropped to the floor.

"No, no," Vekk said, holding her hand out. It placed the plant into her hand and she suddenly felt tension throughout her head. In her mind, she heard breathing that was not her own, followed by a man speaking to her.

What draws me to this place? he asked.

Wh—who is that? What are you doing? she responded in thought, physically unable to release the Floruna in her hand.

Who...are you? he responded.

My name is...wait— Vekk thought as she watched Kol enter the room.

"Are you alright?" her brother asked as her hand loosened its grasp on the Floruna and watched it drop onto her chest.

"Who?"

"What? I asked if you're alright," Kol responded, his brow lowering to convey his confusion.

"Sorry. Yes, I'm doing fine."

"I'm sure you'll be glad to know that since your rescue, I have decided that Reqilar is trustworthy enough to follow," Kol said, deciding to ignore her unusual behaviour.

"I wasn't waiting for your verdict on him," Vekk responded. "That's good to know, though."

"You'll also be glad to know that Arkriat and Kretai are back, along with the keys," Kol told her. "One of the rebels found them in a nearby forest."

"I thought we'd lost them."

"They also found the three keys we had lost. I don't know how."

"That's one less thing to worry about."

Kol nodded and clutched the end of Vekk's hospital bed. She smiled at Kol to mask the agony she felt from the stabbing pain in her chest and the various other injuries that had been inflicted during her capture.

Kol returned the smile and left the room so that she could rest. He left the hospital and met up with Reqilar to discuss their future plans, feeling a grudging respect for the rebel leader since Vekk's rescue.

Working alone for the next few weeks, Kol struggled to lead without the aid of his sister and instead carried out smaller missions underneath actual experienced leaders who could efficiently complete their goals.

He also utilised the services offered by his allies; one of the shops in Modspi had been renovated to offer repairs on items and he managed to find someone who was able to upgrade the map—the tracker was repaired and the location of the final key was revealed, although it appeared to be constantly moving.

Reqilar advised Kol to hold off on finding the key until Vekk was available and the rebels were ready to attack Zrelyar, conscious of the risk of losing it before the final assault. While Vekk did recover in the following weeks, the rebels were not yet powerful enough to face Zrelyar's military.

A week after Vekk had recovered, Reqilar called a meeting to discuss their next objective; it would be one of the final missions before the rebels focused entirely on attacking Zrelyar.

"For our assault, we will need soldiers," Reqilar told the room. "We have located many individual rebel groups who are open to communication—with a little persuasion."

"Are we all splitting up, as we did with the factories?" Vekk asked nervously.

"In a way, yes. Available rebel soldiers will be split into groups and sent to...persuade...

these independent groups to join us,"

"Aren't we supposed to be the good side?" one of the officers sat at the table asked.

"I did not say to beat them until they agreed," he told her. "I hoped that you would infer my meaning—you should speak using language that will subconsciously influence them."

"Understood," she responded uncertainly.

"Everyone will be given a group to seek out," Reqilar said, sliding holographic devices across the table to each person. "Psykier has divided every available rebel into groups depending on their abilities and skills—you will work with them to ensure that the independent groups comply."

"What about us?" Vekk asked.

"What about you?" Reqilar responded. "You will go with Kolansar and your animals to recruit rebels."

Vekk glared at him for a moment, before studying their assigned group on one of the holograms.

"We still need to find the final key for the final assault," Kol said. "When can we do that?"

"Once you successfully recruit the rebels, you can search for it," Reqilar told them, watching as the officers vacated the room

"Why do we get the secretive group?" Vekk asked, looking at the lack of information available.

"You have a good reputation with them," Reqilar said. "They appreciate the supplies you allowed them to steal from my mining operation."

"Hopefully I won't get left behind on this mission," Vekk said in an accusational tone. She quickly left the meeting room, pursued by Kol. They met up with Arkriat and Kretai and boarded a stolen shuttle, departing the hangar and flying towards the snowy forest that they had previously explored.

"He still acts like he's better than us," Kol said, sitting beside Vekk and watching her struggle to control the vehicle.

"I don't understand why he was so aggressive to questions," Vekk responded as she reached across the control panel and pulled a beige lever.

"Maybe it's just stress."

"I expect it's his military past taking over, he has a lot of responsibility right now. Still, I don't appreciate his...arrogance."

They flew near Reqilar's old mining base and saw several military transports nearby. Vekk struggled to turn the shuttle away using the unfamiliar controls, managing to divert them away from the snowy lands. They passed great forests comprised of giant flowers and monstrous creatures, as well as inverted mountain ranges that reached deep into the surface of Quelliare and concluded at a fine point.

"Quelliare is surprisingly beautiful," Kol said as he stared out of the glass in front of him. "Think about the billions of creatures down there...they're completely unaware of our struggles as sentient beings."

Vekk remained silent as she took a sharp turn and began flying back towards the snowy forest. Kol pulled out the map and saw that the final key was nearby, close enough that they could reach it.

"We have to find the rebels first," Vekk told him, seeing the map in the corner of her eye and predicting what her brother was planning to say.

"I know," Kol said with a sigh; he gazed longingly at the pink-stemmed roses beneath them. He looked at his sister to see her focusing on the sky ahead as she resisted the draw of freedom.

They soon re-entered the icy forest and landed in the middle of a blinding blizzard, which masked the night sky above. They vacated the shuttle and pushed through the storm, shielding their eyes to avoid the mix of snow and sand that flew at their faces.

Kol dug his feet into the ground and double-checked the information that he had been given; he struggled to see the location amongst the powerful storm. Vekk yelled to Kol and he called back, running to her.

"I can't find Arkriat and Kretai!" Vekk

shouted as she stopped her brother from being knocked off balance.

Vekk and Kol ran separately through the storm to find them. After several minutes without success, they reunited and stood close as the howling storm grew quieter.

A click was heard. Multiple figures suddenly rose from the ground, creating a circle around the fearful siblings.

"I thought you worked alone," one of them said.

"We work with Reqilar!" Vekk shouted as the screams of the wind blasted in her ear.

"Let's discuss this further, then," one of the figures said as a circular platform detached from the ground and lowered the siblings below the surface.

"Wait!" Kol said. "Arkriat and Kretai are still lost!"

"Again," Vekk said. "We've lost them again."

Once they reached the underground base, the figures gestured for the siblings to step inside but they refused.

"We need to find them," Vekk said.

"Fine. Hurry up."

Kol suddenly stepped off the platform as it rose, leaving Vekk to find Arkriat and Kretai alone.

"Do you need to discuss as a pair or will doing it alone suffice?" one of the figures asked Kol, their faces now visible as they had protection from the storm; the group consisted of both Quarailians and Kerrilas.

"I can...do it," Kol said as he was led to a meeting room. They were inside a grand underground cave, filled with various objects and furniture. Some Kerrilas rebels were present and working on projects or sorting shelves.

Kol and a group of the rebels sat around a metal table, clearly having been stolen from the military, and began the diplomatic discussions.

"Do...you know why we're here?" Kol asked.

"No," the rebel at the opposite end of the table said. "We just knew you were coming."

"Reqilar wants you to join his group of rebels so that we can take down Lasapra," Kol told them.

"What's in it for us?" she asked, narrowing her eyes.

"You won't need to fight the military anymore if we win," he responded. "I imagine that you would prefer to live a more...legal...lifestyle."

"Not necessarily," the woman countered.

"So what do you want?" he asked.

Vekk ran through the cold blizzard, pushing through mounds of snow and sand, and was finally able to find Arkriat standing rigid in the snow. She ran up to him and hugged him, before telling him to follow her. He made a wide array of noises to indicate his displeasure while they looked for Kretai, with both of them knowing that the small Ukrifar was unable to defend herself fully.

Arkriat stared into the storm, which was growing quieter but maintained a flurry of particles that frequently entered Vekk's eyes; she was forced to stop and remove them.

"What is it?!" Vekk yelled, loosely holding her hand over her eyes and looking down at the ground. She stood defiantly in the snow, waiting for the storm to pass, but it continued as she chose not to move.

She heard a sound and looked up, seeing only Arkriat standing in front of her—the noise was not from him. She began to relax and watched the snow drop as the storm calmed; she retracted her hand when it was clear enough to see through and saw many fallen trees, being chewed on by a lone Garisal who proceeded to flee.

"Come back!" she shouted as she sprinted after it; she was outrun by Arkriat, who managed to tire the feral Garisal and slow it down.

Vekk's boots dug up the snow beneath her feet as she ran; she struggled to run in the thick snow and resorted to firing her handgun at the Garisal, missing most of the shots. She threw her dagger and it hit the ground beside the feral Garisal—it slowed down enough for Vekk to catch up and shoot its back legs.

It squealed and dropped Kretai; Vekk picked her up and checked her injuries, noticing deep bite marks in a circular shape around her body. Vekk held her close as Arkriat approached and watched the feral Garisal with distrust.

"We need to get you to shelter," Vekk muttered as she and Arkriat ran back to the rebel group.

Kol was trying to renegotiate the independent rebel's requests for power but was failing, as he did not know what Reqilar's rebel group could offer them in exchange for their co-operation.

"You can live freely," Kol said. "I assume you aren't in this cave by choice."

The rebels began to mutter between them, speaking quietly so that their speech was unintelligible and Kol had to wait for them to present their ideas to him.

"If you kill my daughter and allow me to take her place, I will join you," one of the Quarailian women told him.

"Who's your daughter?" he asked her, doubtful that he could fulfil her request.

"I do not know what name she goes by," the woman said, opening a hologram and sliding it across to him, "but she looks like this."

"That's Psykier," he said quietly, then raising his voice. "How do you not know your own daughter's name?"

"I never gave her a name," she responded.

"She's part of a special forces group and one of Reqilar's closest allies," Kol said. "He wouldn't let me do that, even if I wanted to."

"Would he prefer her skills or our skills?" the woman asked.

"Well—" Kol began as he heard Vekk shouting above him.

"Get her inside," the woman said to the other rebels. They promptly left and stood on platforms, rising into the snow outside.

"Why do you want to kill your own daughter?" Kol asked her.

"I don't want to face her after abandoning her," she told him.

"She's a good person, I doubt she'd want to kill you," Kol said as Vekk walked inside.

"We helped you get supplies," Vekk said. "Several months ago, you stole supplies from a vehicle that we controlled."

"That's a fair point," one of the rebels said quietly to the woman.

"Alright then," the woman said. "We'll join you…if you help us out."

"As long as it doesn't involve killing your daughter," Kol muttered.

"You must kill a ceremonial beast that hides within the depths of this cave," she said. "You must then harvest its heart and detonate it to break into a nearby prison to save our fellow rebels."

"Detonate a heart?" Vekk repeated in confusion.

"The heart of the beast is explosive, be cautious when carrying it," the woman replied.

"Is killing this ceremonial beast going to anger anyone?" Kol asked as he slowly stood up.

"No," she said. "It's only ceremonial to us as we sacrifice our own to prevent it from raiding our cavern."

"It sounds like we have an easy task then," Vekk said sarcastically, taking out her knife and her handgun immediately and holding them beside her. They began to walk towards the door until they were interrupted.

"We can heal your Ukrifar while you fight it," one of the rebels told them.

"How can we trust you?" Vekk said. "You're sending us to fight a beast you can't even kill yourselves."

"Leave someone here then," she said. "It'll make the fight more difficult, though."

"Arkriat, stay here and guard Kretai," Kol said, pointing to Kretai. Vekk handed over the Ukrifar and the siblings began to trek through the dark caves.

"Do you think we can trust these rebels?" Vekk asked as she struggled to move past two thick stalagmites that protruded from the rocky ground.

"I think they'll honour deals, at least," Kol said as he stepped over an area of cracked ground.

"Let's hope they do," Vekk muttered.

The caves were incredibly dark as the torches inside had extinguished long ago. Vekk was able to see slightly ahead with her dimly lit dagger. She did not dare to fire her handgun, as she feared that she would collapse the cave on them.

They heard the crackling of fire and looked to see an opening that was lit from the inside.

"There," Vekk said, walking quickly towards it.

They entered to find a creature sleeping flat on the ground; the only way that the siblings could tell that it was alive was due to its heavy breathing. It appeared to awake upon their entry and slowly stood up, before spontaneously jumping and smashing into the earth, causing the cave to shudder. The stalactites fell from the roof and some drove themselves into its back, causing it great pain.

It effortlessly pulled them out and threw them at the siblings, who dashed behind two large rocks. They had a clear view of the beast; it had deformed, thick legs, which held up its irregularly-shaped body, which included a large portion appearing as if it had been carved out. Part of its rib cage was exposed but its heart was not. Its head hung from the neck like a fruit hanging from its stalk. It was a disturbing sight and appeared to have mutated or have been the subject of experiments that led to its deformed shape.

"This will be the most horrific thing we've fought," Vekk said.

"It's actually worse than anything I saw in The Dystopian," Kol said.

Its hoarse vocal cords roared but had clearly come from a place of pain.

"Let's put it out of its misery," Kol said, readying its spear.

"Do you think it's ever seen sunlight?" Vekk asked as it began to approach.

"Not the time!" Kol called out as he ran under the beast's many arms and jabbed his spear into its foot. It did not appear to be bothered and continued charging towards Vekk. He stabbed his spear into its leg and began to climb, knowing he was beneath the weakest area.

Vekk shot at its face but was mostly unsuccessful at causing any injury. She rolled away from its swinging arms and managed to ram her dagger into its finger. She pushed it through and successfully cut it off, causing the creature to yell in pain.

Is this really worth it? Vekk thought as it grabbed her and tried to throw her into its gaping mouth. She grabbed onto its tooth and stabbed beneath it, giving her time to climb away as it continued to roar weakly.

Kol hung from one of the ribs and began stabbing at the exposed flesh, trying to find the heart.

How could they live with this thing in here?! he thought as he slashed at the bone, trying to hit a weak spot.

Please die, please die, please just lay down and die, Vekk thought as she drove her dagger into its back and began firing inside the open wound. It tried to grab her from its back but she slid away.

Kol kept slashing but made little progress, knowing he had no weaponry that would help him here.

He climbed the ribs as the creature tried to throw him off and he began stabbing deeper. It managed to throw Vekk across the room, leaving her injured but still capable of fighting. She ran between its legs and saw Kol stabbing at it.

"Give me your gun!" he shouted to her as it tried to pull him off. She began to climb the beast using her dagger, aiming for Kol's position.

Once she had reunited with her brother, she passed the weapon and he began firing through its ribcage, causing it to cry out in pain. Vekk quickly made her way back to the ground and ran into the adjoining tunnel, watching from afar, as Kol shot into the beast's chest.

"You'll detonate the heart!" Vekk called out but her warnings drowned out by the beast's horrific sounds.

Kol used the wound that he had created

to reach the heart and shot it twice. It tore through one side of the creature and he quickly jumped away and ran to his sister as it exploded and killed the beast.

"We've lost it!" Vekk said as she ran back inside the cave.

"I would rather be alive," Kol said. "We can get backup from Reqilar."

They looked at the dead creature, finally at rest after years, possibly centuries, of torment.

"I can't believe they let it suffer like that," Vekk said softly, slowly walking away.

"I want to forget that thing ever existed," said Kol as he joined her on their walk back up to the cavern.

They entered to find Kretai sat on the back of Arkriat and waiting for them. Kol checked them over as Vekk approached the rebel group's leader.

"What was that?!" she asked furiously.

"The ceremonial beast," the woman replied. "You were already told that."

"It was deformed, struggling, suffering. Why?!"

"We certainly didn't want to release it."

Kol asked for directions to the surface; one of the rebels complied and showed him a staircase that had been hidden in the wall. He walked into the thick snow and stared at Reqilar's old mining base, contemplating their next objectives.

"You can't just do whatever you want!" Vekk told her.

"Who's going to stop us," she asked. "You?"

"I don't think animal torture is permitted in Reqilar's rebellion," Vekk sneered.

"Then perhaps we won't join," the woman said.

Kol soon returned but Vekk led him back outside, leaving the rebels to discuss their next moves.

"I don't know if this is worth it," Vekk said. "They have no morals."

Kol handed Vekk his earpiece and walked back into the cavern to check on Arkriat and Kretai. Vekk called Reqilar and discussed the situation; he suggested that she should decide alone as to whether the alliance was beneficial or not.

"Come on, Kol. We're leaving," Vekk said as she re-entered the cavern.

"You haven't broken into the prison yet!" the woman told them as she cautiously approached them.

"What prison?" Kol asked, turning to her.

"The prison we told you about! We need you to return our lost allies."

Kol told them, "Give us proof that you'll actually join us, then we'll help." He looked at his sister, who shook her head.

"No. We need proof that you actually care

about our goals—I imagine Reqilar wants committed rebels," Vekk told them.

"You just need us to attack Quelliare's capital city; our perspectives don't need to align," one of the rebels told them.

"No, they need to align. You can't mistreat the innocent citizens of Zrelyar," Vekk said.

"We take care of each other. We wouldn't harm civilians—we don't see the point in unnecessary deaths."

The leader thought for a moment but finally brought out a pendant and gave it to Kol, who placed it around his neck, atop the necklace holding the fourth key.

"This is sacred to us, this is proof of our desire to help," she said bitterly, marking Kol's map with the prison's location. "Return it to us when you are done and we will join you, if you wish."

Kol nodded and Vekk led him, Arkriat and Kretai out of the base to find the prison. They passed by the mining base, glancing at it and remembering their initial encounter with Reqilar.

"I still don't know how you convinced Reqilar to change his entire life for you," Kol said. "Just a moment ago, you made those rebels want to join us!"

"I guess it's just my charisma," Vekk said with a smile.

They walked for half an hour, finding a

small grey building upon reaching the location on their map.

"We didn't find this before," Kol said as he looked around its exterior.

"I think it's new," Vekk said as she studied the weak metallic panelling that struggled to hold the roof up.

"It doesn't look like it's in use," Kol muttered as he walked inside the building and found it to be empty. He walked back outside to see Vekk looking into the distance and Kretai squealing loudly.

"What is it?" Kol asked as he approached his sister.

"I think Kretai has found something," Vekk said softly as she attempted to discern the rigid shapes in the distance.

They trudged through the snow and sand that had settled on the ground. Kol noticed a long white pylon in the distance and checked his map, recognising the familiar structure.

"We're near that superweapon," Kol said. "Someone else must've discovered it."

"It was...destroyed! It's useless now, who would care about it?" Vekk responded, forcing her feet through the thick snow in front of her.

They reached the military base that was attached to the destroyed superweapon and approached a back door. They used their weapons to force the door open and looked into the well-lit interior—a soldier stared at them.

What? Vekk thought as several guns were aimed at her and Kol's head. Arkriat ran inside, giving the siblings the opportunity to draw their weapons. Vekk began firing while Kol ran inside to dispatch the soldiers that Arkriat was distracting.

More soldiers soon arrived and Kol hid behind a pillar, waiting for Vekk to clear the way. However, his sister was unable to do so due to the number of reinforcements; she told Arkriat to run through them and watched as the Alpha Garisal caused havoc amongst the soldiers.

The siblings ran past and found a control room, pulling Arkriat and Kretai inside and sealing the door. They turned to see that the room had been repaired and was in use, its systems modernised.

"They've turned it into a functioning base," Vekk said, looking at the tablet laying on the computer desk.

Kol started searching through an unlocked computer and Vekk stood by the door to prevent any interruptions. She listened to the tapping of keys and reminisced.

"Remember when our mother snuck us into the palace so we could see what it looked like? The control centre was so…loud," Vekk said.

"I don't remember anything like that—I probably hadn't been born then," Kol muttered as he struggled to understand the various messages on the screen.

"I think you're right; I miss those times," Vekk responded. She turned to see Kol glaring at her. "No—I meant I miss being with our parents, without any responsibilities or fear of death."

"So do I," Kol said as he turned back to the giant screen on the wall. Vekk placed her ear to the door and heard voices on the other side of the door. Several seconds later, someone hit the door with a heavy weapon and caused Vekk to move away rapidly, a ringing sound dominating her right ear.

"Delete what you can. Make their work harder," Vekk said as she held her hand to her ear and drew her gun. Kol immediately complied and ordered Arkriat to protect Vekk. Kretai hovered behind a monitor, fearing the loud sounds in the corridor.

The door was broken through several minutes later and Vekk called for Kol to abandon the computer; he had managed to delete a large number of files in relation to the base's operations and military activity in Zrelyar.

Arkriat pushed the soldiers away from the door and Vekk soon followed him. Kol offered his hand to Kretai and she accepted, climbing onto his palm so he could cover her with his hand. The two of them left the control room and Vekk fired her gun at the central computer, causing it to explode.

"They're probably dead. Let's find the rebels!" Vekk called out as she ran towards the superweapon. Kol stared at her in shock for a few moments before following behind her.

They reached the door to the superweapon and found that it had been blocked by multiple secure doors, which closed upon the siblings' approach. The two guards that protected the room began questioning them, but were swiftly killed by Vekk and Kol.

"Maybe we can deactivate them with something in the control room," Vekk said as she sought a switch, stepping over the impaled bodies.

"I would agree if you hadn't destroyed all of the monitors," Kol said. He found a nearby interactive screen and managed to unlock all of the doors, except for the final one, a soundproof metal door.

Vekk knocked and to her surprise, it opened; the officer and two guards inside were surprised to see the siblings enter.

"You're not military personnel!" the officer said in shock, pulling out her pistol.

A firefight ensued and the siblings were able to defeat both guards; the officer backed away, realising she was outnumbered. Kol approached and she suddenly lunged for his spear; Vekk shot her in the leg and watched as the officer grasped the air, seeking a weapon.

Vekk closed her eyes and fired at the woman, piercing her heart and instantly killing her. Kol stared at the corpse while Vekk took several seconds to reopen her eyes.

"Remember when you said you would never kill again?" Kol said as he struggled to look away from the bodies on the floor.

"It...it doesn't feel wrong anymore," Vekk said, suddenly coming to a realisation. "It just feels like I'm shooting at an inanimate object."

"I know," Kol said quietly. "This journey has changed us."

They turned to see that the superweapon room had been converted into a prison, with the roof being changed from a glass skylight to a flat metal ceiling.

Cells were stacked up to the roof, surrounding the entire wall with no clear way on how to reach the prisoners. The remnants of the superweapon had been cleared and a flat surface lay in its place.

The siblings walked in to see the hundreds of people who called out for freedom.

"Are they all rebels?" Vekk said as she looked at the many prisoners, most wearing different clothing to each other.

"I doubt it," Kol said as he walked up to one of the cells; a man sat in the corner and refused to look up at him. Kol ran back to the officer's body and retrieved a key, unlocking the man's cell and three others. The prisoners thanked them and swiftly escaped the room to avoid any soldiers that were bound to arrive.

Kol made his way around the room, placing the key in each lock and swiftly opening the doors. He managed to open all locks on the first row of cages but was unable to reach the rest.

Vekk pointed to Kretai, who was flying around the room and taking advantage of the large room. Kol called her down and instructed her to open the cages; Kretai grabbed the key and jammed it into one of the locks. She forcefully pulled the key and it snapped in the lock, one of its halves falling to the ground and breaking apart.

"Why did they use such a primitive system in the first place?" Vekk said, holding a broken lock in her hand and searching for an alternate method of freeing the prisoners.

"I'm more surprised by the fact that we haven't been attacked yet," said Kol as he left the room. He hid in the shadow of a wall and watched as soldiers patrolled their usual routes.

Why haven't they come for us yet? Kol thought as he waited for a soldier to isolate himself from the rest of the guards.

Heavy rumbling was heard outside of the base and many of the soldiers rushed to find the source, leaving behind a skeleton team. Kol watched one soldier patrol the corridor ahead of him and stealthily walked behind him.

"Hello!" Kol called out. The soldier swiftly turned around and Kol elbowed him in the face.

The soldier stumbled back and Kol threw him against the wall and forced him into a headlock.

"What do you want?!" the soldier asked in a wavering tone. Kol felt guilty for his actions but continued to drag his captive to the prison room. Vekk saw the captive and relieved Kol; she held the soldier against the wall but struggled to keep him from escaping.

"We need to free the prisoners," Vekk said. "How do we do it?"

"I can't tell you that," he responded, fidgeting to escape Vekk's grasp.

"These people have families. Don't you have a family?" Vekk asked him.

"Don't you dare!" he shouted as he broke free. Kol tackled him to the ground and held his spear to the soldier's neck.

"Tell us. Go on," Vekk said, kneeling down to his face.

"The...the...centre of this room," he said. Kol examined the area and found a circular indent in the ground. Placing his fingers into the gap, he opened a large hatch to find a switch amongst intertwined wires.

"L...let him go!" Kol called out as he pressed the switch. Vekk released the soldier and he ran out of the room, disregarding the escaping prisoners. Kol retracted his hand and closed the hatch, turning to Vekk.

Vekk stopped one of the prisoners and inquired about his allegiance, discovering that he worked for Psykier's mother.

"If you're looking for the rest of us, they've been moved elsewhere," he told her.

"Where?" Kol asked, approaching them.

"I don't know, they left about half an hour ago," he replied quickly, desperate to escape. Vekk and Kol thanked him and left the room, taking advantage of the prison break to slip out of the base.

They reached the surface to see tanks hovering towards them. They brandished their weapons buy the vehicles continued moving. They eventually stopped several metres ahead of the siblings and one of the hatches opened, revealing a rebel soldier.

"I forgot we called for them," Kol said.

"Are we still needed?" the rebel asked them.

"Yes," Vekk told them. "There should be a group of rebels being transported nearby."

They were invited into the main tank and the ten rebel vehicles hovered through the icy biome, seeking one or more military transports.

They came across an area with many fallen trees, creating a path through the forest. They followed through to find a burnt area of ground, covered in ash and a lone concrete wall.

Vekk and Kol climbed out of the vehicle and found bodies of soldiers and rebels, clearly having engaged in a firefight. It was unknown what had burnt the ground but the rebels soon determined that explosives were not involved, based on the lack of holes in the ground.

Kol looked at the wall; gunfire was spread along it, as if the target had been moving. A man's body lay beside the wall and was coated in ash.

"I guess the rebels rebelled," Kol muttered, looking over the corpse.

"Don't make jokes," Vekk told him as she held her hand over her nose to weaken the smell of death that engulfed the site.

They returned to the tanks, where they decided to return to the independent rebel group. Vekk and Kol sat at the back of the vehicle, with Vekk placing her arms around her brother as the sight of death rattled around in her mind.

They travelled in silence for fifteen minutes, before reaching the hideout. The siblings, Arkriat and Kretai stepped out of the vehicle and walked down the steps to find the rebel leader sat at a table. She grudgingly stood up and welcomed them back.

"We are grateful that you've returned most of our rebels," she said to them as she stared at the pendant in Kol's hand.

"We searched to find the rest but they were...burnt," Kol said.

"We arrived at an area of scorched ground to find dead soldiers and rebels," Vekk explained to her.

"Alright," the leader said in a suspicious tone. "We will join you. Is there a form of transport waiting for us?"

Vekk ran outside and informed their rebel group about the additional crew, followed by Kol leading them into the tanks. The siblings climbed into one of the hovering vehicles and pulled Arkriat inside, with Kretai flying in behind them.

"What's going on?" Vekk asked as she watched the rest of the tanks hover away from them.

"There's a problem with this tank," the pilot told them as he struggled to increase the slow speed of the vehicle, eventually giving up.

"Why did we have to get the defective one?" Kol said as he watched the crew frantically try to repair the vehicle.

They heard the hum of engines above them, followed by darkness inside the tank; all electrical systems began to spark and shut off.

"We're under attack!" one of the rebels shouted as crew members forced the doors open. Vekk, Kol and Arkriat leapt to the ground and looked up to see two military Hovercles firing at them.

Vekk began firing at the approaching vehicles but missed most of her shots, causing a negligible amount of damage. The rebel crew's weapons had been damaged in the power outage and they were forced to turn their attention to their own disabled vehicle.

One of the pilots contacted the rest of the rebel reinforcements and begged them to return, to which they agreed but stated that it would take several minutes to reach them.

"So what do we do now?" one of the rebels asked.

"I don't…" Vekk began, before pausing to think of a proper response. "Survive."

The Hovercles surrounded the rebels and opened their doors to allow the soldiers inside to aim their weapons at the siblings.

Vekk and Kol stood in defensive positions and waited for the attack to begin. The soldiers dropped from the Hovercles and approached the siblings with their weapons drawn. The siblings drew their weapons and stared into the soldier's eyes, seeing their fear at the idea of consciously killing another person.

Vekk reacted first; she shot the closest soldier's hand and caused him to drop his gun, giving her, Kol and Arkriat a chance to hide behind the broken rebel vehicle. Once the other insurgents distracted the soldiers, the siblings ran for the nearest military Hovercle, pulling Arkriat and Kretai inside.

They managed to throw the pilots out of the open doors and Vekk took control, firing the built-in turrets at the soldiers and forcing them to scatter away from the rebels, who were hiding inside the disabled tank for cover.

"Someone's approaching," Kol said, alarmed by the sound of engines gradually growing louder. Vekk peered out of the corner of the window to see a vehicle spinning rapidly and moving towards them. She immediately stood up and stabbed the windshield with her dagger, dragging it along and creating a crack across the glass.

She pulled Kol onto the control panel and placed her back against the windshield. Stabbing the glass several more times, it quickly fractured and Vekk wrapped her arms around Kol as he grabbed Arkriat's leg.

"Follow us Kretai," Vekk said as she lent backwards and let herself and her brother fall from the vehicle, releasing her grasp on him as they fell. Arkriat descended above them for the second that they were in the air before hitting the ground. While they had not been far from the snowy earth, they still felt the blunt impact of slamming into the surface and the rebels had to help them to stand; Kretai flew down and squealed to alert the rebels to their injuries.

The vehicles collided above and caused an explosion that caught the attention of the nearby rebel tanks that had been struggling to locate them. They began to hover towards the stranded rebels, who were running towards their saviours. Once they met, one of the rebels stepped out of a tank and approached.

"You better stay close this time," she said as she looked at the destroyed vehicles and invited the survivors inside the tank. They hovered back to Modspi, where Reqilar waited for results; the siblings entered the command centre tower and found him in the meeting room.

"I assume all of our rebels have convinced the independent groups to join us," Vekk said as she walked in.

"Not all of them," he said. "Although you were the only one to call for assistance, which turned out to be unneeded."

"Don't tell us how to complete a mission," Kol told him.

"The support was needed—we were attacked while returning to Modspi!" Vekk said.

"Don't argue with me right now," Reqilar said. "We are so close to our final goal! We must focus on Zrelyar!"

"If you don't treat us like people, then you're no different than Zavroon," Kol said.

"No, the difference between me and Zavroon is that I can accept when I'm wrong," Reqilar retorted.

"So you don't want to treat us as people... even me?" Vekk asked.

"No, that's—I...I will adapt my tactics," Reqilar replied. "Your next mission will not be with me anyway."

"The last two missions weren't with you either," Kol reminded him.

"Your next mission will be to claim the final key that you have spent so long searching for," Reqilar told them.

"It constantly moves," Kol said. "I don't know what it's in or who has it."

"We'll pinpoint it soon enough," Vekk reassured him.

Vekk and Kol left the building to see that Modspi was in a state of celebration; the rebels were elated from their most recent success and were becoming closer to their many new allies.

"Finally," Kol said as he entered the city square to see lights and hear music. "Success awaits us!"

CHAPTER 22

"I've cleared you from all other missions for now," Reqilar said, the light from the window illuminating his face. "We'll mostly be preparing our forces for the worst."

"That's the safest thing to do," Vekk said to him. "As soon as we're able to learn more about the final key, we'll seek it out and return here."

"We'll have to catch up when you return," he said to her.

"Let's hope you won't have to wait long," she said, lightly kissing him on the lips.

She walked into the meeting room to find Kol analysing the map. Arkriat was sat beside him on a chair and Kretai was flying around the room to exercise her wings.

"How are we supposed to figure out who has the key from some vague images?" Kol asked his sister as she sat down across from him. He slid the map over to her and she placed one finger on Modspi and the other on the orange dot that marked the final key.

"They're in the snowy forest right now, near the mining base," Vekk said.

"It must be someone in the military," Kol said. "They're the only people in that area."

"It doesn't matter who has it—we'll have to face them," Vekk told Kol.

"I'd still like to be prepared, though," he responded.

"We don't have that luxury," she said.

Kol had spent his limited free time marking the movements of the key from the map and now attempted to triangulate its position. However, the previous locations showed irregular movement and pointed to an uninhabitable area of Quelliare.

"Triangulating won't help us," Vekk muttered.

"They were close to our position while we ventured across the planet," Kol said. "Could it be someone we know?"

"We were alone most of the time…" Vekk said, standing up and walking out of the room to meet with Reqilar; he provided her with a list of every rebel that he commanded and she returned to Kol. Together, they sought through the potential traitors; the majority of recruits had suspicious backgrounds.

They concluded that a young woman with ties to her former military allies was the mostly likely to be deceiving the rebels; her location was near the one dot on the map that represented the final key.

"She's currently on a mission in a place close

to Zrelyar." Vekk said. "The area looks…barren."

She then called Reqilar into the room, and he provided them with co-ordinates for her location.

"This is a key part of our plan," he told them. "Literally."

"If she's a traitor, I guess we'll let you know," Kol said as he picked up Kretai from the table and placed her on his own shoulder.

"I'm sure we can deal with her ourselves," Vekk said as she walked towards the door, with Kol and Arkriat following behind her. They left the command centre and approached the hangar, deciding to take an unused shuttle. Vekk chose the pilot's seat and Kol placed the map on the control panel so that they could ensure that they would land in the correct location.

"This feels identical to the last mission—getting in a ship, going to complete a mission with some rebels," Kol said as he watched Kretai fly and land on the back of Arkriat, who was sitting behind Vekk's chair.

"This is the one of the last steps of our personal objective," Vekk responded as she fiddled with the controls and barely managed to avoid crashing into the other vehicles nearby. They lifted off and flew over the desert, with Vekk reducing the speed of the vehicle as they reached the adjacent jungle.

"Don't fly too close to the city," Kol warned

as he watched a flying vehicle hover in the distance.

"I can't wait to return," Vekk said as she slumped in her chair. "We've spent most of our lives there, but I want to go back."

"It feels like it's been decades since we were there, but I doubt it's even been a year," Kol responded as he tried to locate the Cristrial village beneath him.

"When people—rebels—have asked me to bring their memories to the surface, I would spend that same night dreaming about Zrelyar. In some of those dreams, we're welcomed back and we get to live normal lives; our parents and Thrakalir are alive to help us..." Vekk told Kol, who was now listening intently.

"I'm guessing that the rest involve us being arrested or killed," Kol said as he looked towards the sudden end of the forest and was unable to see beyond it.

"Yes, yes that...happens too," Vekk responded with a quiver in her voice.

"We'll...what is this place?" Kol said as they passed the end of the forest and looked ahead into a white landscape.

"It's otherworldly. Are we in the afterlife?" Vekk muttered. Kol glared at Vekk, before turning his attention back to the quartz moor ahead of them. The crystalline ground was filled with a subterranean white mist that masked anything that lay deep below it.

"It's like a void," Kol muttered, before noticing the various ruins and pieces of debris that had partially sunk into the ground. Brick and metal fragments infrequently stabbed the fragile landscape and some could be seen descending below the surface, above the mist that concealed anything that was more than five metres below the moor.

"Ruins," Vekk muttered as she looked at the objects in an attempt to identify their source. "Maybe the rebel we're looking for is sheltered in half a building or something."

"I can't see a single living being," Kol said, his attention consumed by the strange, empty lands.

Vekk decided to land near a giant dome, where figures could be seen talking and studying the ancient architecture. The map stated that the final key was about five miles away but the co-ordinates that Reqilar had given them pointed to the dome.

They exited the vehicle and were greeted by an absence of ambience; the only sounds were of the people talking and walking around, along with their own steady breathing.

Kol looked down at Arkriat, who was unwilling to leave the shuttle due to the unnerving silence. Kretai was comfortable flying into the still air but quickly chose to land on Kol's shoulder once several figures began walking towards her.

"What do you want?" a woman asked the siblings.

"You," Vekk said, recognising the woman's discontent expression from the rebellion's few images of her.

"Oh?" she responded, glancing at the rebels standing behind her. "What do I have that you want?"

Vekk remained silent for a moment as she processed the question, before responding, "A key, possibly."

"I don't have any keys," she responded. "We're here to kill a commander."

"Are they around here?" Kol asked as he opened his map and showed it to the woman. She nodded her head and stared at Kol.

"What's the map for?" she asked, staring his eyes with a specific interest and making him feel uncomfortable.

"It's…for tracking down military camps," Vekk told them.

"Then we'll target that dot," she responded, pointing to the map. "Maybe your primitive key will be there."

One of the rebels suddenly drew their gun and started aiming into the distance. Vekk and Kol immediately placed their hands on their weapons while the other rebels did not react.

"When you're in a place as quiet as this, you start hearing things; you'll get used to it," the woman told them, her eyes holding silent judgement for the siblings.

"We haven't—" Vekk began, before being cut off by the woman.

"You're Vekkilar and Kolansar; I'm Yaxxnare," she told them, turning away from the siblings and walking inside the giant dome. One of the rebels went to comfort the soldier who suffered from auditory hallucinations while the siblings pulled Arkriat from the shuttle and followed Yaxxnare into the dome.

"My contacts have confirmed that our target is incredibly important to the General of the Royal Guard himself," she told the siblings, who were surprised to find a makeshift base inside of the ruins.

"Where did this dome come from? What happened here?" Vekk asked. Yaxxnare shrugged her shoulders and picked up a gun that had been hidden underneath a metal table.

"Let's go and find your key," she told the siblings.

"Better than you staying here," Kol muttered.

"Why? Don't you trust me?" she asked them both.

"We need proof that you don't have the key," Vekk said as her body began to tense in preparation for an argument.

"Search me," she said, holding her arms out. "You can find the truth yourselves."

Vekk and Kol looked at each other with discomfort until Yaxxnare began to throw everything from the bags beside her bed.

"You don't need to—"

"This is everything I have on me!" Yaxxnare told them, throwing a bag onto the ground.

Kol quickly opened his map and reminded Vekk that the key was not in the camp. Vekk relaxed her shoulders and stared at Yaxxnare, who was picking up her scattered belongings.

"We'll find that enemy commander—he's our best option," Vekk said as she led Kol outside. Kol looked at his map and Vekk glared at the glowing orange circle on its rugged surface.

"It looks like the key is east of here," Kol said. "The commander could be there too."

They began walking eastward through the silent lands, admiring the broken obelisks that had been plunged into the ground and the ruins that had sunk through the delicate quartz.

Vekk began walking faster as she saw a pink object laying underneath the transparent quartz. Kol slowly pursued her, struggling to encourage Arkriat to walk through the unnerving biome. They reached the object and looked down at the giant portrait that lay beneath the ground, several metres above the mist.

Vekk and Kol stared at the face of a Queen, whose purple eyes and pale green skin pierced the ground and stared back at the siblings, as if the portrait was alive. Her shoulders were relaxed and her mouth formed a smile that brought comfort.

Kretai landed on the ground and looked down at the portrait, drawn by the striking colours; the pink and blue background swirled behind the middle-aged woman wearing a platinum crown. Vekk fixated on the face and felt herself involuntarily emulating her expression.

"I don't know who she is, but it's nice to feel welcomed for once," Kol said as he stared at the pastel background surrounding the Queen.

"That could have been here for centuries—everything else here looks to be ancient," Vekk responded, biting her lip before speaking. She walked around the portrait while Kol and Arkriat walked over it, the three of them meeting and continuing their journey with Kretai flying overhead.

Far ahead, they saw giant blue trees and plants sprouting out of a dark, ashy surface. Bioluminescent yellow creatures flew over the biome, using all four of their wings to keep them from crashing into the bright flora that dominated the lands. The wildlife stood out against the setting sun as the world prepared for darkness.

"One place is full of life, and the other is lifeless," Kol said as he first glanced at the glowing biome, and then turned towards the quartz moor.

"The same could be said for Zrelyar and Lasapra," Vekk said with a smirk.

"Neither are full of life—closer to death, really," he responded, beginning to run with Arkriat towards the new biome; Vekk pursued him, enjoying the freedom of the empty lands and a childlike thrill that she had not been able to experience in her youth.

Stepping into the glowing ecosystem, they heard the many sounds of primal creatures calling out to each other, in direct contrast to the silence of the quartz moor. Despite the light from the flora, they struggled through the lands in relative darkness. After around an hour, they stumbled across a small building,

A building stood ahead of them that vaguely resembled the temple from the Cristrial village but this one was shaped differently —the trapezoid structure was comprised of illuminated steps that could easily be climbed. The roof appeared to flatten out, and a giant beam rose from the centre. A square door lay just below the roof, and the siblings could see the outline of a figure standing in darkness.

"It must be in that building," Kol muttered.

"Not necessarily," Vekk replied, readying her weapon, "but clearly someone is waiting for us."

"Come for me, siblings!" the figure called out. "Your interference is irrelevant anyway."

Vekk immediately darted up the stairs and removed the dagger and handgun from her belt. She reached the roof and stood in the doorway, swinging her weapons as the figure ran at her. She blinked and was suddenly blinded; she stumbled back and felt a foot on her stomach, pushing her down the steps.

Her brother ran to the roof and saw the face of Yarsnael watching Vekk's unconscious body roll down the temple. Kol felt around in the darkness and managed to stop her from rolling further, laying her comfortably on the steps before continuing his ascent with his spear drawn; he caught a glimpse of Kretai reaching the roof.

"You've ignored another threat; I'm surprised you haven't noticed it yet," Yarsnael told him. Kol ran at the agent, who grabbed Kretai from the air and threw her at him. Kol moved to avoid her and looked behind to see Arkriat sprinting up the building to reach them. Kretai was suddenly struck with grey powder while Kol struggled to strike his target in near darkness.

Arkriat leapt at Yarsnael, who quickly moved away and grabbed a box from his belt.

"I know what you want," he told Kol, quickly unsheathing his silver sword and striking tactically. Kol struggled to defend himself, with the box just out of reach. Yarsnael discarded the box and Arkriat rushed to grab it, picking up the lid with his mouth.

The box fell open and Arkriat suddenly fainted, causing Kol to run to him. Yarsnael grabbed Kol's shoulders and slammed him into the wall, before throwing him into the doorway of the temple.

"I will succeed," Yarsnael sneered as he held Kol to the ground, his sword to his neck.

"Just you?" Kol asked, before the agent discarded his sword and slammed his fist into Kol's jaw; Kol watched a flurry of powder head towards his face.

Vekk awoke to the sounds of rumbling and rummaging beside her. She opened her eyes to see rebels walking around and organising their belongings. She felt a hard surface beneath her and looked down to see a rusted sword through the transparent quartz.

"Where am I?" she asked, quickly sitting up to see Arkriat and Kretai sitting on the ground in front of her.

"We were patrolling in the Ippleti and found you near a giant temple," one of the rebels told her. "What happened over there?"

"I don't...know," she said. "What's an 'Ippleti'?"

"That's the biome you were found in. Bright blue trees. Ashy ground."

"I don't remember," Vekk said.

"What's the last thing you can recall?" he

asked, helping her to stand.

"We were talking to...your leader," Vekk told him.

"The last time you spoke to Yaxxnare was a few hours ago," he told her.

"We were studying the map and suddenly I woke up here," she said, failing to make sense of the situation.

"She must've found something in the temple," a passing rebel stated to the man questioning Vekk.

"Do you have an idea where your brother is?" one of the rebels asked Vekk, who had stood up and was looking around for Kol.

"I thought he was here," Vekk said. "If not, then no."

The rebel led her to Yaxxnare, who briefly explained the siblings' plan to find the last key.

"Look through the Ippleti," Yaxxnare told her. "He's probably still inside."

"Should we join you?" a rebel asked Vekk. She opened her mouth to respond, before being interrupted by Yaxxnare.

"Reqilar would probably prefer us to complete our goal first," she told the rebel, who nodded and walked away.

"What if Kol is hunting down the enemy commander right now?" Vekk said. "We can complete both objectives."

"Fine, good point. Come with us," Yaxxnare told her as she called a small rebel squad to join them. Vekk approached Arkriat and Kretai and asked them about Kol's location; while she did not expect a response, she could see that they were as confused as she was.

"Something must've happened to all of us," Vekk said.

"Why would your brother be singled out?" she was asked.

"I don't…he has the keys!" she said, her eyes widening for a second.

"We found you under a tree—we have no trail to follow to find him," Yaxxnare told Vekk.

"You don't have any idea where the commander is?" Vekk asked with a tone of suspicion.

"We were planning to target nearby camps; that's our only option."

"At least whoever knocked you out left you with your weapons," one of the rebels pointed out.

"Let's begin as soon as possible," Vekk told the group as she glanced down at her dagger and handgun.

They ran to the Ippleti and began searching with their weapons drawn, with all rebels ready to attack. Vekk was on edge as she was worried about Kol's fate and her own memory loss, suspecting that she had wandered into a trap that she could unintentionally trigger again.

"One of the camps should be close," Yaxxnare whispered to the group, moving quickly between bioluminescent trees to avoid the darkness.

"How many do we need to attack?" Vekk whispered back.

"At least three," she responded.

They approached a busy site and stood beside the metal fence, staring through the gaps to see a few small buildings that served as the soldiers' homes, alongside the soldiers themselves.

Yaxxnare threw a grenade over the tall fence, causing mass panic within the camp and allowing the rebels to climb over the fence to attack the soldiers by utilising the cover of darkness. Vekk followed behind her, helping her to disarm and dispatch her opponents efficiently.

Vekk's ears were suddenly filled with ringing, as she turned to see gaping holes in the ground, decorated with bodies and lit by the red lights that had been set up by the soldiers to illuminate the camp. Her breath became rapid as she watched Yaxxnare kill a nervous sergeant and disregard the bodies littering the camp, stepping over her deceased allies.

The only way to survive this is to become desensitised—again, Vekk thought as she cupped her hands over her ears to muffle the blasts of mines. She forced the thoughts of her family from her mind and ran to catch up with Yaxxnare.

"We've lost half the group!" Vekk yelled as she dodged gunfire and turrets. Yaxxnare threw a grenade at the remaining turrets and destroyed them, allowing the remaining rebels to subdue the few military soldiers that had survived.

They raided the camp for supplies and locked the captured soldiers inside the barracks. Soon after securing the perimeter, the rebels worked tirelessly to extract information from the prisoners but learnt little, despite their efforts.

Vekk was offered to lead one of the interrogation sessions and accepted, walking in with her dagger ready.

"Give me the other camp locations," she demanded.

"We don't know them," one of the soldiers said bluntly.

"Why should I believe that?" she asked.

"The general has them."

"Why wouldn't you know where your reinforcements are?"

"In case of this."

Vekk went silent. She looked around the room to see that the other captives were exhausted and ravenous.

"Where is your general?" Vekk asked the soldier sitting on a metal bed in front of her.

"He's setting a trap. We don't know where."

"Who is your general?" Vekk asked, hoping she could interrogate him to find the locations of the other camps.

"The G.R.G."

Vekk stayed silent, waiting for him to elaborate.

"The General of the Royal Guard," he said, visibly surprised that she did not recognise the acronym.

"Zavroon is here?!" she said, swiftly walking out to inform the other rebels.

Kol blocked the blinding light with his arm, giving him time to adjust to the brightness of the room. After several minutes, he lowered the limb to see a white ceiling above him; he looked down and saw that the rest of the room was identical. He saw someone standing in front of him, dressed in black armour with a black cape hanging from one shoulder.

Who's that? Kol thought as he stood up.

"I'm glad to see I'm not alone," the person said calmly.

"Zavroon? What are you doing here?" Kol asked as he immediately recognised the voice.

"You may have noticed you still have your weapons and armour," he said.

Kol checked and realised that he was correct.

"What sort of mental torture is this?!" he asked.

"One that I didn't expect," Zavroon responded. "Yarsnael has realised his intelligence rivals my own."

"So he betrayed you," Kol said, mentally noting that the room had no clear exits. "He's trapped us both."

"Correct," Zavroon said bluntly.

"Once we've dealt with your rebellion, our focus will go onto him," Zavroon told him, running his fingers along the edges of the blade of his sword.

"He's the second threat you've let escape," Kol said. "I would've thought the General of the Royal Guard wouldn't have let that happen."

"I would rather be trapped with your Garisal than with you," Zavroon said. "It would provide a more stimulating conversation."

"I also would prefer it if you were trapped and I was not."

"Do you really think your rebellion will succeed? This question has lingered in my mind since you first escaped," Zavroon said.

"Why else would I support it?" Kol countered as he began to search for a way out.

"Because you have no other choice," the general responded. "Your perception of good isn't destined to win, despite the happy endings you're taught to believe."

"What's good about killing your own people?!"

"Profit."

"How do you profit from that?" Kol asked, finding the walls to be completely solid.

"Less citizens means less of a drain on the economy," he said. "Goodwill died centuries ago, let it meet its death."

"They will revolt eventually," Kol said fiercely.

"Do you really think they would join you? They see you as murderers who seek to destroy everything they love," Zavroon said, laughing.

"We're saving them!" Kol countered.

"They don't see it that way," he responded, unsheathing his sword and studying the sharp blade. Kol anxiously walked around the room and sought a hidden switch or button to allow him to escape.

"If we both died in here, Quelliare would greatly benefit from losing you," Kol said, losing hope of escape.

"How would your sister feel?" Zavroon asked him. "She would have failed her job as your protector; she would be hopeless and drowning in despair."

"You know nothing about her!" Kol snapped.

"Vekkilar, forty-two years of age, Quarailian, born with a rare skin condition, along with her knowledge that she will inevitably fail every expectation set for her."

"Most of those are facts," Kol told him. "Her passion and strength to do good are immeasurable."

"Do you think you and your sister are the perfect heroes of an adventure?" Zavroon asked, brandishing his sword. "To the people of Zrelyar, you are the antagonist of the same story."

Kol grabbed his spear and stood with the blade facing Zavroon. The general retaliated by running at the lone sibling and slashing at him with his sword. Kol struggled to block the attacks, using the pole of his spear to prevent Zavroon from killing him.

Kol tried to thrust his spear into Zavroon's chest but instead hit the wall, opening up a doorway.

"Your tomb has been prepared!" Zavroon sneered as he swung his sword close to Kol's face, forcing him into the tunnel behind them. The attack suddenly ceased as the general studied his opponent to find a fast way to end the fight. Kol stood defensively for a few seconds before bringing his spear down on Zavroon with such intensity that the general was forced to step away.

Kol attempted to spin his spear and use the blunt end to strike his enemy, but instead lost control and Zavroon kicked it from his hands.

"You were born insignificant, you will die insignificant," Zavroon sneered, pushing Kol to the floor.

Kol swiftly jumped back up and wrested the

sword from his hands but was immediately faced with his opponent's gun. He threw the sword at Zavroon's arm and almost severed it. The general fell to the ground in pain as Kol stole his gun and aimed it at the general's face.

"This is what I'll do to Lasapra," Kol said as he readied the gun. Zavroon stared into the barrel of the gun and watched Kol's hands shaking as the weapon was held to its owner's face. Zavroon quickly grabbed the gun and Kol fired, missing the shot.

Zavroon threw the gun to the floor and reclaimed his sword, slashing Kol's legs and forcing him to fall to the ground.

"You will do nothing to your Queen," Zavroon told him as he swiftly kicked Kol in the face, leaving him lying in defeat.

They struggled to find Zavroon's location as Kol was in possession of the map. The remaining rebels struggled through the darkness, lacking directions to the next camp.

"We should search for Zavroon; he might have taken Kol captive," Vekk said, slashing some weeds with her dagger.

"We need to find the camps," Yaxxnare told her.

"We don't have time!" she responded.

"I'm in charge; follow my orders."

"My loyalty is to my brother," Vekk told her sternly, before beckoning Arkriat and Kretai to follow her. They departed from the rebels and traversed the Ippleti, reaching the area where they first entered.

"Arkriat, Kretai, see if anyone's passed through here recently," Vekk commanded as she stared into the distance and tried to recall the path that she and Kol had taken. Kretai hovered over the ground and analysed the grains that comprised it, seeking footprints; she quickly found them.

Vekk turned her head towards Kretai, who had begun to squeak loudly. She approached the Ukrifar and saw the footprints on the ground, dimly lit by the rising sun.

"Lead the way," Vekk told her as she followed behind Arkriat, who was clearing the way of predators so that Kretai could lead unharmed. Vekk began to fear the loss of her remaining family and urged Kretai to hurry.

They pushed through the Ippleti for around an hour before hearing a gentle humming in the vicinity; they turned to see a great beam pummelling out of a stone building. Vekk stared into the beam in awe, suddenly stumbling backwards with an influx of memories.

"Kretai, check the roof for Kol!" Vekk swiftly commanded as she ran up to the entrance. She walked inside to see a circular stone wall around the centre of the room and two staircases on either side that led deeper into the temple.

Vekk, Arkriat and Kretai wandered down the left set of stairs to find a pentagonal room covered in irregularly placed metal panels on the wall. They walked through an archway on the back wall and entered another room where glass cubes were placed on the floor like soldiers waiting to march.

Someone has already passed each challenge, Vekk thought as she walked past the completed puzzles and reached a square room with a computer terminal embedded in the front wall.

She approached the terminal and tapped on the screen to reveal a menu. The text on the screen was blurry and almost unreadable, forcing Vekk to navigate the controls based on imagery alone. She tapped on the pixelated face of a snake, which brought up a 3x3 grid.

Kol's face suddenly appeared in the centre square, with Yarsnael and Zavroon in the upper and lower right squares, respectively. Vekk stared at the screen and watched as Zavroon's face leapt diagonally over Kol's and captured him, causing his face to disappear.

Vekk blinked and saw that the grid was empty; her hands clutched the edges of the screen and her shoulders rose. She closed her eyes for a couple of seconds, before opening them again and tapping on the lower left square.

The squares shifted, with four of them forming a diamond shape while the rest disappeared. Arkriat barked and Vekk turned to see that a physical diamond had appeared on the wall beside her.

She pulled the diamond out of the wall and it shattered immediately; the walls shifted and turned to reveal a pure white room, significantly brighter than the rest of the temple. Vekk ran down a concrete corridor that branched off the room and found an observation station that overlooked a giant reactor core containing various unlabelled controls. She looked into the core and saw her brother's body lying inside, unmoving, and his spear out of reach.

She instructed Arkriat and Kretai to stay in the observation room and she sprinted down the stairs into the core itself. She ran to his body and grabbed his hand in a desperate attempt to ensure he was alive.

"Kol," she said quietly as she slid her hand onto his chest and felt his beating heart, causing her to relax slightly.

"Vekk…" he said weakly, his arm sliding away from his side and turning to point towards the spear. Vekk looked towards the weapon and stood up to grab it, walking over and retrieving his weapon. Returning to Kol, she held the weapon above him.

"It'll be alright," she told him softly as she prepared to stab him with his own spear. She closed her eyes and suppressed a rising feeling of guilt as she drove the weapon through her brother's body. He let out exclamations of pain as the initial shock gripped his body.

Vekk immediately dropped the spear and stayed by his side as his body slowly began to heal enough for him to move.

"We're getting out of here," she told him as she held onto his wavering body and slowly carried him out, clipping the spear to her back before they left. She eventually made it to the control room and lay him down, allowing him to rest for a moment as she approached the controls and attempted to stop the reactor.

She struggled to navigate the controls and instead decided to grab her handgun and aim it at the controls. She glared at the reactor, knowing it was likely to explode based on the deafening sounds that quickly grew louder.

"Arkriat, take Kol outside," she commanded as she steadied her hand, rising it to face the glass in front of her. Arkriat complied and began dragging him with the help of Kretai, who gave directions.

Vekk fired into the reactor core, first smashing the control room window and then piercing the weak glass around the reactor. It began to become unstable and threw shards of glass and metal beams around the room. Vekk quickly fired one shot at the exposed core and one at the controls, before retreating as the room began to collapse in on itself.

She caught up with her brother and began to drag him by herself, pulling him out of the temple. Outside, the beam began to flicker and then shut off, with no possibility of being repaired.

"We need to find Yarsnael," Kol muttered to his sister, who was more focused on his health.

"We'll find him soon," she said, calling the rebels in Modspi for another shuttle. They were refused as a shuttle had already been lent were asked to make their own way back to the city. Vekk held back her insults and politely ended the call, helping Kol to place his arm around her shoulder.

"Call Reqilar," Kol muttered.

"He won't have time to help us," Vekk responded. "Kretai, we need to go back the way we came."

Kretai immediately relocated the path they had made in order to reach the temple and Vekk followed her, placing her arms around Kol's chest and helping him to keep up with the rapid pace of the Ukrifar—Arkriat ran in front of the siblings to protect them and Kretai from predators.

They returned to the rebel camp in the quartz moor and found it deserted. Vekk placed Kol inside the shuttle that they had arrived in and closed the ramp; Arkriat and Kretai sat beside him as Vekk activated the vehicle and flew towards Modspi.

Once they had landed, Vekk brought Kol to the hospital and sat beside him as a medical bot analysed his injuries.

"Thank you," Kol said to his sister, who was caught off guard and smiled in response.

They remained at Modspi for two weeks, with Vekk tracking the final key with Reqilar while Kol recovered.

Kol was invited to a meeting fourteen days after being admitted to the hospital, despite not having fully recovered. They sat and discussed their next move, including analysing the map to locate their target and studying Kol's conversation with Zavroon to construct a sufficient understanding of the situation.

"He's in the Cristrial village in the jungle," Kol said. "That's too close to Zrelyar."

"Everyone probably knows that he's a traitor," Vekk said.

"We still need to catch him," Kol said to her. "I think we should take the risk."

"We need the key, and yourselves, for our final mission. Don't die," Reqilar told them both. The siblings nodded in agreement and left for the jungle, closely following the plotted route so that they would not be discovered by military vehicles that patrolled the air.

They landed close to the village and stepped out of the vehicle to see Cristrials leaving the village in large groups, screaming and yelling.

The siblings ran inside to see the entire area burning, with Yarsnael at its centre.

"Come here, you liar!" Kol called out, quickly drawing the attention of the Kerrilas himself. The former agent drew his weapons and waited for the siblings to approach, which they did with their own weapons ready.

"I don't know how you found me," he told them, "but I'm going to end your little lives."

"You hurt these innocent people." Vekk asked as she watched people flee their homes in terror. "Why?!"

"To send a message that I am to be respected —I am not Zavroon's servant," he told them as he flourished his sword in preparation for the battle. The siblings ran at him and he quickly blocked their attacks. Kol commanded Arkriat to attack and he complied, forcing Yarsnael to focus on defending himself. He suddenly began slashing at Vekk and Kol, focusing on the latter while Arkriat was forced to retreat due to a falling tree.

Yarsnael kicked Kol's knee. Kol stumbled back, loosely waving his spear in front of him. Vekk ran at the former agent, who quickly turned and almost decapitated her— she dashed away and ran towards Arkriat, who was now watching beside Kretai.

Kol thrusted his spear in front of him. Yarsnael sidestepped and drove his sword towards Kol, who barely managed to block the attack. Vekk ran towards them, dagger drawn and watching as Yarsnael lifted his sword and swiftly sliced between the metal plates on Kol's armour, cleanly removing his left arm and shoulder.

Kol watched his arm drop to the ground and felt agonising pain in his elbow. He stared at the dead limb and remained silent as the pain worsened; the pain of the wound quickly became stronger than his shock and he fell to the ground and cried out in pain.

Vekk gripped her sword tightly and swiftly impaled Yarsnael as he watched Kol suffer, causing him to fall to the ground. She leapt over his body and ran to Kol, now audibly crying. Vekk looked at him, her face pale and her breaths irregular. She felt tension grasp her body as the reality of the situation set in—she fell to one knee and placed her hand on his right shoulder.

He was unable to speak but pointed at Yarsnael with his left arm, expressing visible surprise when his finger did not appear. Vekk stood up, Kol's spear in her hand, and walked over to Yarsnael as he began to rise.

"You can't stop me," he said with great anger, before darting at Vekk and attacking her using as much strength as he could possibly summon; the sight was almost feral as he clawed at her arm and tried to grasp her wrist.

Kol looked at the village through his tears;

the Cristrials had returned and had begun throwing water at the fires that engulfed their homes, knowing that Vekk was distracting the arsonist that had set their buildings on fire in the first place.

Vekk managed to shoot Yarsnael's hand and knock his sword onto the floor. He reached for his pistol but Vekk thrust Kol's spear into Yarsnael's chest once more, causing him to collapse to the ground in agony. He lay on the charred ground, elevated by one arm and staring disgustedly at Vekk.

"I have plans beyond your comprehension," he told them. "You'll doom this world if you end my life."

"From what we've seen, your plans don't seem to be worth it," Vekk said, holding Kol's spear to the former agent's neck and tightening her grip on the wooden shaft, causing it to slightly splinter.

"It's too late, anyway," he said. "You two and Zavroon will destroy each other and leave me as the rightful ruler of this world."

Vekk looked up and withdrew the spear from Yarsnael's neck, instead throwing it over his head.

"That's...not happening," Kol said as he impaled Yarsnael from behind and kneeled on the ground as the pain persisted.

"He's finally gone," Vekk said as she shot Yarsnael's body once more to ensure he was dead, before running to Kol.

"I want to get the key," Kol muttered as Vekk helped him to reach the body in front of him. He used his remaining hand to search through pockets and bags, finding a small wooden box. Vekk opened the box for Kol to reveal the decagonal, star-shaped golden key that lay inside on a cushion, which fit it perfectly. Kol slowly removed the key and placed it in his own bag, completing the collection.

"We need to get back," Kol said as he carefully stood up and fought back the pain. Vekk called Arkriat and Kretai and helped Kol make his way back to the shuttle. Vekk helped Kol to sit in the chair beside her as she prepared to take off.

Kol opened his mouth to speak, but instead fainted and slid onto the floor. Vekk gasped and immediately moved to return him to his seat, with Arkriat helping to push him up. Arkriat sat with his paws across Kol to hold him in place while Vekk piloted the ship back to Modspi.

They returned to the city and Vekk ran to the hospital to call for help. A team of medical bots soon arrived at the shuttle and carried Kol to a bed, cauterising the wound to prevent further blood loss.

"We will attach a prosthetic arm once the wound has healed," one of the doctors told Vekk. She sat beside her brother as they performed tests on him, choosing to remain with him until she was asked to leave—Arkriat and Kretai were taken to a veterinarian clinic to check for wounds.

I'm a terrible guardian, Vekk thought as she entered the command centre to update Reqilar on their latest mission.

"We've found the final key," Vekk said. "We're almost ready."

"Now we can focus on our actual mission: assaulting Zrelyar," he responded.

"What do you mean by 'actual mission'?"

"This was a personal mission—" Reqilar began.

"This mission is an integral part of the final plan," Vekk told him fiercely. "Kol lost his arm to complete this!"

"He lost his arm?" Zavroon asked with a tone of confusion, as opposed to the horror on Vekk's face. "Anyway, the mission was the one you set out to do, not us."

"It's one of Lasapra's sources of power, you *prixtibba!*"

"Vekk!"

Vekk narrowed her eyes as he watched him study her expression. "Since you are so focused on the mission, you should know Yarsnael is dead."

"Good," Reqilar muttered. "You better prepare yourself for what's to come."

"Kol and I have already suffered enough; I

want to save this world so that my family—and other families— won't have to suffer any longer."

"Once we're done, I expect to see you alive," Reqilar said, pulling her towards him for a kiss.

She pulled away but smiled at him. "Trust me, I'm not dying at the final stage."

CHAPTER 23

The training of that particular day was more difficult than usual but Arthur had prepared rigorously for the physical prerequisites of his dream career. He jumped from bar to bar that had been placed on the low ceiling and dropped to the floor, into thirty push-ups. He then ran through the maze that had been set out ahead of him and swung over a pit using a metal bar that had been installed between two walls.

He swiftly completed the rest of the course and stood beside the other astronauts who had finished earlier than him. They were then joined by the remaining two trainees, who Arthur was secretly relieved to have surpassed.

The instructor briefly congratulated them and began explaining the next activity of the day—Arthur had been intrigued by the weightlessness exercises and was glad that it would be the next aspect of his course—after the human centrifuge.

The astronauts were led to a large building in a field on the outskirts of York. They were led through the building and into a giant room with spherical walls; in the middle was a human centrifuge, characterised by a large metallic arm that stretched across the room, from the centre, towards the wall, holding a pod for the astronauts to climb inside.

The astronauts watched as an instructor led one of them inside, giving the astronaut the necessary equipment and performing safety checks. The door then shut and the human centrifuge began to spin the compartment slowly, then gradually increasing its speed until it was moving rapidly.

"Your ability to cope with this will determine whether you have the necessary skills to continue your training," the instructor told them.

Arthur was surprised at the momentum that the compartment was swung at and was beginning to feel anxious at the thought of sitting inside. However, it appeared to be incredibly stable as the arm was able to handle the rapidity and Arthur knew it would make the final journey into space easier.

When the astronaut was able to leave the vehicle, she was slightly disorientated and struggled to move normally as she stumbled outside. The rest of the astronauts were left to watch the training once again as another was subjected to the human centrifuge.

The instructor was unable to explain the reason for the training as the sound of the machine spinning was too loud to speak over, especially considering that the astronauts were given noise-cancelling headphones.

Once it was finished, the woman slowly walked out to rejoin the group and Arthur was invited inside.

"This is about 6 g," the instructor said as he checked the equipment while Arthur strapped himself into the chair.

"I assume I won't black out, then," Arthur said as the instructor stepped out.

"Not if you want to become an astronaut," he said as he shut the door.

That's not a choice I can make, Arthur thought as the machine slowly began to spin. He tried to clear his mind to make the experience more bearable but the increasing speeds stopped him from thinking anyway.

He felt several times heavier and the pressure inside was unbearable; he was barely able to see properly as the machine increased its speed further.

He felt as if he was going to be violently ill and his vision was beginning to lose all colour —something he did not expect. He clenched his muscles, which did not reduce the suffering as he had hoped. The pain became overwhelming and he was preparing to quit his training when the human centrifuge slowed and he was able to think again; the colours returned in front of his eyes as the instructor helped him out of his seat.

He stayed outside as the final astronaut experienced the human centrifuge; Arthur rejoined the group when he had recovered.

"Well done everyone. Take some time to recover, then we'll return to the training room for an agility workout," the instructor told them, leading them to the van waiting outside.

I'd have been kicked out if they hadn't simplified the training, Arthur thought as he stared at a distant office building. *I'm lucky space travel is becoming more widely available.*

He completed his day of work and returned home, immediately collapsing on his bed. He glanced at the degree hanging from the wall and sighed, instinctively reaching for his new phone due to boredom.

Arthur slept little during the night, knowing that the following day would be as intense as usual. Dreams of the two figures became sparser as the weeks continued, forcing Arthur to wonder if it had just been his mind creating random images. Still, the figures remained in his thoughts and he had grown accustomed to them in his dreams, choosing not to keep track of them after roughly his eighth otherworldly dream.

He awoke to a week of survival training that would slowly pass. On the following Monday, Arthur and the other astronauts prepared for the next phase of their training; they were led to a reduced-gravity aircraft that awaited them in a large hangar.

They geared up and boarded the jet, standing away from each other and waiting for gravity to leave the vehicle. The vehicle soon rolled out of the hangar and lifted off the ground, preparing to provide the astronauts with a parabolic flight.

Minor weightlessness soon took effect; the astronauts had few instructions, other than to grow comfortable with the new environment that they were in, one that resembled the amount of gravity on the surface of Mars. Arthur enjoyed the feeling of relative normality—basic activities such as walking took less strength.

The gravity further slipped away and Arthur struggled to stop himself from floating backwards from the centre of the room. He watched as his fellow astronauts tried to reach the other end of the tube while he relished the unique experience by jumping to reach the roof and floating away from the walls of the aircraft.

Once the tube was gravity-free, Arthur refocused on the reason for the training and began making his way towards other astronauts, exchanging brief remarks about the strange feeling of being closer to the ceiling than the ground.

Even if I didn't go to space, this is one of the

best experiences I've ever had, Arthur thought as he narrowly avoided bashing his head on the roof of the tube. He allowed his body to fall to the ground as he repressed the urge to vomit, seeing that the other astronauts were mostly unbothered by the strange environment.

Luckily for him, they soon began to descend. He moved into to prepare himself for the changes in atmospheric pressure, almost disappointed when the gravity returned to the jet and they hit the rough asphalt surface of the runway.

They safely returned to the hangar and congratulated each other on coping with the descent, walking in a disorientated manner as they continued to readjust to the weight of gravity.

Arthur quickly returned his borrowed gear and walked home, having to stop and vomit while walking. He reflected on the experience as he returned home to his parents and their adoptive son, who were watching an animated programme that Arthur did not recognise.

He walked inside his room and went to bed in an attempt to reduce the minor headache he had acquired from the flight, eventually falling asleep while appreciating the gravity that held him to his bed.

He was inside a cave. He began walking through, despite being unable to see much ahead of him; it was incredibly dark but something told him that he was in a cave. He found that he had his weapons that had been recovered from the vault under the university. He made his way through the cave using the small amount of light provided by the glowing weaponry, passing a couple of stalactites to hear shouting and slashing nearby.

He saw light and ran towards it, hearing the chilling screams of a monster. He saw its carved-out body, with the ribs hanging grotesquely and its rigid body was struggling to deal with those who were trying to kill it. The neck held the head on the end, like a lamppost, and its mouth hung open in search of its next meal. The two attackers were separated, one on its back and the other climbing the ribs.

What is this? Arthur thought as the one on its back was thrown and the remaining attacker called for something that was unintelligible to him.

The injured attacker began to climb the creature using their dagger and threw something to the other figure, who used it to fire into the creature's chest and brought it crashing down—the other figure protested for an unknown reason.

They appeared mournful towards the creature and discussed something in a dialect that he felt he recognised but could not understand. Arthur could see that they wore grey armour with helmets that concealed their faces as they approached him.

He felt the sudden urge to run and did so through the caves behind him that were suddenly lit. He ran into a lit metal room, which quickly collapsed before he had any chance of examining it. He was forced to retreat into the cave, where he ran into the two figures, who suddenly fell into a white light that appeared from behind them.

He woke up in the early hours of the next day with scattered emotions and reached for his laptop to divert his focus. He searched through various websites to find information on rocket modifications but only found results that detailed the inner workings of a normal rocket.

He placed his laptop in the draw beside him and fell back to sleep, hoping that he could ask a YAATO employee for more information in the morning.

He awoke several hours later, almost late for work, and rushed to get ready. He was able to arrive on time but was later than the other astronauts were, his face becoming red as he rushed inside.

Arthur and the other astronauts were instructed on the class that they would be faced with, after being led to a training room where they completed another round of agility training.

Once the course had finished, the astronauts were awarded a break—Arthur took the opportunity to visit the mechanics, who were working on the rocket that Arthur planned to board.

A woman walked towards him as soon as he entered, making him think that he would be asked to leave.

"We're getting it done," she told him in a calm yet confident voice.

"I—I wasn't checking on the rocket," Arthur responded as he admired the nose cone hanging in front of him. "I just wanted to see one in construction."

"We're just assessing the quality—"

"Sayuri!" one of the mechanics called out and the woman walked towards the nose cone. Arthur watched as she checked the cone for scratches or holes that could jeopardise the trip.

"I'm—I'm Arthur," he said as he approached the mechanics and saw the immaculate surface of the cone.

Hi Arthur," she said. "Is our work up to your satisfaction?"

"I don't know, that's only a nose cone."

"Have you learnt about the specifics of a rocket?"

"Yeah—I studied Mechanical Engineering at uni."

They spent the rest of his break discussing

their passion for space travel and the rocket that was being built for the astronauts; Sayuri gave a short explanation of how each component of the vehicle functioned, particularly focusing on the nose cone as it was directly in front of them.

After his break, Arthur was called to a public speaking class, something that was mandatory and included within his training—something that was vital for him to improve.

Walking into a small classroom, he was greeted by his fellow astronauts and an instructor; they were sitting around a C-shaped table and watched Arthur pick up a wireless microphone headset and attach it to his ear.

He stood in front of them, his eyes darting between the faces of his fellow astronauts. He slowly raised his shoulders, before lowering them upon making eye contact with the instructor. His breaths were fast and short as he recalled the short speech that he had previously written in preparation for his return to Earth—assuming he would return.

"In 2028 I began my training at the York..."
What's the name?!
"...Aeronautics and..."
Next word begins with 'A', then it's 'TO'.
"...Aircraft Travel Organisation."
That's wrong. Move on.
"The journey to...reach where I am now has been hard but I am forever grateful that I've—"

Speak more formally.

"—I have had this opportunity thanks to the instructors that guided and supported me throughout everything. Despite my difficulties and issues that I have faced to get here, I am—"

Should I have said 'the difficulties and issues' instead?

"—honoured to have the chance to further humanity's space exploration efforts, to tell you about them today."

Arthur stared at his critics, their faces falsely conveying support. He focused on calming himself down as he listened intently for questions.

"Okay, Arthur...what does YAATO hope to achieve on this mission?" the instructor asked, his face expressing little warmth.

"To determine whether or not it is possible to set up a colony on the Moon based on data we've already collected, currently stored on the ISS; we'd like to humans permanently living on its surface by..."

Not 2030. It's...

"...2050?"

He responded to several more questions, generally focusing on his rigorous training routine and mission, before he was granted a chance to stop speaking.

"Not bad..." the instructor told him. "...it could be better, though. Your body language is too defensive and your knowledge isn't particularly accurate. Dom, your turn. Arthur, try again at the end of the class."

The classes continued throughout the week; Arthur spent longer revising the knowledge he needed, hoping that he could reach the standard that his fellow astronauts had set with their powerful speeches. Between lectures and training sessions, Arthur would converse with Sayuri, initially hoping that she could help him reach his extraterrestrial destination.

A couple of weeks later, he hesitantly entered the Vehicle Assembly Centre and found her sitting at a table eating her lunch. She offered him a seat across from her and he accepted, staring at her uncomfortably.

"Do you know where I could find parts of a rocket ship—"

"The parts aren't for sale," she told him.

"—to reach another planet?"

Sayuri laughed. "Our rockets are not equipped for that."

"But where could I find the parts that are?" he asked.

She stayed silent for a moment before responding in a quiet voice, "A couple of months ago, there was a piece of alien technology recovered at the bottom of the ocean—all over the news. It's now inside a vault in Canada, apparently."

"Are we forbidden from discussing it?" Arthur asked.

"No, I—I don't think so."

"Ah, thank you so much. I'll leave you to eat," he said to her as he stood up and left the room to return to complete the rest of his training for the day, thinking about a way to secure the technology without flying to Canada.

Once his work day was complete and he had returned home, he called Rose and immediately asked if she was able to contact Sarah. She fulfilled his request and their former roommate soon called Arthur, who was eager to speak to her.

"Hello?" Sarah said as she glared at her webcam.

"Hi," Arthur responded. "I need some help."

He vaguely explained the situation but she was unable to help him since she was in Poland. However, she gave him Steven's phone number, as she was unwilling to cut her holiday short. Arthur called, feeling relieved as he finally had the opportunity to see potential evidence that could verify the sights in his dreams.

"I need a piece of a rocket," Arthur said. "It's in a vault in Canada."

"How am I supposed to get that?!" Steven asked in surprise.

Arthur gave him the same explanation for his request as he had to Sarah, knowing that he would need more information and money to find the part.

As he tried to reason with Steven, Arthur's

father walked in and told him that someone was waiting for him outside. Arthur walked out, phone in hand, and saw Sayuri standing at the door, visibly desperate to speak to him.

He led her into the dining room and closed the door. He sat beside Sayuri and placed his phone in front of them, with Steven smiling back. Sayuri spoke in a calm voice, telling them that she had close friends in North America who were willing to steal the component and deliver it to Arthur for a large fee.

"Are your friends part of a gang?" Arthur asked with an incredulous glare.

"No, they're just well connected," Sayuri responded.

"This borders on illegal activity," Arthur said as he wondered if he would be able to cover the costs, knowing that no one else would help him to pay the fee.

"They need to get into the country, bribe guards, transport the massive piece out of the facility and get it across the Atlantic Ocean," she said.

"I'll pay a percentage of the shipping costs," Steven said. "If you tell me what this thing is for."

That's a good point, what is it for?" Sayuri asked Arthur, who was beginning to turn red.

"It's…um…I want to leave the solar system," he said after a long pause. Steven mumbled something while Sayuri stared at him.

"You're…you can't. You'll die," she told Arthur. He felt pain travel up his arm and he slammed his fist down on the table in an attempt to repress the ethereal daggers that fought to strike from his hand.

"It's not our fault," Steven said, staring at his clenched hand.

"No…I was just crushing a bug," Arthur said as he relaxed his hand. His eyes darted around the room, before looking at Sayuri and nodding; she left the room to contact her friends.

"This is a really bad idea," Steven told Arthur, who was staring at the table in front of him.

"I know, but I'm doing it anyway," Arthur said quietly. They sat in silence as they waited for Sayuri, who soon returned. Arthur ended the call with Steven and switched to his banking app, hesitantly depositing the funds into the account that Sayuri detailed.

He spent the next few weeks asking around and researching the next pieces needed, which soon led him to seek out a modified engine kept somewhere in Wales.

Remembering that he was relying on others, he informed his parents as to where he was going and quickly called a taxi that would take him to his destination. Shadow jumped at him as he left the house, causing Arthur to feel guilty about leaving him for a short time—he felt even worse about preparing to leave him permanently.

He had compiled all of the information he could find and learnt that the part was near Aberystwyth. The taxi stopped in the town centre and Arthur climbed out, seeking out the nearest garden centre. He bought a shovel and a pair of gloves, before asking around about historical sites.

He was directed to a set of ruins in a field, loosely resembling a temple. He found it devoid of visitors and stepped inside to find it entirely abandoned. As he pushed past the scaffolding and tape, he walked through a mossy corridor that led deeper underground, into the main building.

Entering the main room, he found that the interior was surprisingly well-kept, suggesting that it had been recently visited or that it was still used; some of the flooring and walls looked as if they had been recently replaced.

He walked through more dark corridors to find a door that refused to move. He was able to break the thin metal that held the door shut but opening the door proved to be a more difficult task. He took his shovel and was able to jam it into the edge of the door, bending the tool but allowing him to get into the next room. As he removed the shovel and slipped inside, the door shut once again and he was unable to find a way to open it back up.

He walked through a few more corridors, which became increasingly modernistic, and finally found a giant, ancient room where only parts of the floor had survived while the rest of the room was comprised of a crumbling dirt. Inside were three giant engines that were not designed to be carried by one person.

He tried calling Rose but found that he was lacking signal since he was in the middle of the countryside. He was left to marvel the ancient engines and the brilliant patterns that ran down the sides, with a glow from a type of technology that he had never seen or heard of.

Someone must've got the engines in here somehow, Arthur thought as he searched the room for an escape route. Looking up, he saw that the roof was simply dirt held up by metal scaffolding; it did not appear to have a simple method of collapse but he quickly searched the room for something to dislodge it.

Walking behind the deactivated engines, he found a half-buried chest and dug it out of the ground. He pulled it beside him and knelt down, pressing the button in the centre to open the lid.

Inside were a couple of deactivated landmines, below a single sticky grenade. Beneath the mines was a lighter and some rusty nails, which suggested to Arthur that it was the belongings of a long-dead soldier, likely discarded in the last two hundred years.

This seems too coincidental, Arthur thought as he carefully rolled the grenade out of the box and lifted up the landmines, placing them on the floor beside him. He glanced back inside the box and grabbed the lighter, noticing a small notebook underneath.

Arthur quickly shoved the notebook in his pocket and lifted one of the mines in the air, holding it away from his head, as he feared dropping it. In a sudden burst of adrenaline, he threw the mine in the air and it magnetised to the metal scaffolding above, despite being several metres away.

Why did you do that?! You could've killed yourself! Arthur thought to himself as he picked up the next landmine and threw it as high as he could, watching it attach to the scaffolding.

Once they were all placed, he picked up the sticky grenade and stood in the centre of the room. He threw the grenade above his head and heard a clink as it secured itself to the scaffolding. He crouched beneath one of the engines and heard a ticking sound, which stopped and presented him with a large explosion that caused dirt to rain down on him

He saw that the entire roof had collapsed and direct sunlight shone into the ancient room. The three engines were covered in dust and mud but otherwise undamaged, despite the explosions that had occurred above.

I'm glad no one was walking over this place, he thought as he climbed one of the engines and leapt onto the grassy surface above. He stared at the unearthed room for a few moments, before running to the nearest road and calling a taxi.

He reached a nearby town and called Sayuri, who grudgingly agreed to meet with him and to hire two lorries that he would pay for. He thanked her and jogged back to the engines, where he began digging a slope so that the engines were easy to reach.

Sayuri and the lorries arrived after four hours to find Arthur laying on the grass. He quickly stood up and greeted her, before approaching the lorry driver and paying the £200 owed for the two vehicles. The drivers left in a separate car while Sayuri and Arthur entered the pit, listening to the hum of the engines as they approached.

"Give me a sec to take a look at them," Sayuri told him as she opened her toolkit and placed her hand on a metal panel. She then knelt down and tapped on the glass that covered the lights, before grabbing a screwdriver and hitting the glass with it.

"What are you doing?" Arthur asked as he cautiously approached her.

"Trying to figure out how to get in," she responded. "There's no cords or screws or anything. I don't know what's holding it together."

Arthur wandered around the back of the engine and looked inside. Stepping into darkness, he fumbled around for his phone and used the torch to look around inside, hoping that the knowledge from his university education would help him.

"There's nothing in here!" Arthur called out after several seconds.

"Why would there be? There has to be a barrier between the fire so the engine doesn't explode!" Sayuri replied as she managed to remove a panel by jamming her screwdriver into its edge. "Also, don't...go in the end of an engine you know nothing about."

"You'd have no idea that I have a Mechanical Engineering degree if I hadn't told you," Arthur said, holding back a smile. Sayuri let out a short laugh and began prying the rest of the panels off the first engine, muttering the lyrics to a song under her breath.

"Can I borrow some of your tools to start on the other engines?" Arthur asked, before walking towards her toolkit after receiving verbal confirmation. He picked up a screwdriver with a glass handle and looked at the small picture laying inside, showing the portrait of a young man and woman standing in front of a river.

"Can—am I able to use this?" Arthur asked. She turned around and stared at the transparent handle, opening her mouth slightly; her eyes displayed apprehension as she fixated on the tool.

"Yeah, sure. Don't—worry about the picture, that's just my brother and sister: Finn and Mia."

Arthur glanced at the photo once more and quickly walked over to an engine to begin disassembling it.

Sayuri appeared to relax as she turned her attention back to the component she was removing and let out a sigh. "I took that photo when we were visiting my gran in Osaka—I distinctly remember how happy she was after my parents told her that I was named after her."

Arthur smiled, remembering his own grandmother before turning his focus back to dismantling the engines.

They worked until night, when they could no longer see what they were doing. Arthur sat inside the engine he had been disassembling and looked at the photo in the screwdriver.

"I miss them."

Arthur dropped the tool and turned around to see Sayuri standing behind him. He quickly picked it back up and looked at her pensive expression as she stared at the portrait inside.

"What happened to them?" Arthur asked. *I shouldn't have asked her that—too insensitive.*

Sayuri stopped working and inhaled the stale air. "Finn and Mia got into a car crash last time we visited our grandparents," she said, crossing her arms and continuing to focus on the photo.

"Sorry—I didn't mean to make you uncomfortable," Arthur responded, giving her a weak smile. "Not to take away from your grieving, but I lost my grandmother last year."

"I bet she's proud of you, going to space—my brother always wanted to go, but he was too scared to do it. It hurts me to know he never got to go."

"Did he manage to work in aeronautics?"

"He became an instructor, helping others to become something he wanted to be. He would've loved to work beside me, but he couldn't beat the other applicants—he tried for two years before applying to teach."

Arthur glanced at the photo again. "When did he teach here?"

"He started when your group came in," she told him. "Did you meet him?"

"I think I did," Arthur said. "He looks like the guy who encouraged me through one of the hardest aspects of the course—well, it was hard for me."

Sayuri sat on the ground and gestured for the screwdriver. Arthur passed it to her and she looked at the photo more carefully. She stared at it failed to fight back tears, looking at the smiling face of her deceased brother. Arthur hesitated to move towards her, instead deciding to walk out.

"Don't leave," Sayuri said as she heard his

foot exit the hollow engine. He returned to her and consoled her, knowing he had been in a similar situation several months ago.

Sitting beside her, he looked into the darkness outside and said nothing. *Death is permanent. How can someone bring themselves to kill another person? How is it fair to steal someone else's life?*

"Think about the time that they got to spend with you," Arthur said in an unsteady tone. He briefly glanced at her to see that she was no longer crying, instead staring at the giant engine they were inside.

They suddenly awoke at midday and weakly smiled at each other, before continuing to dismantle the giant engines. They managed to remove the majority of the alien technology and elected to hire a couple of mechanics to help them disassemble the rest.

They were finished by the evening and had piled the pieces into the back of both lorries. Neither Sayuri nor Arthur had spoken a full sentence to each other since their last conversation and drove separate lorries to the border.

They were briefly checked by security, who did not find the engine parts to be suspicious and let them back into England. They returned to YAATO's Vehicle Assembly Centre and unloaded the parts, with Sayuri briefly checking her phone.

"My friends got the pieces—the fins—from Canada. They're already inside," she said. Arthur nodded and smiled as he dragged a giant metal panel inside. Once they had finished, Sayuri stopped him from leaving and stared at him.

"Last night, I didn't—"

"Don't worry about it," she told him, watching his brown eyes as they stared back at her. She placed her hand in his. "It was nice having you there."

"If I'm going to space, I'll have to leave everyone behind," he said, glancing at the rocket modifications behind her.

Sayuri's calm expression wavered as she spoke but quickly returned to its relaxed state. "I know."

He slowly moved his head towards her and kissed her; she joyfully reciprocated the gesture but broke away, moving her hands away from his.

"I'll help you out, but this isn't what I want," she told him, watching disappointment form on his face.

"Sorry, I get it." Arthur said. "We've only known each other for a few months. I think we're just desperate."

Her face indicated she disagreed. "I had no one else to confide in. You were there and cared enough to help. That's all."

"Sorry, I'm not—"

"I know, just don't worry about it."

Arthur repressed the urge to try to explain himself and instead stood beside Sayuri; both were silent, watching the sun setting over the green fields. The sky was filled with streaks of yellow and blue; the air was still and the car park was silent, unlike their minds that were occupied by a flurry of thoughts. "I think we're both looking for someone to comfort us."

Sayuri continued to watch the sky grow darker, crossing her arms as the air became cooler. "As long as we can stand up for ourselves, I wouldn't say there's anything wrong with that."

They stood in the car park for half an hour, silently contemplating the futures that awaited them.

A couple of months passed before Arthur was given a lead on the next rocket modification. Rose had contacted him about an ancient rocket nozzle that had been found in New Zealand as she had been asked to write a story on it; she offered to attempt to recover it for him using her contacts if he compensated her for time and money lost while getting it—he agreed and wished her luck.

This is getting expensive, Arthur thought as he browsed his laptop for more information on the final piece; he had extensively studied the components of a rocket and felt that there was only one other part that mattered, although he planned to check with the mechanics to see if there was anything he had missed.

He searched the internet for an hour, before finding what he was looking for. The entire guidance system of a rocket was for sale as a replica, but the design seemed otherworldly and resembled the other pieces that Arthur had recovered.

I guess I won't need money once I've left Earth, he thought as he bidded £5000. He immediately moved to retract the offer but ultimately decided against it, instead choosing to wait a few days.

Come on... Arthur thought as he checked to see that he had won the bid. He immediately checked the address of the seller and hired a taxi to Bristol, meeting with the driver outside of his parent's home.

He sat in the back of the taxi and watched as they passed YAATO's training facility. He checked his pocket for his phone, only to find the notebook he had taken while obtaining the modified engines. Opening the book, he read the first page and realised that it was a diary.

My name is Harold Brookes, writing to chronicle my many thoughts. I am enthusiastic about what is to come in the decade ahead, for it cannot be worse than the previous year. I cannot lose my cat Peter twice! In spite of this, I hope to record a plen-

tiful number of positive experiences as we enter the 1930s! Dad has finally agreed to teach me about archaeology so that I can discover the world using my own hands, I will write about the results at a later date.

That explains why I found his notebook underground, Arthur thought. *But was he the one to leave it there?*

He skimmed many of the entries, learning that Harold eventually became an archaeologist and married a woman called Dorothy, having many children—one of the grandchildren had the same name as his grandmother.

Wh— Arthur thought as he was shaken by the idea that he was reading the notes of his great-grandfather. *That's impossible—that's too much of a coincidence.*

He read the final account, desperate to know his fate.

I have reached the Engines. They are not of this world. I write this as I stare at the glowing green lamps that look like they came from the future (like in the illustrations of the 2000s)! They do not resemble anything I have ever seen, although I am not a mechanic. That man is still chasing me, clearly hysterical about me finding these magical inventions. If he succeeds in murdering me with that tiny knife, this will be the last entry. I will hide this notebook for my children to find and remember me by (I expect it will be James). I do not know where this technology is from, but I hope that it can be used for good by a heroic soldier, or someone similar. I must stop writing as

Arthur sat back in his seat and closed the notebook. He looked out of the window and wondered if he could track down the man who killed Harold, but ultimately decided against it as it was a not a role he was suited for—regardless, the murderer was likely dead before Arthur had even been born.

Arthur turned away from the window and picked up his phone, deciding to ring a furniture removal company—partly to distract himself and because he could not transport the guidance system alone.

A couple of hours passed and Arthur reached the seller's house. He got out of the taxi and approached the door, trying to shake the images he had conjured in his mind after reading through the notebook.

He knocked on the door and it was opened by a middle-aged woman, who seemed irritated by his presence.

"I'm here for the guidance system...replica," he told her. She led him to a living room, where several well-built men watched him enter.

"Are you the one who wanted furniture moved?" one of them asked.

"Sorry, yes. I should've clarified that this isn't my house," Arthur responded.

"Would've been nice if you'd said something—I thought they were breaking in," the woman muttered behind him. She led them to a large room where an assortment of parts lay on tables and the floor.

"This was my great-grandfather's," the woman muttered. "No idea where he found it."

Was he the one that killed Harold? Arthur thought as he helped them to move the pieces into a truck, managing to get a ride back home with the movers. Once they arrived in York, he directed them to drop the pieces off at YAATO's vehicle bay. Luckily, Sayuri was outside and helped him to hide the pieces within the facility, understanding the purpose of his visit by his presence alone.

"Only one more part left—my friend is getting it for me," Arthur told her as he put away the final sensor.

"Okay," she muttered.

"I know we haven't spoken much, but we will talk before I go…forever," he said.

"Before launch day, hopefully," she said as she locked the parts away in a storage room. "That reminds me—I've convinced YAATO that we can't fit the five of you in a rocket, so you'll get your own."

"Thank you so much, I've been worrying about that for a few weeks."

"It's fine," she said, admiring the alien technology beside her. "Just don't tell the public.

Rocket's aren't cheap."

"Let's hope I actually find something in space, then," he said with a smile, before leaving to check on Rose's progress.

With two months to go before launch, he had mostly left the modification duties to the engineering crew, who had no idea what they were installing. Rose had delivered the final piece, which had turned out to be as alien as the rest of the technology, and Sayuri was able to oversee the project, along with working on it herself.

The final months training was incredibly intense for Arthur and the other astronauts, but the instructors were also carefully supervising the candidates and ensuring their health was a high priority.

Arthur reduced his physical training at home to spend more time relaxing from the stressful work days, as well as talking to his friends as much as possible. Alex promised to visit on the day while Rose managed to convince her boss to let her report on the event, meaning that she could say farewell to him.

The day of the launch came and Arthur woke up at 3am, earlier than usual. He rushed to dress into some casual clothing and feed Shadow, before stopping and forcing himself to calm down. He left his room and entered the kitchen, quietly pouring a small bowl of cereal to avoid waking his parents.

I'll see them at the launch, Arthur thought as he began to eat. He glanced around the dark room and reflected on the memories he had with his parents, knowing that he would likely never see his childhood home again. A rosary sat atop a box in front of the window; Arthur's face was blank as he reminisced on his religious childhood.

I may not be a Christian anymore, but I know what it's like to have an...otherworldly experience.

Once he had finished his food, he walked to his room and carefully removed the alien weapons from a box that was under his bed, planning to conceal them in his spacesuit until he could unload them in the rocket; he also took the relic as he hoped he could find a tooth-shaped key that would fit inside.

He placed both the weapons and the relic in his backpack, before creeping around the house in search of Shadow. He found him in the kitchen, eating from his food bowl.

"I'm going to miss you," Arthur told him, kneeling beside the bowl and smiling at his dog, who was blissfully unaware that it would be one of their final times together.

"Alex'll pick you up later," Arthur told him as he stood up and walked back to his room, grabbing his backpack. He slung it around his arms and quietly opened the front door, slipping outside.

He walked quickly to YAATO and rushed into a vacant lecture room, where he abandoned his backpack behind a table. He then walked into the suit room, where he was helped to dress into his space suit.

"I'll be right back," he told one of the YAATO employees once it had been fitted, before walking back to the lecture room and reclaiming his backpack. He had come to realise that they would not fit under his space suit and approached the Vehicle Assembly Bay, where he was able to hand his bag to a mechanic so that it would be stored on the rocket.

Please don't look inside, Arthur thought as he left the room, knowing the bag would be checked anyway. He walked into the lobby to see Rose standing in front of a group of camera operators, talking to the receptionist.

I didn't know journalists could be reporters too, he thought as he waved to Rose and she waved back, both of them holding a stare for a few eternal seconds. Arthur walked up a wide staircase and reunited with the other astronauts, along with one of the instructors.

"Hi, Arthur, I was just telling the others that the rocket we have prepared only fits four people," the instructor told him.

All of the astronauts appeared concerned; they had come so far and were at risk of being turned away.

"Luckily, our engineers have designed a separate rocket which can be operated by one," he said. "That person will have a great deal of responsibility on them."

"I'll take it," Arthur said. "I want to prove that I can do it."

The instructor was surprised but nodded, leaving to inform the mechanics and the mission control centre.

"Are you sure? I don't mind taking it," one of the astronauts asked, taken aback by Arthur's calmness.

"I think it's for the best," he told them. "I want to make it easier on everyone else."

He felt guilty about his selfish actions, knowing that his family and friends would be upset by his departure. Furthermore, the separate rocket likely costed millions of pounds that he would be unable to repay, along with him being unable to pay off his student debt.

He reassured himself, fully aware that it was too late, and remembered the alternatives; taking the other astronauts with him without their permission, or staying on Earth and being forever haunted by visions.

However, he was terrified by the thought of being stranded in the middle of space, far away from Earth—if he could not return to civilisation, no one would come for him and he would die alone.

He called his parents, who were jolted

awake by the ringing of the phone. Hearing their voices caused his own to wobble; he struggled to cope with the thought of speaking to them for the last time.

They arrived three hours before the launch while Rose was reporting on the situation, speaking with confidence to mask her worry for Arthur; she was unwilling to lose her closest friend.

The doubts continued to flood into Arthur's mind as his parents arrived with Patrick, a brother he had had barely any time to become familiar with. Arthur met up with them in the lobby and pulled them away from the receptionist's desk.

"Mum, Dad," he said. "I'm in a space shuttle…on my own…but I'll have full control of it."

"I hope you're trained for that!" his father responded.

"Kind of," he replied. "I'm…going to go beyond the space station, beyond the solar system…"

His parents were shocked and confused as they had thought that he would return in a couple of months or years—visible concern took control of their expressions and Arthur immediately noticed.

"That's supposed to be the plan, but I'm going further," he told them, frozen by anxiety.

"Is that safe?" his mother asked.

"Probably," he said, with a fake smile that

disappeared quickly. "I—I hope…so."

His parents did not appear to be convinced and hugged him tightly, clearly terrified at the concept of losing their child.

"You should've told us this earlier, I…" his father said, letting go of Arthur and standing at a distance.

"My rocket is equipped with modifications that should protect me," he told them. "They should keep the rocket working in an environment that a YAATO rocket is not designed for."

His parents looked increasingly concerned, as he had feared, and were clearly holding back tears. His mother held Patrick tightly as Arthur justified his actions.

"I've had…dreams. Dreams of two alien people who seem so realistic…I have an unexplained confidence that they exist and I need to find them," he said. "I don't know why, but I just do. Please trust me."

They hugged him again tightly, with Patrick joining in despite not understanding the circumstances.

"I'll do my best to return," he told them, his breathing quickening.

He was informed through his earpiece that the rockets would be taking off in a few hours, and that he would have to begin preparations.

I hope this isn't a mistake.

"You'll be in our prayers tonight," his mother told him, followed by his father nodding.

"Thanks Mum," Arthur said with tears in his eyes, leaving his parents and climbing onto the shuttle bus waiting outside. He looked away from the other astronauts so they would not mention the many emotions plastered across his face.

They reached the launch pad and Arthur entered the facility, standing by a window for around half an hour as he watched his fellow astronauts cross a bridge to enter their rocket. Arthur heard constant orders in his ear and ignored them, knowing he would have to wait for the four-person rocket, Sunlight, to launch first.

He carefully continued making his way through the facility, watching the larger rocket prepare for takeoff.

This is the last time I'll ever be on his planet... possibly.

"Sunlight, prepared for launch," Arthur heard in his ear.

I've just realised that that's a strange name for a rocket.

"T-minus one minute."

They have no idea what I'm about to do.

"T-minus thirty seconds."

I hope their flight goes as smoothly as possible—I doubt mine will.

"T-minus ten seconds."

Arthur ran up to his rocket and stared at the

bridge between him and the hatch.

"Three, two, one, zero. Lift-off for Sunlight. Prepare Moonlight for launch."

Arthur watched Sunlight force its way into the sky as he stepped onto the bridge that extended to Moonlight, thinking of the six years that had led to the moment. YAATO professionals rushed past him, as he stood stagnant, his legs refusing to move until he had mentally processed the situation.

Only six years ago, he thought, briefly flashing a smile. *Six years ago, I worked for King Cut at Cakecut Bakery—becoming an astronaut seemed...unrealistic.*

The sun beamed through the immaculate windows that extended from the floor to the ceiling. He could see the hills behind the facility, the hills on which he had spent many days of his childhood running around and playing with friends—only one of which he had kept in contact with.

"Wait!" he heard behind him. He turned around to see Rose, running with her notepad in her hand. "Do you know what you're doing?"

"No...but I'm doing it anyway," he said quietly, looking away so he would not see her initial reaction.

"Please," she told him, staring into his fearful eyes. "Come back. We'll sit on the hill and have a picnic, like we used to."

"We can't—I'm...so sorry, Rose," he told her

in a sombre tone. Rose let her notepad slip out of her hand and she ran and hugged Arthur, the tears sliding down their faces.

"Write the best damn story about this mission," he told her as he released her. "If anyone talks about me, you'll know where I am."

Rose opened her mouth to respond but instead remained silent, wiping the tears from her eyes. She picked up her notepad and looked at her friend's face with sadness, as he reciprocated the expression.

"We've saved each other more than once. Save me one more time by surviving this trip," she said.

"I will, if you save me a copy of your report for when I return," he said as he began to approach the airlock, taking a moment to compose himself.

"Arthur!" Alex shouted from behind him, holding Shadow on a lead.

"Thank you so much," he said as he began to stroke and pet Shadow, who was excited to see him. He became more emotional as he was told to finally enter the space shuttle. He hugged Shadow and looked into the large eyes staring back.

"I love you so much," he told him quietly. "Someone, please look after him while I'm away."

"I can look after him," Alex said, "but we've been through too much for this to be our last conversation."

"If I return, I want to hear about everything you've both done since this moment," Arthur said.

"I'll wait for you on the hill," Rose said softly, her gaze briefly switching to the landscape outside.

"Bring yourself back soon, mate," Alex said. "I want to see you before I die—to know where you've been."

"There's no way I'm leaving you both forever," Arthur said with a smile as he opened the airlock.

"Arthur Brookes, enter Moonlight immediately," a voice commanded in his ear. Arthur's hand shook on the airlock door and he quickly let go, turning to see Shadow staring back at him. He ran back towards his loyal dog, hugging him tightly.

"You've been here since the start," he said. "You have no idea what I was doing, or what I'm doing now."

Rose urged Arthur to board the shuttle; he released Shadow from his grasp and jogged up to the airlock.

"Au revoir," he told his friends with a smirk. Taking one more glance at the hills, he stepped inside Moonlight and heard the airlock door shut firmly behind him.

Alex and Rose pulled Shadow away from the

bridge as it detached from the facility. They exchanged a couple of brief words, before Alex headed home with Shadow and Rose continued to report with false enthusiasm, clearing the running tears and makeup off her face before starting.

Sayuri emerged from another room and helped Arthur to secure himself in his seat. She then checked the cockpit for any damage or faults, opening up several parts of the room to expose the wiring.

"I may never see you again," she said, reaching into a jumble of wires.

"We said we'd talk before launch day—I wish we had spoken more before I leave," he said to her as he ensured his helmet was secured to the rest of his space suit.

"It's too late now," she muttered. "If you come back, we can talk again."

"Thank you for all the help you've given me—this would've been impossible without you," Arthur said as he watched her close a panel and open the door to the adjoining corridor.

"I wish I hadn't helped you to leave," she said sombrely. She closed the door and walked out of the shuttle, into a private room where she could mourn the loss of another person she had begun to feel close to.

You've done it, you've done what you wanted to do, Arthur thought to himself as he activated the control console and responded to the many voices in his earpiece. Moonlight lifted off, preventing the lone astronaut from abandoning his mission.

The rocket broke through the atmosphere and entered space, the nearest space station glowing in anticipation of his arrival. His rocket lit up and he sped up where he was meant to slow down.

The other rocket docked at the space station while he pushed his way into the void that was space, ignoring the voices warning him.

"You're going too far!"

"The rocket isn't designed to go beyond Earth's orbit!"

"Arthur...what are you doing?"

His fellow astronauts spoke into his ear and begged him to return.

"I'll...I'll see you again," Arthur told them, hearing the cries for concern grow louder, before they were drowned out with static—then silence. He pushed his engines into overdrive and hurtled through space, disappearing from the sight of human civilisation.

CHAPTER 24

The assault was almost ready to begin, but Vekk had another priority. She entered the giant underground hospital and asked for directions to Kol's room. She reached the door after a couple of minutes and walked inside to see him lying on a bed.

"Are you...you..." Vekk said as she stared at Kol's pale face. She rushed to hug him but he was unable to reciprocate the gesture.

"Don't do that, it hurts," he muttered. She quickly let go and sat on a chair beside him.

"This is probably the third time one of us has needed medical assistance," she said.

"Do you think we're ready for Zrelyar?" Kol asked as a medical robot entered the room and began looking at his wound.

"We'll have a ton of backup," she said. "I doubt we're ready to take them on alone, though."

"We'll can train more, once we've won," Kol said, with complete confidence.

Let's hope we do, Vekk thought as she nodded in agreement.

Kol looked at the ceiling as he felt a device being attached to the area where his shoulder once was. He suddenly felt numb—his neck would not move as he tried to see who had just entered the room.

It was a bot carrying a metal arm, equal in length to Kol's remaining upper limb. It was pure black, the exposed wires and pieces of plating being painted to match the modern design. The two robots lined up the metallic shoulder with his wound and slowly attached them.

Kol was visibly shocked by the sensations but said nothing. His head fell to the side and he looked at Vekk with fear; his sister struggled to watch the procedure.

The arm was attached within an hour but Kol remained in the hospital for a couple of weeks as the robots checked the prosthetic to ensure that it would not cause discomfort or injury.

Once he was discharged and had mostly recovered, Reqilar ordered them to train for the final assault alongside fellow rebels who had little experience in war. They practised for months as supplies were stockpiled and alternate plans were created in case the main mission failed.

After five months of preparation, both of the siblings were called to a meeting with Reqilar—

one of the final conferences in Modspi.

When the meeting began, Reqilar spoke with a renewed passion, commending each rebel that was present before getting into the specifics.

"Assault vehicles?"

"Ready."

"Rebels?"

"Ready."

"Armaments?"

"Lacking."

"Have we been discovered?"

"Not yet."

Reqilar looked at his notes in silence and began typing something. He then looked up and requested further details on the gear and weaponry supplies from Sydrilla, the head of war supplies and original founder of the rebellion. She slowly nodded as he made more notes and then looked up with concern.

"This is going to push our plan back by a couple of days," he said. "We need to acquire more armaments."

"Each of us could scout out locations," Psykier suggested. "Each of our commanders has a reliable team that could get around without raising suspicion."

"Yes. Contact Vekkilar and Kolansar once you're sure of a location; they will distract the guards so you can get inside," Reqilar told them, much to the surprise of the siblings.

The meeting concluded and the siblings waited around Modspi, waiting to be called for combat.

"I just want this to be over," Vekk said as they walked around the city.

"It'll be strange," Kol responded. "It's been like this for a year, I think."

"Almost a year," Vekk corrected. "Let's hope we won't miss these days."

They admired the city for three hours, until Reqilar approached them and briefly instructed them on their penultimate mission.

"You will distract the guards at a hidden storehouse so the rebels can sneak inside," he told them. "After that, you'll enter the robot city of Drixav and disable the beam that has been set up there—I believe it is identical to the one in Zrelyar."

"Where is the storehouse?" Vekk asked.

"Right next to the city."

"Alright," Kol said hesitantly.

"Good luck, don't die," Reqilar told them, walking off to the command centre.

"I just want this to be over," Kol said with a sigh, shaking his metallic arm as he continued to adjust to its presence.

"Thrakalir would've been a better protector than me," Vekk said as she watched the arm move around. "Let's get to the shuttle."

"I couldn't have done what you have," Kol reassured her.

"You already have...and much more," she muttered as they turned towards the hangar and were directed to a free shuttle, where Arkriat and Kretai were waiting for them. Vekk looked up at the buildings around them while Kol tapped on the shuttle with his metallic fingers to test them.

Vekk soon led him inside the vehicle and the four of them flew to Drixav, admiring the tall buildings of the lifeless city.

"Zrelyar and Modspi must be the only cities with underground buildings—even Modspi has a lot above ground," Vekk muttered as a giant skyscraper came into view.

"Must be," Kol responded, stretching his new arm and clenching his fist as pain seared through his left shoulder blade.

"Medical care is better than I thought," Vekk said. "I thought it'd take you longer to recover."

"Maybe my body repairs faster than others," he said, relaxing his hand. "I'm just hoping my metal arm will still be there after Zrelyar."

Vekk piloted the shuttle over the city, letting it hover over a nearby ravine. A small door was embedded in the cliff wall and was guarded by two robotic soldiers standing on a platform. Kol looked to the left to see rebels waiting on either side of the ravine, waiting for the siblings to move in.

Vekk moved the shuttle close to the platform and Kol leapt onto it, quickly destroying the two robots with his spear. Vekk and Arkriat joined him as he tried to enter the passcode.

"Let me try," Vekk said as she approached the keypad on the wall. She tapped four random numbers, causing a small metal stick to protrude from the wall and shock her. She shot the stick and it fell to the ground, before she shot the keypad as well. The door opened and the siblings ran inside, with Arkriat and Kretai retreating to the shuttle without them realising.

They hid behind a wall as a small patrol ran at them. Vekk destroyed the robots using her handgun and the siblings ran into a small room, with three other rooms branching off it.

Vekk ran into the left room while Kol entered the right. Vekk quickly destroyed the robot guards but struggled to face off against the two turrets, forcing her to hide behind a shelf.

"Kol!" she called out. She did not hear a response. Turret fire pummelled the shelf, eventually creating holes that exposed her to the relentless assault. Vekk knocked the shelf over, damaging one of the turrets but leaving her vulnerable.

Gunfire pierced her arm but she managed to take out the last turret before falling to her knees. She grimaced in pain and stood back up, watching rebels flood into the room to gather a variety of weapons.

"Are you alright?!" Kol asked as he walked in to see Vekk holding her arm.

"I should be fine," she told him.

"We can loot some medical supplies while we're here," he said.

"We'll clear the last room together."

"I'll get some other help, stay here," Kol said, helping her to the ground before walking off to speak to the rebel commander.

Kol and three other rebels stood beside the door to the final room. They then ran inside simultaneously and quickly destroyed the remaining turrets, with one person being gunned down without remorse from the machines. The rebels looted the room, finding a variety of medical supplies, and returned to their commander.

Kol stared at the corpse beside him, then lifted his head to look at Vekk sitting on the ground; she clutched the railing behind her as she looked back at him.

"Commander...we've lost someone," Kol said. The commander ran over and called two rebels to carry the body outside.

"You'll see a lot more of that later," the commander told him. Kol reacted in disgust as he turned away and picked up a bandage. He approached Vekk and placed it over a small section of exposed arm.

"Thanks," she said as he helped her back up. "We need to get going."

Vekk and Kol grabbed a large amount of medical equipment and sprinted for the exit. As they escaped, Kol bashed his elbow on a grey wall tile and heard a click, followed by a constant beeping that quickly grew louder.

"That'll stop Zavroon taking anything that's left!" one of the rebels shouted as she loaded supplies onto their ship.

"It's underneath the city!" Vekk shouted as an explosion burst through the walls behind her. She and Kol narrowly escaped the building as it collapsed and the platform fell into the ravine below. They threw the stolen supplies into a compartment and sat inside the shuttle, ready to takeoff once again.

"Are we better than Zavroon?" Vekk asked as she stared at the burning plaza through the window.

"We don't just leave the dead in the streets, do we?" Kol responded, looking down at Arkriat sitting beside him.

"The killing will stop once the rebels are in charge," Vekk said, placing her hands on the controls. "It's for the greater good, at the moment."

Vekk landed in an open area within Drixav, taking advantage of the distraction that the explosion had caused. The foundations of a skyscraper had collapsed and caused it to lean dangerously to one side, distracting the robots from the siblings' arrival.

They ran to the city square to see that the beam was unguarded. Kol took the five keys from a small pouch and placed them into the slots in the door. Arkriat and Kretai waited beside them, unsure about what was to come.

"Good practice," he said as the door swung open. Entering the room, they were faced with a glass tube that allowed the beam to continue, uninterrupted, into the sky. On each side was a metal ladder, which the siblings climbed down to see a room lined with turrets. They focused on the siblings but did not fire, as if waiting for something.

"I think we should disable the turrets first," Kol said as he helped Arkriat down the ladder.

"We might accidentally activate them instead," Vekk responded as they walked down the corridor to find a room that was empty, except for a ceiling light and a large glass door in the centre of the back wall; Vekk pushed the door but it did not open.

"There's something written above it," Kol said, squinting to read the faint text. It read:

She creates an artificial day but ages as you do, until her death. However, she can be reborn by skilled hands and the cycle will start anew.

Break her.

"Is it supposed to be a living being?" Kol asked.

"I doubt it," Vekk said. "It's compared to something alive, so it probably isn't alive itself."

"'An artificial day'?"

"A day...light! Light doesn't age..."

They looked around the room for prompts but nothing appeared to have ageing qualities.

"How could light age?" Kol asked as he walked around the room.

"Artificial light dies," Vekk said, moving her attention to the light in the middle of the ceiling.

"It's reborn when you replace it," Kol said as he approached it.

He thrusted his spear into the light, smashing it and watching as a device fell onto the metal floor. He picked up the keypad and placed it on the door, to which it magnetised.

"Glass isn't magnetic," Vekk said with a puzzled expression. Kol saw that five of the buttons had been worn down and he pressed them, causing the door to open. They walked through to find a ramp that led into a darker section of the underground building.

Passing through yet another corridor, they found a large circular room that was seemingly empty, except for a glowing pillar in the centre and the sound of howling wind. A wall surrounded it, the top half made of metal while the bottom half was reinforced glass that allowed the siblings to see inside the room.

"The metal walls look quite damaged," Kol

said as he walked around the hall that wrapped around the outside of the circular room.

"They're just corroding; they've probably been here for centuries," Vekk responded as she studied the loose bolts that had failed in their responsibility of holding the wall together.

Kol pulled a panel off the wall opposite the circular room to find a giant boulder lodged behind. He removed another panel and saw the edge of a second boulder that was directly in line with the first.

"I've found something that could help us out," he said quietly, pushing the first boulder to see if it would move; he was too weak and began looking around for a mechanism that would help him.

He quickly found a lever and pulled it, watching the boulder retract into the wall and hearing a rumbling around him, which grew gradually fainter. Rolling was heard along the roof, before the boulder tore through the ceiling of the circular room and threw its full weight onto the pillar in the centre, tearing it down.

Vekk turned to see the boulder being lifted from the ground and being thrown around by an invisible force. It split in half as it was slammed into the walls and thrown at the glass that refused to break upon contact with the heavy rock.

"We need to get out of here," Vekk said as

she began to run towards the exit. Kol pursued her, stopping at the doors as she ran through. He turned back inside and saw that the boulder had broken into the circular corridor and shattered on the ground.

The walls clunked, followed by the sound of rolling across the ceiling. Kol saw Arkriat and Kretai cowering on the ground as the sounds surrounded them. Instinctively, he ran towards the two creatures and forcefully pulled Arkriat from the ground, commanding him to run.

Several boulders broke through the ceiling and began rolling through the area, some smashing into others or setting off levers that released more boulders.

Kol saw rocks rolling towards the door and grabbed Kretai, throwing her at towards Vekk. Arkriat leapt between two boulders as they collided at the exit, breaking into thousands of smaller rocks.

Kol rushed through and reunited with Vekk, who was waiting at the bottom of the ladder.

"That was easy," she said as she began to climb up.

"For you, maybe," Kol responded as he placed Arkriat on the ladder and climbed beneath him, pushing him up as he ascended. Kretai flew beside them and darted towards the entrance door, squeaking loudly.

"The door's locked," Vekk said as she

twisted the lock several times. The floor cracked beneath her, splitting the once-sturdy concrete. She looked up at the tiny glass windows in the door and pierced one with her dagger.

"We can't fit through that," Kol remarked as he moved away from the crack that split the ground.

"Kretai, get us out of here," she said. Kretai did not respond and instead stared at her. "Kretai, go through here!"

"What've you done?" Kol asked as he looked at Kretai for any obvious signs of distress.

"Nothing!"

"Kretai, get us out," he commanded. Vekk watched in disbelief as Kretai passed through the window and turned the lock from the outside, opening the door.

"She must've understood me," Vekk said as she began walking away from the group in search of Psykier. Arkriat, with Kretai on his back, followed behind Kol as he pursued his sister.

They found the rebels waiting in the city centre, silently surveying the damage to the skyscraper.

"Sydrilla and Reqilar are waiting," Psykier told the siblings in a calm tone as she watched them approach. "They'll lead the assault once you're ready."

They returned to Modspi and Kol entered an armour shop with Arkriat and Kretai. Vekk entered the command centre and approached Reqilar, who was eagerly waiting for her.

"Were you successful?" he quickly asked.

"Very," Vekk responded.

"Elaborate. I'm curious."

"Kol pulled a lever that launched a boulder—it destroyed the source of the beam."

Reqilar smirked and looked down at the hologram in front of him.

"This planet holds many surprises," he said. Kol suddenly entered, flanked by Arkriat and Kretai. Both were wearing full body armour, excluding a helmet for Kretai. Arkriat's brown body armour blended into his fur while Kretai wore some incredibly light metal plating that provided minimal protection.

"Seems like we're mostly ready," Vekk said with a pleasant surprise.

"We will begin tomorrow, when we're calm and rested," Reqilar said. "Do what you want until then, just as long as you are ready for the assault."

"You're not our father," Kol said as he left the room with Arkriat and Kretai.

"I'd rather not be," Reqilar muttered.

"We'll speak before the battle," Vekk said, smiling as she left to find her brother.

Kol heard Vekk behind him and walked into

the centre of Modspi to find the heart of the rebellion; a grand ice sculpture, depicting a headless rebel stabbing Zavroon. The transparent statue glimmered in the desert sun, its melting point high enough that the ice could withstand moderate heat.

"The head got lost in transport," Psykier told the siblings as she welcomed them into the city square that was filled with rebels.

"I thought it was an alien or something," Kol said.

"Perhaps it is," Psykier said, returning to the crowds.

"How're we going to defeat Zavroon?" Vekk asked calmly as she stared at his icy depiction.

"We'll have enough soldiers," Kol said, smirking and walking off.

Vekk stared intensely at the statue; the headless rebel made her reach for her bag and grab a Floruna. She suddenly diverted her attention to the rebels surrounding her and dropped the flower to the ground, integrating herself into the congregation.

That night, the siblings slept more than usual, focusing on the day's events to block out fears of the following morning.

As soon as they awoke, they dressed into their armour and met up with the rebellion's leaders in anticipation of instruction.

"The day has come!" Reqilar announced.

"The Assault of Zrelyar. Our opportunity to deliver salvation."

He checked the supplies, armaments and morale, finding each to be high. He then produced a hologram of Zrelyar—Vekk and Kol were taken aback as they had not seen the city in such detail since their escape.

"We will break through the lower-class section of the city with a couple of soldiers, where there is minimal security." Reqilar told the room. "The majority of our forces will attack the front gate to distract the Zrelyarian military."

"Vekkilar and Kolansar will arrive in my ship in case the rest of us are attacked en route," he continued. "Once they've infiltrated Zrelyar with the small group of soldiers, they will sneak through the chaos and disable the Beam of Zrelyar, joining us at the palace once finished."

"What about Zavroon?" Kol asked.

"Undoubtedly, he will be part of the defence force and we'll deal with him as we do with any other enemy," he responded.

Vekk looked unconvinced, yet eager. "Maybe he's not even near Zrelyar."

"It shouldn't matter if he's there or not," Reqilar said. The console in front of him began beeping and he pressed a button to silence it. "Psykier says the rebels are ready. Any questions before we begin?"

The commanders in the room launched several queries at the rebel leader, which he easily responded to with a series of short answers.

"What if we fail?" Vekk asked.

"We fight until there's nothing left of us, or them—whatever comes first," he said.

"Hopefully there will be something left—of us," she muttered.

"Of course. Let us move, before the General of the Royal Guard comes to join us," Reqilar told the room, who promptly stood up and began crowding the lift outside.

"The people will hate us if we destroy their homes," Vekk said to Reqilar as he left the meeting room and she waited for the lift to return empty.

"That is why we're initially sending in soldiers instead of tanks, but I will inform Sydrilla —we will keep that in mind." Reqilar responded. "I will see you in the palace."

They kissed and Kol quickly gestured to her to join him. Once outside, they were escorted to Reqilar's personal ship, which was heavily modified and had far more weaponry than an average shuttle; they entered the vehicle to find Arkriat and Kretai sitting inside.

"I would've thought that he'd want to be in his own ship," Kol said, familiarising himself with the controls.

"He has to lead thousands of rebels into the city. He and Sydrilla are the two leaders of the rebellion, and they've got to act like it," Vekk responded, pushing her way into the pilot's seat.

The pristine ship lifted off like a bird of prey that knew where its next meal lay. The shiny black hull absorbed the heat of the sun, making the exterior untouchable while the interior remained cool due to the built-in air conditioning.

They slowly flew over the rebel forces below, advancing towards the jungle that stood ahead. The giant cliff that separated the two biomes remained as a barrier, causing the rebels to diverge to reach Zrelyar.

Vekk quickly contacted Reqilar and Sydrilla through the built-in communication system.

"We wouldn't recommend ploughing through the jungle," Vekk said quickly.

"Why not?" Sydrilla asked, her voice calm to protect her aged vocal chords.

"Yarsnael recently attacked the villagers who lived there—they wouldn't appreciate another round of threatening vehicles travelling through the area," she told them. The two leaders muttered in agreement and ended the call, commanding their soldiers to find an alternate route.

Vekk and Kol flew over the jungle, noticing an area that had been previously dominated by ancient trees.

"I hope the Cristrials have recovered by now," Kol said.

"I doubt it," Vekk responded. "Yarsnael did quite a lot of damage."

Passing over the charred Cristrial village, the siblings saw the field of Florunas that lay ahead. Vekk made an emergency landing, her silent goal remaining inside her quiet mind.

"We don't have time for this!" Kol said as she stepped out. Vekk ignored him and walked over to a Floruna, carefully pulling it from the ground.

"There are things I need to know," she said as she slowly walked back to the ship. She took the opportunity to check on the rebels through the ship's computer screen, seeing that they were far behind.

"I guess we do have time for this," Vekk said. They stared out of the window in front of them, seeing the edge of the wall that wrapped around the circular city.

"Imagine if Zavroon returned to find Zrelyar under our control," Kol said, holding out his hand for Kretai to land on.

"I really, really hope he's not there," Vekk responded. "I'd love to see that."

"I thought he was going to arrest us when we first encountered him," Kol said, retracting his hand as Kretai perched on his shoulder.

"He'll be wishing he did," she responded. They waited for around an hour before the rebels arrived, noticing a small number of vehicles beside the wall. The main gate was out of sight, but the siblings assumed that Reqilar and Sydrilla were creating a distraction.

Vekk quickly reactivated the engines and flew closer towards the entrance to Zrelyar, until she and Kol could see Reqilar standing in front of an army of tanks. The tanks quickly began firing at the gate once the Zrelyarian guards drew their weapons.

"Let's take advantage of this," Kol said. Vekk nodded as she flew towards the small group of vehicles that sat a couple of miles away. Landing beside the small rebel squad, they disembarked Reqilar's ship and watched as the men tore a hole in the thick metal wall.

The rebels ran inside, causing the nearby civilians to retreat into the safety of their homes. Vekk, Kol and Arkriat, with Kretai on his back, stepped through and watched as the rebels began to assault the city that was once their home. Arkriat whimpered and looked up at Kol as bombs dropped near the palace.

"It'll be alright," Kol told him as they began to run through the streets. They briefly glanced around the area that they had entered into; dirt was scattered around the ground, working in partnership with the discarded litter in the area to create an inhospitable environment that housed many lower-class citizens.

"I can't believe people have been living like this," Vekk said as she stepped over a bundle of cloths. They saw that the people of Zrelyar cowered upon the siblings' approach; they sheathed their weapons to prevent further panic and calmly walked past.

Kol looked to his side to see a hologram projecting from the wall, depicting the four of them. He looked down at a man holding his young son close to him, visibly prepared to give his life to protect his child.

"I think it'd be better if we hurried up..." Kol said as he began to jog, before breaking into a sprint. Vekk and Arkriat pursued, with Kretai flying overhead. Soldiers began filtering through the area as the four of them slipped into the nearest middle-class housing district, the smallest class-based area in Zrelyar

Some of the civilians began to block their way, standing in the middle of the roads and on top of homes. Vekk exhaled loudly and began pushing her way through the crowds, holding her weapons for additional encouragement for the citizens to disperse. Kol slowly pursued, apologising as he walked past.

They swiftly turned onto a wide road to see Reqilar's forces advancing towards them. They looked to the right and saw their childhood; the street remained, as it had for decades, and led to two of the buildings that they remembered well.

"We need to go back, to see what's happened since we were...forcefully evicted," Vekk said. They walked down the road to see a tall fence around the hatch that led to their house.

"We can't go in there. Let's see if Leritri's still around," Kol said as he walked to the house across the street to find the hatch open. They walked down the stairs, into the kitchen, and looked at the new technology that graced her home. In her redecorated living room, she sat in the same chair that she always had—one of the only items that had not been replaced.

"Leritri, we're back," Vekk said as she approached her.

"I know," she said in a harsh tone.

"We can't stay for long, but—"

"I can't wait for your attack to fail."

"What?" Kol asked, repeating her words in his mind as he tried to rationalise them.

"You've hurt me—I hope they hurt you," she said, standing up with ease and walking towards a bookshelf in her house. She stared at it for a few moments, before grabbing the wooden sides and throwing it to the ground—a door had been hidden behind the bookshelf, and Leritri stepped through it.

Vekk and Kol opened their mouths to speak but remained silent as the elderly woman gestured for them to follow. They did so, with Vekk tightening her grip on her dagger.

Walking down a narrow staircase, they entered a room that mimicked a field at night, with burning hills in the distance. Meteors collided with the frail ground and caused dirt to leap into the air like weak fireworks, before falling and crushing the green grass.

"You cut me off from the organisation I worked for," Leritri sneered. "I'll get some revenge before Queen Lasapra has her chance."

Vekk and Kol watched in utter confusion as Leritri stepped outside and locked the door, which swiftly blended into the landscape around them. The siblings turned to face each other, exchanging fearful stares instead of words.

"We need to figure this out," Vekk said as she wandered around the room. She walked west until she hit an invisible barrier—the room was deceptively small as the walls were invisible.

"I think it's an illusion," Kol said as he reached in front of him and felt the concrete wall behind the rolling hills.

"It's...like the end of time," his sister responded as a distant hill imploded. She looked up to see a meteor heading towards the four of them and ran—it suddenly disappeared before it could reach her.

Kol stepped forwards, feeling the raised ground beneath his foot. He walked forwards to find that it had become uneven, as if walking through a real field.

Kretai landed on the ground and walked around, confused by the appearance of grass that had no depth. She squealed at the moment that thunder was heard—lightning struck the environment around them a few seconds later.

Vekk suddenly shoved Kol away and commanded Arkriat to run as it struck her, causing her to collapse to her knees. She looked to Kretai, who began flying towards her.

"We need to get going," Kol said as he attempted to reach through the wall to find the exit.

Vekk cautiously drew her weapons as she watched a dead man approach her.

"I want to leave," she said in a panicked tone as he stood over her.

"Let the woman take her revenge," Yarsnael whispered loudly, quickly fading away once his message had been delivered.

Kol's hand fell through the scenes and gripped a door. He pushed it open and called Vekk, who quickly stood up and pursued. Arkriat waited for Kretai, ensuring that she was hovering up the staircase before he left the room.

Running up the stairs, Kol broke through the door using his spear to find Leritri sat in her chair, once again.

"Listen up, you old witch," he sneered as he and Vekk approached her. They swiftly turned their heads to see soldiers running into the living room, weapons drawn.

"Armour," Vekk muttered. Kol nodded and pointed to one of their opponents, who was quickly taken down by Arkriat. Vekk supercharged her armour and dashed at the soldiers—once Kol joined her, they managed to swiftly defeat the ambush and redirect their attention to Leritri.

"We helped you for years," Kol said. "You told us to rebel!"

"I have learnt that rebelling doesn't bring salvation," she said, straining her vocal chords to deliver the words.

"Is that from experience?" Vekk asked.

"I was told by my employer," Leritri responded.

"Who?" Vekk asked. "Don't do anything to avoid the question."

"If you ever find out, I won't be the one to tell you," she said.

"W—what about your daughters? We saved them!" Kol told her.

"I'd rather you hadn't—they're dead to me."

Kol looked at Vekk and told her, "I can't kill an old woman."

Vekk stayed silent for a moment and then grabbed Leritri's shoulder, watching the elderly woman's arm reach beneath her seat.

"We'll be back when we've conquered this place," she told her. Vekk knelt down and grabbed the knife that was attached to the bottom of the seat and threw it at the fireplace, causing it to shut off. The siblings left her home and reminded themselves of their actual objective, running through the city once they had remembered their objective.

They sprinted towards the beam that pierced the purple clouds, sprinting past civilians and soldiers who watched them with suspicion. The siblings entered the upper-class zone of Zrelyar to see the streets desolate and the homes covered by a variety of coloured glass barriers.

Security bots stood in front of the doors to the houses and fired when the siblings walked past. Vekk, Kol and Arkriat opted to run between buildings, climbing over garden walls to bypass lengthy roads.

They soon found the building that housed the Beam of Zrelyar and saw that thick walls had been installed around it, along with additional security that patrolled the area.

"We entered the sewer when we first came —we should try that again," Vekk whispered.

"I can't wait," Kol responded in a sarcastic tone. Vekk ignored him and leapt into the garden of a vacant house as gunfire echoed in the distance. Kol, Arkriat and Kretai followed her as she sought the nearest platform that would lead them underground.

They soon found a panel beside a power station, which was surprisingly vacant of guards; beside it was a platform that was labelled as sewer access.

"I don't think we should destroy the power

station—electricity's the only thing keeping some of the civilians safe," Kol said. Vekk muttered in agreement and activated the platform. The three of them stepped on while Kretai floated above, watching the daylight disappear as they were lowered into the dark and damp environment that existed in the sewers of Zrelyar.

"Any prior knowledge of these sewers has left my mind," Vekk said, admiring the cleanliness of the platforms, which had clearly received regular maintenance. There were no guards patrolling the corridors that the siblings walked down, despite the Zrelyarian military knowing of the siblings' mission to disable the beam.

They crossed over the glass floor to the other walkways, the fear of falling into waste occupying their minds. A gate soon stood ahead of them, blocking passage into the sewer depths.

Kol ordered Kretai to find a method of lifting it while Vekk stared at the sewage below, taking note of the cleanliness of the air that had been absent during their first visit.

"The security's better than before," Kol muttered, watching Kretai return to him while whimpering due to her failure.

"Don't rely on what the builders made," Vekk told him as she drove her dagger into the glass floor. She began stabbing it repeatedly until her foe shattered and dropped her into the flowing waste.

"I'm sure the builders made some of that," Kol said as he crouched beside the hole in the glass and watched his sister be carried past the gate.

Could be toxic, he thought, directing Kretai to follow Vekk. She resisted and hovered above Arkriat, who soon jumped into the sewage. The Ukrifar pursued him while Kol waited for them to reach the other side.

Vekk waited on the other side, watching her brother follow close behind Kretai and scramble to escape the sewage. They wiped off most of the waste and climbed the steep stone staircase, remaining as flat as possible to avoid detection.

They lay at the top of the stairs and watched the guards talking beside the door. Vekk gripped her handgun and carefully placed it on the ground. She stared at the face of one of the guards, who was looking at the wall above her, and fired at him. He instantly collapsed to the ground.

She then began firing rapidly at the other soldier as he ran towards them. Kol grabbed his spear and stood up, before immediately retreating down the steps to avoid being shot. Arkriat appeared from the shadows and sunk his teeth into the guard's leg, giving Vekk time to shoot him dead.

"I'm starting to feel like Zavroon," Vekk said as she stepped over the corpse. "Murdering people."

"Hopefully he'll be one of the last people we need to kill," Kol said as he rejoined his sister and approached the nearby door.

"One of the last?"

"Maybe Lasapra too."

Arkriat watched for patrols while Kol hurriedly shoved the keys into their respective slots. The door hummed and automatically opened, inviting them into a corridor that was entirely distinct from the architecture of Zrelyar or Modspi.

"Crimson red walls and ceiling. Lit by orange lights. Interesting," Kol said as they wandered towards a triangular door on the other side. "Kind of ugly, but interesting."

"Do you think it's..." Vekk said, staring at the broken windows that revealed metal scaffolding behind the walls. "...part of the survivor's ship?"

"I never imagined the founders of Zrelyar having much technology, but they must've gotten here somehow."

"This is definitely the site of the crash."

They passed through the door to find the cockpit, complete with broken controls and half of the pilot's chair.

"I thought this ship would've deteriorated by now," Kol said as he began looking through the hidden compartments. Finding nothing of value, he quickly shut the drawers and looked to his sister for guidance.

"We can't wait around. The rebels are fighting for their lives up there," she said, leading him and their creatures through a pristine white door that revealed a well-maintained corridor. The walls were glass, displaying holographic portraits of former leaders behind them.

They quickly walked to the other end and opened the door, entering a dark room that was lit only by fire. In the centre was a small table with seats around its edge, currently empty.

"Who would go this far underground just to have a meeting?" Vekk said as she tried to open the next door with her dagger.

"Do you really want to know?" Kol responded as he attempted to comfort Arkriat in the dark.

Vekk soon broke into the next room and they were greeted with an observation room, with the beam's reactor laying on the other side. The deck stretched around the entire core, giving them a full view of their target.

"Another reactor," Vekk muttered. They walked around but only found a small hatch that could fit Kretai.

"Kretai could drop it inside," Kol suggested as he ran back to the previous room to search for armaments. He swiftly returned with a crimson sphere that shook in his hand.

"How do you know this'll explode?" Vekk asked as she took it from him and placed both hands on it, quickly learning that she could not repress its movements.

"I don't, but it looks like a grenade."

Vekk handed it back to Kol, who gave it to Kretai. The Ukrifar flew through the hatch and carefully approached the reactor. Dropping it in the middle of the room, she darted out as it exploded.

Kol silently celebrated his luck while Vekk urged him to flee. The four of them ran through the ship and ascended a spiral staircase that led to a small metallic room on the surface.

"Get the keys," Vekk said. Kol obeyed and ran back inside to seek out the sewer entrance. Kretai hovered hesitantly by the door while Arkriat stood beneath her, both watching Vekk.

"Kretai?" Vekk asked as she studied the hesitant expression on the small face. "You've avoided me since we...left you at that factory."

The Ukrifar descended and landed on Arkriat's back, releasing a high-pitched snarl from her small vocal chords. Vekk raised her eyebrow, before turning away to look through the tiny glass window in the door.

Kol returned, the colliding of keys in his cupped hands alerting Vekk to his presence. He squeezed past Arkriat and unlocked the door in time to see a chain of explosions in the air. Vekk took the lead and quickly killed the guards outside using her handgun. Kol looked behind him to see that the beam had disappeared from the glass tube in the centre of the small room.

"This armour's the only thing keeping me alive," Vekk muttered as she stepped into the street, glancing back at the corpses behind her.

"We did it! We're finished!" Kol said, his eyes wide with excitement.

"We did agree to help the rebels with their objective."

"I know. Just enjoy this moment before we almost die for the thousandth time."

Vekk hugged her brother and looked at the sky, slightly disappointed that it had not immediately cleared.

"We've done all we needed to do. The rest is just fulfilling a debt and then we're free," she said. "We'll discuss it later."

"Whatever we do, I want to be remembered as a hero," Kol said, smiling.

"You—we will be," Vekk responded.

Wounded and determined, they walked through the empty streets to meet the challenge that they expected to be the last obstacle to salvation.

CHAPTER 25

The rebels converged on the palace, pushing through the rain that slowed their approach. Lightning broke through the crowds but struck the field surrounding Zrelyar, as if it was purposefully avoiding the invaders.

Vekk, Kol, Arkriat and Kretai watched the two rebel leaders push through the city, demolishing gardens and huts as they rolled over the crowded homes of cowering civilians. Running down a ramp and over flattened ground, they slipped behind the rebel army and continued towards the lower-class zone of Zrelyar.

"Where are we going?" Kol asked, his eyes fixed on his sister sprinting ahead of him.

"To sort those out," she said, swinging her hand to point at the turrets lining the road to the palace. "They'll wreck the tanks before they even get a chance to reach the palace."

"Sounds like you've already put thought into it."

"I saw them on the way to the Beam of Zrelyar. I d...don't want Reqilar to die."

"We need help!" Reqilar's voice called out in

the distance. The siblings ran to his ship and climbed back inside, catching their breath as they took off.

They watched the battle from above as they cautiously approached the turrets; Reqilar was perched atop his tank and regularly looked behind him for rebels that would never come—every rebel soldier already stood by him.

Sydrilla began waving her arms in front of her from the relative safety of her own tank. The rebels scattered and were quickly divided by a seemingly infinite supply of Zrelyarian soldiers, who were fiercely loyal to their Queen.

Kol looked to his sister as her breath rapidly slowed and her eyes fixated on the turrets that had turned to face Reqilar; lasers smashed into the rebel leader's vehicle and he disappeared inside, the exterior melting around him.

The turrets eased their attack once their targets had concealed themselves. Sydrilla climbed out of her vehicle and cut into Reqilar's tank, allowing him to escape. Vekk exhaled loudly as she watched him speak to his fellow rebel leader and continued the assault on foot.

"Are you alright?" Kol asked.

"We need to decimate those turrets," she said, focusing all of her attention on the buttons and screens in front of her. She swiped one of the screens in front of her and the ship produced lasers of its own, cutting into the houses beneath them.

"Avoid the people!" Kol said in a distressed tone.

"I know, I'm trying!" Vekk responded, aggressively swiping her finger back and forth across the screen. Watching the lasers slice a garden in half, she let go for a moment and stared at the controls in front of her.

"Draw it," Kol suggested. Vekk slowly moved her index finger back onto the screen and slowly drew across the turrets. The thin blue beams caused the turrets to explode, the debris causing minimal damage to the palace steps.

"Is that it?" Kol asked. "Are we going back down now?"

"I suppose so," Vekk responded as she pulled her fingers away from the laser interface, resisting the urge to draw a line across the fortified palace that was protected by centuries of rare technology.

As they flew towards the palace, Vekk sought out and destroyed the soldiers that swarmed the rebels, using the lasers to slice them apart. Kol watched in a mixture of surprise and horror as bodies collapsed around the advancing tanks.

"The way should be clear now," Vekk said as she piloted the ship towards the wide street that led to the palace. Landing atop the flat entrances that lead to many underground homes, the siblings stared at the hundreds of rebels running up the stairs to the palace that stood ahead of them.

An assortment of stolen vehicles hovered behind the army and decimated any soldiers that dared to approach. They then reorganised themselves and formed a line in front of the palace, aiming their weapons at the doors.

Vekk stared blankly out of the windshield of the ship, watching a soldier run and be shot down. She turned to Kol to see him staring at her.

"What?" she asked.

"What happened to 'one more death'?"

"I didn't kill that one!"

"What about the others you burnt to death with lasers?"

Vekk's lips shaped several different letters, as if trying to find the one word that would absolve her of guilt. "Y...you've killed people too."

Kol stood up and walked towards the exit, with Vekk following behind him. He pressed the button beside the door to reveal the rain dripping off the back of the ship, as well as the destruction in the distance. Even after the door had opened, his metallic finger had not moved.

"I wish I hadn't," he said. "Look what it did to me."

"Our last obstacle is the palace," Vekk told him. "That's it, then we're done."

Kol nodded and stepped outside, briefly looking around to see if there were any imminent threats. Vekk stood on the nearby road and looked at the metal steps that led to the palace. She looked to Kol, Arkriat and Kretai, who followed her as she sprinted towards the stairs.

Sliding between tanks, they ran up the stairs and stood behind the rebels; they had formed a semicircle around the doors, each person aiming their weapons at the purple-hooded guards that stood by the door, their quarterstaffs drawn.

Vekk, Kol and Arkriat pushed their way through the crowds, with Kretai hovering above, to witness the guards stepping away from the door. The rebels lowered their weapons and formed a sea of confused expressions.

"What is coming?" Reqilar said in a calm tone that failed to mask his intrigue. Vekk looked to him while Kol grabbed Kretai from the air and held her in his hands. The doors carefully parted and gave the rebels a glimpse of the Lasapra's home—along with her greatest asset.

Zavroon stepped out into the pouring rain, his eyes fixated on Reqilar; the rebel leader held fear in his eyes as his posture became more rigid. The General of the Royal Guard had been outfitted with new weaponry and held a helmet that the siblings had never seen before.

"This is far beyond anything I expected of you," Zavroon told them, "which is why it won't continue."

He glanced at the rebels, each individual standing in a defensive position with their weapons drawn. He casually turned his head to look at Vekk and Kol, seemingly unbothered by their presence.

"You destroyed our lives, we'll destroy yours," Kol sneered.

"Anything to say, Vekkilar?" Zavroon taunted. She stayed silent, knowing he expected a verbal response.

"Each one of you intends to hurt Queen Lasapra," he told the rebels. "Her life is worth far more than a hundred of yours."

"You seem close," Reqilar said with a smirk.

"Not as close as you are with your subordinates," Zavroon retorted; Reqilar's smile quickly disappeared.

"The woman is corrupt!" Vekk said.

"She wasn't the one to ruin the lives of millions for a short-sighted goal," he told her, smiling at her. Vekk's face froze as the images of burning buildings occupied her mind, her eyes moving to focus on the smoke in the distance. Kol looked through the crowd of rebels to see the damage that they had caused to his and Vekk's city.

My home. My home is burning because of me—because of us, Kol thought, softening his grip on Kretai and allowing her to return to the air.

"I've struck fear into your leader and terrorised both your heroes without resorting to violence," Zavroon told the rebels. "You could all learn something from me."

"That's why people follow you—you manipulate them," Reqilar said, his attention partially occupied by Vekk as she stared at the ground and attempted to resolve the moral dilemma that had overwhelmed her.

"Don't dismiss your opponent's ideas just because they are different," Zavroon said, turning to face Kol. Kol stared back, a mix of fear and hatred in his eyes.

"If you hate violence and chaos, why do you ignore it inside of Zrelyar?" Kol countered. "I ran through poverty to get here."

"Zrelyar has been ruined by you."

"I'm tired of your hypocrisy," Reqilar told him.

"Interesting choice of words for a betrayer."

Vekk grabbed Kol's arm and dragged him into the vacant space in front of them, occupied only by Zavroon.

"For what you've done to me and Kol...I will end you," Vekk sneered, grabbing her dagger and handgun, as well as supercharging her armour to enhance her natural abilities.

"We will," Kol added, grabbing his spear and looking up at Kretai, who did not understand the situation.

"I will fight them alone—it is what they wish," Zavroon said, drawing his jet-black sword and placing his helmet on his head; he smirked at Reqilar, before swinging his weapon at Vekk. Arkriat lunged and unbalanced him, which did little to deter Zavroon from his attack. He stood on the Garisal's back and brought his blade down on Vekk. She slipped to the ground and crawled away, as did Arkriat.

Kol thrusted his spear at Zavroon's chest but the general dodged and stepped back to refocus on his enemies. Arkriat lunged at him and he kicked him away.

"Get off, beast," he snarled as he watched the Garisal cautiously move away. He looked up to see Kretai flying in the air and then focused on Vekk running towards him.

Kol moved into the centre of the area and watched his sister hold her dagger against his sword, both combatants refusing to yield. He saw Vekk turn and throw her gun at him; he grabbed it and began shooting at Zavroon.

The general slipped away from Vekk and ran at Kol with his sword in a position to stab his opponent. His sword clashed with the spear, with both surprised that Kol's ancient weapon did not break upon contact.

Vekk ran behind Zavroon. He moved his torso away from Kol and swung his sword backwards, slicing across Vekk's lips and raised hand. She stumbled away and placed her uninjured hand over her mouth while the rain washed her bleeding palm.

Kol quickly backed away from Zavroon and glanced at his sister. He swiftly turned his head to face his target once again and ran at him with his spear. Zavroon smirked and raised his sword to strike Kol, who had drawn his attention away from another threat.

Kretai darted at Zavroon, her small body moving through the air as a blur. The general's focus was on the wrong target, but his reflexes acted in time.

The jet-black sword sliced through the centre of Kretai's fragile body, immediately killing her. Kol stopped charging and lowered his spear, watching as Zavroon was caught off guard—Reqilar grabbed the general and drove him into the closed palace doors.

"I—I...no! No!" Kol said, ignoring Vekk's incoming footsteps.

Vekk looked at Kretai's lifeless body and stared in confusion. Kol had collapsed to his knees; his tears fed the puddles beneath him while the rain became lighter and a small amount of light reflected off the tiny bodies of water.

"We need to deal with Zavroon," Vekk said, her worried face focused on Kretai.

"Don't you feel anything?!" Kol asked her in a distressed tone, watching as Arkriat sat beside Kretai and placed his head by hers, whimpering loudly.

"I don't—I can't," Vekk responded, listening

to the rebels behind her running towards Zavroon. "I think it's...shock."

Kol placed his head in his hands and screamed, before slowly rising from the ground and turning to face his sister. She embraced him, holding him tight as Zavroon began to shout taunts nearby.

"We will kill him," Vekk told Kol, releasing him so he could grab his spear. They ran towards Zavroon, who was surrounded by rebels.

"I can deal with him." Reqilar said. "Get to safety."

"No, he needs to know what he's done!" Kol said, approaching the defeated general. Reqilar backed away but stood close enough to intervene if necessary while the rebels fought off the incoming palace guards.

"Making you die in disgrace is the best thing I can do for me and my brother," Vekk said to Zavroon, the corners of his eyebrows upturned, as he finally feared her.

"Queen Lasapra will be pleased with my work, regardless of what you do," he told her.

"Shut up about the Queen!" Kol told him, grasping his ancient spear tightly. Zavroon responded by grabbing the spear and pulling himself to his feet.

The spear was wrested from Kol's hands, forcing him to use Vekk's gun. Zavroon swung the spear at Kol but quickly turned to Vekk when he saw she had a dagger.

Kol stood back and held Vekk's handgun in case Zavroon escaped. Vekk slammed him into the palace doors and stabbed him repeatedly in the stomach, aiming for the fabric between his armour plates.

Zavroon slowly fell to the ground, shocked by the strength of the badly-trained civilian. The siblings stood over him as he placed his hands on the palace doors which refused to open for him.

"Those who rebel are those who rule," Vekk told him confidently.

"It doesn't matter," Zavroon said, turning to face Vekk and Kol. "As you've left a...mark...on me, I've left a mark...on you."

"The murders you've committed." Vekk said, watching him slip into a sitting position and clutch his bleeding chest. "This is how they felt."

"I've...killed very few people," he told them, breathing heavily. "I work...I worked through fear...and intimid—"

"You've failed your leader," Kol taunted, with Vekk glaring at him.

"If you do take this...place...you will mature and you will...learn...real struggle," Zavroon said, slipping onto the ground and clenching his teeth in pain.

Vekk knelt down. "You've been our greatest threat," she said softly.

"You should hope that it stays that way," he

replied, closing his eyes and allowing the pain to leave his body.

Vekk and Reqilar dragged his body aside while Kol reclaimed his spear and watched Sydrilla's group of tanks blast a hole through the palace doors. Rebels rushed in, firing at the well-trained guards who were quickly overwhelmed.

Kol remained outside, crouching beside Arkriat as the Garisal mourned for the loss of his best friend.

"Why did we have to take her to her grave?!" he asked, unaware of his sister watching him.

We need to go inside, Vekk thought as she stood still and forced away the memories of their time with Kretai. She saw Kol's grief pour from him, his pain on display for anyone to see.

Just let go. Cry, she thought to herself. She allowed Kretai's gleeful face to enter her mind as she approached Kol and stood behind him.

"Get inside!" A rebel yelled from the palace entrance.

Vekk looked down at Kretai and hated what she saw: an innocent creature murdered in war. She did not cry, instead kneeling beside her brother.

She understands, Kol thought. *She feels the same way I do.*

"We need to go. We need to go," he said, standing up alongside his sister. They turned away and walked into the palace, with Arkriat hesitantly following behind as Kretai lay in the light rain.

"Thank you for that," Kol said to Vekk. She smiled and unsheathed her weapons.

"We'll get more than enough revenge today," she said. Leading Kol and Arkriat, she walked to the right and ran up the L-shaped staircase to reach a grand hallway that was littered with corpses.

"I don't want to see another dead body after this day," Kol said as they followed the purple carpet to find a black marble corridor where the rebels were fighting against the palace guards. Running through a side room, the siblings soon reached another hallway; this one was empty.

"Pass me my handgun before we reach Lasapra," Vekk said, pushing the urge to mourn from her mind. Kol handed it over and grabbed his spear, walking cautiously through the building. One of the nearby doors burst open and several dead rebels fell onto the pristine purple carpets; their killers were palace guards, who quickly noticed the siblings.

Arkriat sprinted at the nearest guard, his attacks more vicious and deadly than usual as he sunk his teeth into the kneecap of his enemy. Vekk ran a couple of metres away and began shooting while Kol struggled to defend himself.

The siblings supercharged their amour and lunged at their attackers, swiftly throwing the trained guards off balance. While their strength was augmented by the armour, Vekk and Kol still struggled to survive as they lacked proper training.

"Follow me!" Vekk shouted as she shoved her way through the guards and pulled Kol inside, with Arkriat slipping in beside her. She quickly shut the door and hesitated over locking it.

That could affect the whole building, she thought. *I don't want to block the rebels from getting further inside.*

"That could lock down the whole building—that'll stop the rebels from joining up with us," Kol said.

"I just thought that," she responded as she began to run towards the door on the other end of the corridor. Kol and Arkriat joined her as she opened it to find a dining room, adjacent to a kitchen.

"Far better than our old dining slab," Kol said as he inspected the unfinished buffet that had been laid out. He reached for the pole that held it to the roof—a previously unseen security camera fired at him and shot through the pole, sending the delicate slab crashing into the ground.

Vekk fired back as Kol retreated into the adjoining kitchen and hid behind a wall. Her armour protected her as she demolished the automated security and rammed her dagger between the doors at the other end of the room, forcing them open.

"I thought they were all automatic," Kol said as he rejoined her.

"Maybe someone else locked them down," Vekk suggested as they strode through a hall and walked up a grand staircase to find several groups of rebels facing off against palace guards.

"Our forces are everywhere," Vekk said, looking down the hall to see a damaged door that revealed the locked guest rooms beyond it. "I don't understand how they got here."

"We don't have time to find out," Kol said as he walked away from the chaos and through a vacant hall that led to many more rooms.

"It's a maze—one we're supposed to die in," Vekk said as she looked down the endless dark corridor.

"It's not where I wanted to die," Kol muttered as he broke through the nearest door to his left. Vekk embraced him from behind without warning, preventing him from exploring further.

"We need to go," he protested.

"You're not going to die here," Vekk said. "It'll be me before you."

"Hopefully, it'll be neither of us—especially after Kretai," he said as he broke away from her grip and wandered into the next room; a small area that split off into two opposing corridors that curved into darkness.

"Let's split up—take Arkriat with you," Vekk told Kol, who immediately agreed. They walked through separate corridors, red lights activating upon their approach.

The corridors curved around to a single lift that stood in between them both. Vekk and Kol were relieved to see each other as they walked inside the lift and stared at the controls.

"What if this takes us straight to her?" Kol asked.

"Then we'll face her; she's not a warrior," Vekk said, pressing the single button that worked. "If we can defeat Zavroon, we can defeat her."

Upon reaching the next hallway, several palace guards were waiting for them as the doors slid open to reveal a small room. They held their swords defensively, as if expecting the siblings to attack first.

The door opened behind the siblings' opponents and two of the guards were hurriedly impaled by Reqilar, wielding his double-bladed sword with skill. Vekk shot at the disorientated guards while Kol held Arkriat back to avoid the swinging blades.

Once the guards had dropped to the ground, Kol released Arkriat and opened the door to see that the carpet had been torn up.

"That was from my weapon," Reqilar said as he looked down both sides of the hallway; one was heavily damaged from his assault while the other was untouched.

The building shook and cracks formed across the walls—the pillars that stood in the centre of the halls threatened to collapse and desecrate the well-protected palace.

"I will personally help you dethrone the Queen," Reqilar told them as the building threatened to collapse around them. "She knows this palace; she will activate everything to stop us."

"Are we too incapable to do it alone?" Vekk countered.

"You struggled against Zavroon—I won't let her kill you," he told them, particularly focusing on Vekk.

"Let's move before the building kills us," Kol said, looking worriedly at the walls.

They ran down a hallway, ignoring the doors on their right and turning left twice to find a ramp lined with red lights.

"The rest of the building uses staircases," Vekk said. "Something's up there."

Footsteps approached quickly and the four of them ran up the ramp to find a locked door.

"No, no, no, no, no," Reqilar said as he tried to break it open. Vekk and Kol stood either side of him, watching as guards ran towards them and aimed with rifles, their arms shaking.

"Do we want to know what's inside?" Kol said as he held his spear towards the enemies that were hesitant to fire.

"Yes," Vekk said confidently as Reqilar suddenly turned around and lunged at the guards, struggling to avoid his own blades as they sliced through the air on both sides of the hilt.

A small group of rebels joined them, the rest having been dispatched by palace security. Reqilar pointed to the door and a rebel nodded, placing explosives around it.

Vekk, Kol, Arkriat and the rebel backed away as the door broke apart and revealed a second ramp. They ran up, into another hall; half of the floor had caved in and made it impossible to reach the other side from the interior.

Unlike the rest of the building, this area was lit by natural light—the windows had been smashed by the explosives and exposed them to the toxic air outside. They could see beyond the walls of Zrelyar; the corridor stood far above the palace roof.

Kol leapt over to the window frame and pulled himself onto the exterior of the building. Vekk and a couple of rebels soon followed him as he climbed across to the other side.

Reqilar tried to conceal his surprise at their plan as he prepared to jump. Arkriat began whimpering beside him; the rebel leader commanded some of his subordinates to carry the Garisal across as they pursued Vekk and Kol.

They passed the door to see another hall,

filled with guards that stood against the purple-black pillars that were now against the wall as opposed to centre of the corridor. Vekk took the lead and broke the window with her dagger; rebels piled inside and defended the siblings as they fought to survive in a room that had been upgraded with additional security.

Reqilar leapt through the window and joined the battle, dashing around to avoid being hit by swinging swords and his own blades. He mercilessly sliced through multiple enemies at a time, at a pace that seemed almost unnatural.

Once the guards dropped dead and the security cameras had shattered, Vekk helped Arkriat to get inside and joined Kol and Reqilar as they discussed the door ahead.

"S—she's ahead," Vekk stuttered, fixating on the grand door that awaited them.

"The palace guards were terrified because they know they cannot fail their Queen," Reqilar told them.

"I'll be terrified if she succeeds," Kol said, his words followed by an explosion behind them. They turned to see Psykier and her squad of elite soldiers, who quickly took notice of the door behind the siblings.

"We're here for you, sir," she told Reqilar, who smiled and nodded.

"Your skills will be invaluable. Thank you,

Psykier."

Together, they slowly wandered down the wrecked hall. Tanks fired outside, their ferocity incomparable to the might of the Queen of Zrelyar. They approached the giant entrance and Kol took his spear, sending it through the door —which opened before the spear could touch the lock.

We've been granted entry, Vekk thought as they slowly walked inside the small room, briefly glancing at the balcony to her right.

Queen Lasapra sat on her throne, immediately shutting down her robot servants and calling in a group of palace guards, wearing purple robes that heavily concealed the armour underneath.

She had piercing red eyes and long grey hair that trailed across her throne. Wearing purple robes that flooded the floor, she resembled an evil goddess—her throne room provided her with the power of one.

"You've threatened my people," she said in a deep voice. "Does that make you feel powerful?"

"They die from your inaction, you ignorant *prixtibba*!" Vekk countered, her face illuminated by the hanging white lights that descended from the slanted ceiling.

"Zavroon!" Lasapra called out, clearly infuriated by her insult.

"I don't think he'll be participating in this

battle," Vekk sneered.

"Scum!" Lasapra shouted suddenly. "You've killed my general!"

Kol smirked at her. "He deserved it."

"I don't need him," Lasapra said. "What do you want with Zrelyar, anyway?"

"We will rule the planet with a supporting hand," Reqilar told her. "Unlike the iron fist that you control it with now—that will be used to destroy your achievements."

"Your disillusioned soldiers won't get you there; why would they give it to you, as opposed to taking it for themselves?"

"As you're about to find out, they wouldn't have a chance at defeating us," Kol countered, his spear gently swaying in his hand.

"If you believe that you're strong enough to dethrone me, try," she sneered.

Reqilar ran at her but was swiftly thrown back as a transparent barrier rose over the Queen and her throne; the guards walked out of it and positioned themselves to attack the rebels.

Psykier's elite rebel squad immediately attacked as the siblings and Reqilar repositioned themselves to the right, carefully walking over the glass floor that exposed the wires below.

Lasapra called more guards; Vekk, Kol and Arkriat joined the fight while Reqilar worked on disabling her barrier. Kol impaled several guards, alongside his sister, and felt disheartened when ten more ran inside.

Is there a guard factory just…pumping out an army every minute?!

Reqilar saw his allies struggling and unsheathed his sword, forcing Lasapra's reinforcements to disperse. Vekk and Kol supercharged their armours while Psykier commanded one of her soldiers to shut down the Queen's barrier.

"We won't die here, not today!" Reqilar shouted as he struck down two guards simultaneously. One of the rebel soldiers pushed him away from the door and threw a grenade outside of the throne room; the adjoining hallway, already unstable from the sieging tanks, broke away from the rebels and plunged one end into the palace roof.

The rest of the guards were hurriedly killed and the rebels stood directly in front of Lasapra's barrier, watching as she failed to mask her surprise.

"Surrender, or—never mind, you will not survive this," Reqilar said.

Lasapra hurriedly tapped the buttons on her grand throne and the outside of the barrier became electrified, stunning Reqilar and knocking him unconscious.

Kol fell to his knees as the pain from his prosthetic arm became almost unbearable and forced him to crawl away. Arkriat shook off the electrical surge and ran to his owner, who was dragging himself across the metal floor.

Vekk managed to step away and persevere through the pain, helping Psykier to escape the dangerous defence mechanism.

"Need some help," one of the rebel soldiers called out as he attempted to gain access to the barrier through an exposed electronic panel in the wall. Psykier was informed about the issue and returned to Vekk as she looked for unorthodox routes to reach the Queen.

"We need the name of a potential mentee of hers," Psykier whispered to Vekk, who nodded.

I'd read her memories if I could reach her, Vekk thought as she approached the barrier, standing far enough that she would not be electrocuted.

"What if we all die here?" Vekk asked. "Who will take your place?"

"I will not answer to you," the Queen told her as she tapped on the arm of her throne. Robots dropped from the ceiling and drew their guns, aiming at the weakened rebels.

"Conformity guarantees security," Lasapra said, clicking her finger. "You shouldn't have rebelled against me."

The robots immediately began firing at the rebels, gunning down most of Psykier's squad. Psykier ran for the wall panel and smashed it, causing the barrier to malfunction and stretch across random parts of the room.

"What have you done, Psykier?!" Kol

shouted as he took cover behind one of the newly-formed obstructions.

"The wonders of technology!" Psykier said as she shot five robots and ran to Reqilar, pushing him behind a barrier.

Vekk hid and shot at the robots as they sought her out; they resembled the bots in Drixav but appeared to have been modified with mismatched parts, as if they were unfinished.

Arkriat leapt from behind cover to tear through one of the robot's wires, before moving onto a second bot. Once he had cleared some space in front of Kol, the latter ran into the fight and helped Arkriat avoid being shot.

The robots were swiftly destroyed; Lasapra was left with few options. Her eyes darted around the room and she clutched her throne, feeling inclined to remain bound to it like a part of a machine.

Purple wires lit up beneath the transparent ground as the gears in Lasapra' mind turned and delivered an output of scorn, her emotionless voice seeming almost unnatural.

"I will make you suffer for as long as I live," she told the rebels who threatened her.

"Then our suffering will be temporary," Kol said as he stabbed his spear through the glass below and split one of the wires, shutting down her shield.

Vekk ran back to wake Reqilar as Psykier,

Kol and Arkriat approached the Queen, alongside the two remaining rebel soldiers.

Lasapra looked at them with a bored demeanour, switching suddenly from the fearful expression she had shown.

Electricity leapt from every corner of the throne. The Queen smiled as she switched to another button and pushed down on it with her index finger, causing the centre of the room to erupt with an uncontrolled current of power.

"Seems like her last source of defence!" Psykier said as she ran from the throne, before being struck down by the electricity that conquered the room.

Vekk and Kol moved against the wall, watching as their allies were shocked and left unconscious on the ground for a few seconds. Vekk fumbled for her handgun but was struck and dropped it on the ground; within seconds, both of them had fallen to the floor and struggled to avoid Lasapra's powerful last stand.

Vekk grabbed the grip of her gun and held it unsteadily at the Queen. Kol crawled in front of her, crying out in pain as he acted as a barrier to allow her to steady her hand and aim carefully.

If you don't calm down, we'll all die, Vekk thought, her hand beginning to shake. She stared at the Queen, her smug face watching Reqilar as he was repeatedly struck by electricity, and fired. The first shot missed while the second struck the Queen and left a hole in the back of the throne as she fell from the seat of power.

The rebels watched her collapse to the ground and cry out in shock and pain. She glanced up as Reqilar carefully stood up and looked down at her.

"Does she deserve death," he asked, "or imprisonment?"

"Let her die," Kol sneered, his mind flashing to the death of his elder brother.

"Wait," Vekk said, removing a Floruna from a small pouch. She grabbed Lasapra's hand and placed the flower on it, before putting her own hand over.

"Why did you do this?" Vekk calmly asked.

Vekk saw a happy childhood, filled with activities and games to stimulate the mind. Lasapra aspired to become a scientist. She had completed many courses by the age of forty—the beginning of adulthood for Quarailians—and was highly intelligent.

Her sister died a year later, leaving the throne vacant. Lasapra's parents forced her to take her sister's position, going as far as to ban her from work outside of the palace. Faced with the opportunity to inflict suffering that was not her own, she became Queen and imprisoned her parents for the crime of stripping away her passion for science.

"Oh...my...I'm so sorry, Lasapra," Vekk whispered to the dying Queen. She nodded at the young rebel.

"You and your brother will face the same fate—most rulers do," Lasapra told her, before relaxing into the void that awaited her.

"Where do we go from here?" Kol asked as Vekk walked towards him.

"Away from the throne," Vekk said, briefly glancing at the balcony as the sound of engines reached her ears. "Leave it until someone's ready to rule."

"Understood," Kol replied, looking down at the deposed Queen.

"Success!" Psykier said, receiving nods from the other rebels.

"Well..." Kol said, seeing that the room was littered with corpses.

Vekk stared at the body of a fallen rebel. "We're going to have to walk past Kretai when we leave."

"That little Ukrifar saved your lives," Psykier said. "You wouldn't have survived without his sacrifice."

Kol displayed a sad simile on his dirt-covered face, wincing from the sound pummelling his ears. "We had no chance against Zavroon alone—she gave us one!"

Incessant rumbling filled the room. Reqilar walked out onto the balcony to see smoke filling the air, forcing him to retreat inside.

"Someone has arrived," he muttered, looking at the collapsed hall that lay against the throne room doors like a ramp.

Arthur slowed the rocket as much as he could using the alien controls, having no one to guide him on how they worked. His heart beat quickly as he allowed the shuttle to designate its own landing site and sat back, looking at the world outside his window.

The rocket gently hit the ground and he remained in silence, hoping that the strange city that surrounded him was filled with welcoming inhabitants.

He sighed and detached his seatbelt, before clipping his alien weapons to his spacesuit and grabbing the alien relic. Climbing through the space shuttle and locating the door, he glanced through the tiny glass window to see groups of aliens standing outside.

He pressed the button to open the door and watched it slowly rise. Smoke dispersed around him as he stepped onto the hard concrete floor below and looked at the strange people who watched him; they resembled the figures from his mind but were not the same.

Vekk and Kol ran out of the palace and down the steps to see that an alien vehicle had landed. The inhabitant of the vehicle had stepped out and turned to stare at them as they approached. They walked towards the alien, its face concealed by a helmet. However, the body language showed that it was confused and defensive towards them.

Arthur slowly removed his helmet to reveal his stunned expression. He turned to the two figures and held the relic up, hoping that it would match some of the architecture behind them.

Vekk and Kol watched in awe of the strange, yet familiar, species as it spoke a language that they did not understand, its eyes locking on Arkriat's necklace.

"Oh, thank God you're real—I'm Arthur."

Printed in Great Britain
by Amazon